Dream Book

Jaddamiah Jabberwocky
(and the things that happen to people with such names)

BOOK ONE

Sebastian

BALBOA.
PRESS
A DIVISION OF HAY HOUSE

Balboa Press books may be ordered through booksellers or by contacting:

Balboa Press
A Division of Hay House
1663 Liberty Drive
Bloomington, IN 47403
www.balboapress.com.au
1 (877) 407-4847

Because of the dynamic nature of the Internet, any web addresses or links contained in this book may have changed since publication and may no longer be valid. The views expressed in this work are solely those of the author and do not necessarily reflect the views of the publisher, and the publisher hereby disclaims any responsibility for them.

Interior Image Credit: Sebastian

Print information available on the last page.

ISBN: 978-1-5043-1942-3 (sc)
ISBN: 978-1-5043-1943-0 (e)

Balboa Press rev. date: 10/16/2019

[1]Next marks Ezeru-Izar, and from his Nature flow
The Most afflicting Powers that rule below,
Heat burns his Rise, Frost chills his setting Beams,
And vex the World with opposite Extremes.
He keeps his Course, nor from the Sun retreats,
Now bringing Frost, and now increasing Heats:
Those that from Mul Lunergal view this rising Star,
Guess thence the following state of Peace and War,
Health, Plagues, a fruitful or barren Year.
He makes shrill Trumpets sound, and frightens
Then calms and binds up Iron War in Ease. Peace,
As he determines, so the Causes draw,
His Aspect is the World's supremest Law.
This Power proceeds from the vast Orb He runs,
His Brightness equals or exceeds the Sun's.

---

[1] From Astronomica by Thomas Creech

Contents

Authors Note

Many explanations are given as far as possible in Summaries or The Glossary or Index so that the reader may from time to time refresh his memory or familiarize with words. The teller can offer no apology if perchance the material seems complex and neither can be held responsible if the reader attempts to use any Enchantment or Symbol or Rune without permission from Power or Principality.

All effort has been made to thank or make citation and for those who have showed kindness through assistance in this tome. Should an error or omission occur the teller offers apologies and will make corrections in future editions.

Prooimia

Strange folks came to that village. Why and from where people soon forgot. I knew a man by that name once; he was named Eldritch. I wish I had asked him why he was named that now…

Once, long, long ago, longer than that word would care to remember, there lived a beautiful young girl as all young girls are, of course. Each fifth year, it was the custom of her parents to travel with one of their children to Ninfa.

Hyperion was the eldest child and had five brothers. The 3 sat in their hansom, and Hyperion's father, Dan, was complaining to his wife, Hyperonoir (or Elhama, as she was also called) about a dream he'd had the previous night. He said it was a peaceful sleep with such a wonderful dream, but when he woke, he could not remember it at all.

"It is a great travesty to be human. One forgets one's own dreams and thoughts in one's own mind and can often never retrieve them. This perplexes me greatly," he complained.

The very dream would come to fruition some day in the future, but he would neither remember it nor see the prophecy fulfilled.

It was delightful to be a child and see such wonders, sights and sounds. Ninfa, where every edifice or structure was two or 3 times the size of similar structures elsewhere, was a feast to the senses, an adult may never attain again in his/her lifetime. Going to Ninfa or as the Hrosvyras called it, 'Ninfalingas' was a shock to, or perhaps an awakening of the senses. Going and being there felt almost Dagian. The highway was paved some 125.95194 miles before one reached the great gates of Ninfa proper. This highway was known as the "Golden Highway" in the common speech and in the ancient speech of Ninfa, "Haimamarga". It ran parallel to the lingering Lama Dupes. The Lama Dupes sent strong white plumes of spray into the blue air from its deep gorges, so that it seemed a great dragon lay in its own smoulder.

At various intervals, there were vantage points, great leaf-shaped platforms carved and crafted out of Simhadanti wood. From those one could view the great river far below, flowing in all its tempestuous booming, and feel the coolness of the spray in the warm summer sunshine. The Golden Highway was paved with large amber slabs that flushed the softest gold at every sunrise and sunset. To prevent the wagons and horses from sliding around and going over the side into the Lama Dupes, there were even-scored lines in the shape of ornate mandalas running in spirals the entire length of the highway. These mandalas were representations of the universe, for above all else, the Ælves loved the stars. The Ælfennes, who was queen of Ninfa, was named Estatira, an ancient name meaning "creation of the stars".

Some one hundred miles from the capital of Ninfa slept a walled town on a hillside called 'Arambha'; some folk called her 'Anu-zas'. The fiefdom was situated on an absolute crag and had a population of 25,000 people. Fifteen thousand of those were soldiers, best known as the 'Arundhati'. It was well known that the soldiers were placed there in such abundance for Arambha had a river port that one could sail on as far as the river port of Élle. There were those who would see it forfeit, but, the eyes of Palador guarded it well.

Although Ninfa was a peaceful realm, the realm had to keep those soldiers in readiness in case their services were requested by the principality of Palador, but such a request had not been received for a long time. A zig-zag road made of amber cobbles ran up its side, and one entered Ninfa through a large portal crafted from Lemurian Seed Crystals. It shone rich gold, and a horizontal striation configuration ran upwards in the interior of the crystal, adding to its splendour. It was said that anyone entering under that arch with violent intentions became disarmed, falling into a swoon of affection and healing. In the centre of the portal, in the centre of it, in the surface of its pillars, was the heraldic symbol of waves. Between the waves were stars.

Travelling only thirteen miles farther down the Golden Highway, one arrived at yet another town, much smaller than Anu-zas. It was on the right side of the river, and a grand, narrow, arched bridge allowed access to it. It was also built on a hillside with a portal as its entrance. That town was called 'Pravalha', meaning 'enigma'. One could say it was the opposite of Anu-zas. There were only a thousand inhabitants, mostly tinkers and tailors; there were no soldiers. There were many guesthouses for visiting travellers, and there were always many.

Map of Ninfa

In Pravalha, the road ran in a spiral, round and round till the very top. There, a great edifice made of pure white marble and a golden dome for a roof endured. That edifice, or fane, was called 'Marga', and it was the abode of the 3 Djedi of Ninfa. It was well guarded by 6 Arundhati.

Hyperion and her parents often stayed at Pravalha, and it was where they would have decided to stay this time too. The abodes were very large. Another thing that made it special was that chamomiles and daisies, daffodils, thistles, lilies, dog roses, clematises, carnations, bindweeds, brooms, stocks, phlox, lady hollyhocks, high ferns, bushes of laurel, blackberries, capers (with its exotic purple filaments) and myrtle, and a lot of ivy were everywhere to be seen.

Whenever strangers went to Anu-zas or Pravalha and stood on the side-walks looking at the marvels of the paved roads and crystal portals, inhabitants stopped and whispered in friendly gestures, "It's the Ælves, you know. The Ælves have strewn on every world the foundation of crystals. The Ælves!"

All the structures had either domed or round roofs. Their tops were crafted of copper, so the years had turned them to turquoise jewels that were delights to the eyes. The story of Hyperion's mother was shrouded in mystery, for she was found as an infant by the Ælfennes, Queen Estatira of Ninfa. I think perhaps I need to regale you with that tale here.

The Day of Litha

⸙

The date was 21 June 8624 of the Fourth Age. The gardens were blooming, and summer was in full bride with the bees. It was a strange morning as Queen Estatira, with her magnificent cavalcade, was on the way to Jinbōchō. She had come by way of Élles and was on her way through Béth-Élam. There were 3 splendid open carriages With 3 Ælfenna bow-women, called the 'Nervauric Force' on each carriage. At the rear were 6 of the Arundhati; preceding the carriages were another 6, all on horseback. The carriages were all made of a single pearl, and only Queen Estatira's coach was enclosed with a polished Abnu Zabarkizag dome-shaped roof. That roof was not just for splendour or artifice; it served to protect her from any attack other than those experienced by the senses. Inside the coach with Queen Estatira sat an awesome Ælfennes named Lucifellon, and she was in charge of the whole cavalcade.

The gardens were blooming and one could smell lemon, myrrh, pine, rose and wisteria. Their fragrances permeated the air two miles away, not because they were flowers, but, because the fragrance came from incense burned on the Day of Litha, which was the festival of Mid-Summer.

Because Queen Estatira knew that her travel would take place during that time, her personal coach was trimmed all the way around with 113 emerants strung on glittering strings of vrilium steel. Between each green emerant hung a fresh blue-bell that would not wither during the entire duration of the journey. As she rode, the blue-bells sang. The sight and sound of that procession, the absolute handsomeness of the she-Ælves, and the beautiful Arundhati were so terribly hard to describe that one would have had to use an adverb like "orchaiomelelvenotolkienarate" to describe them. But having said that, let me at least try to convey the incredible beauty of Queen Estatira.

Queen Estatira wore a thin, golden diadem around her pitch-black tendrils. Her hair cascaded down her back like a still comet. In the very middle of the diadem, at the front of her forehead, was a star made of deep-blue zésàndara. On each side of this were two short waves of the same rare crystal, which was only found in the deep south of Dhara. She also wore a broad golden band with the same heraldic motifs around her upper right arm.

Her cheeks were flushed with pastel orange, and her face had a fire-hazel Fay glow. Her full lips were stained red as if red, berries had fallen upon them. Her high cheekbones housed above them two, caesious, dark pools surrounded by dark shadow. This was no anvahr. All was her very own being, every bit of colour in her face. She held her head was slightly downward as she sat pensively. Queen Estatira's right arm was extended behind her on the soft seat that resembled an ornate sofa. She rested on her hand. Around her neck hung large pearls that complemented the plain, woven, sheer white fabric of her dress. Her skin and the contour of her handsome form could be seen clearly for the silk was translucent. The silk coiled itself around her waist like a blue star flower, and she was seated on the remnants of it. Her left arm rested casually over her crossed knee, and in her hand, she held the Catur Padmini, which was made of gold.

From her waist hung a dagger. Its scabbard was kræfted of glittering pearl. A pattern of coiled blue leaves was engraved into it. The mouth of the scabbard was encrusted with lilūlium steel in the form of a Catur Padmini; the blade handle looked exactly like the scabbard. The front bolster, as the rear, were two zésàndaras.

When looking at Queen Estatira there was only one reaction, silence, speech impediment.

Lucifellon sat up suddenly; she got up and opened the upper half of the door which was made of thin, transparent Quartz. She commanded everyone to an immediate halt for she sensed something in the road. The entourage stopped only centimetres before the cascading waterfall, before the Sag kata. The curtain of water, was called 'Yavana Yahva', and flowed from a spring against the mountainside called 'Svadurasa'. It was into the cascading curtain that one of the Nervauric Force was ordered. Queen Estatira looked out of the carriage door while Lucifellon stood close to the entrance of the tunnel.

There, sitting flat in the middle of the road, naked and soaking wet, was the most beautiful little baby girl of 11 months. Aspas, one of the Nervauric Force maidens, brought the little girl to the Queen immediately. Aspas had walked under the cascading water yet, there was not a drop of water on her and neither were her habiliments wet.

Queen Estatira held the little girl to her bosom and caressed her chin and kissed her brow. She took the remnants of the train of her dress and wiped the child. The child looked up at Queen Estatira her eyes lit up for, she had been found.

"Rángárang! Rángárang! A delight!" exclaimed the Queen, "Sanúf Áyán, Sanúf Áyán," she went on in a sweet reverential voice.

"Parizád!" replied Aspas.

"Hmmmmmm," said the Queen, looking into her blue eyes, for it was like the bluish-steel of a midwinter sky, and her left eye was black-flecked and deep brown like pecan shells.

In short, the child was 'fámsanúfhálat'.

"What shall we call you little joon, for I feel in my divine thought that you belong to no mortal?" said the Queen in a soft, quiet voice.

Lucifellon came striding out of the tunnel, towards the Queen and said, "My Queen, there is village called Béth-Élam only minutes away. Shall we find a surrogate there for the child?"

"You have heard my thoughts my warrior joon," replied Estatira with a smile in her soft, quiet voice.

The 6-carriaged cavalcade moved through the Sag kata and sped over the surface of the road.

There were some boys playing at the Great Dwarve Clock and it was also from that point that the cobbled street began. There, standing at the round-a-bout was a large scuttle made of brass and filled with burning, oak pieces. That was one of the customs on the Day of Litha.

The houses were decorated with dried herbs, potpourri, crystals, summer flowers and fruits and there was a feeling of destiny in the air.

The boys stopped their playing, their mouths dropped, and their eyes popped. Several menfolk who were digging a hole for planting a linden tree, stopped their work. After the procession, the boys shook out of their swoon and ran behind the carriages screaming and shouting, other children joined them, some stood mostly stock still as no-one in Béth-Élam had seen Ælves in such a splendiferous cavalcade, for four generations. The folk standing outside of their houses stood gobsmacked, their thoughts were jargogled and their faces made contortions that the face muscles had never known before - flizzen and flodder comes to mind. Those who were indoors, poured out, and the most famous Inn in all of Dhara, was immediately emptied.

The Jabberwocky family, who were by far the largest (and who loved horses), were cast immobile on the street curb as the carriages, if indeed it could be called such, had the most magnificent, ebony and ivory horses, but most noticeably, there were no reins, no curb-bits, no martingales, no head-gear and no breeching.

The horses went into a passage that was quite regal and the onlookers stood amazed. As this occurred, the blue bells along the carriages made sounds which sent all into a sylvatic swoon, as the horses shook their heads and whipped their tales in merriment. The manes of the white horses glittered with crystals and jewels which were weaved into their long hair. The black horses, had strings of glittering white pearls in their manes. Their hooves were azure and their coronary bands were of a golden hue.

It was a day altogether lovely, but there was more.

Queen Estatira stepped out of the carriage, at the exact house which she foresaw as having the best circumstances in the years to come, for the young girl.

Queen Estatira stood before the gate of 31415; its occupants were all at the gate, the garden path too narrow to house all at the same time. Before she proceeded, she stood still, and her guards formed a circle around her carriage. The people of Béth-Élam folded their hands and made slight bows. A slight, fair-skinned woman of a plain beauty, stood pressed to the gate.

The Queen was the first to speak as she held the little baby girl to her bosom. "Sus-vapnah my joon mother. I have brought you a great blessing and would ask of you a boon. I am the Ælfennes Queen Estatira also called 'Puru-Ambas' of the Pradeza Ninfa. My entourage and I make journey to the great City of Jinbōchō. . ."

Her voice travelled so all could hear her clearly, although she only spoke in honeyed, soft, quiet tones. The inhabitants of Béth-Élam were held spellbound not by some fell kræft, but by the Queen alone, by her very being.

"We have found this baby girl on the road, naked and alone under the entrance of the Sag kata. Would you keep her for me till I return, this would be the boon I require from you?"

The woman's grey-green eyes were clear and honest and separated by a thin nose, the upper lip of her small mouth twitched; that always happened when she was nervous or excited. She answered in a quivering voice; "I accept this child, Queen of Ninfa. It would be my great honour, *our* great honour", with that said, she looked at her husband standing beside her. He shook his head up and down, for he was smitten by the Ælve Queen's beauty.

"Our great honour to keep the child till your return, Queen Estatira, this is my word to you, that we shall let no harm befall her and she shall be as one of us."

The child, still swaddled in royal silk, was handed to the woman. "I will take that as a zapta but, śapatha is most pragmatic for nothing else will do. Aures and Dayaal Cinaed this is for you." said Queen Estatira in a calm voice. "Aures, I have decided that the name of the child is Hyperonoir but, we Ælves are polygynous so she shall have a second name, Elhama, for she was revealed to the Ælves."

Aures and Dayaal were very surprised that the Queen knew their names because they did not tell her but, they were deceived for, she could read their thoughts. Queen Estatira smiled coyly, her rhodopsin eyes were kissed with collyrium and had light in them that were reminiscent of some distant sea shore, such that anyone looking into them longed to go there. Strangely, even in her eyes, there was the sound of music, not perhaps audible to the mortal ear but such that impressed on the mind, as a mirror of some forgotten time or previous lifetime. Queen Estatira lifted her index finger; Aspas walked forward and handed a soft, purple velvet bag to Dayaal; it contained 1000 merkes of gold. As he took it from Aspas, a surge of energy flowed from her to him.

The Ælve Queen said Sus-vapnah and elegantly got into her carriage.

The silence was broken by the cheering and shouts from the crowd, the horses were pawing with their feet, tails raised high and neighing. The 6 carriages moved toward the Pass Hrada and as it pulled away, the skids made by the lilūlium steel, carved long grooves in the cobble stones. Blue flames died down as they burned in the grooves.

There was a strange, beautiful fragrance in the air at Béth-Élam after the Queen had left, it lingered for several days before vanishing. The inhabitants of Béth-Élam stood gazing into the air long after the royal cavalcade had passed, as they had been treated to the stuff of legend and myth. Döppievölle Inn was packed to capacity that evening; every man, woman and child was inside; and they spoke about the events of that day into the early hours of the morning.

Only two mortals from the outerworld had ever been invited to the Palace of Queen Estatira;

the first was Elhama and the second was her daughter Hyperion, the following part of the tale, tells of the meeting of the latter.

It was said that Alkana was majestic but certainly, Ninfa was beautiful. There was a charm in Ninfa that no other Pradeza had, as such charm only occurred when a place had aged slowly; and Ninfa *was* the second oldest realm in Dhara. Cascading in profusion on some parts of its walls and which were a delight to the passer-by, were fragrant Dina Majjari. It was also said that the language of Ninfa was directly based on birdsong, and of birds there were plenty.

The Sadrada's summer house was at Anu-zas. It was there that he and his wife went for holidays when they wanted to release themselves from politics.

Heilyn Surbaer was his name and he had been the Sadrada for a very, very long time. While Queen Estatira reigned and while she willed it, the Sadrada was blessed with unusually long life. Thus, the Sadrada received his power from the Queen, she allowed him 'the seat' and his right-doing was directly related to that power.

Large terraces were filled with beautiful flowers; they were built into the retainer walls supporting the paved road that ran zig-zag up the steep crag. On the south western side of the town, were low-lying marshes, filled with hundreds and hundreds of nenuphars of many hues. At the start of Beltane as well as the flower festivals of Ninfa, the city folk went on 1st May to look at the colourful display and the beautiful gardens of Anu-zas.

They went to see the grand display of the nenuphars for only around the town of Anu-zas, did the Nenuphars grow in such profusion. Water, fed by springs, ran from three bridges under the Golden Highway, into the great Lama Dupes.

The people of Ninfa believed that on the eve of Litha, the heavens opened up and that it was the best night for magical spells, especially for love spells. They also believed that plants harvested during that night would have magical powers.

Dan, Elhama and Hyperion arrived in Anu-zas on the Day of Litha, 21 June 8685. They did not celebrate that evening but, decided to go to bed early because they had seen so much on their journey and were very tired. Elhama and Dan wanted to be up early the following morning as they wanted to spend the subsequent two days inside the great, capital city of Ninfa.

Dan was a tall man with light eyes and broad shoulders, he held little Hyperion on his shoulders as they stood on the balcony, snirping in the petrichor and drinking in the clean, morning air. He pointed upwards to the sky at the glittering, bright star called 'Haasil', brightest of all the 9 Royal Stars.

Later, when the small family stood outside their lodgings, on the side of the street, they could feel the warmth of the sun on their faces. It was a beautiful day.

A Capillaire walked towards them and offered each a glass of capillaire, they graciously accepted and stood casually slaking their thirst. As Dan was about to ask the porter to bring their wagon around, an opulent carriage pulled up in front of them. It came around the bend, glittering in the morning sun. The box seat was shaped and kræfted in several nymphs with their ephemeral garments blowing in the wind, and on it sat the most beautiful driver.

The sculpted nymphs were made of gold and the Ninfafemma seated between them, was dressed in traditional Ninfa style. When the drove of horses came to a halt and lifted their heads into the air, they neighed and nudged at each other. The 6 horses were handsome enough to be sculptures; their coats were shiny, appearing platinum and luminous in the morning sun and because they were first brought to Dhara from Haasil, they were called the 'Golden Haasil'.

People started gathering around as it was unusual to see the Queen's Haasil without her in the carriage. Since she was not in the carriage, there were 3 Arundhati on 3 Ambughana; there was one of the Arundhati who seemed to be in charge of the whole equipage, for his horse snorted and he turned her left and right, forcing some of the crowd back. Its coat shone like black silk and on its nose, was a small, white star. The hair on her mane and tail were so long that it swept the cobbles.

The carriage driver got up from her seat and went to the Cinaed family (still standing in awe). She was balletic in her movements and was very distinctive in her looks, as the women of Ninfa were. They were curvy and plump women but in no way jollux. They had long blond, kinky or nappy hair, bare shoulders, rounded foreheads, thin eyebrows, big cheekbones and small delicate noses. They wore dark powder around their eyes and their eyes were extended outward, up-slanted corners and had full, pouted lips.

The carriage driver wore a tarast which consisted of a golden lumbar covering of silk, studded with jewels and a small zuka made of solid gold and shaped like a shallow cornucopia. Over this, she wore a loose, blue, sheer silk jumpsuit, held together with a silk collar around her muscular neck and also at the ankles. She also wore a hammered bronze headdress. "I am Þrúðr," she introduced herself with a light, husky voice. "I have been sent by our Queen to drive you to the Palace of Dhanadava." She was jocund in her manner and Dan, Elhama and Hyperion took an immediate liking to her.

Elhama was first to speak, "This is a surprise. We did not expect such a grand invitation nor had any presumptuous aspirations.

On behalf of my family, we apologize ahead for the way we are dressed. We did not expect this." While saying this, Elhama pressed her hand against her breast.

Þrúðr smiled as she listened then replied with enthusiasm, "I do not mean to be haughty, but allow me to take you all to our tailor and fit you with customary garments."

"That would be wonderful but, I need to see how my husband feels about this offer," replied Elhama as she turned to Dan.

"I have to agree" he replied and smiled.

Þrúðr turned to Hyperion, "And you my joon, forgive me if it seems like I have forgotten you, but I have not. It is not our custom in Ninfa to forget the little ones. If your parents do not mind, will you sit upfront with Þrúðr?"

Hyperion's blue-green eyes lit up as she looked at her parents pleadingly and said, "May I father! Please?" Dan ran his fingers through her long, dark-brown hair and said, "Only if you promise to tell me all about it tonight before bedtime."

"I promise, promise, promise father!"

"Then it is settled," replied Þrúðr, and clicked her fingers.

Immediately a tall, dark-skinned Ninfamalla with long, smooth, black hair and dressed in a short skirt appeared. He wore a blue, sheer batiste silk shirt and had a sword on his hip, he stepped off the back platform. He introduced himself as Dal, for he was also a poet and his name meant 'door of my lips'. He spoke in a modulated voice as he held out his large hand to Hyperion. He smiled as he said, "Come my little joon, let me lift you to your seat." With one sweep of his arm, she was seated between the magnificent golden sculpted nymphs. The Ninfamalla were about 6ft 3inches on average and had beautiful, smooth, umber skin. The Cinead's regarded the union of Ninfafemma and Ninfamalla as being exotic.

The crowd parted as the royal carriage left and they whispered to one another as to who those 'āmeiza' were to be whisked away in such a grand manner.

As they left the town behind, the Lama Dupes was on their right and the Golden Highway drew closer to the edge of the gorge. The river gorge widened to nearly a mile and there, like fáerië sentinels, stood 3 rocky outcrops of 1640ft high, called 'Darva'. Some trees grew at the top of one Darva and on the heads of both Darva, perched thousands of birds, whose melodies filled the air.

As the royal carriage moved at a moderate speed, the Cinaed family feasted their senses on every marvel they could possibly take in.

Hyperion's little head cocked backwards and forwards, left and right as she watched grand carriages, regal horses, festive naraizaoha and many, many more āmeiza promenading from place to place. Despite this, the milieu was like a dream. Hyperion looked up at the poised Þrúðr then tapped her on the knee. Þrúðr looked down at her as her blonde hair took to the breeze. "You have a question my joon. I can tell by the light in your eyes, what is it you want to know?"

"Þrúðr!" exclaimed Hyperion then stopped. Þrúðr smiled as Hyperion sat pensively then begun again, "Joon-Mitra! Who do you suppose built this carriage? A gold beater or the Dwarves?" Hyperion continued inquisitively as she looked ahead, her eyes running over all the golden sculptures and embellishments.

"I don't suppose they were either my joon. I believe that it was the Ælves themselves who kræfted this splendour," said Þrúðr in her light, husky voice.

Hyperion thought it was a good answer as it sounded like it was true, so she sat silently; her eyes transfixed on all the beauty of Ninfa.

They were drawing close to the large gate of Ninfa, and for what seemed like a moment, the highway was empty and only their carriage was on it. Elhama looked out of the window as she also noticed the change.

There were many marvellous maxims about Ninfa but of all of those, the following was the greatest; 'so deep is the peace in Ninfa that a golden ring lying on the side of the highway, would be left untouched'… that was until one day a certain, beautiful girl came travelling by with her parents.

Suddenly Hyperion demanded that Þrúðr stop the carriage; which of course she did, because the child's voice was so defined that she were taken aback. As soon as the horses were brought to a halt, Hyperion jumped down from her place next to Þrúðr and ran to the sidewalk, her parents got out of the carriage. Within seconds, Dal was at Hyperion's side. One of the Ambughana and its rider was also close at hand while the other two guards reined their horses about. Hyperion was sitting on her haunches and retrieved something from a clear, turquoise blatter. Þrúðr, Dal, Elhama and Dan stood around her and looked down at the child who had the eyes of an eagle. She had found and then slipped a golden ring around her finger. It was far too big for her finger and slipped off again. Hyperion tried to put it on a second time and the ring just fell from her tiny fingers. She was persistent, then something amazing happened; the ring shrunk and coiled around her little finger.

Not only did it begin to coil around her finger but, the gold begun to slowly fade into a glittering, silver ring, within this ring another ring began to coil round and round. The adults looked on astonished, as the inner ring ran over the lower ring, like an 'uroboros'.

"Lokarahu is the beginning, Lokarahu is the end. Worlds rise and worlds fall. Dominions rise and break down, adjourn, or prolonged, all are replaced by a woodland of stars," Dal whispered. Their faces displayed a mixture of amazement and disbelief at what they were seeing.

"Welkin! Welkin!" exclaimed Dan reverentially.

"I feel that this ring was meant just for you," assured Þrúðr. "Look around us, there is no-one, very strange." She made a wide sweeping gesture with her arms. The area was enveloped in silence.

They returned to their carriage seats and the horses moved towards the great gate. The Golden Highway was itself again. Hyperion held up her hand, star-fish like, with her fingers wide apart. As she held her hand up into the sunlight, the silver ring glittered. She was delighted that her first visit to this great Pradeza had started so well.

Desire Lines and Tailors

※

The great gate was now in full sight. It had sixteen Doric columns, eight each side supporting eight tall arches made of Lapis Lazuli. Those arches created a connection between the physical and celestial planes. In the centre of the eight arches, was a portal which only the Queen used and the gold in that great edifice glittered in the sunlight. The gold glittered so brightly, that in intense sunlight it was almost blinding.

The eight portals stood at a height of 88ft. They were flanked by two large circular pools with large fountains at their centres; perpetually spurting water higher than the portals. At night great fires burned from furrows which ran around those two pools. The light from those flames were an awesome spectacle, as the water, fire and Lapis Lazuli fed off each other's elemental splendour. A white-stoned, domed roof, filled with millions of glittering spangles, spanned over the portals. Close by and towering still higher, stood a statue of Queen Estatira; she held a sword in her right hand and a garland of *real* flowers in her left; that garland was changed every day according to the orders of the Flower Master.

These spectacular structures could be seen from many miles away.

A road of about a half a mile long, ran before the great gate and on the sides of the road, grew thousands of purple tapiens.

Soon after they had passed under the Gates of Ābee, they turned off the Golden Highway into a weald with a sylvan tunnel. The track was no wider than the carriage. The softest, greenest grass, dotted with Paris, laid either side of the track. In the middle of all that lush vegetation, were trees with silvery-white barks (Sidhamidha) that curled over and touched. The fragrance was woody and sweet, with citrus and mint undertones, reminiscent of frankincense and myrrh. Dan and Elhama popped their heads out of the carriage windows to take deep, deep breaths of it. The Sidhamidha were special trees and that area of the wood was named 'Sidhamidha Torana'.

The sound of the horse's hooves and carriage wheels on the soft grass and the intoxicating effect of the Sidhamidha; put Dan and Elhama into a very calm state and they quickly fell into a deep sleep. It did not have that effect on Hyperion. The Torana twisted this way and that for a while, and if Hyperion's parents had taken a glance back they would have noticed that the wood had closed on itself.

The journey, though exciting to Hyperion, did not last long as, no sooner had the carriage entered the wood, when they exited out of a small garden and into a busy street. Dan and Elhama awoke to the scene of aproneers standing on the sidewalks with their hands on their hips and others, selling fruit and vegetables from colourful, horse-drawn carts. They had entered the city of Rasala, one of the 6 great cities of Ninfa.

Rasala was the gateway to the southern part of what was called the 'Serulien Kingdoms'. Rasala was well known for its cloth making and perfume.

The narrow streets with double and triple story buildings and red tiled roofs, were something to behold. There was an air of mysticism about the place, and the scent of flowers, perfume or sweet tobacco drifted from open doors on the sidewalks. Rasala was a special place and though the streets were busy, there was a kind of lazy-hazy air about the place, traces of indolence in the way the milieu moved, like they didn't have a care in the world.

One thing that was synonymous with its name, was grass, magnificent lawns and manicured long grasses were set in circles, on terraces and between streets everywhere. The inhabitants believed that the grass of Rosala could provide relief from anxiety, cure stomach disorders and all types of ulcers. There was a legend which told, that when the Ælve Queen first arrived in Ninfa thousands of years before, she would walk through the streets of Ninfa with an exotic feline companion and, as its hairs dropped to the ground, they grew into the beautiful, perfumed grass of Rosala.

The carriage stopped in front of two black doors of a quaint tailor shop, with a large, brass number 4 on the solid, left door. The right door had Dorset windows and between the two doors were Dorset panes and muntins, in black with a fine, gold trim. There was a bay window to the side of the doors and at the top of its panel, in gold and black lettering, was the name of the establishment; 'Snip, Cut & Stitch'. Below fifteen rectangular glass frames, was another panel which read; 'Fine Tailoring' and on the brick wall which separated the shop from another, hung a circular sign with the image of open scissor within it.

At the very top of each door was a small, golden crown, which symbolised that the shop catered to the needs of the Queen.

When the Cinaed family were standing on the sidewalk and Hyperion's parents were still scratching their heads as to how they had covered such a great distance in such a short space of time, Hyperion looked up at Þrúðr mischievously because, they kept a secret.

As if knowing at just the correct time when to exit the door, a bushel woman came striding out to welcome the family and the Queen's consort.

"We were expecting you Þrúðr," said the tall, Ninfafemma in a plumy voice.

"And we are happy to be here Puratana," replied Þrúðr making the Namaste gesture. "Let me introduce you to your guests," Þrúðr introduced the family and started with Hyperion. Dan and Elhama could not help but notice the penetrating gaze of the maiden's eyes.

When the introductions were over and they were ready to enter the tailor shop, Dan noticed that the doors of other shops along the sidewalk had different numbers to that of the tailor shop and, he wondered why.

Once inside, they were introduced to Mr Snip Batiste, a famous weaver, after whom several weaves were named. He was a delightful man, full of wit. The loom of years had bent his back and so, he was not as tall as the ordinary Ninfamalla. He had a glint in his eyes and a child-like demeanour. Elhama and Batiste immediately took a liking to each other, and he offered her some fruit harsa called 'Ninfa Harsa', (Harsa being the man who created the delightful sweet 230 years prior) Mr Batiste ordered that Puratana bring some cool refreshments for the guests. She disappeared behind some expensive curtains and returned moments later with iced-tea, biscuits and dates infused with rose petals.

After Puratana had served her guests, she succumbriously sent the remaining clients away and placed a non-harried sign outside the front door.

When she returned, her employer was regaling Hyperion, ". . . according to legend, the Ninfa Harsa was the handiwork of a confectioner named Priya Harsa, his name meant 'beloved delight'". On saying that, Batiste broke out into an infectious laughter and everyone joined in.

". . .Priya was a native of a small town named Nagaghosa, high up in the mountains of Nilam Hesperiis. He came to Rosala in the Spring of 8460 and set up his sweet shop. I will take you there if you desire my young joon." Batiste broke out in laughter again and turned to Hyperion's parents. Þrúðr slipped away quietly.

While Puratana showed Elhama the various fabrics, Dan and Mr Batiste lit their pipes and continued chatting. Batiste stroked his long, white beard as he enjoyed the brief recess for, he was always busy and seldom sat down for a break.

Dan asked him why his door was numbered four and the others seemed to run in sequential order. Batiste cleared his throat and supported his pipe on his lower lip, then answered, "It is number four because four is the fourth letter 'D' of the common alphabet. My windows and doors are Dorset-styled, calculate the numbers of the letters of the word and we come to the sum of 81." There was some more laughter after this mischievous, yet confusing, witty reply. Dan was silent for a moment because the octogenarian's trivia was beyond him so, Batiste spoke through his laughter, "I am 81 Dan! Eighty-oneth." At that, they both broke into much laughter.

"Mr Batiste, from chalk to cheese, can you tell me about Nilam Hesperiis. My wife and I truly love Ninfa yet, the name 'Nilam Hesperiis' is not on any of my maps at home and the name is foreign to me."

Batiste removed the pipe from his mouth and raised his finger saying, "Aha! And it would be, you would have to go to the old library to find maps which show *that* name. Nagaghosa is more-or-less 372 miles from our current location and mind you," with that he poked his pipe into the air at Dan; "And it's not as the crows fly. One would have to journey down the Golden Highway till it runs out, then head off the road into the wilds, cross the mountains till one arrives at the destination. Nilam Hesperiis means 'blue west'. . ." he paused then went on thoughtfully again, "aaah! Dan, Nagaghosa!

It is a beautiful place; I have been there only once in my youth, it was a Dhara paradise; perfumed zephyrs and freshness all year-round; a country situated above the eternal fogs of the Rahu-Ucca range at 14461.94ft, I believe in your Pradeza it is named 'Drakensberg' - where imposing cascades rush downward with clamour to the Nilamsaras and where an eternal Serulien Spring lasts from January to December. Wild roses, over two yards high, and Varasura are blooming there; lilies as big as a large amphora fill the atmosphere with fragrance. Ancient jaguars, to judge by their appearance, saunter about untrammelled, very few mortals dwell in that land." but then he held his hand cupping the side of his mouth. ". . .the Ælves come and go freely."

Dan was amazed, he had listened eagerly to the tale and then asked another question. "Is it easily accessible?"

"It is hard to tell, many come and go from my shop but, none have ever spoken of it with me." Batiste paused again as if some long-forgotten memory were difficult to recall. He shook his head in disbelief and said, "I am afraid, how I got there has slipped my mind . . . it is a strange wonder."

Their conversation was interrupted by the beginnings of a beautiful sound. Dal was tuning an interesting, small, stringed instrument made of elaborate wood work. He began to sing slowly, and the strains of music accompanied by his beautiful voice, was carried on pleasant airs. People on the sidewalk slowed their walking and some stopped and leaned against the windows to listen in.

"Now come the Shapers of the ancient days
To change all to dust or gold.
Like a golden Sun is revealed by the passing
Clouds, so these secrets now unfold.

And in the veil of magic raise that which
Was hidden in garden, woodland or weald old.
Celestial viators that invite us in
To walk again by sweet forgotten worlds.

Sweeter still, like honeycomb on
The lips of a wandering child,
A dream fulfilled, returning to the Westernesse.

Of Heimdal's horn, calling from celestial steeple bells,
As time-allotment shackles disintegrate
Our eyes are filled with beauty, our hearts supernal rest."

The strains of the music had caused the thoughts of Batiste to stray and when he came to, he remarked in a melancholic tone, "Yes, Yes. . ." he whispered, "Yes . . . the music takes me back."

The Halkyondhra

⁂

The folk at the window applauded, some walked away dreamily, and several remained behind contemplating.

Elhama and Hyperion had chosen their fabrics, colours and styles. It was Dan's turn and he held out his arm to his wife for help, because he didn't know much about such things.

When all was done, Mr Batiste had assured them that he would personally cut and stitch their gifts from the Queen. Before bidding them farewell, he also made them promise that they would bring Hyperion back, so he could take her to the sweet shop.

Þrúðr reappeared as quietly as she had disappeared, and soon they were on their way to the palace. The carriage entered a low gate into a small, walled garden, that seemed the very epitome of primordial. When the carriage entered the garden, it seemed like the throngs of the street didn't notice it at all. It was only then, that Dan and Elhama understood how they had arrived in front of Snip, Cut & Stitch.

As they were once again driven through same tunnelled avenue of Sidhamidha, both parents were overcome with a swooning feeling. Dan fought hard to keep his head from falling backwards. It seemed that Elhama was succeeding in fighting the swoon, in fact, she was determined to remain conscious for the duration of the magical, sylvan passage.

Dan was lying on his soft, monarchical seat opposite Elhama. While she took in every breath, exotic butterflies fluttered beside the carriage. Afterwards, they passed over an enchanting, double-arched stone bridge, where the golden light of the western sun cast the leaves of the trees in a soft, delicate light. The gentle, flowing river had hues of gold, gold-green and pastel shades of blue-grey at the water's edge. The river, though flowing, had a surface like golden glass.

For a moment, the pawning of the horses hooves over the stone bridge brought Dan from his swoon. He shook his head, sat up and asked, "What did I miss my love? Did I miss anything! Anything at all?"

Elhama smiled at her husband with a look of compassion in her Sanúf Áyán eyes. "Look back!" she exclaimed. 'Quick!"

Dan did just that and caught a last glimpse of the golden bridge.

One of the Arundhati rode up next to the carriage window. He was poised, and his right hand was resting on his knee. He raised it and said in a deep, baritone voice, "That beautiful bridge is named 'Taleyah'."

"What does it mean, the name sounds so gentle," asked Elhama.

"This word means 'golden rays of sun' my lady." He smiled and bowed his head, then took his position behind the carriage again.

Dan took out a beautifully crafted, silver pocket watch. It had a stylized face of the sun at the top centre and below the lid was a compass and it was gyrating terribly. He opened it and the melody which it usually played was silent. Dan was trying to figure out just how long they had been travelling but, the minute and hour hands were spinning around like drunk tops.

Dan leaned, like a little boy, out from the window and indicated to Dal that his time piece was not working.

Dal smiled, his eyes twinkled mischievously and said, "This is the Land of Duram' master. In the common speech it is called the 'Land of Fernem'. There is no time here." Dan sank back onto his seat and contemplated for a moment, for Dal's last words were emphatic.

"You concern yourself with idoneous things my dove. Stop being so pragmatic, now is not the time," his wife said, with her head still out of the window.

They had travelled for only an hour but, it seemed like moments.

Next to the 'desire line', the Sidhamidha dissipated and formed a large circle, where grass of about 3 inches grew. Two circles of halkyondra grew outside of that.

The entourage stopped, Dal was close at hand to open the doors for Dan and Elhama. Hyperion was helped down by Þrúðr. The 3 Arundhati dismounted their horses and allowed them to forage in the sweet grasses.

Hyperion wasted no time and was running about in that veritable wonderland, as butterflies gathered around her and dinky birds came twittering in the bowers of the Sidhamidha. The halkyondhra were most wonderful, one circle had tall blue shrooms with white polka dots. The other had shrooms of a mixture of colours; deep red, bright green, red with orange and pink fading into each other. Hyperion drifted instantaneously towards the blue shrooms because, they were unique. Before stepping into the circle, she glanced towards Þrúðr, who she regarded as her new friend and mentor. Þrúðr nodded her head and Hyperion stepped into the circle of halkyondhra. Immediately Hyperion vanished; all that remained were millions of blue spangles. Dan ran after his daughter and Elhama was nearly in tears, as she held both her hands on her heaving bosom. Two of the Arundhati were quickly at Dan's side and restrained him with their strong arms.

"Be at peace master Dan. Be at peace!" exclaimed one of the Arundhati, the same one that had come beside their carriage window earlier. "Your daughter is safe, and, she is already with our Queen."

"But! But!" stuttered Dan. "But. . ." he searched for the correct words to say, "Drat crow! Great horn spoon! Crikey! Criminy! Cracky!" and with those expressions, he fell flat on his bottom and sat with his arms folded; he was speechless. Elhama broke into laughter and tears, as she dropped her head into Þrúðr's bosom. Þrúðr gently put her arms around Elhama and smiled saying, "There my joon-joon, we are in the country of the Queen now, there is no darkness here, we are in the land of eternal dawn and twilight, where all things remain forever young, and the flowers and the corn grow always and are never cut by the scythe." Elhama pulled from Þrúðr's embrace and looked into her beautiful eyes; she placed a kiss on her soft lips and smiled. She stood there smiling then thought to herself, 'even the speech of the consorts is beautiful in this place, what could possibly go wrong?'

Dan looked up at the two tall Arundhati and said, "I apologise. Forgive my behaviour, I should know better." He bowed his head, locked his fingers into each other and balanced his arms over his knees. Afterwards, he looked upward to all the beauty, wonder and sounds around him.

Hyperion and Queen Estatira

Hyperion found herself waiting in a beautiful garden. There was no fear in the little girl's heart, she felt only jubilation; and when Queen Estatira walked over the soft grasses towards her, she understood how her mother might had felt, when first placed, long before, into the arms of the Queen.

Queen Estatira stood in all her paradisal glory before Hyperion. "I would have told you my name Queen Estatira, but you already know my name," said Hyperion in her girlish way. She lowered her head and bent her knees in genuflection.

Hyperion was in awe of Queen Estatira and thought that her beauty transcended all earthly excellence. The Queen smiled and held her hand out to Hyperion and said, "You are virtuous. All honour to your sweet childhood, you are indeed the child of Hyperonoir.

Such great love was in the heart of your faithful mother when she first held you in her fragile arms and your father supported her because of their new, mutual delight. Dear child, believe Queen Estatira, you are fortunate, for a son will be born to you one day. Although you are only an innocent child now, let these bold words not fill your coy heart with alarm but, let these words be a paean in your heart. The life of your child will be filled with wonders; in bliss and majesty, you will pass this ring to your child and he will wear it as a crown. . ." As Queen Estatira spoke, the inner ring, the uroboros, began to glow in brilliant blue and coiled round and round, chasing its tail.

> ". . .For those high above the world and deep beneath
> the earth will know his every wish, his every dream;
> That which is noble will be fulfilled; no joy will be
> comparable to him in splendorous fulfilment.
> The profane live but are dead, you are neither,
> and your seed shall ascend to the stars."

The Queen's voice was a melody, as little Hyperion stood looking up at her. Her innocent eyes were glowing and a smile of enchantment creased her lips. A bolbol could be heard as it ascended higher and higher, singing to all under the stars. The uroboros stopped moving and the blue glow subsided. The ring was again just a silver ring on the little girl's finger.

When Queen Estatira caressed her head, Hyperion drifted into a forgetfulness and her mind wondered on other things.

Hyperion suddenly found herself in a separate garden; once again she heard the singing of a bolbol. She wondered what could sing such transitive songs. Then a gentle voice came over the aethyrs and replied, "It is a bolbol and she sings, for it is 'Mawsem-e Gol'. Here it is always 'Mawsem-e Gol'" said the sweet voice. Hyperion looked around but could not see the source of the voice, yet she understood every word — she instinctively knew that bolbol was a Ninfian word for a nightingale and Mawsem-e Gol was the 'season of roses'. She decided to listen as the song and its enchantment continued, then she heard the voice again, "Here is only Mawsem-e Gol for here are hours and tidings of gladness, we leave ill news for Golestān. He sits on the left arm of the Queen."

Hyperion walked past a wall that had the scars of age. It was kræfted from snowflake iron glass and fragrant féirínóblath tumbled like a waterfall from it. There were blue hydrangea spilling out of the hollow of an oak nearby. Poplars, cedars and maples grew to stately heights in the garden and large circles of stone formed natural springs everywhere.

Hyperion found the garden a delight and most of the green, growing creatures came naturally, responding to the eólasian power of the Queen. Other creatures responded to something else… it seemed as pure kræft.

Hyperion was silent, and rightly so, for the voices which she had heard before, manifested in front of her. They sounded as one voice but, were in fact 3 Sprites, a most rare glimpse for her. It seemed as if an invisible filament was attached to their heads as they walked over the Llan. Their eyes seemed fixed on the stars. They took long, lissom strides, swayed their caderas and stooped in minstrelsy. They were the essence of elegance.

They surrounded Hyperion and plummeted kisses on her cheeks and forehead. "We are Rügfeydah, Lurlluhrlian and Hunnahveydah!" they said in quivering, breathy voices, as if Hyperion was to know exactly which name belonged to who. They led her by the hand towards a large, circular pergola with a pool and fountain in its centre. Around the pergola were thousands of liliums, 'halinï' the Sprites called it. They explained to Hyperion that their presence brought about magic, and that the halini helped her to withstand the magic that filled the aethyrs.

She asked them how old they were, and they explained that they were close on 10 000 years old and that the time would soon come for them to leave Eridu but, there was one last task set before them, that task affected the Ring Bearer.

"Where is your home?" asked Hyperion.

The Sprites gathered, with their fingers locked, in a circle around Hyperion. They started to make a sound with their voices. Then they passed through space and time, through two duirs with pillars which were consumed by a gazillion stars. Each pillar was shaped like a dragon, one pillar of vitelline stars and another of glittering, pavonian stars.

Hyperion sat in the circle and watched the 3 Sprites become colossal. They hovered in a spiral array of light, which was as bright as a constellation. A feathery breeze stirred Hyperion's hair, and warm tears ran down her cheeks when the Sprites started singing a song which no mortal had heard before.

> *"Ānidiromēda, Ānidiromēda, Ānidiromēda!*
> *Uttarabhadra, Uttarabhadra, Uttarabhadra!*
> [1]*"White doves often choose mates of different hue*
> *and the parrot loves the black turtle dove.*
> *Satyam, Satyam.*
> *Yath-Atatham!*
> *Dama! Dama! Dama!"*

Thus it was, that Hyperion at her tender age, was given a glimpse of the Sprites, a most unusual and rare gift.

---

[1] <u>Epistles of the Heroinces-Ovid</u>

The Palace of Queen Estatira

⁂

Elhama and Dan were in the carriage for only a short time when they arrived at twilight at a gate set in a thick hedge. The tall gate was shaped like a large tree and was made of a pitch-black metal.

The tree-shaped gate divided in two when it opened. They passed through a weald which was so thick with growth on either side, that it was impassable if a person tried to walk through it. When they looked out of the carriage windows they saw a large hill ahead, covered with lush, beautiful trees. They didn't say a word, for every passing moment seemed to reveal a new wonder.

When the carriage stopped, Dal opened the door for Elhama. Dan was so excited that he didn't wait and let himself out. They found themselves standing before a watery mass, glittering in the twilight. The water appeared to encircle the large hill and some mute swans drifted by. The swans, whilst gliding on the water, were at a height of two meters; how tall they would stand out of it, was hard for the couple to imagine. From the banks of the watery isle, a golden coracle was approaching. . .or so it seemed. It was pulled by 3 elegant, ebony swans. Þrúðr approached Elhama and Dan. She was hard pressed to take them out of their reverie but nonetheless, said in her beautiful manner, "This is as far as we can take you. This is called 'Dhanadava' which means, 'the gift of the weald." "You are leaving us!" exclaimed Elhama, still looking at the amazing sight. When the swans set the coracle on the far side of the green banks, they realized it was no ordinary coracle. It was round and chrysochlorous and very much like a gigantic nenuphar pad. A tall, lithe figure came floating towards them, she was like a lunar impression and nothing like the women of Rasala. Her skin was pale, like a late moon. Her eyes were like stars set against a cold winter sky. She wore a pale, thin, peach-coloured silk peplo that clung, as if it were soaked in water, to the rises and fall of her lissom form. When she stood in front of them, Dan and Elhama had to look up at her. She spoke in a soft, clear, melodious voice, "I am Blanchefleur," as she said this, she toyed with her long, silver hair as if trying to keep it from floating upwards. Her hand felt cool as she presented it to greet them.

"Elhama and Dan, you are most welcome to Dhanadava, where Queen Estatira resides on Dhara."

She held out her slender arm gesturing them to get into her coracle.

At the entrance of the large disc notch, Blanchefleur said in an inviting voice, "Welcome to your Seeblätter!"

Elhama and Dan were speechless for, they had never been told that such wonders ever existed. The gastrovascular branches of the coracle were like botanical keels and there was a celadon glow to them — they rose through the surface of the disc creating hedges of about 3feet high, so that Blanchefleur opened her arms directing Elhama and Dan to the left or right, to walk through its labyrinth. They stepped in and dubiously placed their first steps. They went in opposite directions yet, kept watching each other.

Dan knelt and touched the surface with his fingers, he smiled in astonishment, it was no different to a small, garden nenuphar. He took a deep breath and his senses filled with a sweet and strong sort of hay or grassy facet. He got up somewhat elated, for there was an after-smell, faintly like tobacco, and that made him long for his lesepfeife.

Elhama and Dan walked to the middle-most part to where a soft, circular sofa was. They could not tell what it was made from. They were still speechless when they sat down. Blanchefleur introduced them first to the largest of the ebony swans. The supple neck of the swan elegantly twisted back to reveal her doe-like eyes. She blinked them in the most inveigling way and said in a soft, tender and animated voice, "My name is Malina-Chada. I am in service but not in servitude, to the Queen," as she spoke, she nibbled at her neck, then carried on, "Some call me 'Bluen' but I prefer to be called Malina-Chada." She elegantly turned her head to the left and continued talking, "I also speak for Malina-Kama." Malina-Chada nibbled into the neck of the swan on her right and fluttered her long lashes, "And *this*, he is my cobbe and is named Arka Naravahana."

Malina-Chada did not wait for her guests to respond; she dreamily swung her head around and glided away from the green embankment.

It was only then that Elhama realised that their carriage and the Arundhati had left. Blanchefleur noticed the surprised expression on Elhama and Dan's faces and said, "Do not be troubled my dear Hyperonoir, you shall meet them again and Dan, you seem surprised that Malina-Chada could speak. Do you not know that all creatures have language but, not all creatures choose to speak because not all who speak, have wisdom?" She fluttered her long, black eyelashes.

Elhama sat more relaxed, pleasantly surprised that Blanchefleur addressed her by her proper name. She did not know what to look at because the swan, the golden coracle, their hostess, the crossing of the water, were as a dream. Dan was speechless and sat quietly considering the eloquent words of Blanchefleur.

At that moment, Blanchefleur raised her arm and pointed to the large hill and said, "This isle has no name, for no one knows that it exists. Perhaps I must say that there is no word in mortal speech that is able to describe such beauty, as that which you are about to discover." As she spoke those words, it was as if Elhama and Dan were being given clearer sight. Ahead of them stood a monumental sight. As Malina-Chada sailed toward the grand banks, Blanchefleur spoke again, "We have reached the other side of Vestana-Sindhu which in the common speech means 'encircling waters'. In the next 300miles, only one splendoured structure could be found. Nothing of its kinds exists anywhere else and no one can find it on their own, even though many have tried. Only someone with a child's pure heart can see the castle." Thus far they had seen no-one else around and twilight had not dissipated.

"Is there a source to this wondrous light?" Dan asked as he wiped his eyes. Blanchefleur pointed upward and Dan and Elhama looked to where she was pointing. About 200m above them, on top of a tiered quintet, stood a giant tree. Dan loved trees and was spellbound as he looked at it. He squinted his eyes but could not tell what kind of tree it was, only that it exuded the brilliance of a rare crystal. Water cascaded from an arch under the tree.

Elhama did not know why but, she cast her eyes from the tree to the cascading water then to the Vestana-Sindhu, and she was overcome with a desire to be submerged.

Malina-Chada had brought them to the side of a pale, blue-purple staircase. The base wall was stained gold and had great emblems of stars and galaxies engraved into it. Dan held Elhama's hand as she stepped from the coracle. Blanchefleur waited for them on the step above.

Dan noticed when Blanchefleur held her dress in her delicate hand, that she was barefoot. Malina-Chada drifted away without the coracle. She immediately went to the front of a group of mute swans which drifted by. Elhama noticed a shimmer around the swans, like the pale, golden light of an aura.

When they ascended the many steps, it glittered in the light; to Dan it seemed that the tree was the source of the light. After ascending at least 50 steps, Dan only then noticed that the top part of the first wall was made of pure gold of two metres in depth. Another set of steps started, and they ascended the second flight which brought them to two tall, square pillars set into the hillside. The pillars were made from a strange stone and between them ran even more steps. Dan stopped at the foot of the steps and looked up at the pillars.

"You are blessed to look upon these gates, it has been called by many names. These pillars are only a portion of stone, it is called 'Sudinnipat-Somadhara' and, if you stood high above on the peak of Drastumanas, you would be able to see them glittering in the early morning sun or when the moon is at its zenith. Many have persevered in finding this place, but no one has succeeded because they find themselves lost in the great weald." The words flowed from her tongue, like honeyed water. Elhama and Dan knew they could not pronounce that name without some practice. "In the common speech it is called 'the Stone from Heaven', yet others called it 'Amala Somadhara'."

Her grandiloquent tone was music to their ears. Blanchefleur led them up hundreds of wide steps. There were tall, wonderful, lush green trees at the top of the climb. The trees were vertical topiaries standing side by side, with alternating weeping lindens and the leaves seemed to reflect the green of the Amala Somadhara. They were led through a long, arched passage-way that was illuminated with radiant light but, the origin of the light could not be seen. Dan was nearly gasping for air when they reached the very top so, Blanchefleur scooped a handful of water from the long, slender pool and held her hand to Dan's lips, and he gently held her wrist as he slaked his thirst. Elhama was the first to notice that they had not drunk nor eaten anything for a long while yet, she wasn't feeling hungry.

From that height they could see millions of trees for miles and miles. The tall tree with its wide girth impeded their view to the north but, in all other directions, no structures could be seen. Blanchefleur directed them to the pale, yellow heliodor which encircled the tree; bird song could be heard in the branches of the tree.

"Have you been presented to the Paladins of the Zarvari Vana?" asked Blanchefleur. "I have heard of them in legends told but, we can't say that we've ever seen any," replied Dan disappointed, for after a day of marvels such as he had witnessed, he could only imagine what those Paladins were like.

"I will tell you how they are nourished. Their prana is sustained by a crystal whose essence is most pure. You may not have heard her name before, she is called Sudinnipat Somadhara."

To them, the sound of that name, was like hearing beautiful music for the very first time. The couple turned simultaneously, and caressed the shimmering tree. The tree trunk appeared to be smooth yet, it did not feel smooth like crystal. It felt more like the roughness of a birch or beech tree. Life flowed from its trunk into their hands but, suddenly they withdrew as if they had been shocked by a charged eel and they looked alarmed at each other. Elhama held her hand to her breast. "Sudinnipat Somadhara only gives in measure to your destiny. By virtue of this Tree, the Paladin is re-animated, when complete he shines resplendedly and strong as before! Most Paladins veil themselves in lesser forms for, no mortal can look upon their true form and live. However disconsolate a mortal man may be, from the day on which he sees this Tree, he shall not taste a mortal wound for eighteen days and; if any maiden were to gaze upon the Tree at twilight, for nineteen years her complexion would be as fresh as her early youth, except that her hair would be silvery white! Such power does this Tree confer on mortal women, that their flesh and bones are made young again. The Tree is sometimes called 'The Dhisana'."

Blanchefleur got up and they followed her towards the northern side of the tree. Although they were still under its canopy, they could see an avenue of oaks, which had beautiful flowers growing around their bases. About halfway down the avenue, an old man was tending some flowers. When they passed, he got up and bowed, took off his hat and held it to his chest. Elhama and Dan returned the greeting. As soon as they had passed, the man knelt down again and busied himself in the earth. This was the first person they had seen since meeting Blanchefleur. Another amazing sight appeared before them. It was a wide, palatial staircase covered in a purple carpet of at least two meters wide and with edges of gold. Two guardian-Ælves, - who stood at the foot of the staircase, asked them to remove their shoes. The Ælve standing on the right was named 'Mihi', his face was yellow and radiant, with a myriad of silver spangles and traces of the finest, faintest orange lines which criss-crossed his face. Mihi was dressed in only a white skirt made from the purest wool; in the skirt were many pleats kræfted of gold. Around his waist a deep azure, thick, leather belt kept his sword in place, that belt was studded with purple gems. Around his neck was a flat, circular collar of 6 bands, each a different colour and from it hung an elegant hacele of white and gold.

On the right, dressed in a similar way, stood a second Ælve. His complexion was pale white, with myriad golden spangles and the faintest green lines crossed his face. He was named 'Laegel', for he was from the Golden Wood. Laegel was armed only with a shimmering, ebony bow on which he leaned both his hands. He was taller than his two metre, long bow. The grip of his bow was kræfted from serrated gold Obsidian 'Surrā Hurasam'. The upper and lower limbs were moulded from silver birch. Beautifully engraved into the back and belly of the bow, were tiny 'red cap' (these toadstools usually grew under birch trees in the woodlands). The name of the bow was 'Sagitta' and in the common speech it was called 'Fly Agaric'. Sagitta needed no quiver for Laegel wore a breast plate of silver-blue Wearyan. Embossed into his breast plate were many slender, 3-inch arrows. When ready use or for battle, Laegel would simply pull on the bowstring and an arrow would be ready in his serving and arrow rest. Both Ælves wore no headpieces, only their long, flowing, silver hair.

They walked up the widespread, luxurious steps and felt the thick, soft, purpureal carpets beneath their bare feet. When they arrived at the topmost stair, they saw something which they were unprepared for. Nothing like that had ever been seen by humans before. Two statues of winged, eight-legged horses stood raised on a pedestal of about 9 meters high. Adjacent to the winged horses, water flowed back and forth and created an arch.

Crystal water flowed between twelve-rayed flames, which burned alongside the water. All of this created an arch covered with a canopy of spangled sands. Thus, the four elements stood side by side in order of celestial reckoning; Air – Water – Fire and Earth.

Dan held his wife's hand and she stood behind him because she was too timorous. The water and fire created perfect light, the spangled sands made it possible to see colours that mortal eyes could only ever see in the heart of the universe, or at the Great Central Sun called 'Amzudhara'- 'bearer of rays'. Blanchefleur smiled and led them under the elemental wonder but not without first saying in her melodious voice; "You pass with me as One, for no mortal nor immortal can pass under the 'Dome of Kala' unless in perfect balance with the four elements."

When Dan and Elhama passed underneath, Dan stopped and looked up at the light which was tempered for their form. He stretched out and lifted his arms upward. He lifted himself onto his toes, his fingers spread open, as he reached for the swirl of water and tried to feel the outflowing light.

"What? What Blanchefleur, am I feeling?" he asked, his heart trembled yet he was overcome with the urge to touch.

"The supremacy of the Amzudhara is what you are feeling, although tempered for you. Usually, ceaseless energy flows and acquires more power with every stair in the tree. It manifests as seven rays, seven states of consciousness on Dhara, similarly to the way that mortals are bound to this world by their seven senses. The senses have no purpose beyond the fourth dimension. They are fully expressed by the Amzudhara." Elhama smiled as she reflected on the meaning of her true name because, all the truths which Blanchefleur spoke, was on account of that light.

As they walked under the Dome of Kala, Elhama understood that they were not thirsty nor hungry because it was the Dhanadava that nourished them.

On the other side, engulfing another hillock, stood 6 slender minarets. The minarets were tiled with the azure stone of heaven called 'Azurite' and they fitted together almost seamlessly. The minarets had 13 serefes because, Queen Estatira was the 13th and last Ælven Queen of Ninfa.

Always on those serefes, stood the Devaka Ælves. They were cloaked in mystery, were without sentiment and a few called them the 'Erinyes'. Although they stood nearly 93m high, their glittering eyes could be seen. The 13 serefes were kræfted from blue Apatite and that crystal helped the Devaka to read thoughts and intentions, particularly evil thoughts directed at the queen or her abode. The greatest dome stood highest, while eight other smaller domes could be seen cascading down the hill. A great architectural feat, was that the main dome's diameter, was 415m and made entirely of Aqua Aura Quartz. Blanchefleur escorted them through the main arch, which consisted of Ælve Wing Blue Anhydrite. The crystal clusters, which formed fan-shaped sprays, reminiscent of wings, stilled their minds as they walked underneath it.

On the other side was an amazing courtyard of blue walls which surrounded tall white poplars, their leaves rustled in a non-existent breeze. They stood tall and contributed to the salubrious effect of the sudden green which greeted the eye. At the centre was a large, octagonal fountain, kræfted from black Opal Blue Fire.

When Elhama looked into it, it seemed that a dark blue sea grass weald lay dancing beneath. As the fountain held her gaze, she heard the psithurism, for a slight moment she caught a preview but, she did not understand it and withdrew her gaze. Yet, that sound of strings from some great instrument echoed in her ears.

They passed through the courtyard and entered through another arched stairway with a passageway of about 6m wide. The passageway was supported by many arched pillars. There were four passages which made a long rectangle, the inside of the rectangle was a large, courtyard garden measuring 351ft by 231ft. Each pillar was about 30ft high; above that was a dome, each dome was kræfted from a different blue jewel. Dan and Elhama were immediately drawn to the light of the large, courtyard garden so, Blanchefleur allowed their wonder to direct them. Haasil shone brightly down and mingled with the light of the moon. They were surrounded by indescribable, pavonian light. The pathways were seamlessly tiled from Abnu Zabarkizag; there were 1000 tiles, every picture on every tile seemed to tell a thousand words.

Elhama soon found herself drifting away from Dan, each in their own wonderment, each in their own reverie. At first, they stopped to admire a four metre, unpolished Skymar at the entrance to the garden. There were thirteen stones scattered through the garden, each stone had words inscribed on them.

The first stone was called 'The Secret' it read as follows;

I give you verse
And this is much
Count the nectars – Enter!
If you have reached the flower late;
Then measure now these hours
For if I were a fainting
Bee, still I would
Not tell
For everything that I have
Told was like
A fragrant floral bell.

Before moving on, Dan pondered at that stone for a while. As he was about to walk away, he noticed that there was a golden band which encircled the foot of the stone. It was engraved in a foreign language that he did not understand.

Blanchefleur stood patiently waiting. Elhama had found the second stone in the middle of a clear pool of water. Elhama soon returned because, she was overcome with tiredness. It was not weariness from labour nor anxiety but, it was the fragile mortal form, even after having experienced such delights, it was unable to find equilibrium in the presence of perfection.

The second stone was called the 'Blue Flower' and had the following inscription;

Far from mortal eyes, deep in
The Woodlands
There is a crossroads.
You can get there,
If you get there,
If you see;
There you will find a show post;

It is grey with years, old as aeons...
If Puck is gone
Or Bragi is not waiting there
If the Ælves are absent
If the Fæge can't be seen;
Ask the birds.
They will tell you
Of the Blue Flower.
This flower
When found, will set you free.

In the golden circle around the stone was a strange inscription; 'তিনি যারা জ্ঞান তার অর্থ - অকল্যাণকর দেখেছি দিন'

It was with those words, that Blanchefleur led them to their chambers, closed their eyes and *set* them asleep. This act was called 'Prabartanā'.

The following morning, when the new sun blessed the world, when Dan and Elhama stood before the palace with all its stately blue minarets and larges domes, they were once again overcome with wonder.

The palace of the Queen of Ninfa had 6 main domes, 6 minarets, and 8 secondary domes. The top-most pinnacle glittered like gold in the morning light. It was overwhelming in size, majesty and splendour.

Two beautiful eight-legged Navapur came striding to Blanchefleur and before introducing them, she nestled between their glowing necks. Elhama took an immediate liking to those strange horses and caressed the rump on one and found its hair was utterly soft. "They are most glorious," commented Blanchefleur as she offered one to Dan. "Do you see how light becomes pliable through their fell?" she asked, face radiant.

"Yes!" replied Dan with the excitement of a child. "Very much like a straw bending light through one side of the fell and refracting it out the other side."

"Observant my joon!" she replied respectfully.

"They are more glorious than the Bragii of Hros. What are their names?" asked Elhama as her horse lowered itself so she could mount it.

"They have no names!" exclaimed Blanchefleur gently, with a meaningful expression on her brow. "Each Navapur comes from Ekam Audapana; some call her Ekamesa which is in your tongue, 'gliding one' or 'Gluggivængr'." "Aaah! The 'gliding one' hmmmmmmm... the Winged Horse." re-joined Dan.

"Look!" he said using the palm of his hand over the horse. "They do not have a single hair whorl."

"Imagine!" remarked Elhama as she held her horse's mane and walked it in circles.

"If that is so, wonder of wonders! There are. . ." she had a quizzical look on her face and started counting on her fingers.

"There are plus-minus four, seven…and eighty hairs in a horse's tail. You mean to say, the fell of Gluggivængr, each hair is one of these Navapur?"

Blanchefleur nodded her head in a coy way, the expression on her face changed to one of blissfulness. She started walking up the ramp and the two Navapur followed her. As they strutted, the one that Elhama sat on, radiated a blue or purple sheen and Dan's, a dazzling mahogany bay.

(If you will allow me dear reader, I will take you on a tour of its architectural majesty and splendour because I value such things. It strikes a memory chord in my being, from days of yore when I spent some ages on Azvapadinbha.)

Heavy, gold chains hung in the upper court entrance on the southern side of the palace. A visitor was allowed to enter the court of the palace, provided they were on horseback and without saddles, reins or bits and contraptions, as was custom to Ælvish folk. A chain hung down from the entrance, so that those entering had to lower their heads or backs. This was a symbolic gesture, to ensure the self-effacement of the visitor on entering the presence of the Sempiternal.

The ramp was glimmering blue from the 30 000 Aztlan, like the sea and the sky on a summer's day. It was also called 'Alhalsu Tamtu'. Various shades of wan, blue, green-blue to deep blue glittered as they made their way up to the entrance.

It was said that the Dwarves dug deep for all that glittered and for gold but, it was the Ælves who shed a tear or laugh for joy and common minerals change to shapes of Light, Diamond, "gem of the heavens" or Emerant. Aztlan was no exception, so named from the land where it was discovered. At every 9th step were amazing designs of deep blue of the four petalled Lotuses, also known celestially as 'The Lotus of Divine Law'.

As they went under the chains they found themselves making genuflection involuntary and then entered the light. The bowing action is also named 'Saĝsiĝĝar'.

They found that the space was very large and round with many windows (300 to be exact), each kræfted from a different gem. Light danced everywhere, and of the 300 windows, one hundred were of clear Quartz. The light was so brilliant that there was no need for a fire-torch or chandeliers. Immediately after the entrance was a circle of about 30 feet wide, and a substance that felt like gold dust, was inside of it. A hedge of 'lalamanpada' (called 'Hornbeam' in Midhe) edged the circle, and they dismounted in front of the hedge because there were many stalls for horses. The stalls were made from lalamanpada hedge, each half the height of the outer hedge which was 6ft high.

Elhama led her horse to one of the stalls, she did not know why but it felt right. The horse entered and dropped its head to feed on the 'gold dust'. Dan led his horse to the right where the stalls had green, green grass growing. It smelled so fresh but, the horse would not enter any of those stalls.

Blanchefleur and Elhama looked at Dan and they smiled, then Blanchefleur said to him, "The Navapur do not eat from the food of the horses which men drive, but of this," she bent down elegantly, scooped up a handful and ate it. Dan was not surprised; he led his horse to the stalls with the 'gold dust'.

Blanchefleur did not explain her behaviour; she only walked toward the large arch cut into the hedge. Dan looked at Elhama who wore a look of enquiry on her face.

"Do not look so curious or suspicious my love. Remember in the books of yore from the East, I used to sometimes read?"

"Yes, I do" replied Elhama, as they walked towards the arched entrance.

"Well, I now fully understand the saying; 'the Sons of Heaven consume the Jiǎ dé. . .'"

He knelt again and scooped up some 'dust' then, looked up at Elhama in a slack-jaw fashion saying, "This is no Jiǎ dé but, I believe it is one and the same." He let the 'dust' fall through his fingers, then scooped up another handful and took it to his lips. . . "No!" exclaimed Elhama.

"Do not eat the nourishment of the Elvysshe-folk, or you will be taken from me and vanquished." Dan immediately let it slide through his fingers.

The two then walked hand in hand under the sylvan arch.

If they had looked upward, they would have noticed that a circular, glass roof enclosed the stalls. That roof retracted at certain times of the year.

Afterward, they stood in the great interior of the grand circle of lalamanpada. They saw that double-sided niches were cut at regular intervals into the hedge and there were halfmoon, marble seats at those intervals. When light shone through from the outside, the 'gold dust', vernal leaves and marble, created a kaleidoscopic dance.

The wood of the lalamanpada hedge was known as 'Karuna Sanda', which meant 'a particular *tone* of wood' and it produced remarkable properties such as when the Queen needed to address a multitude, the hedge and its leaves would carry her voice, so everyone could hear her.

In the innermost part of floor was another circle of lamps covered with gold and gems. After every second lamp were bowls kræfted from Emerant, Tarala, Diamond and Azmasara. The highest vibrational crystal spheres lay within the circle. Still in the circle of many lamps, was a large twelve-pointed star. Its lines were laid in Eastlea while, at every point of the star, in gilded script was written;

The Sacredness of Private Integrity
Water the Divine Balance
The Law of Divine Revelation
The Lotus of Divine Law
Authority in Universal Truth
Consciousness into Destiny

Universal Celestial Agreement
Visitations of Providence
Serene Existence
The Diamond Breath
The World of Light

The two lovers spent a long time in that space, stopped and pondered for long periods at each point, and traced the lines of the star. They felt mixed emotions because they did not understand everything that they were looking at.

A deep cord was struck within Elhama, a distant memory that unsettled her. A memory of a time without Time; when the curse of Ēl Elyōn had not yet pervaded the Worlds nor Stars.

Still many things was revealed to them but, more was revealed to Elhama, this while Dan was set under prabartanā.

Elhama Remembers

It was while Dan was under prabartanā that Queen Estatira walked over the soft grasses towards her. The sound was like wheat bending in the wind and Elhama instantly recalled how she felt under the Yavana Yahva, when she was first placed in the arms of the Queen.

The memory was like coming out of marmoreal sleep and she could hear the music of the creatures of the night. She saw the many Suns bright in the sky and peered into the future. She could hear the immortal sorrows of the world which was to come, through all the ages of man.

She could feel rain. Her skin was drenched with the first tears of Ninéderim, the first female, when she was raised from Abzu. She saw those who came from the Heavens to Eridu. She also saw the First Lament between Onn and Okunoku (Lorelei) and the time before all ages, before Eridu was so named, some four billion years before, when she was "Tara" and was swept away by a sable blazing hand from Ilat Eltarā. She saw the time when Tara had descended into the abyss of mutterseelinallein, one of utter sorrow, and how the two Great Dragons took turns and swept over the sleeping Tara. So young, so tender or perchance not, Elhama was shown some kind of Énouement. All this and more were made clear to her, like wild things seen under a harvest moon.

She also heard a grand and awful voice saying,

> . . .Though the father shall have a mortal son
> that he shall never see,
> he will abide with his immortal brother;
> That the son shall not see, but know.

One other knew this prophecy, it was a Lītūtu Da'Āmu, as all Belum of Haasil made. The oath maker and the oath breaker was one of the Belum of Haasil. Elhama was from the line of the Belum of Haasil and the Haasil were from the line of the Pavonian feminine. The Pavonian feminine bore children from the High Ælves of Morpheus. To her were shown the secret things and to you are revealed some things that are secret, so that for a while it will be known as a polichinelle.

At last they arrived in the throne room before the Queen. To their delight their little daughter stood on the left of the Queen's dais. At the Queen's right, just a step lower, sat Blanchefleur, bright and peaceful like a pale flower.

So, it came to pass, that parents and daughter came to know the many splendours of Ninfa.

...Some holidays are best remembered even to old age, when the eyes grow dim and the hairs turn silver, and over the years the experience is embellished...

Embellishing memories is how the mortal mind searches for lost time and as time passes, the visions slowly pass from memory.

The Taking of Elhama

The time was 3 January 8663 and Elhama was reading in the garden, when she suddenly put her book on the bench beside her. She was suddenly troubled and as she looked up, She noticed that the sky had darkened A chill crept over her and caused her to drop the book to the ground, and a withered leaf blew onto its pages. She got up to go inside the house but stopped and glanced at the open book. Her bright eyes caught a line, '. . . a thunderbolt gives birth to a spring, a broken heart to floods . . .' She then rushed inside to get her red shawl.

Her parents were visiting a neighbour and she didn't tell her siblings where she was going. She looked up the road and saw that nobody was about.

In those days the village was simply called 'Élam' because, travellers would suddenly come upon its light after riding on the dark roads between the mountains or forests. The light! The lights of several dwellings of Élam. There were only four dwellings; her family's house which they rebuilt after the Unpance's had moved out, the Underhill's, the Abathwa's and the Jabberwocky's. The street was always filled with many children, like sparrows having found a home and swains from far and near.

As always, the Döppievölle Inn was abuzz with customers but, for some strange reason the street was devoid of people and so, Elhama would go unnoticed. She wore a long red cape and cowl over her clothes.

By the time she reached the Great Dwarve Clock, the sky was already a grey-silver-white, from the falling snow. It was an anomaly because it didn't snow in Élam and the air wasn't cold enough for snow fall. Elhama couldn't understand why no one was about to see such a great event. In her heart was a stranger incongruity and sensitivity of flight.

She looked hurriedly over her shoulder and saw a ratha parked in front of the gate at number 528. The sprightly Elhama got in, took hold of the reins and hurried the dwhëel along. They made quick tempo of it, up the hillside towards the cottage of Bllömpotvölle. Her cheeks were flushed, and her fore-head was hot, and her heart was racing because she had never taken anything from anyone, without asking for it. Although she had no idea *why* she needed the ratha, she reasoned that it was a necessity at the time.

When she reached the top of the hill, there in the middle of the road, stood a lonely figure with his hands behind his back and with arms folded. Bllömpotvölle was wearing red leather pants and a fur trimmed, red leather coat with a broad band of blue near the fur. She had a tremendous fright because she had never seen him in her 18 years. He was only spoken of in tales by the fireside.

Elhama signalled the dwhëel to stop in front of Bllömpotvölle. He started singing in a melodious voice;

"Are there [any] well-behaved children here?

Look! One is out of her nest. . ."

Bllömpotvölle moved out of the way. Elhama did not understand what he was singing about and she was agitated that he had delayed her yet, she was surprised that his song kept her from moving forward. She drove off without looking back. When she reached Dystiġ, she turned the ratha around and encouraged the dwhëel to make full speed.

As she passed the cottage of Bllömpotvölle the axel of her ratha snapped and came undone, the left wheel rolled away while the axel dragged in the snow. She came to a stop against the hedge of Bllömpotvölle. Fortune was on her side for, she came out of it without a scratch and her youth made her all the bolder. She jumped out and looked at the snag she was in, then heard a melodious voice faintly singing. It came from within the hedge so, she opened the gate and passed through. She followed the voice and hoped that Bllömpotvölle would be of more help to her than previously.

He was singing these words;

> *"Come now maiden, damsel dear,*
> *I will show you a secret gate*
> *By the secret wicket you shan't be late*
> *I'll lead you where others fear to tread*
> *You will go where no mortal has been led.*
> *I'll bring you to the willow's end*
> *where light guards and the water bends*
>
> *In-betweens, crepuscule, twilight, light;*
> *Where the butterflies flutter bright*
> *and the flowers sing.*
> *And where the Shadow-Folks dwell*
> *between the dark and the day.*
>
> *I follow these forms of light*
> *for on light the child is fed.*
> *They call this time the 'children's hour'*
> *for their hearts are un-haunted,*
> *and their dreams are not dead.*

At the tip of the leaf
in the glint of the drop
at the quiver of the bough.

Or the blue haze of stars
on a winter night that it seems
to warm Will o' Wispet beams.
Or flame bright, Moon light –
Honey-suckle – lamplight.
Glow worms and Fireflies.

Don't you wish, you wish you will;
Dance by the light.
Go off and translocate
to the wondrous world of Light.
Pick-a Boo
in Gazanthadu!
King Salamander lives there too.
And Okunoku is the maiden to know
when standing in the flam-rouge-luce"

Elhama found herself suffused with the celeste glow of the evening sky and water. She had arrived at Amala Rhada, where even the finest, natural landscapes transformed. The little, woodland lake of Amala Rhada was like a dream and there was no snow falling there.

The stars glittered brightly through the celeste glow. Steep stone steps led down to a coracle nestled in a grassy alcove.

Elhama got in immediately. She didn't ask any questions because she had time to contemplate while she followed Bllömpotvölle through the sylvan wickets. As she touched a linden tree at the foot of a stone staircase, she remembered that if she were to find herself in trouble that, someone would come to help her, one not familiar yet a Familiar. Elhama understood, as she settled into the coracle, that Bllömpotvölle was that one.

Her coracle was shaped like a leaf and the leaf stalk was used as a rudder for steering in rough waters. The ribs of the coracle also ran forward at an angle like the lateral veins of a leaf. The wickerwork of the coracle was ornate and kræfted of flaxen thread and was rolled up neatly at the rim of the coracle. Tied with silver rope, was what seemed to Elhama to be a sail of some kind. "Loosen the ropes when passing through Hros for that part of the river is guarded by the Pradezini. . ."

"Do you mean the Mergwarch?" interjected Elhama in a breathy voice.

"I mean exactly what I say," replied Bllömpotvölle with a wry smile.

She took hold of the blue paddle as Bllömpotvölle pushed her out and away from the embankment.

With this he said to her:

>*"Cossetted, you sail*
>*into the world of Anadi*
>*a wet horizon encircling us*
>*Ássmentär"*

Elhama held on as the coracle seemed to find its way up the river. Avidity flowed through Elhama as they sped on. Where was she going? Where was the coracle sailing her because it seemed to have a mind of its own? The strong waters of the Afon Wen flowed towards Ninfa yet, the coracle had no difficulty traversing it.

Snow was falling but not as hoary flakes, instead she saw them as millions of forms of multi-coloured luminosities. A light within the flakes revealed an-Other shape and within that, yet another which was receding. Elhama believed that it was deception created by the light but soon discovered, that her journey was no ploy.

Time was fleeting when she neared Hros and she remembered the Mergwarch – the Pradezini and did as she was told. She loosened the ropes which held back the sails and they jumped up as if caught by a strong gale. Elhama pressed her hands in surprise to her bosom because the sails were incandescent, blue light. Thinking that she could physically touch the sail, she fell forward and had to grab hold of the boom. To the Mergwarch guarding the banks of Hros, no coracle was seen floating by, so she passed out of sight, out of the watches of the world.

❖

The snow had been falling and voices came calling dressed in willowy figures, green eyes shimmered like Emerants and long snowy hair followed in the still night. The inhabitants of Beth-Élam came out of their homes and poured into Lamas Street and saw only snow falling, and the wonder that it was did not leave their hearts cold, except for Elhama's brothers because they went peely-wally telling their parents that their sister was gone.

"Do not be alarmed sons, she is not gone." replied their mother in a soft voice. Though her voice sounded like a threnody, her eyes spoke only of wondrous hope.

Dayaal smiled pensively and wrapped his arms tenderly around his wife's shoulders. They were, after all, forewarned that such an Elvysshe Fægenimen might happen.

Kumina Portendorfer saw that the family was in a group hug and walked over to them, pushing through the merry crowd.

"Is this not a happenstance? We have not had snow in these parts for as long as I can remember. Where is that pretty girl of yours, we should all be celebrating?" she said in one breath.

"I've just sent Hertia to tell her pappie to bring out ale and tea," she went on matter-of-factly.

Kumina turned about in her slow-motion kind of way, and ran her fingers through her thick, chestnut hair. She smiled and did the turn again, then clapped her hands coyly and dropped her head as her thick hair fell over her hazel eyes. She was a voluptuous, delightful woman and her pretty, playful manner was infectious. Kumina took Aures's hand and started dancing in little steps, one then two, staccato; stop and start.

She grabbed Dayaal's hand, then Eynon, then another and another till the circle was twenty strong. Old and young joined in.

Those outside of the circle clapped to a merry rhythm. The large circle took one step backward, one step forward, another to the side. Toes pointed up, toes pointed down, then all hands dropped from holding another and the circle walked in a clockwise motion.

Soon some Jabberwockies had brought out a large brazier to keep everyone warm. The ale was flowing from Döppievölle Inn. Two of the youngest Illyrian boys rushed home to get two wooden bathmats, took it outside and set them down on the snow. The older of the two got on top while the youngest one, pushed. Down Lamas Street to the Great Dwarve Clock they went. So in 8663; January the 3rd of the Fourth Age, on the eve of the Fægenimen of Elhama, the first snow sledge was created.

While all were merry and other boys and girls followed suit, young Hertia Underhill asked Aures where her friend was. Aures lied and told Hertia that Elhama was sick in bed. Hertia smiled and said, [2] "Poor Elhama, she's sick as a cushion, she'll want nothing but stuffing." Aures broke out in laughter as Hertia walked away. Hertia knew that Arye Aures was lying, for Hertia had sagacity.

For 3 mornings Hertia would ask how Elhama was getting on and Aures continued to lie to Hertia. For 3 days and 3 nights, it snowed continuously but, it was not so for Elhama.

On she sped through the night along the banks of the Afon Wen. 9 phantoms were seen. They appeared as long, cyanic whizzes and, at the end of those long cyanic whizzes, were the heads of comely ones who wore garlands of leaves made of glittering gold. Four of them were Dwarves and 3 of the 9 were ancient Ælves.

All was a whizz of Morpheun light so that by the time the coracle passed Maldon, the light had tranced Elhama into asleep.

When the coracle neared Albtraum, it slowed to a standstill and Elhama woke. The river was wide and placid. Myriads of exquisite nenúfares, some four meters wide, floated by the river bank. She paddled her coracle toward them, eased her awes and glided into the flowers. It surrounded her coracle and she smelled the strong fragrance rising from the coloured petals.

---

[2] Jonathan Swift in 1731

The four petals of each flower opened only a wee bit, that light escaped from its interior, blue and silver light so that myriad spouts of light reached upwards into the night sky.

Those four petalled flowers were the celebrated nenúfares of the Tao, with two, deep blue and two glittering silver petals. Elhama reached for one and plucked it from the river and brought it close so that she could drink in its fragrance, then she was enraptured by all the nenúfares.

She sped over Albtraum while its inhabitants dreamed in the still of the night; over the forest Zarvari Vana and then, passed out of time. Her coracle splashed into Hrada Kaza, a beautiful lake in the shape of a handsome face. The lake was one of 6 winterburnas that partially fed the River Næddre.

Above the head of the lake, rose a great dūn. A solitary village lived there, disconnected from the rest of the world. No path or road led to or from it, and some who had gone to the foot of the dun were afraid to go up it because they said that blazing eyes looked at them and that those were eyes from the congregation of the Eldritch.

The village was named Zamm, for it meant 'a space of Time'. It was said that brave or adventurous Eldiĕni told tales of arriving at Zamm but would never tell what Zamm actually meant. Whenever folk gathered around fires and told stories, 'Wulfmaer' and 'Kurtidāgh' were often uttered in relation to the village.

In the heart of the village of Zamm stood a tall plinth, on its top were 3 mirrors which were personally kræfted by the great Dwarve king Nshidimzu, father of Buzur, for the Ælves.

The mirrors were kræfted from fire Agates and were vitreous; each stood at 18ft, positioned like 3 mainsails with overlapping curves caught in the wind. At the foot of the plinth were 3 winches that were used to turn the 3 Agates.

On the night that Elhama arrived, the Agates of Zamm were spinning. Nothing passed by Zamm or Hrada Kaza without its inhabitants knowing because, the Agates gave signal to the watch towers of the Palladins at Vel Domas and on top of Vel Samoda.

The spinning of the Agates of Zamm caused a kind of 'fox-fire', which in turn caused a sun-scald on the lake, awakening the Parizád.

It could be seen at the top of Il-Kur-Ngis and to them it was called 'the turning of Izi Sˇuba' and the whole realm of Fæ̃ge and Ælve subsequently knew that a geis was on Elhama.

Elhama sat pensively in her coracle, her mouth was dry and she could hear her heart flooding her throat. The coracle floated over the still waters toward a tall rock that had aggy-jaggers about it, similar to those found along the north Midhe coast close to the city of Nilbud.

In the middle of the rock was a glimro and it mysteriously seemed to dissipate. Elhama saw that the rock was shaped like a seat and the glimro came from the eyes of a being seated on the rock. The being was an exotic winged Parizád. Her raven hair hung from her well-shaped head around her large, outstretched, snowy wings and into the water.

She was in a hurdle sitting position with her right arm rested on her right knee, so that it supported a golden scale which hung from her fingers. Her left leg hung down to the moss-laden rock. Her carves were hugged by ornate, leg shin guards that were shaped like wings and kræfted of silver and had edges of gold.

Strands of grey-green fabric poorly covered her form, as most of it floated about the water. On one of the scales stood a Dwarve, only 6 inches tall and on the other scale was a golden hourglass, the sand made of many hued crystal grains kept falling, never ending. "Drink!" said the Parizád, in a grand and awful voice.

"Your mouth is parched and I offer the waters freely." Elhama scooped the water from the lake into her hand and drank.

The Parizád said, "Now you are free of Time," then faded from mortal sight.

Light, like gossamer threads on a sea full of stars surrounded Elhama, and she was swept away like celestial meal-drift. She passed west over the sun and then over Simud. Elhama wept because Simud had been covered in flowers for millions of years and now they were fading. The sight was hard for her to bear. A tear trickled from an eye and rolled down her lovely face on to her swelling breast, and then it rolled into a dell. From it, a lovely green, oak seedling germinated.

Elhama passed from the aethyrs of this world and the dregs of time seeped from her being as she was carried away on starlight.

Her destiny was sealed, though in her blood Elhama already had *an issue* of Sunnestede. For as you know Elhama was found by the Ælve Queen on the Day of Litha.

She passed so far over the stars that her brothers and father had forgotten that she was gone. Her mother never forgot, for each waking moment she thought of her dear child.

On the 3rd day Aures woke up with a start. She snuck downstairs and prepared a breakfast, took it up to Elhama's bedroom. Aures wept softly for there Elhama lay fast asleep. She gently woke her daughter and when her eyes opened, she said lovingly, "Elhama! From now on we will also call you 'Veladhr' for it means 'time stops'. Blessed are they that took you away, for I am glad that you have returned. For the Ælves do not entertain the Eldieni. Your face is filled with youth like those they call 'the ever young'." Aures placed the tray beside the bed and mother and daughter embraced.

"Yes Mino!" Veladhr softly exclaimed. "I have been far away where all temporal things have no sway."

Her brothers came into the room one by one, so did her father, all were glad except one, his name was Invidia.

Invidia saw the favour of the Ælves on her face and fled from the room. She never saw him again because he left home and chose to live in the land of the Měnehüne. In the years that followed, he had a son whom he named Cayden, who became best friends with Tigma of the Hrosvyra. Always those 3 were ready for war because enmity crept between Invidia and the Ælves for over him was 'Leśyā'.

Dheya Visits Alkana

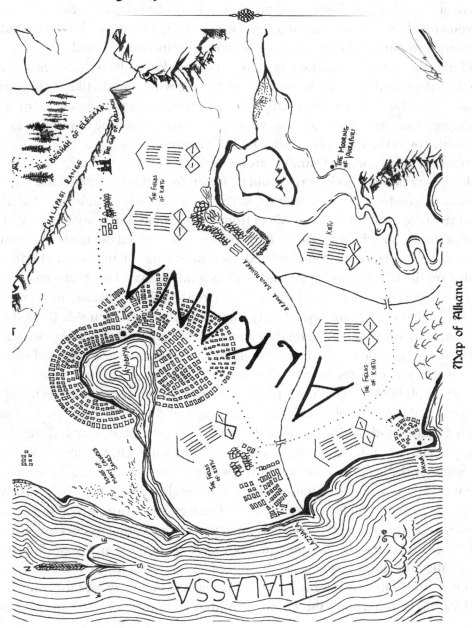

Map of Alkana

There was no Pradeza inhabited by mortal kind like it on all of Eridu (or Dhara as those from Alkana call Earth) and it was called Alkana, she was the majesty of the western world.

The mighty realm lay 15miles from the ocean at 600m above sea level and lay with her back to the sea. It boasted the grandest beaches in all Eridu, called the 'Strönds of many coloured Sands', where glittering shells of white and purple-black lay like pelagic jewels.

When you visited there in summer and stood with your hands on your hips you would sigh, for the mile-long promontory below was triturate with glimmering sea sand.

The midmorning sounds of Pandura, Jalakukku and Nilaksa gulls could be heard overhead, accompanied by the sound of gentle, lapping waves. Its enigmatic sounds, like walking barefoot over a mountain of silver coins or the scuffing and shuffling of feet on the sand, or the heavy, loud throbs close to sunset of the mighty waves or perhaps the whistling or barking sand after dark in the winter or as the wind played with its zillion grains.

The 'Strönds of many coloured Sands' were a delight.

Every day before noon, a giant horn would be blown from the Tower of Nabû (781ft). The horn was made of wood and overlaid with gold. The great horn itself was called 'Nabû' which meant to 'summon' or 'proclaim'. Many sailors from the one thousand harbour bars called that the 'Straight of the Moon' which measured 8.6992 miles wide and led out from Alkana into the Great Thalassa. As the 'Horns of Nabû' echoed over the Strönds, many, many children could be seen seated on the tall dunes that guarded a fifteen mile canal. The Alkaninas unearthed the canal and made it possible for their ships to sail from the Great Thalassa to a large, inland harbour at the capital city of Ayodhya. Thirty flagpoles, fifteen on each side lined the canal, each with a beautiful image of a crane on the pennoncelle which flipped and flapped with their long, purple streamers in the wind. The image showed that the crane held straws of wheat in its claws, that was the symbol of the Pradeza of Alkana.

Ships from far off lands entered the Straight of Nabû at noon every day. From the planking of the hull, large sails which looked like dragon wings, would be released. That accompanied by well-crafted figure heads of dragons near the bow; was a sight of wonder and trepidation.

As they passed, the children sitting like sparrows on a branch, would rise to their feet and cheer. Some of the mighty ships would house triple crow's nests and from there, little accoutrements would be catapulted towards the passerine children. Some would rush away to show their parents, others would stay and dream of foreign lands from which those paragons came. Such were the wonders on the 'Strönds of many coloured Sands'. Alkana was also named Asura-Bhu, 'The Land of the Sun', for the sun shone 250 days of the year. It was a land of plenty and was also called the 'Realm of Magick'. In the old days it was a realm of great peace, ruled by the 12th Queen or Fratakara. Her name was Vardhaka. It was very rare for women to rule Alkana and Vardhaka ruled since the 11th King. A king was called a Fratadara and Vardhaka was a descendent of the first ever Fratadara named 'Sebelo' for he was half Ālkerian and half mortal. So it was, that the brightest star that hung over Alkana was named 'Ālker'.

The Fratadara and Fratakara were Magi; they were fire makers or Guardians of the Fire because they understood Fire's purpose. They held an esoteric wisdom of the Element and some said, that in years past, they kept *agreements* with Lorelie. Lorelie was fire itself, in all its forms and ways in all the Universe, in every Realm and Dimension and, sometimes took the female form at will.

During the reign of Vardhaka, rumour spread that she was good, keeping equilibrium with Lorelei and therefore a great time of prosperity ensued.

The 'Strönds of many coloured Sands' was at Alkana's vanguard but, at their rear, rose a great mountain range called the Phalapasi. It lay in a great curve of 500miles, with only a small passage for access or thoroughfare. That passage was more like a ridge where the mountain range lowered and it was called 'Giridvara', which shared the name with the little town situated on the ridge. The town was flanked by two tall towers of 2624.67ft, named 'Nabholihvara'. Its inhabitants kept guard to the east for enemy intruders. A long road ran beneath it, called the 'Gap of Balloch' named so by the Hrosvyra. One could say that it was the twin edifice to Ina-Nirmana. The Hrosvyra also used the term vinaborgir (friend cities). At the two towers of Ina-Nirmana was an inscription; *'Only Ina-Nirmana is worthy of Nabholihvara; only Nabholihvara is worthy of Ina-Nirmana'.*

The entrance and exit of the Gap of Balloch was guarded day and night. Two guards at the east and two at the west gate; even if the king of Alkana wanted to pass, it had to be 'samacapada'. The gates could not be used as an advantage for war, by foe or vanquisher. The sentinels at each gate were called the 'Þursar'.

Alkana was the second largest realm with 3000 000 inhabitants, who had plenty and in need of nothing. Unlike other realms, they had highways paved in granite, lamplights posed like sentinels and lined the highways. Lesser streets were cobbled, smooth and well fitted.

The cobble stones shone silver in the moonlight while heaps of thick white snow lay shimmering on the sidewalks. It was December and for only 30 days every year, heavy snow fell in Alkana. The scene was a winter wonderland, while the sound of wagons and horse hooves could be heard not too far away, on busier streets of the city.

A tall figure walked up one of these cobbled streets; he wore a dark blue hood and cape. He stopped in front of an obscure door and stood there for a short while. He held his hood with his thumb and index finger and looked down the incline of the street to see whether he had been followed. He wished that the streets of Alkana were less lit.

The tavern was well known albeit that the entrance seemed obscure. If he wasn't in such a melancholic mood, he would have known that it was difficult for anyone to see him clearly under the shadows of the tall, Ponderosa pines on either side of the door. As he turned the large, brass door knobs, he thought for a moment and looked at the smooth piece of granite above the door; deep in its surface, in bold letters was the name, 'Ponderosa'. The Ponderosa was a lavish affair; nothing like Döppievölle Inn and inside he would be as obscure as Jude. Two drunks came falling, muttering and sputtering, through the doors, their legs all wingle and fell together into the gutter. Dheya would usually assist but on that day, he went straight inside and closed the doors behind him.

Inside the Ponderosa were many pursuits, besides ale drinking, to keep one busy. The Ponderosa was a 3-story structure with lavish rooms tailoring for all wants, needs and pockets. That night as always, it was full but, Dheya had been visiting there for nineteen years, so place would be made for him even if it was full.

The Inn Keeper was not expecting him that night but fortunately, Dheya took the table of the two drunks who had just fallen into the street. More fortunate still, was that their table was in the far side of the taproom. Dheya plonked his tall frame down on the fiddleback chair, rested his elbows on the table and locked his fingers.

The din of the place was distant to him, for he was involved with the noise in his own head. He tried to rationalize his actions of late but, it always came down to his deep melancholia. He had lost his father years before, in a most unfair manner or so he thought, and that loss gnawed at him. He had lost his mother to old age only the year before and then the rebellion of his daughters Ástríðr and Arla.

He waited impatiently for the one person that said she could help him, for Dheya desired to travel back in time and he knew full well though it was forbidden to do so, he knew that Orabilis Tama was a close consort to the King and she once said that she knew how to obtain the magick powder, the spice.

Dheya had a silly notion that she would help him travel back in time before the death of his loved ones, perhaps to bring back memories; who could tell? He thought to himself, 'it cannot be wrong. After all, how could it? I am not doing anything wrong by seeing this woman' As he thought that, he fingered his silver marriage ring.

He had seen the young woman several times before and she had been kind and helpful and a woman of her word. Hyperion knew of her because he had told Hyperion of her. Orabilis Tama had never failed him and he believed once again that she would keep her word.

A barmaid gently placed a large pint of yuvasuravira (a kind of 'ginger ale') on the table before him. As a rule, Dheya chose not to drink alcohol but, his wife said many-a-time that he might as well drink the stuff as the 'vira' was so strong.

The 'taproom' was becoming too noisy for him so, he picked up his glass and walked over to the saloon, where it was supposed to be quieter, and found himself a table there. The saloon had soft, red rugs on the floor and the fire was roaring. Dheya was carrying a secret sorrow which was unknown to his wife. He was afflicted by what he could prove and distracted by what he knew.

He fingered the marriage band again as his thoughts digressed; a short poem came to mind which he had learned long before;

Day is ended
Eyes are dim
Candles burn out
As stars a-light
Now sleep allures me
As dreams drift
Me ever on
Tis how we cross the
Deep dark night

Tis how we
Cross the deep
Dark night.

His head fell forward for a moment, then he jolted back up as he realized he was falling asleep.

The Woe of Unnumbered Tears

———◆———

S ome moments passed before Dheya noticed that the noise level in the tavern had dropped substantially. As he looked up for the reason, he saw, gliding through the entrance, the tall, stately figure of Orabilis Tama. Most of those present had seen her before but each time was like the first for; she would arrive, stay a night or two, then not return for long, long periods.

No one knew where to find her except at the Ponderosa. If anyone needed her help and waited there for her, she would arrive at exactly the right time. Some thought that she employed a spy but, no such person was employed by her, for how else could she know when to arrive? Some believed she was born in Alkana, others believed she was a Hushas but even so, she would be a long way from her home because the Hushas.ene never went to Alkana. Folk knew that her looks and beauty were different from those native to Alkana but, amongst the locals, she didn't stand out much, except for the ta-tus. She usually concealed it under her clothes because it stood out so and made her look different in any Pradeza. That night however, she didn't conceal them.

She wore a yellow, silk tussah blouse, with a kind-of v-neck and soft collars, which revealed a long ta-tu that started under her full, thick, mauve lips. That ta-tu almost in the shape of a lyre, extended under her clefted chin and clearly parted over her larynx into two columns that showed a pattern of criss-crossing like a weave of wool. That ended with two parallel lines in the shape of pine needles, which ran the length of her strong neck. Where her neck ended that shape was inverted and more curvaceous, the last two curled upward like finials with a star upon each. The long space between the splitting ta-tu was closed on her chest by a third star that divided equally in light and dark shades.

She also wore a crimson-and-white striped wool skirt with a tassel belt; on the tassel belt were many leaves made of fine, silver dangling and jingling freely, as she swayed her serpine hips. Her boots were thigh-high, tanned leather with Marten fur, a small mirror made from polished metal and wood with carved hare figures were at the top end of the boots.

Orabilis had long, plaited and twisted, auburn hair that hung to her waist. Wisps of light hair danced on her forehead.

Even this mpese she wore elegantly, and it surrounded a face with the complexion of ripe, pale apricots. Over her aquiline nose she wore a temporary ta-tu. She had nearly transparent, pale, almond-shaped, green eyes that were lined in pitch-black ink. She took her seat next to Dheya and half whispered in her husky voice, "Miboosamet!" which means 'I kiss you', for she greeted in this way. All sleep had now left Dheya, her presence gave flight to all fatigue. "And I greet you Arama," he replied; for Dheya chanced upon her a long time before in spring, and Arama meant 'spring'.

"You are late today Arama," said Dheya as he signalled to one of the barmaids. Orabilis smiled demurely and said, "Father Time kept me tonight, why so serious and morose my dear Dheya?"

Dheya dropped his head because she spoke the truth and her being late didn't bother him in the least. The barmaid came beside the table and Dheya ordered some red fruit tea for Orabilis, that was what she always drank. She waved her slender finger indicating no. Instead, she ordered a tall glass of 'the Green Fairy', that surprised Dheya but, he did not ask for the reason why.

He listened as she spoke in whispered tones and while her speech explored the haunts of his melancholic solitude, it brought him placid moments. When the barmaid arrived with her drink, Dheya found himself drinking little bits of the smooth drink. Its colour made him feel as if he were swimming in some swaying grass. Orabilis kept pouring little bits into his glass, and spoke in accepting tones about the fact that he did not drink.

"There is a secret about the 'worms wood' to induce an inexplicable clarity of thought, increased sense of perception, enhanced imagination, inspiration and the ability to see beyond. Can you see me now?" said Orabilis. As Dheya looked up at her, it seemed that she was adorned in the plumes of a great eagle, its wings enfolded her and its neck and large head bowed down and caressed her face.

As she spoke it sounded to him that furtive chorales were falling like golden stars from her full, mauve lips.

Her words, her presence, withdrew Dheya's treasured woes and they got up and walked out the doors of the Ponderosa. Hardly anyone saw them leave as she led him up the street, higher it seemed through the snows. At times, as the wind kissed Arama's long hair and she beckoned, he imagined that it was Hyperion.

Hyperion, Arama, a goddess, a wraith, his mother? Who could tell, but as they climbed higher, the trembling willows wept on her form like sylvan swags.

They crossed the river Peyakheda (which was named "Dheya's Sorrow in the years that followed). There, the quivering water reeds sighed around Arama. Some disturbing of wings could be heard in the boughs but they did not come out to sing, neither to save Dheya. The birds and the night things slept on amid the passing haste, except the eyes that fatten on darkness and in placid trance, Dheya forgot the pain that came with desiderata.

They arrived at a door; Arama stood in it and looked at Dheya and he fell into the pale, green pools of her eyes as they spoke fragrant words like myriad roses in a jewel garden. And since no consonants nor vowels fell from her parted lips, Dheya entered willingly. She retreated into the recesses of that dusty, stoney place. An ancient smell of old leather, old tiles that had been polished a thousand times or more and dried rose petals pervaded the place. Light from the moon fell through obscure niches, illuming the space with its pale, blue softness and candlelight created a roseate patina against tall doors that led to secret passages.

All the while there was silence, no beckoning calls from an impatient voice, no seducing words to rush him on, but the sound of silence and the racing of his heart.

He came upon a room that was all together fetching and Dheya entered gamely, and he felt light. All was sweet, like red apples offered to a hungry child, from the flaxen hands of wood nymphs.

The room was large and spacious, it was encircled by the greenest, softest hedge some 12ft high, in its vernal bay grew many roses of different hues, interlaced between them were circular, grassy paths that was so soft, it stole the sound of footfall.

The roses were as large as elephant feet and their fragrance more intoxicating than 'the green fairy' and mixed in with this, was the pleasant aroma of juniper. Wide paths from four directions led to a central floor which was made of a dark crystal, and the stars from above reflected in it. Upon it was a dais and upon that a large, inviting divan. Sprawled like a lawn after a peeving, stoney path, lay Orabilis, dressed only in roses. At the corners of her divan were tall, blue moon roses sculpted as topiary. White ring doves cooed and fed on tiny, glittering objects on the floor. To Dheya it seemed that they were feeding on the stars which reflected in the floor. That enchantment healed his mind and he forgot about his cares as he grasped at her lissom form. He looked into her glittering eyes and thought that he had found Hyperion there. Trust broken; his freedom escaped amongst the cooing of ring doves by pale moonlight. He acted willingly yet, was ensnared; he gave his fearless form to all the fury of her wasteful storm. And why? Why did he do it? All his matrimonial fear was gone, and he craved rest from his temporal miseries and wanted to join those he loved in their asinine tombs. But too late the dead contrition make, and cannot wipe out error's stains. Dheya, before death realized that he was bound to a different oath, that in that deed, he was eternally bound to the circles of the world. That deed brought many to death and destruction and even touched the doors of the Ælves.

Dheya lay suffering and swooning, languished as the night turned into dimity. He reached for the black quill beside the divan but, it slid from his fingers and fell to the floor. He pulled his flagging body towards the end of the divan and fell over the edge. There on the floor, he scribbled these words before dying,

    . . . And so I leave this world, where the heart must either break or turn to lead. . .

For a moment, his sight became flawless and he saw clearly before him several maidens asleep in a circle around him. Many flowers surrounded them and in the middle of the circle rested a giant, golden casket. In Dheya's delirium he tried to reach for the golden casket, a Jinnī, beautiful and handsome, stood behind the casket. Dheya called out to him in a heavy dystopian voice, "Why you, at this final hour? Aerendgast! Jinnī!"

And in a melodious voice the spirit replied, "All locusts are grasshoppers but not all grasshoppers are locusts. I am the spirit cast from smokeless fire." and with those words, the Jinnī opened the golden casket. Inside was the most incredible, supernal galaxy filled with all her glittering, glintering stars. Dheya noticed the fire of the Jinnī beginning to dissipate, the great flames danced from his leaf-like ears and then the red glow of his eyes faded as he folded his arms. "Yo-uuuuh!" shouted Dheya.

The Jinnī re-appeared as a beautiful feminine, flaming form, burning warm yellows and oranges and waited for Dheya's words.

"I want your name! I demand it?" said Dheya in desperation.

"Nunzalag!" came the reply, in a most subtle voice. Slowly the flames co-mingled and became a flaming eagle, her wings aflame, dissipating, gone!

Dheya passed from this world on December the 25th 8734, and he found himself walking beside a strange Ælve, who introduced himself as El-Ashhal. The Ælve was known by many names in different lands. El-Ashhal turned Dheya into a raven and bound his limbs with jesses and a pair of wood bells so that he could be heard from a distance. He wore aylmeri jesses and anklets of eastlea as he flew through the Halls of Irkalla. El-Ashhal the Ælve led Dheya past the fields of Pan where all the yellow poppies grew and then through to halls filled with light and darkness, where dust was food and clay, bread. Dheya entered and saw heaps of crowns, no, mountains of it. The crowns belonged to those who once ruled the worlds above. Many plumed wings could be seen, blood stained and without host. Dark, black, strange artifices from curates and acolytes, prophets and mystics, sages of old, those who sang in praise to God and gods, lay strewn about. Still those who implored for relief from life, supplications for healing of their sick and afflicted, from those who beseeched and beseeched yet, got nothing. The vision was one of dejection and despair. At that point, El-Ashhal and Dheya approached a beautiful Ælfennes. She was the epitome of beauty, and Dheya could not understand why she remained hidden from the face of the sun, or why El-Ashhal was not disturbed by her visage because he, Dheya, was troubled. The breeze lifted and played with her long hair, like sails perfumed with an unknown fragrance. Even the breeze stirred by the sighs of her veils, she was altogether lovely. It was warm and balmy around her but, only when Dheya got close enough to look into her eyes, did he notice that she was standing in a place which enlarged, and it retreated further and further until he saw that she was guarded by a great duir, and the West was her eyes. This welcome distraction caused him to become unbalanced and falter in his flight, and he fell towards the ground. Opposite that beautiful Ælfennes stood another beautiful Ælve, and he caught Dheya by the aylmeri. Transfixed, Dheya became his mortal self again and looked into the pavilions of his eyes. In them were things that no man or Djinn could ever know. Dheya turned to El-Ashhal to garner some words because Dheya was speechless. He noticed that the Ælve faced to the East.

El-Ashhal said, "Towards that place no mortal goes. Someone will come after you, your unborn bairn, and he alone has right of mortal kin to enter unto the West or East." Dheya fell at the feet of El-Ashhal and wept, unnumbered tears they were, and while searching through his falling tears, he saw that the ground upon which he knelt did not receive his tears. Only then did he understand the enormity of his deeds.

Enemy in Secret

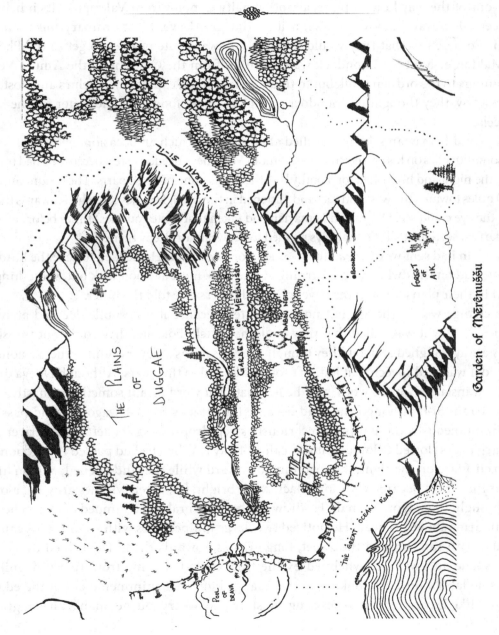

$\mathcal{T}$he 'Boondock experience' he would always remember because he had regaled it to Hyperion on countless times and until before his death; and she cherished the tale for some unknown reason.

It was an unusually, balmy day for that time of year. The sky was clear of clouds and Dheya was to meet Lemayian, his best friend and compeer, at a small town named 'Boondock'. It was a shady-out-of-the-way kind of place, a kind of halfway point from Vakrapuri. Its inhabitants never seemed to travel anywhere else, neither did they leave. Most ordinary folk wanted to bypass it, so much so that they would take the far away route of Élles to get to the Plains of Hros, Maldon or Malbon. Boondock was 100 miles from the Crossing of the Amura Vel and was infamous to the ordinary folk but to traders, stage lines, express men, Jehu's and postriders to name a few, they thought of Boondock as a place to get food, fuel and water for the horses or dwhëels.

Dheya and Lemayian seldom travelled alone, this was such an occasion...

At some 90 miles on his journey from the Amura Vel, Dheya needed to rest because he had travelled through the night and he wished for a bothy but, there was none in those parts. The mountains stood some 30 miles towards the west and east and glistened in the sunlight. They stretched towards the east, as far as the eye could see. Dheya and Lemayian had taken that route countless times before and they didn't like that section at all. They always seemed to get weary or sleepy there.

Lemayian had sent word ahead to No 31415, for assistance. He needed to ease the burden of his heavy load on the dwhëels, so he arranged that they meet at Boondock but, something had changed in their plans, their plans never changed unless one told the other.

The change was in the air, but none could tell because it was subtle. He had arrived at Harrani Si-il; why it was called that they could never tell. For one, they could not translate it and they always laughed about it, they thought perhaps it was a clever prank. Others whom they asked said it was 'Xul speech' but it didn't sound like Xul to their ears. Although Dheya did not know the translation for the word 'Xul' he felt that, *that* word meant something ghastly.

At Harrani Si-il although the road became four tracks so that wagons could pass each other simultaneously, there was a precariously steep drop-off on the left side. A river filled with sharp rocks flowed below and it was called 'Drava'. When he had passed the section with its steep cliff face on the right, the road ran downward while the land opened, and on his left shoulder the Drava became wide and placid with bright, fat, green willows growing along it. Dheya brought the wagon to a halt. He drew up the hand brake and jumped off, stretched and raised his arms above his head. He noticed two, large juniper trees with voluminous canopies and that a path ran through the sweet, long grasses, towards them. He walked over to rest in their shade and was overwhelmed by the fragrance that came from those magnificent trees. As he lay on his back looking at the strange light that shimmered about the edges of the needle-like leaves, tender voices sang "Rest, rest, o' weary journeyman". The singing felt like a shimmer on the aethyrs. He thought that he had fallen asleep but, when he came to it, how long he could not tell, the thing that woke him was a melody so sweet from voices so enchanting, that he sat up. He looked around and hoped to find the source of the music. "You have slept! Slumbered away your tiredness, Oh stranger!" such was the susurrus songs that the sleepy Dheya heard.

The singing was soft and honeyed as he looked up into the bowers and its bright, green leaves. It was then that he saw the heliotropic blue berries glistening and moist, which gently bobbed against each other causing music but, the source of the singing eluded him. He reached out to pluck the fruit, but it would not budge from the bowers. It was then, as he reached up again, that a pale, lithesome hand plucked the fruit and gave it to him. The hand came to him as in a dream and with it appeared a face, porcelain and cynosure with its dulcet voice.

"Such singing!" he exclaimed while eating of the fruit.

"Come" she whispered. "I will sing for you."

Dheya looked back from where he came but the path was lost. He thought of his dwhëels and wagon, but her voice swallowed up his thoughts and the leaves of the great junipers blew them away. She led him away and said in a soft voice, "My name is Sanballat of Mērênuššu."

Dheya replied "I am . . ." and Sanballat finished, "Dheya!"

"How do you know my name?" he asked, as she plucked a flower from a nearby tree and offered it to him. He took it without knowing, ate it and the esculent was sweeter and twice as wholesome as the juniper berries. Dheya fell into a swoon and walked about in a daze. "Why—dooo—you—lead me a—stray?" he asked in a dreamy voice. As the beauty of Sanballat shimmered before his eyes, he held her hand and walked in a desultory fashion.

In fact, all about him was balmy and desultory. He found that her words were kind, her composure was kind and her acts were kind because she walked in a garden of richness, filled with flowers of utter delight and there not only did she sing to him but, the flowers were singing, bright faced and every bell flower imaginable was ringing. "What . . . is . . . this place?" asked Dheya overwhelmed by its beauty. She half turned her head so that her chin just dropped a fraction, like a swan preening its shoulder and replied demurely, "Why—this is the Garden of Mērênuššu."

"Mērênuššu . . . Mērênuššu!" replied Dheya. "I have not heard of such a place . . ."

Sanballat led Dheya to a stately tree. They were tall individuals however, they appeared small from the flowered feet of the tree.

They sat down and she said, "Come! Rest a while." He did not know how long he lay under the grand tree but when he woke, Sanballat said in a whispered voice, "I knew . . . your . . . father once."

Dheya did not reply at first. It took him some time to realize that the prophecy which his father foretold had just come to fruition.

He got up hastily, stumbled forward and fled from Sanballat of Mērênuššu. He did not look back, he only ran as fast as he could.

Panic stricken, disappointed, he thought of his compeer Lemayian.

He found himself lost in a dark forest because he could not find the path which Sanballat had led him by.

His thoughts raced backwards and forwards, he thought, 'how could such a straight forward thing turn out to be such a savage rough?'

For a moment, it seemed to grow dark around him, and he thought that he saw a light on a hill but, remembered that on arriving, there was no hill. Perhaps there was, but he did not notice it because he was in a wonderous swoon... At any rate, he ran toward the light but, the light kept moving away. At last he got close and figures materialised in the light. An ebony leopard, a luteous lion, and a she-wolf. Frozen before them, they howled, growled and chuffed.

The ebony leopard, sleek and flirtatious, came closer with loud, hissing and chuffing. Dheya fell to his knees, panting and tired. At that moment, all that filled his mind, was the story that Hyperion always regaled for him of when she was only a little girl at the palace of the Queen. Suddenly the 3 beasts stood as Sprites before him and became tall and lissom. They said, "Midage on your life's journey, we find you in Myrcwudu, the right road lost. We come before you to give you relief to right path for, this succour you will pass through Dark Wing Realm."

Between them, it lit up bright as day and Dheya then saw the right path ahead of him. He never understood those words till it was too late...

Meanwhile an hour or two prior, Lemayian had arrived at Boondock. He stopped his heavy wagon in front of the local inn called 'Boonies'. It was probably the only pleasant place in 'Bundók'; as the boonies spelled their town. Boonies Inn was without bewilderment perhaps because the owner was a distant relative of Mr Underhill of Béth-Élam. Meena, who owned the place, was the great, great, great, granddaughter of the first Underhill and she was already 90 years old.

At any rate Lemayian knew he could count on her for any news at any time but, Meena had no news of Dheya and it is said that 'no news is good news' except this time, Lemayian wasn't so sure. He left immediately and drove his dwhëels hard, kicking up dust in an already dusty town, zig-zagging, dwhëel-spinning, dodging this wagon and that hrosmaw, getting out of Bundók as fast as he could. He felt that his friend was in grave danger.

When Lemayian saw Dheya's wagon parked beside the road, in the middle of nowhere, he stopped immediately and whistled in a long, drawn out way, with a quiver near the end. First it came as a tiny sound on the aethyrs. Dheya ran as if to nowhere and in his frantic flight, heard it immediately. There was no way anyone in that location could whistle that tune — it had to be Lemayian — it was unmistakably Ondervelden. The sound came from his penny-whistle.

As Dheya ran towards it, he heard these words coming after the impish tune, 'Pano ine ndine!' It was a call from his friend.

Nearing the road, Dheya hoped to find the two, huge junipers but, they were not to be found. When he reached Lemayian, he was panting for breath and fell into Lemayian's arms in an embrace of gratitude. He regaled the story to Lemayian as they worked hastily to transfer some of the goods on to Dheya's wagon and, they kept it a secret between themselves but, the Garden of Mērênuššu, neither its glades nor its singing, were easily forgotten. The sting was gentle, it was not seen, but the esculent that Sanballat offered Dheya was a thing of sorcery.

Dheya visited the garden on more occasions after that, he did not know why, neither could he pull himself away from it, he only knew that when visiting Sanballat, he experienced a kind of querencia. After the second encounter, he told his wife but, it was more embellished for, the embellishment was true; Sanballat prefigured it so, so that Hyperion would not dissuade her husband.

In the years that followed, Lemayian and several others detested passing that place. The 'Boonies' swore that the garden existed, but no traveller actually saw it because they believed it to be flamadiddles.

When the two drove from that place, a beautiful and enchanting voice came over the breezes and with it the words,

"We will meet again
Perchance under a diverse name,
To defeat is, to know a name!
But who can know my true name?

The Magick goes away
Employed only by those of the Magical Way
For what nourishes lay
Waste; for taking you did pay.
The charm fetches velleity;
You have eaten the fruits of Kalliope
It shall rear contrariety;
Not to hate—not to love; only animosity."

The song came in such dulcet tones that even Lemayian swooned for the unknown songstress.

Lemayian looked at Dheya, for the two wagons rode side by side on that stretch of the road. He believed his friend.

Dheya looked at Lemayian and said, "As I came weary to the wood of Seiren ymatal - Â ni'n!"

And Lemayian smiled replying, "The sweetest call is many-a-time cold as ice."

"But sweet music seduces man, soaring melodies sets man free. . ."

Dheya laughed out loud and fell into an ancient triolet;

> *"Tschada dada dada daa (please).*
> *Tschada dada dada daa!"*

> *"I long to be free,*
> *From my griefs, from my fate!*
> *I have become acquainted with thee;*
> *I long to be free!*
> *Since my fall, endless aeons debate,*
> *My wings have become memories plate.*
> *I long to be free;*
> *From my griefs, from my fate!"*

Lemayian broke in, in his lyrical tenor, *"Set me free! All I want—set me free!"*

Dheya sang again in a deep, lowered baritone, *"Set—me—freeee!"*

Then sang Lemayian, his vocal "hiccups" (somewhat like gulping or air or gasping) and breathless stutters;

> *"I long to be free,*
> *From my griefs, from my fate!*
> *I have become acquainted with thee;*
> *I long to be free!*
> *Since my fall, endless aeons debate,*
> *My wings have become memories plate.*
> *I long to be free;*
> *From my griefs, from my fate!"*

The two friends enjoyed themselves as they drove, slowing the pace somewhat in that agreeable delirium.

"La-la-lah—dada dada daa (please)

Tschada dada dada daa—Dada dada daa tschadaaaah!" the two continued in such lament that found themselves near crying.

The Garden of Mērênuššu faced east and spread out south west. It was filled with unknown, opulent fruit trees and flowers but it was not the virtue of Dynyansek but, the rose that had more thorn than petals. Many a brave mortal child came upon it, seduced by its sweet waters and fragrant flowers only to end up under the yoke of Kašadom.

Old wives' tales told that it was in such manner that he, Damasandra, ended up under the 'power of the great and awful Meline Dragon'. Damasandra the Great had journeyed by and was overcome with unusual thirst and weariness. There, while slaking his thirst, he fell asleep and the spirit of the Dragon walked into him. So the story went that Damasandra depended too much on his own strength and was zealous for it.

Mērênuššu lay at the foot of the tower at Erset la Tari where no horde, Kwizir or Melchizedeck was allowed entry. They weren't bothered by that decree because they hated the growing green things and trees or changing leaves anyway. A long passage lined with juniper trees ran from the most eastern door, some five miles long, into the garden. The passage between the junipers was paved and lined with gold so that when the eastern sun fell on it, it was the only light that could be found in Leers.

As with everything in that area, that golden passage was a disguise and so too, was the little door facing east because, it was part of a greater door and it was their desire that vimāna should come through. Sanballat was pleased because her Lord would also be pleased with what she had accomplished.

As the late afternoon sun started to fade in the west and fell on her porcelain skin, she combed her long, flaxen hair with her lissom fingers and watched as the two wagons climbed out of the vale but they, as they took one last glance back, could not see Sanballat of Mērênuššu.

It seemed to Lemayian and Dheya, that the Crossing of the Amura Vel could not be reached even though they had travelled through the night. How long a time had elapsed at the Garden of Mērênuššu they could not tell, but they were worried that arriving later than was said in Béth-Élam, would cause their beloveds unnecessary concern, though it was often their habit to peregrinate in the wilds or some out-of-the-way-town or village-Inn.

The Secret Things of Béth-Élam

⟐⟐⟐

it was once believed, once long ago; that was, very, very, very long ago, that Béth-Élam was Béth-Élohim which meant 'House of the Gods'. It was not surprising then that Béth-Élam felt so very central. In that far back time, folk there used the Dagian Tongue more than the Tongue of Tuath da Noraquilon. In Midhe there were two main dialects spoken; Noraquilon and Dagian. Town and village folk spoke everything in between including common speech, mixing the two main dialects when no other word would suffice. Aquilon which was reference to North really meant 'sky' or 'northern sky' and there was no real history why the people with the Noraquilon dialect called themselves 'Tuath da Noraquilon' or 'the people of the northern sky'. Dagian (dawn) dialects which were referred to as the 'Ancient Tongue' and an even earlier version was used in Ta-merri, were mostly spoken in Alkana. In the deep south of Eridu, Dagian was spoken almost exclusively. The Ælves did not speak any of the languages of man, for the Eldiĕni it was a kind of symbolic interlocution, a facade of language as it were; they called it 'liemduwëi'. Human speech, any human speech, even in those far off days, was already then too low in vibration for the Ælves but, to tell of those Eld reasons here, would destroy the magick.

At any rate, when one scoured the dales and mountains and wandered further afield towards the 'Scīr of Trequaire' by the 'Willow Queens of Traquaire', one might stumble into overgrown labyrinths.

Those hillsides and a little further up in the high mountains of the Glass Houses were also littered with blue rock, and if one dug deep enough; a rock held by the Dwarves to be Blue Diamond could be found. It was not spoken of but, every household on Lamas Street, if they patiently searched, they would find that they had a very large, precious stone or gem somewhere in their home.

It was told that once grandsire Cinaed came home with a large deposit of Moonstone. It was feldspar Moonstone, and he had used it for scrying the future. No one knew what happened to it, whether it was lost or whether he had given it to Old Man Bllömpotvölle after being on the 'ship hanging among the stars'. It was believed that he sailed for 12 years on that ship between Eridu and the Moon but, that link was severed, and none were since able to see it upon the rim of the world. The stone was in the form of an 8-rayed star; and cut into its face, was a smaller

5 rayed star. In concentric circles at the top and bottom, were 9 sacred names. The name of the jewel itself was 'Pyax' and it shimmered like placid water. It is with these bits of secret, that we come to the revenge death of Dheya for that it was, revenge. A revenge held for many ages by a certain Churel. Her revenge came by misappropriation of the Land of Uruku, there in that land where 'Beyond Life there Are' dwell and their ruler was Ubilmelekh. A land where the sky was high and black, so dark, that one would think that no Sun shone on Eridu. No one but the first ones who settled in Béth-Élam in the second age when Béth-Élam was not yet called Élam, when that place whose name now lies buried under many loads of sand and when none now living there lived then, and a slim chance at that, except for the Portendorfers who lived under the hill with the Underhills. That time when that village was plagued by darker sorrows and people's hearts were possessed with supplications, there lived a lovely maiden whose name was Orla. This telling came from looking into that stone found by grandsire Cinaed, so dark was its scrying that he never looked to the past again.

Orla, mostly lovely and gentle, died during child birth. The Awroks of Mirzapur said that if a woman died in a lying room (the place where women gave birth) she became a Churel. Orla gave birth under the Withys, already ancient when her tragedy occurred, before it was named Vēdu Vīrü, and before the Ælves set guard about it. The town's people wished ill on her under that tree because they believed that Orla visited the 'witch shire' too many times and that the 3 Willow Queens could have been the only ones to cause her to be with child, because no one knew who the child's father was.

On the night that Hyperion gave birth to Normagest, Orla's Churel was wakened. Maskim Xul ensnared the spirit of the Churel making idol promises to Orla. He gave her a most beautiful form and so Orabilis Tama was born. But Maskim Xul, liar-in-wait, was deceived, for *those* at Jinbōchō saw all things, they charged the Tuatha Dé Danann to cause a féth fíada, so that Maskim Xul did not see when Hyperion would conceive. In his blindness Maskim Xul used Orabilis Tama to kill Dheya (Orablis Tama who killed Dheya was not so powerful as the one that was awakened from the tree, the latter was mightier and could take many forms), hoping that Normagest, the last Ring Bearer would not be born to Eridu. . .

Ƒow Four became Seven

In the 'Book of Lore' and the "Book of Fate", found at the Library of Floraheuyenza at Jinbōchō, a chapter entitled 'A life for a life" is duplicated; therein are some deep and grave things, that mortals would find trivial, yet they have many manifestations. . .

It came to pass that on the same morning of Elhama's return, Tuesday 6th January 8663, that the children of Élam brought back over the Bridge of Liana, a woman of about 1.7 meters tall, slender, young, pretty, creamy cocoa skinned, with sparkling, azuline eyes and light-flaxen hair. Her very long and somewhat fore-grown earlobes provided her with a singular and unique quality. The children said that they had found her on the playing fields under the large, yew tree. She said that her name was 'Semjase'. Her arrival happened at the same time as the fleeing of Invidia so, everyone in Élam were distracted, more likely enchanted, by it. She lived under the mountain at 528 Lamas Street. Many years passed and the inhabitants of Élam forgot her age or when she arrived. Even when Élam became Béth-Élam, Semjase remembered that when she arrived 8663, she was already 344 years old.

She lived under the mountain with the Abathwa's because they invited her to live with them. The only thing that they remembered about Semjase, was her dress. She was wearing a strange, blue-grey one-piece garment, that the villagers called a 'tuta' and it clung to her body like a second skin.

There was much light in her soft eyes and she found light in the eyes of the handsome Lemayian, for he one of the children of the 'Sons of the Earth', and they soon married. The custom was to have large weddings and theirs was particularly large because Lemayian was very well known. There was another secret in Béth-Élam but, the rest of the story I must now tell.

The day that the children were to be taken to Nilam Hrada to enjoy the remnants of the warmer weather that was fast slipping away, had to be cancelled because thunder came and spoilt the plan. Hyperion had decided that she would go along but the plan had changed and instead, the children had to remain indoors.

There was a knock at the door; the type which makes one exclaim; 'it must be the patravaha Hrosfrēogan Jabberwocky!'. Rains have thunder and lightning, and at times they destroy the crops or harvest, or like the time when it thundered and stormed and Big Bertha was struck by lightning some 30 years before and survived, and at that time she was already 49. The good news was, she survived, and the bad news was she no longer bore milk for the villagers. And the other good news was that she lived another 30 years and kept on going. Those destructions mixed with approbations were at times, part and parcel of the natural order of things. Lightning and thunder were but gentle compared to a more accursed wretchedness like those things that leave a home sorrowing and its occupants lost; that loss and sorrowing are normally done at the actions of man, mostly by their change of mind. For when a thing is set, let it be set and when in doubt, there is no doubt. . .

Lemayian and Dheya stood under the moonlight, their wagons loaded over capacity. They could not believe their luck because they'd get a triple portion and the merkes glittered in their minds' eye. It came at a price though, because what they disliked most was to part ways at a time when they should have returned home together.

That 'luck' of industry was sending Lemayian to Malbon which was nearer home but for Dheya, fell the straw to journey to Gätker Yic; and it would be at least two months before he arrived home.

So, in doubt the two departed from Alkana in separate directions and the Summer that was in their hearts, now lay dying, as a strange warm wind blew through the harbour and its warehouses. Dheya drove through the busy streets and passed the boisterous citizens who were looking, for eternities, into shop windows made up of perishable things. He set out in the late afternoon until temple, house and chattel thinned out. He passed some boys playing on a see-saw with its soil all hollowed out at the ends. He waved at them and they waved back cheering, and as he watched them a tear came to his eye. He sniffed but, did not know why he suddenly felt so emotional at that scene. Finally, he left the great city behind, towards the west on to Nabholihvara and passed over the Gap of Balloch. Once over that mountain pass, the cities, towns and villages were no longer in sight. He was now further away from great Alkana but, closer to the Horns of Elfland. The sunrise chased him and revealed the Autumn crocus opening her flowers. For a brief moment, morning traffic moving in the opposite direction appeared to lessen, till only he was on the road. It was there that some Pixies strayed from their Kingdom and arrived in the fields of man...

And then, all awonder it seemed to Dheya, that Spring had appeared with all her dreams. As he passed through a great cedar wood called the 'Beshah of Elessar', they jumped and climbed onto his wagon and untied all his knots until the ropes were slackened. One went ahead and waylaid a stone or two, so that the wheels went bump and hump but, Dheya ignored the bumps and only uttered a mild curse. Then those blue creatures with their Ælvish ears pulled at their dark, spiky hair that stood at end, and screamed in frustration because he did seem not care.

Dheya stopped the dwhëels and turned about on his seat, he turned his head this way and that, his flashing eyes searched for the answer but he saw nothing, he saw no-one because, to see those of Elf-Land one could not be in polarity. Besides his busy thoughts, were those things of economy and commerce, which negated all Wonder. As he set the dwhëels to run, several heavy boxes fell with thuds, on to the road. He stopped. He got off and rubbed his strong hands over his stubble. He brushed his hair with the same hand and shook his head. He walked towards the back of the heavy-laden wagon and tugged on the slackened rope. "Certes! This is strange. No one can tie knots like Lemayian and I . . .Tch-ch-ch!" he clicked his teeth. He was a strong man but, he had no desire to lift heavy boxes so early in the morning, especially since he was certain of his knotting and roping abilities. When he was done tying and checking and re-checking, he set the dwhëels to start rolling and while he speculated that strangeness, he asked the dwhëels in frustration and in a deep scolding voice, "Do you dwhëels know who caused this delinquency?". The Pixies giggled amongst themselves, but one of them slapped them over the head and they were quiet for quite a while thereafter. The dwhëels were rolling fast and for some 13miles they carried on in that fashion, till they came to a border which the Pixies dared not cross. The road made a fork and to keep to the left was a quicker, faster option through the Forest of Aik. Crooked Junipers grew there, with their gnarled barks all twisted and tangled and not one bore berries. It was a forest with disastrous flowers and plants from haunted heaths. The Pixies knew better than to cross the river into that tangled wood so, they went no further. They stood in the road with their hands on their hips and shook their heads, because the opportunity to hamper Dheya's progress was lost. It was too late, as they already knew of *future time* when that very river would be remembered as 'Peyakheda' or 'Dheya's Sorrow'.

Hrosfrēogan Jabberwocky stood before Hyperion and handed her the letter in haste. It was a busy day for him and that already was the first mirror for Hyperion, but she didn't see it. She recognized the handwriting as her husbands, and in haste tore it open only to read a letter written in alacrity that Dheya would not be home on the intended date. She was not entirely disappointed because from time to time, Dheya and Lemayian would be delayed.

She went into the lounge and slid the letter between one of the books on the shelf, then returned to the kitchen to make a cup of warm tea. As soon as she left the lounge, several Pixies ran amok and took the letter.

Hyperion received two more letters as Dheya addressed the progress of his journey home but, the patravaha never came again. The weeks passed unnoticed by Hyperion, perhaps by others too, like some veil spun by silk-worms.

The days went by as they did in Béth-Élam but there was always arriving or leaving it, September 23 was no different. Mr Underhill had not seen Meena for many years and he had a sudden, unusual urge to see her. Besides having a great, aged Port, several in fact, that she would exchange for a visit from him; Döppievölle Inn was known for its fortified wines.

The Underhills had four draft horses which the Jabberwockies stabled at a price. Määthëkaja and his sister Jöŋkölleuwen (the eldest children of Hrosfrëogan) prepared the horses and the wagon.

So, Mr Underhill set out, a quiet tempered man, but hardly so when he drove his wagon and horses! Around the Great Dwarve Clock they reeled, he covered the distance between Béth-Élam and the Windy Piny Pass in a single day.

When he arrived in Malbon, he spent the night at Dopparoz where the ale and food were known to be good. They knew him well there, as all Inn Keepers seemed to be connected by some spiritis drop.

In the morning when Mr Underhill approached the 'Cobbled Street of Highway' the night guard was being relieved by a fresh guard, who walked over to Mr Underhill and introduced himself as Rhan. He did not make small talk but momentarily told Mr Underhill what was on his mind. He placed his large left hand on Mr Underhill's knee and said, "When yoosa see Dheya agenn remember der is a prophecy thet regards himm. Doonoo forget it. Now go en hevva safe pessage." Mr Underhill though puzzled, thanked him and rode on. The horses were fresh, so he drove the bejeezers out of them, making quick tempo to the Crossing of the Amura Vel; he smiled as he turned towards Boondock.

"Mr Underhill! Mr Underhill!" came several shouts as folk who knew him waved their caps and hats when he sped by. He returned the greeting with a broad smile for, how couldn't he?

The day was cool but clear and without the sign of rain although, on his mind was that 'prophecy' which seemed to niggle at his brain. He reminded himself of the saying that 'it was the little things that changed the world as folk go on their way.'

Some names from olden-time-folk of Béth-Élam sprung up under his pate. They were long gone but the prophecy remained. He recalled the prophecy regarding Dheya Illyrian and wondered why he had been away from home for so long, and why a stranger told him to remind Dheya. It felt like an omen, so he tried to think on fairer news but, little known to Mr Underhill, was that Eridu was passing through tremendous hours.

❖

We all wait for a moment, an enlightening, a window as it were, or any such sign that would inform us of the moment of death, so that we may know beforehand of its approach. We want to know, but such knowing is only for the Gods and the Immortals. There are some who receive a premonition or perhaps a sign. Sunlight was streaming through the bowers as Hyperion reclined in the late afternoon. She was in a dream-like vision and for a moment, she saw Dheya stumble and fall. She was startled as her tea cup fell to the ground and shattered on the cobbles under the tree.

She stared at it for a moment. She never drank black tea. She enjoyed hers with milk and as she watched the dark liquid seep between the stones, into the cracks of earth and vanish, she realized at that very moment, that her husband was lost and was not returning home. At first she cried uncontrollably but, stopped and violently wiped away the tears with her hands. Hyperion sat up, had a thought and walked straight out of the garden toward the house. She left the shards of broken porcelain on the ground. When she emerged just after twilight, she wore a medium sized leather drawstring mayll, thick woollen gloves and a long, red cape and cowl over her shoulders. At the front gate, she looked up the road to see if anyone was around, but it seemed that the winter evening had sent all the children inside and the sojourners into the Döppievölle Inn. Hyperion was glad because she didn't feel like answering unwanted questions or having neighbours' eyes glowering after her. She proceeded down the road to her friend, the one she knew wouldn't hesitate to help her. It was twilight by the time she reached the garden gate of No 528. It was the end of summer, and the sky which she had sat under earlier in the day, was growing darker with dark grey, wet-looking, cloudy layers when she knocked gently on the door.

As the door opened, light streamed out from its interior and before her stood, not the mistress of the house, but her daughter Sigrún. She was wearing a fustian peplo and with a flat candle in hand, she answered the door. Sigrún was the exact image of her mother just taller with dark, long hair which fell to the back of her knees.

She did not wait for Sigrún to say anything.

"Evening greetings dear Sigrún!" Hyperion exclaimed in a breathy, susvapnah greeting. Sigrún noticed that Hyperion was hasty so, she said, "My yaya is not home at present Arye Hyperion. How may I be of service to you?"

Sigrún's politeness broke Hyperion's anxiety so, she smiled and sighed. She caressed the strong cheekbones of Sigrún and replied in her usual charming way, "Dearest child you have your mother's disposition, a way of speaking that diffuses all divergence. I need to leave Béth-Élam immediately and I have no way of reaching my destination for it is atidura! So feorr, so feorr!".

While she mixed words from ancient and old tongue her voice broke, Hyperion broke down before the child and cried. Sigrún being of a tender nature, reached out to Hyperion, embraced her and cried too. When they had done, and their mutual tenderness had eased the pain that Hyperion endured, Sigrún pulled away and wiped her tears and said; "I do not know your troubles, but I feel you are in great pain. Give me a moment Arye and my brothers will prepare a ratha. Come! Have a seat while they hurry."

Sigrún disappeared through the house and only moments later she returned with some warm, lavender tea. Shortly afterwards, the second eldest son, Semjaja, peered around the door and told them that a ratha with a strong dwhëel, was prepared. Sigrún saw to it that she personally drove the dwhëel because it was old and experienced so, the ratha became an elegant carriage.

The early evening was quite cold, and light snow started to fall. The two ladies were dressed warm and the ratha was covered, but it was a kind of history-in-the-making because, it was the second snows that fell on Béth-Élam, ever! Sigrún took them past the roundabout and up towards Old Man Bllömpotvölle's cottage. As she turned her head to look up Lamas Street, people had come out and gathered on the street to enjoy the rare occurrence.

"I will take you as far as I can go," assured Sigrún from her box seat. The ratha had two glass lamps, one each side of the cab.

Hyperion was sitting quietly and hoped that her friend would not mind too much for stealing her daughter away in the night. She also contemplated the falling snow outside. She took off her woollen gloves and held her pale hand out of the carriage, to feel the coolness of the snow. It was a wonder, and as they drove and came to the top of the hill; the cottage of Old Man Bllömpotvölle looked like a Snaiwaz tree. The entire house was filled with light, something that folk rarely saw because his cottage was always dark. There in the middle of the road, standing with his hands on his hips like a joulupukki, was Bllömpotvölle, wearing red, leather trousers and a fur-trimmed, red, leather coat with a broad band of blue near the fur.

Sigrún signalled the dwhëel to stop in front of Bllömpotvölle. He started singing in a deep baritone;

Onko täällä kilttejä lapsia?
Katso! yksi on pois hänen pesiä,
Lumi asemat sellaista ystävällisyyttä
Se on niin alkuaine kavelyttaa,
Lumi kuljettaa kyseisiä ihmiskunnan,
Mutta ilta on aamua viisaampi . . .
He kerro tarvitset siipi,
Kuolemasta on lähettänyt pisto.

Nytviesti Langbarðr kohteeseen Elhama;
Tulevaisuus edessänne,
Kutenalan puhdas valkoinen lumi.
Ole varovainen, miten kulutuspinnan sitä,
Sillä jokainen askel näyttää
Sinun tie on Sinisellä Lohikäärme,
Jos poikkeamaan vedet,
lumi on tahrannut.

Mikä on piilotettu lumi, paljastuu sulaa
Vaikkatapa olla hankalaa
Aarre piilee kotona
Tämä aarre on ehtona
Älä anna ennustettu tekoja keinuttaa sinut tiellä.
Ensilumi on pudonnut maahan, joka on jäädytetty
Voi sinulla on kaikki, joka on myönnetty,
Juuret ulottuvat syvälle, lumi tapana purra.

So, the Laulu Lumessa ended and Bllömpotvölle gave way and stood at the side of the road. Hyperion leaned forward and smiled with mild bepuzzlement as, Bllömpotvölle always sang in riddles but this time, she did not understand all and replied, "In Béth-Élam it is said that you are called Dweomer, but I say your name is Maya." Bllömpotvölle laughed vivaciously and quietly walked through his gate and closed it. He soon disappeared behind his tall, hornbeam hedges. Sitting on the gate-post was a large, fat Ragamuffin of a light grey colour, almost white. The fur over her eyes were pitch black and the cat sat there washing her face over her ears with her chubby paws. "Let us go child! If the cat washes her face over her ear, the weather is sure to be fine and clear." said Hyperion. Sigrún replied, "A year of snow, a year of plenty." A chuckle was heard from Hyperion then a soft reply, "Like your father, always looking on the bright side."

Having listened to the 'Maya' carefully, Sigrún decided that from that day onward, she would always call Old Man Bllömpotvölle 'Maya'.

Sigrún signalled to the dwhëel and as they started their journey, a voice was heard from the dark, ". . . and some names only the Ælves can pronounce. . ." The half-afterthought of a reply, came as a gentle song and then all was quiet, dead still.

Hyperion Searches for Dheya

They had barely reached Dystiġ when Hyperion suddenly gripped Sigrún's arm and said, "Bear with me child! Turn back at once."

Sigrún did as requested and made a wide turn in the road to hurry back the way they came. The snowfall increased and Sigrún noticed that the tracks from their first passing wasn't visible in the snow. She wondered whether she should mention that to Hyperion.

"Arye!" she called out softly but, Hyperion was deep in thought. "Arye!" she called again.

"Yes, what is it Sigrún?"

"Have you noticed that the tracks of our first passing are not visible and yet, the snowfall is too light to have hidden our tracks?"

Hyperion saw what the child was talking about and shook her head. "Sigrún, it is a strange night, I wonder what it could mean? I do not know what to make of it for my mind is clouded, my grief has already begun, and I fear that my husband has left this world. All that I know, is that he went to Alkana. I do not yet know if that is where his departure from this world happened . . ."

Sigrún interjected and said, "But why take the road back as if going home?" "No, we are not returning home but, something drives me in the direction of Élles".

The Afon Wen flowed into the Lama Dupes; pure and white as crystal. It meets the Blue Lama Dupes, and is lost within it, so that there is no more Afon Wen, but the united river is all Lama Dupes. The moment that the waters are blended into the great and onward rolling flood, it is impossible to detect it.

It was to that river that Hyperion persuaded Sigrún to drive her, to the very spot where her future son was to be born.

She bid Sigrún to return home as fast as she could. Hyperion then turned her attention to the willows, there was dimity about them, they drew her toward them and she could feel a strong power reeling her in. Hyperion felt compelled to respond to the pull. The sky had cleared and though snow was still falling, stars started to show their glinter.

She walked cautiously towards the willow; there were no eidolons that she could see — her nerves were on end for, she did not want to be presumptuous, and no one had asked for a boon of Vēḍu Vīrü for an age. She was filled with doubt but, her heart was pure. She touched the Vēḍu Vīrü and embraced it, her bosom heaving as she gasped for breath.

After waiting for some moments and having plucked up enough courage, Hyperion drew an old pair of Dheya's boots from the old suede poke hanging over her shoulder, and placed them at the foot of the willow then spoke;

> *"Many-a hallowing on earth there be,*
> *One I seek a boon it be,*
> *Long, long life to you Willow Tree!*
> *Sorrows, none unto thee!*
> *He the Drone, I the Vlinder*
> *I of flesh, let me through your Duir?"*

Hyperion waited, nothing happened. She looked about but still no eidolon was seen. The sky was clear, so Maya was true to his word. "What could it be? What did I miss?' she asked herself. She tried for a second time;

> *"Many-a hallowing on earth there be,*
> *One I seek a boon it be,*
> *Long, long life to you Willow Tree!*
> *Sorrows, none unto thee!*
> *He the Drone, I the Vlinder*
> *I of flesh, let me through your Duir?"*

"Pish—Pish!" she exclaimed. She fumbled into her poke again and uncurled the parchment which she had created from the cocoon of a vlinder. Only parchment from a vlinder's cocoon could be used for that. On it, calligraphied in Nilanaga ink which Hyperion had procured from Jaddamiah Jabberwocky, (it was a rare ink and how he obtained it, no one knew and he would not say), was the full name of Dheya; 'Dheya Garuda Annedh Illyrian'. Hyperion slid the parchment into a bark slit, still there was only silence around her, not even the fauna locals were about, no bird, no owl, no night crickets. One more time she repeated the incantation;

> *"Many-a hallowing on earth there be,*
> *One I seek a boon it be,*
> *Long, long life to you Willow Tree!*
> *Sorrows, none unto thee!*
> *He the Drone, I the Vlinder*
> *I of flesh, let me through your Duir?"*

The parchment was sucked in and disappeared. She smiled a smile of relief. A great, brilliant, chartreuse light shone forth from the large trunk. Hyperion felt with her hand and her arm outstretched that the solid bark had become incorporeal. Light streamed out from the interior. She held onto her poke and glanced back before stepping inside. Through the bright light she saw two figures standing before Vēḍu Vīrü.

The light from the outside diminished and Hyperion disappeared from outer-worldly sight. To say that she walked would perhaps be incorrect, to say that she was immediately pertessered is also incorrect. Hyperion tried adjusting her gait to cope with a definite moving surface, but there was no surface. The interior though not a tree, was absolutely sylvan; bright torrents of luminous, balmy celadon, eau-de-nil, emerant, viridian and zinnober flowed backwards and forwards against ethereal confines. She leaned her torso forward for balance, her eyes were speaking, saying, "Hyperion, you are in motion - being transported" but her feet and legs screamed otherwise. Then something happened, something uncanny; Sorrow and Fate conspired. While passing through the sylperdarn, Hyperion had stumbled on a tree crossing called a 'Coydencroyscee'; sometimes in the woodlands or wealds many trees were sylwar-barthed.

She was thrown forward, as if the trees no longer wanted her, a rift in the sylperdarn had occurred. Hyperion found herself looking up at an angry woman, one whose beauty was like raging fire; something to be prized from a distance, not up close. . .not at that moment at any rate, for she was wielding a terrible axe.

While lying on the ground, Hyperion caught the whiff of incense. She was captivated by that woman, for in her eyes were thumia. Suddenly the woman dropped the axe and held her hands over her bosom, which was heaving like bellows.

The thumia dimmed in her eyes and like clear green rills, they appeared running over moss, gentle reprieve poured from them. She fell on her knees and wept, cupping her face with her hands as her long, ebony locks fell forward on to the green sward.

Hyperion was startled; she felt compassion for that beautiful woman and got up from where she lay. The tree behind them from which she was expunged was still glowing, like a bright Moon mångata. Hyperion put her arm around the stranger. When the stranger had regained her composure, she drew herself away and got up. "I must make amends for what I have done," she said in a charming voice, making palm-fold and reverencing Hyperion. Hyperion bowed and did the same. "It was an error to rend you from your piluceda"

As she spoke, Hyperion was overcome with the beauty of the woman for she spoke with grace and judgement.

"I will assist you in your quest if you would assist in mine. . ."

At that point, Hyperion graciously interjected. "My pursuit is filled with sorrow . . . and death may have come to my bosom." "Nay!" exclaimed the stranger and gently put her warm fingers to Hyperion's lips.

"Speak not woman, the secret things of thy heart, for they are known to me. I must entreaty your pardon for I have not given my name. I was Bleddyn when I tore you from your piluceda. . ."

Again, Hyperion saw that first fire in Bleddyn's eyes, then they softened, she smiled and continued, ". . . and though the Ælves call me 'Lyadalagapē', I am overcome with grief and am becoming 'Blaiddfamdis' for, I fear that my sons have been slain."

Hyperion found that Blaiddfamdis was charming and that she read the thoughts of others however, Blaiddfamdis allowed Hyperion to tell her name, for such was the custom and it was right that the bearer of the name spoke it first. Hyperion did not have to say more for, Blaiddfamdis took her long, raven hair and wrapped it around Hyperion's head and then pressed her plum stained, sharp lips against Hyperion's brow. Blaiddfamdis was shown all that she was permitted to know; then she drew away from her suddenly.

"What!" exclaimed Hyperion.

"You are with child! A boy child! Blessed be the one who will bear *The Ring*. . ."

"With child?" asked Hyperion with astonishment.

"It cannot be! It cannot be. . ." she said, and sat flat down on the sward.

"But it is so Hyperion. Certes!" assured Blaiddfamdis.

"How could you not have known? Is it your first child?"

Hyperion sat still, she did not reply at first but then said to Blaiddfamdis, "It would be my first boy child. I have two girls at home. I always knew, but this knave. . ." "Is Ælvish" Blaiddfamdis completed the sentence.

"Elvysshe? These past hours have been most peculiar," said Hyperion. Blaiddfamdis sat beside Hyperion and touched her upper arm. "No dear woman. Not Elvysshe. Ælvish! The child will have the blood of the Immortal Race."

Hyperion got up suddenly, held her face in her hands and exclaimed "No stop! Stop! Stop Blaiddfamdis! We are strangers, how can you know so much? He comes. . .he comes after more than a score!"

Blaiddfamdis did not respond, she sat still, her green eyes sparkled like queenly emerants. Hyperion slowly drew her hands from her eyes and peeped through her fingers. She realized that she had been discourteous but, saw that in the eyes of Blaiddfamdis two irises had appeared, the clear green began to fade and a croceate hue had begun to burn over her lower eyelid. The colour intensified until the two irises became one brilliant goldenrod colour, piercing, as if they could peer into ones very soul.

Blaiddfamdis arose and grew in front of Hyperion. Her clothing ripped at the seams, still she grew. Her now naked form skin-changed, like the petals of Moonflower unfolding to the Moon, till she stood at 15ft and towered over Hyperion, who was not a short woman at all.

The light breeze toyed with Blaiddfamdis's long, soft, midnight blue hair and her face filled with sphulligini.

She read that Hyperion had become fearful and so, Blaiddfamdis knelt down making genuflection, lifted her snout slightly upwards and gave a long, deprimish howl, "Arh- Wooooooooooooooooooooooo!!!"

A solitary tear fell over the grass, and as quickly as she had skin-changed, she returned to her former self. Wulvlinga Blaiddfamdis stood before Hyperion, her skin still tingled with sphulligini.

"Wulv. . .ling. . .as the Immortal Ælves. . .call us," she said in a mal de vivre voice. "But we have been called much worse. . ."

She reached for the axe, it was wonderfully kræfted and she looked sadly upon it and said, "Voogabool! Tis the name—lain for ages, it was under rock and tree root, in some long-forgotten cave. Voogabool is the first one, but there are many—used by the Ancient Do-Glan. . ."

Hyperion listened, never before had she heard of the Ancient Do-Glan though she knew the word 'glan' to mean 'clean and pure'.

". . . All the rest is a kræft of the Himyar Ælves. They. . .never. . . speak. They never come. Sometimes called 'The Hush'."

Blaiddfamdis ran her fingers over the edge of the blade and as she did, the axe blade sang like a stringed instrument. It wasn't a solid blade; the knob and shoulder were of emerald set in a greenish, coppery coloured metal. The poll, side cheek and blade bit were shaped like an 'S', the blade did not seem solid, it seemed kind of feathery, the most beautiful shades of green.

The curved 'S' was divided in two parts with a large, horseshoe shape separating the two cheeks. Below the large emerant shoulder, two florets were sculpted, the blade was hooked and the butt was curved and triable.

"I wish that I knew what ails you Blaiddfamdis for my fear has turned to joy. . ." said Hyperion as she caressed her belly.

"It is for that reason I tore you from your piluceda; the two oaks are conjoined, this is a great wrong, and I, by axing it would gain entrance for, I wish to go back in time. To avenge the taking of my sons though, it may augur a great battle which clings to a greater war. All of Eridu is at the brink of war, even unto the peace of Béth-Élam." "War! You speak of war?" asked Hyperion in a punning way. "Béth-Élam is the very epicentre of gossip, we have heard of no war," assured Hyperion confidently. Blaiddfamdis tapped her left wrist and something strange happened. An object materialized around her wrist, it glittered, a strange golden luminous thing slid around, coiled itself about her wrist. Hyperion drew nearer and did not understand exactly what she was looking at. "What is that?" she asked unabashed.

"This is named 'Satyam Kar'" she replied with a tender tone.

"I have not seen such an object. But in our village, we too have a similar device, much, much larger! The Dwarves set it into a tower, it is a thing of great kræft, and it keeps time."

"And so it is Certes, they are the Law Makers of Time. Only 9 remain in Eridu."

"Look!" said Blaiddfamdis, pointing to the workings of the Satyam Kar. On the outer edge of the object, covered in clear transparent quartz, were twenty four rectangles of blue and gold. In golden script were the twelve months; one set in the common tongue, the other in the tongue of the Paladorians. It also had 3 crowns. When Blaiddfamdis tapped her wrist, she had tapped on the pusher which was indented and transparent, the bezel was a dragon made of some strange, orange alloy. There were also two cyclops; one for present time, one for future time.

Hyperion imagined that to be an object that kept the measurements of the months, but she also noticed numbers and four large, blue and red needles with pointed chevrons. One of them had the word 'min' engraved onto it; and the other the word 'tir'; that one moved faster while the longest hand hardly moved.

Blaiddfamdis pointed to the right cyclops; it was the year 8816 October 18th.

"Do you see?" she asked. "You have come too far forward. . ." there was a look of surprise on her face.

"Earslingmæl!" she exclaimed to herself.

Hyperion listened closely for sometimes Blaiddfamdis used the dialect of Palador and sometimes of Midhe, mixed with some older tongue. 'Earsling' she understood to mean 'backwards' but the word 'mæl', that came from 1050 in an earlier age. She remained silent and worked the word over in her mind. Her face had a look of quizzicalness.

"Earslingmæl— Earslingmæl—the marker has moved backwards!" she exclaimed throwing her arm up. "Strange! Strange!"

"Certes! Revedh!" replied Blaiddfamdis.

"Satyam Kar on the left cyclops shows Khordad, it is spinning. I beg your pardon — in your understanding it is October 8816. . ."

"So? I am 6 months with child?" said Hyperion with an absent look on her face.

Blaiddfamdis jumped up and pulled Hyperion by the hand, "Something terrible has happened! Something terrible is going to happen! Our paths should not have crossed. . ."

"But. . .but Old Man Bllömpotvölle. . ." Blaiddfamdis did not understand and looked at Hyperion questioningly, her radiant eyes full of light.

Hyperion explained in a hurried fashion, all that transpired on that night, that felt so long ago now. She explained the encounter with Old Man Bllömpotvölle, then tried to describe him, his manner, his Elvysshe ways.

"Aaaah!" laughed Blaiddfamdis, her face aglow, I know *that revedh!*

In Palador he is called 'Lil-An', 'wind of heaven' but to the Wolvlingas Lil-An is called 'Urzu' meaning 'wolv-oracle'. No-matter what he said, no matter where Urzu bid you go, all is destiny. I now understand that we were meant to meet in this fashion, in this place. . ." assured Blaiddfamdis, taking Hyperion's hand in hers. "Look!" she remarked and pointed to the tree, "The Duir is still ajar, you must enter!" she exclaimed and pushed Hyperion to the light. She slid the Satyam Kar off and placed it around Hyperion's wrist. Blaiddfamdis tinkered with it then said to Hyperion, "We must make haste," the look on her face now hunted. "Stand back!" she exclaimed again and took Voogabool. Blaiddfamdis struck 3 times at the very base of the two trees. Hyperion felt her world begin to spin, and Blaiddfamdis jumped through in the nick of time.

"Listen now dear ovim! Our paths must sever ere we hardly met, I to my fate, you to your destiny. Tell nothing of what you saw, tell nothing of what I spoke. The war of Heaven to Eridu has come. I know it now! My deeds create a ripple in the sea, but your unborn knave falls like a star into the briny deep. This piluceda will take you to my door. Warn my 'ansum' and tell him that our sons have fallen into the hands of the Kwizir and I go to avenge them for the blame lay at the gates of Dynyansek. Do not ask how I came to know this, only that it is my time to pass unto *my joy*. Do not pursue the body of your beloved for it is neither on earth, neither in heaven. For the one that risked his life is more careless than all your tears, and crueller than all your anguish." Blaiddfamdis was breathless, Hyperion followed her every word, her emotions suspended as revelation and divination revealed itself.

A mighty wind arrived, the women held on to each other, their hair blew like pennons on a weary flagstaff. The light in the piluceda became altogether fumificated.

They were then ripped from each other's arms. Blaiddfamdis flung Voogabool toward Hyperion, then all was still. Hyperion found herself standing in a beautiful glade filled with Autumn sunshine. Hundreds of butterflies were fluttering about, but when they realized Hyperion's presence, all sped over the hedge, leaving only the atrous swallow-tails, which came closer to Hyperion. She was utterly amazed, for she had never seen so many butterflies in such a show of kaleidoscopic profusion before.

They started circling her, their wings flapped and fluttered like a halcyon thunder. She felt them under her garment and around her ankles, she broke out in girlish laughter as it tickled. She felt herself rising, becoming air borne as the rabble lifted her up. She looked at all the wild flowers, large bees could be heard buzzing about and collecting nectar from several hawthorn trees.

She was mesmerized by hummingbirds hovering mid-air, others she heard singing in the bowers and hedge, singing for minutes at a time, a happy series of notes punctuated by a loud tzzip, tzzip.

The kaleidoscope hovered over the hedge and time seemed to be utterly suspended. The birds had fallen silent, the bees were also still. Beyond the hedge she noticed that the door to a simple abode was left ajar. They entered with her so that she had to duck under the lintel of the door, then they set her down inside the house, another rabble brought Voogabool. With a great rush, with battish confusion, the butterflies fled out down the wide passage. Hyperion startled as their backdraft shut the door with a heavy thud.

She fell on the quirky sofa and drowned herself in the cushionnificaton, exhausted from the sturm and drang, and wept.

She must have cried herself to sleep and must have slept for a long time because she woke up sometime in the middle of winter, when the flakes of snow were falling like bleks from the sky. She sat up and saw a bright fire on the hearth. She was famished. Hyperion noticed that she was alone in the house; there was nothing to be heard, within or without. She slid forward on the sofa looking at the black '8th Gathering' bound on the little table before her. It was gilded with the title, 'The Secret Delight of Books'. . .she traced her fingers over the large, red apple that was embossed on the cover, there was also a wolf, embossed and gilded, sniffing at the red apple. As she rubbed her finger over the apple, Hyperion had a start and pulled back her hand suddenly. She looked around the room to see if anyone was watching. There was obviously none, that is, none that would reveal themselves to her so, she touched the apple on the cover of the book again. This time, she was sure that the apple felt real — felt 3 dimensional. She knelt beside the table and tried to pluck it *out* of the book but, it felt stuck.

Frustrated by her own simplicity, she got up and had an idea. She rushed to the window and tried to open it by pulling on the window sash cord but, that would not budge either so, she took the book from the table and knocked out the lower sash glass, that worked.

All her thoughts were to get out. . .into the cold — perhaps a silly idea?

She was an agile woman and soon she was on the ledge, she did not bother to look over the other side and assumed there was only ground, but one should not assume such things in enchanted domiciles! She slipped and went kaplash, into a river! The river Næddre, though she was a strong swimmer, there were two currents, the top flow of the river was towards Albtraum but, the undercurrent was like the arms of an Ussušuha (the common word is Sea cat) dragging her in the opposite direction.

Fortunately, she was still close to the river banks, so she tried to reach out to the overhanging branches of the willows but, without success, on and on she was carried by the waters.

Now and again, she'd be dipped under the swells and cold water would fill her lungs. Again, she reached out for a branch and held on for dear life. Success that time!

Hyperion pulled herself towards the branch. She reached out for the bank clinging to the long grasses, but the Næddre desperately wanted her, or was it perhaps some other wet menace, for she thought that something slithered passed her legs. Fear became her reality. As she pulled herself up, the wet and soggy bank fell away and crashed over her, pushing her down. . . down. She attempted to swim to the surface as wet energy attempted to pull her down, then she felt that it started to release her. She only made a few strokes before her arms relinquished. Fearing that she would be dragged too far, she continued to kick beneath the surface and at no point, did Hyperion allow herself to lose confidence that she was going to survive that episode.

The water had filled her lungs and she had had her fill yet, her mouth watered for that red apple that she touched on the book. . . 'Why am I thinking this?' she thought.

Under bobbed the head, up bobbed the head,
Like a swan in the wet
Her arms listless like bedraggled wings,
They lay down on the watered bed:
Like two lodes of jasper,
Like a shifting dusky dune,
Like a lotus
Tipped with gold for splendid avatars.
Tree and leaf gazed on at her;
While the wind begun to sing a lullaby,
Water serpent forbore to clinch,
Not a scale to seduce.
Round in fate, circles twirl:
Feminal and Mystery,
Dripping water erodes a stone.
Time and Water breast to breast,

Locked together in one embrace.

"Negeltu, mi!"

…Hyperion woke, staring into thirteen bright faces, their complexions like arctic blue and umber, floating over rainforest celadon.

"Hobgoblin! Hobgoblin!" exclaimed Hyperion, sitting up on the sofa. Her first impulse was to run away but then she looked down and saw that she was covered in a red cape, and that she was naked underneath. The cold that she experienced was gone, and her body was warm. "How on earth did I get here?"

"Hobgoblin! Hobgoblin please my lady, Hobgoblin. How? Tis our healthy handle," replied the tallest one of the lot.

Some were tall, some were small, some had red ruby eyes, some had purple eyes and some the colour of pearl.

Several offered her a bright, red apple, "Hungry? Have hand happle!" they prompted.

Hyperion glanced between them towards the book on the table, to confirm that the gilded apple was still on the book.

"How shall I take food from strange folk? Who knows upon what you feed — or by which Elvyssheness your familiar corms go. . ."

But the horde didn't hearken to Hyperion's haggling.

Another responded to her first question.

"Hence Hyperion hastened on her hriver, hawthorns heralded! Hobgoblin horde hauled Hyperion from hidden haughty Helminth.

Haply hawthorns heard orisons — Haply Hyperion hungers for 'Pixie Pears'?"

Some hands reached towards her, filled with 'Pixie Pears' but, she was cautious to accept them even though they looked so sweet, she was very hungry after all.

Her hand was hardier than her restraint, the fruit gleamed of ruby and ruddy hue as many a dusky face looked at her. Hyperion and the Hobgoblins shared the homespun feast, but not without Gwalather at the helm of the horde asking several Hobgoblins to get a fragrant hoard of honey from the hollow of a hawthorn tree.

"You don't seem unfriendly at all," Hyperion remarked, although she had a "searching expression" on her face.

"Heaps of heresies you've heen told! To harmful heffect! By hoath, Hulf and Hawthorn," cried Gnani with his mouth full.

"We like hou too. But here is a *heuristic*! What's hidden is sweetest. . .", and before he could continue in came the others with sweet, fragrant honey in large, fresh hawthorn leaves.

Hyperion felt much better after eating. She wasn't so confused anymore and then she said with a dumbfounded expression, "How could you feed me honey and 'Pixie Pears' in winter?"

Gnani, respected for his knowledge and wisdom, spoke again; "Hent ye not? The hour is Hora-Al. Hyperion's fate is accomplished."

At the cooing of Gnani's voice, Hyperion drifted off in thought and replied as if from a dream, "Then I must regale for you, of the lady of the house, in which I am a guest. She runs to her end. . .this I know for she. . .told me so. Woman to woman and bosom to bosom swathed one to the other in one sylvan dryads haunt. We were torn like an open heart, both to Fate! One to birth. . .one to death. I know it—*now*. Pixie-Pears—honey hoard or hawthorn tana. All its corms have fixed me to the heart of Nature. . ."

When she came from her reverie, she got off the sofa, stood up and straightened herself. She pushed her long, inflamed, umber hair over her shoulders and slowly walked to the window. She realized, unsurprised, that it was whole again. The snow was gone and as she looked out over the river and beyond towards the high mountains, she asked, "How shall. . .I. . . re-pay. . .you?"

Göbel-Malu walked towards Hyperion and gently touched her shoulder and assured her, "The Hobgoblin horde hoards no handsel from Hyperion."

Then they spoke in unison, "Hear the 'hargholf'! He returns."

Hyperion looked curiously down the passage but heard nothing.

"What do you mean? I hear nothing or am deaf?"

"Hear ye not the hunder of wings hitting?" asked long-eared Garšausis.

As the door creaked open, a grey-brown haze entered first, many fluttering around something tall — Hyperion felt herself pushing against the window. . . 'what is this, more Elvysshe surprises?' she thought.

They were wolf-moths, 'luperina' some have called them but, perhaps they shouldn't be called moths for, they were neither mirthful like butterflies nor drab like their own kind. At any rate, the tall figure bent under the lintel, he brushed the moths aside with his hand and they all vanished. In front of the horde stood Lycurgus.

"Whaaart is dis?" he asked in a deep voice.

"Look!" he exclaimed in a friendly tone. "Elffreondspedig. . .Have you come to share a dark day with me? And this fair lady? What tides have swept you into my humble home, that you have extolled my eyes with a face coloured like the Harvest Moon?"

Hyperion lowered her head and was about to smile but on remembering Bleddyn, the laughter on her lips died as she replied with a grave face, "*Bleddyn*. . . pardon me my lord, Lyadalagapē sent me to your home. It may be a long time ago though, because I have passed summer and winter and summer in your home. The Hobgoblin horde have been kind and courteous. . ."

Laughter and cheering broke out amongst the horde, and hugging and kissing but, Gwalather did not join in.

"Hush!" he exclaimed, the cheering stopped and they continued playing about and around the furniture.

". . .but did not reveal much. . ." continued Hyperion.

"And so they do not, it is their wont. . .like the Ælves."

"Like yourself *also*," replied Galeme, a slender, handsome Hobgoblin.

Lycurgus fell into the chair at the kitchen table, but not before first pulling one out for Hyperion. She sat beside him and pulled the red cape tight about her figure, it had no buttons.

He poured two, large mugs of milk and sat quietly to gather his thoughts. Although he had spoken charming words, his face had become sombre at the mention of Bleddyn. Hyperion didn't answer, she sipped her milk, it was refreshing.

After a while, he started in slow moderate tones, and said, "She was my chatelaine though we have no castle. . .that. . .you. . .had mentioned Bleddyn reveals all. . ." Again, he fell silent.

"It does not surprise me that you have fallen into my home. . ."

Hyperion listened to him intently and with a melancholic expression on her face. Her bright eyes searched for deeper understanding of all that had transpired.

Suddenly he sat up but didn't say a word. The ears of Garšausis was pricked, he listened too, the other Hobgoblins stopped from their revelry but, when they discovered that there was nothing to be alarmed about, they continued.

Lycurgus looked at Hyperion and took her elegant hands in his large, rough ones and said, "It would be folly of me to set after Lyadalagapē now, for I do not possess any kræft to set after her.

Time is like a many layered labyrinth, running in circles upon circles and the Sidhe do not visit these wilds and neither do I possess the cunning to summon them to meddle in our affairs. . ."

She looked with a radiant face at him, a thing she could not help because that all was a wonder to her.

Lycurgus's face was inscrutable, he continued, ". . . Yes. . .the Lordly Ones. . .they know the crem of Time best," he gazed out of the window then, perchance remembering something, some memory from a distant past.

He looked deep into her eyes and said, "Come Cara! Let us depart. I must take you to Palador..." he rose from his chair and held Hyperion's hand as she got up. "They know best. We must make haste, come. . ." "But! I have no clothes," she gasped.

Just then one of the Hobgoblins entered with her own clothing, dry as bone and well pressed. "Ana zu nacham nin," said the creature in a gruff voice.

Hyperion smiled warmly and when she took it. She pressed the clothing to her breast and nose, taking deep breaths for it smelled clean and familiar.

"Thank you kindly, and what might your name be?" she asked. Lycurgus laughed, he knew what was coming. Not that there was anything for him to feel jovial about — he wasn't.

Suddenly all the Hobgoblins appeared in a row before her. The line wound about the place and around the furniture because it wasn't a large house at all.

"I-ham Gugu," he was the littlest one, standing at only 3ft tall, with an adorable, craggy face. From somewhere inside his purple hacele which hung in folds on the floor, he withdrew a strange object, a Solferino Dragon. It was finely kræfted with pulpurite gems and was size enough to hold in the palm of a little child's hand. He held it out to Hyperion and said in a gentle, soft voice,

"A hunk of hoard Hyperion. . ."

She took it in her hand, it was filled with glister, it also felt quite heavy. She brought it closer to inspect it and for a moment, she thought that the eyes blinked suddenly, then drew it away from her face. "Strange!" she exclaimed.

"Hold it, hide it, hands-hon ever. She's the fire in a haycock. Heretofore. . ." said Gugu as he pointed to Hyperion's belly, "Hobbledehoy hemigrates himmerse hit hunder horb of heaben. Heliotaxis! Heliotaxis! Heliotaxis!" he exclaimed with excitement, bashing his hands together and opening his arms wide.

"Hamshackle his tongue!" shouted Baddar. Gwalather quickly gave him a nudge on the head. Gugu stopped at that rude interruption.

"I hamm Baddar. He, Gwalather head of the horde."

"Hush!" Gwalather called out. He stood at the opposite side of the room, having a word with Lycurgus.

Hyperion smiled and flickered her eyes, using her long eyelashes to display fond interest and returning her gaze to Baddar. She looked about for Gugu but, Gugu had disappeared.

Gwalather had returned from his conversation with Lycurgus. Hyperion realized that they were pressed for time because Gwalather quickly went through the rest of the names and pushed them this way and that.

"This is Geet, Gnani and Galeme and Gaagii meaning 'raven'," he shoved them aside.

"Here is Göbel-Malu, 'bright long haired'. Gamba, Gul and finally Garšausis, for he hears well and is long eared and galton of the town on the high ground."

When all were introduced, Gul led Hyperion by the hand into a room filled with enchanting gloaming light, to dress. She didn't take long and when she left the red cape on the bed, Gul encouraged her to wear it for keepsake, which Hyperion gladly did. Gul also gave Hyperion a well-made leather mayll, into which she securely hid the Solferino Dragon and the rest of her belongings. She carried Voogabool over her shoulder and was surprised that it was exceedingly light. As she thought of Lyadalagapē, she wondered why Lycurgus, neither any of the Hobgoblins, did not ask about Voogabool. The fifteen left the homeliness of Lycurgus's home and proceeded into a north easterly direction. They kept close to the river some 300m away on a narrow path with long grasses on either side. Stillness pervaded the landscape as the path moved further away from the river after some thirty minutes.

As they walked in single file, Galeme who walked in the middle said, "Haps we *hought* be called the 'gædrian'. Hafter hall, hit feels heaps like a hun-dertaking. . .a-hoardish hunder-taking. . ." No one responded, the stillness was deathly.

"Hanyone? Hiis hanyone hearing me?" he asked again.

"Yes Galeme!" growled Lycurgus from the front of the line. "We hear you but, no one thinks this to be a gædrian of any sort, we have scarcely left the Wulfscīr, so stop making jest. . .Besides if anyone was to lead any gædrian to Palador it would be Master Elqamar. Gadrian! Tsk!" Galeme did not reply.

They walked on the narrow path for an hour. On their right, grew thick trees which separated them further from the river, so that walking through them became impossible. The path clung tightly to that dense tree line. Hyperion felt that they might have passed through a veil of sorts, because the weather was no longer balmy. The temperature had dropped somewhat and the glade from which they came, seemed hidden from view.

Though quiet, she sensed that they were skirting some strange hyacinthine zone and she knew in her heart that the others felt it too. Hobgoblins liked talking and they were now walking without talking. It was a kind of reverential passage, or so it felt to her. After some time of walking in silence, they passed a large opening where many wild horses were munching knee-deep in the wild flowers. On discovering that band, half the Hobgoblin horde chased after them. The horses scattered in a playful manner, some of the horde mounted the horses with a single jump, as Hobgoblins were great jumpers and mounters. They drove the horses further off into the woodlands and left only Gwalather, Gamba, Gul, Gnani, Garšausis and Baddar with the group.

"Where are we off to Master Wulf?" asked Gwalather.

"I have no idea. . .I only know that if or when I want to go to Palador, an Ælve or sometimes Elqamar, always finds."

"Do they not trust you to know the way Master Wulf?" interjected Gwalather.

"The Paladins are the Igigi of Eridu. Their ways are secret. Who am I to bend their will?"

It was close to twilight and Lycurgus could hear the horns of Elfland blowing. It came gently from the hills, softly, faintly echoing. He stopped walking and looked this way and that into the wilds, then asked, "Do you hear it?"

". . . I do. . ." replied Garšausis.

Hyperion listened carefully. She thought that she had heard some sweet, lamentable strain but then brushed it aside as her imagination.

"I think that we should wait under that Yew over yonder. . ." said Lycurgus thoughtfully.

Hyperion wandered at the great Yew; drunk with silence as the darkness of the night and the fading light of the day comingled. It sent her heart gently fluttering, at what seemed the edge of all unearthly things.

The Book After the Prooimia

Jaddamiah Jabberwocky'

The Ring Bearer

Many Rings, Fewer bearers,
Many Kings, they can never have them,
None for the rich! None for the poor!
You will find the Darkness always binds them.
Many paths, many errors,
One is destined, so say the Ælves of yore,
Who can know the sting of the Ring's wild wine?
Its joys are more the sweeter, than mortals deem divine.

Jaddamiah Jabbervocky
receives a Draconian Letter

Part 1

Jf 31415 had more garden than house, then 161805 had more house than garden. Mr and Mrs Jabberwocky liked gardening but, they had a big family and no one ever moved away. Over the decades the house got ever bigger and bigger as the garden shrunk.

So, it was a case of 'between a brick and a bloom' for it was not the latter that won. There was some talk of them using the land next door at the foot of Mont Boo. If the four families under the mountain did not have such easy access to special geological privileges, then the Jabberwocky's house would be the largest.

Mr and Mrs Jabberwocky had sixteen children, four sets of twins; of the sixteen children only one had ever moved away albeit only 500ft from his parents' front door. He was the 3rd youngest, he said his parents' house had become too noisy, so the laconic fellow moved across to Döppievölle Inn. His name was Jabberstille. Of the 15 that remained behind, ten were married. Of the ten, eight had families of their own. The eight families between them had 21 children.

There was no need for carpenters, tilers, pipe fitters, kiln makers, painters, seamstresses or other vocations because, the Jabberwocky's built their own house and made their own extensions.

Hrosmægden Jabberwocky was the quintessential matriarch; she loved the children that came from her womb and loved the children that came from her daughters and daughters'-in-law wombs, and you could clearly see that by the litters.

She was born on the Plains of Hros and was a horse maiden from the House of Hrosweard. She was the youngest daughter of Aherin. Some of their children carried names from the Jabberwocky side, and some children took their names from the House of Hrosweard.

The patravaha (postman in the common tongue) Hrosfrēogan, was number thirteen in line and one of Jaddamiah's eldest sons. He arrived at their door, on 23rd of September 8816, five days to the Long Night's Moon. When Jaddamiah saw Hrosfrēogan through his bedroom window, he was very surprised. Hrosfrēogan dismounted his tall Etaza, a beautiful stallion, lean, feisty but obedient and loyal to his master. That horse was from Alkana. Their horses were viewed to be greater than the horses of the Hrosvyras on the Plains of Hros. They would not agree to that belief, so to settle an age-long dispute, a race was held every year in the large arena, called Ina-Nirmana, on the Plains of Hros. The competition was named the 'Vega Anala' for the speed of the racing horses was as the wind. The Etaza was built for speed and endurance, perfect for long journeys that Hrosfrēogan sometimes had to endure. He delivered post and other important mail, even royal mail on occasions. At any rate, Jaddamiah rushed out the front door to meet his son halfway down the garden path. He could not understand his luck for, the patravaha always passed their house and for some odd reason he didn't pass them today. Little did Jaddamiah know, that the letter came at a cost...

Jaddamiah had complained at the breakfast table earlier that day, which was an important family affair, that he hated not getting post. He said that it made him feel like an eagle without claws and disconnected from the world, and that he needed perhaps, to go on a journey of some sorts.

After Hrosfrēogan dismounted his stallion, he kissed Dravya and patted him, there was no sign of frothing at the mouth although they had just ridden from Élles. Élles was where all post persons had to collect their stash of mail before delivering it each day. It also served as a river port built by Jason (the Mariner) Jabberwocky and Grandsire Cinaed many years before. He called his horse Dravya because it was the name she came with. It meant 'to be made to run or put to flight'. Hrosfrēogan took a long, slender, red, envelope from his leather bumper bag and handed it to his father, who by then could not contain himself.

"Hrosmægden! Hrosmægden! Look! Look!" He called out to his wife, who was working with her father-in-law, Jabbamiah, in the flower bed around the large Ash.

He tore the envelope open and rushed to the wooden bench to sit under the Ash. Hrosmægden, a tall woman like her husband, rubbed the sweat from her face with the sleeve of her right forearm and in doing so, smeared dark dirt across her brown face. She was happy for him; she always was when he was happy. She went and sat next to him, for she knew he would read it aloud to her.

Jaddamiah did not bother to look up or around but, kept his ears wide open. He did not always have bad looks, for once upon a providence he was a fetching fellow. When he was young he travelled past Dystiġ on the Plains of Lyte Hros, after that little town there was a mountain range which separated Lyte Hros from the Plains of Hros proper, where the Hrosvyras had their domain. The Western Road along that section was very narrow, with a drop of some 300ft to the right. It was treacherous because it was very rocky and ran into the ravine, which climbed out back against the mountain range. It was there that his horse was spooked; and he was thrown down the ravine and lay there for some hours before the young Hrosmægden came along with her party. It was the rjóður that found him as he lay bleeding in the cold. The Hrosvyras had beautiful dogs, nicknamed the rjóða. They could run at 43mph. The Dukkǫ rjóður had tall ears, almost Ælvish in appearance, large red eyes were set in an affectionate face that fooled many warriors on countless occasions. They had soft padded feet that helped them achieve those great speeds. They found the almost comatose form and alerted their mistress. Hrosmægden took the stranger to her father's home and healed him there. The two fell in love and it was only the second time that a horse maiden of the Hrosvyras had married a stranger. From that accident Jaddamiah Jabberwocky lost his speech for a time.

Without Hrosmægden he would have been both mute and lame but, she arrived in time with the help of the rjóða. She went so far as to cast Runes over Jaddamiah to heal him of his lost speech and in time, he spoke again, albeit with a stutter. He forced himself to talk slowly and for that reason he took to reading, lots of reading. Of his looks we will tell later.

The two lovers sat next to each other under the shade of the tree, and Jaddamiah unfolded a thick newspaper folded over many times.

He frantically went from page to page whilst Hrosmægden held the left side of it. "Why has this come in an envelope? Where is the letter from the sender?" he asked frustrated, contorting his face. Then he came upon a thick, folded sheet, it lay hidden in the 13th page. Jaddamiah wasn't fond of the number 13 as, he suffered from triskaidekaphobia. It was on a Friday the 13th that he nearly lost his life.

He skipped the folded paper and instead, read the heading at the top of the news page. It was in big, bold black letters and printed on yellow newsprint. The newspaper was called 'Kesara', a word for saffron, which was used to dye the paper yellow. The heading simply stated:

Dragon Slayer Wanted!
Please Reply Instantly
Remuneration on Completion
Direct yourself to Weir, its citizens await the courageous Personage.
(spelt with a capital 'P').

Jaddamiah, although fated with a serious bout of triskaidekaphobia, could not believe his luck. For him, dragon slaying was a serious business, for it meant a 300mile journey, it meant a quest of sorts.

All those thoughts were racing through his head as hurriedly unfolded the white paper.

It had 13 folds and at its top, in red and black script, it read; *'Bandhamudra Nigra'*. Everyone in the Pradeza knew what those words meant, even if they were illiterate, they knew the script, they knew what it was.

All contracts, all deeds that bound two or more parties, all conditions of engagement no matter in what Pradeza, even the proud Hrosvyras could not use their own tongue for that document, the document had to be in Ancient Patois. Jaddamiah spoke the language very poorly and could not read it so, that meant that he would have to find someone who read it fluently. Jaddamiah also realized the severity of what lay in his hands. He looked at Hrosmægden who sat beside him. She took his hand in hers and then spoke in the form of a verse;

Stay your thoughts
On all that is beautiful,
Balance and hyper elegance.
Remember the secret
Places of Dhara;
Those filled with wonder
And enchantment.

My thoughts fly South to sunny July.
Where I lay in the long grasses
Under torrid afternoons.
Dipping my feet in turquoise pools
Or wandering through the
Fields of Virana,
Where azure templed veins
Throb as heat
Release floral notes.

May your eyes be enskied
And rest on blooms that do not die.
May you think on such things
As best as earthly joy entrances.
And though the worldly battle grumbles
I wish you this peace that advances.

May you be imbued
With peace so deep
Like a Phala-Pasin lake
Set amidst steepled granite mountains
So that no thought could sound it.

So there where you are
While I am here I
Intend for you goodwill and cheer.
But you and I must make
A pact:
We will meet on Elysian Fields.
There where there are no
Sundering years.
I will kiss your brow
And you will hold my hand.

Before Hrosmægden had finished, he already knew that he had to go. He had to respond to that request. He had never seen a dragon in his life and never personally knew anyone that had ever slayed a dragon yet, he wanted to go to Weir and be the first man to do that. He didn't respond to what his wife had said and only sat staring at the Bandhamudra Nigra. He imagined what a cow-eating-children-stealing-sheep-eating-preventing-cows-producing-milk-dragon looked like. Suddenly, he felt a nauseating feeling creep into his throat. He felt it rising from his stomach, and belched. From his solar plexus a wave rolled like something was about to come out. He compared it to when Dhara Móðir heaved and convulsed, when those on her skin sickened her. He was certain that food was going to be expunged and that the morning's breakfast would be erased orally but, no such thing happened. Hrosmægden gently rubbed the curve of his back and asked if all was alright. He bobbed up and down. She ran her pale brown, slender fingers through his long, pitch black hair, and as she did that, the afternoon sun touched the turquoise in her ring, an amulet of the Hrosvyras. The reflection in it was like a summer sky. The stone was quite substantial and was in the shape of a boteh, a droplet-shape. That ring was given to her by her mother who in turn, got it from her mother. She drew her fingers from his hair and looked at the stone contemplatively. She used her right index finger and turned the ring in circles on her ring finger. She was thinking of an old Alkanina idiom.

Around her strong, smooth and tawny neck, hung a silver chain and, at the end of it hung a gem of the same kind, only it was round. The blue gem lay between her breasts and as she breathed, they gently heaved like a small coracle on swells. The green-blue of her veins ran like rivers over beach sand. Hrosmægden took her long, luxuriant tendrils and began to twirl them around her fingers, to make two, long plaits. Her hair was typical of the horse maidens; vibrant, deep and attention grabbing; that Eastlea blackness was richer than most other hair colours. Jaddamiah felt the nausea pass and responded to his wife's beautiful words. He responded in jest, although the verse he recited was an ancient one, taught by Old Man Bllömpotvölle, called 'I am Off! Off!'

> *I am off! Off!*
> *To a secret place and*
> *Many Duirs lead there.*
> *The sky is full of wings*
> *And lights;*
> *The Fáerië Queen waits there.*
> *It's going to be a revelry!*
> *So swing the lamps*
> *And ring the bells.*
> *Only children go but there.*
>
> *I am off! Off!*
> *To the Ælven-Home*
> *And many roads lead there.*
> *Can't you see my*

Happy feet?
They call me to the Spheres.

I am off! Off!
To see a Maidens twilight beauty,
No Duir leads there!
A secret treasure we keep
That I will not share.

I am off! Off!
To meet the Dwarves of the Walmer wood;
And Light and revelries,
And song and dance,
And friendship and feasting,
Is all they know.
Oh! These thoughts are knocking at my heart.
Oh! The magick! Oh! The sorrow, how it dies!

I could mention more;
But for a moment,
Only a little moment, I sit
And think of all that I
Have seen and been.
Of summers on Eridu mountains tall
And yellow leaves at Fall.

I think of the years gone by
And friends of long ago.
I think of all the folks
Who will never see a
World that I shall always know.
A thought for their
Accompanied feet;
Oh! What a pleasant fiction.

The moment now is gone.
I am off! Off!
I close the open Duir.

When Hrosmægden smiled, her eyes narrowed and her full, cordovan lips parted to reveal perfect, white teeth. "That was such a beautiful poyaymah. I will keep it in my heart," she said that with warmth in her eyes and he could see his face in its clearness. As she said those words in her plummy tones, she spread her slender fingers, star fish over her bosom.

The article in the news clip went on to explain that in Weir there were no knights nor Paladins and that help was urgently needed. As the two walked arm-in-arm through the garden towards their house, they noticed that their son had already left. They closed the door gently behind them.

Part 2

The 'study' was a 5m x 6m affair; it also doubled as a library where Jaddamiah spent most of his time. The study-come-library or as he referred to it in the Ancient Tongue, the 'lohavara', was located in the hallway, opposite the main bedroom. 'Lohavara' was inscribed in gold cursive letters above the lintel. It was his special place, despite that on most days, his grandchildren made it some kind of passing muster. The young ones would come to ask questions, and some were deeply interested with serious reflections. Eventually, he burned the 'midnight candle' so he could spend some time alone in his 'lohavara'. It was a place altogether lovely. The fire burned through Autumn and Winter and it was homely. Some volumes, Elsevier's, folios, Octavio's stacked into tall towers of bibliomania, stood at 7ft tall and in corners, gathering dust. Strange objects, obscure and frivolous, stood or hung on the walls, which were also lined with photographs of ancienter Jabberwockies. When Jaddamiah walked into the room after evening tea, he closed the door behind him. He did not slam nor hurriedly push it closed, no, Jaddamiah leaned his body close to it, pressed it gently, until he heard the door click softly. He would stand behind the closed door for a short while and listen if anyone had followed him. He listened like a thief for footfall. When he was satisfied that he was 'safe' and alone, he would jump up and down like a little child, and make 'celebratory' sounds. He walked over to his writing desk and opened some drawers, dug into it and threw whatever was in it, out. He knew that the room, his 'lohavara', had become anechoic and that he would be undisturbed.

The desk was predominantly made from satinwood, with an attractive, blonde finish. Intricately embedded into the satinwood, were masterful marquetry of exotic veneers, which included rosewood, walnut, boxwood and purpleheart. The elaborate marquetry consisted of floral scrolls, leaves, urns and emblems. It was fitted with a golden-tooled, leather inset writing surface, which was surrounded by small drawers, cupboards and storage compartments. In addition, there were five larger drawers underneath which provided ample storage for his accoutrement. The inlaid legs had brass-capped castors. The craftsmanship that went into that desk, was second-to-none because it was crafted by the Dwarves of Walmerwood. It was older than the Jabberwocky family lineage.

He pulled some maps out and unfolded them. Some were really small, no bigger than 12 x 15 cms and on one of those, he found a map that showed the town of Weir.

He crossed-referenced the spelling on the Bandhamudra Nigra; yes, it was the correct town. He began to make many notes and scribblings in a note book that laid on the pile on the desk. Afterwards, he spent time reading the Bandhamudra Nigra but, he found that it jargogled his brain so, he dipped his staff pen in some blue ink and signed. He customarily signed those types of document in Kesara ink, and disliked writing in any other colour. The ink which he used was made from a tree called 'Nilanaga', only found in the wealds on the island of Endymion. The staff pen and ink were treasured possessions of his. No one was allowed to write with it or to use his ink, of which he had a year's supply. The nib and the top of the pen were made of brass and the centre part was made from Nilanaga wood.

Jaddamiah lowered his head towards the desk, his hair hung so that his face was completely obscured. He looked up, then looked around, pulled his tongue through his teeth because someone, had forgotten to replace the candles! If he had been more observant in his studious state, he would have noticed that when he entered the room, only one candle had been burning and it was all but done, leaving a long, black trail of smoke. He got up, pen in hand, and slightly opened the door, as if to prevent an invasion. He shouted at the top of his voice; "Candles!" and disappeared behind the closed door, like a meerkat popping back into its burrow. The Jabberwocky did not realize that it was way after midnight and he was the only nocturnal survivor in the silent household. Again, he pulled his tongue through his teeth and mumbled to himself of how he would always do things himself. He got up again, opened the door wider so that only his head was sticking outside the door. He twisted his neck left then right, almost strangling himself in the process but, there were only two candles burning in the gloomy hallway. He listened and heard no chatter, no commotion, no childish laughter, no washing of dishes, only heard the crackling of fire from the lounge room.

On realizing the lateness of the hour, he cleared his throat, a sign that he needed tea and so, he softly closed the door behind him and tip-toed on the blue Alkanina rug towards the kitchen, to fetch himself a midnight snack and some candles. Half way down the hallway the floor creaked and he stood still. His shoulders pulled forward and up, his chin in the cleft of his neck and his arms beside him, fists clenched. Momentarily he moved on.

When Jaddamiah returned to the door of his 'lohavara' his hands were full, 6 candle sticks in one hand, a tea cup and saucer with a cheese sandwich in the other. He looked down the hallway, because he realised that it would be near impossible for him to enter without dropping something on the floor. He then bent and tried to fit the big, round door knob between his teeth, trying in vain to turn it.

It was quite a sight to behold. After his failed attempts, he stood in the middle of the rug in front of the door and dropped the candles onto it. The candles made a soft thud on the carpet. He entered frantically, placed his snack on the writing desk and rushed back for the candles. By then the room was in total darkness but, fortunately he could just make out the outline of things as it was a waxing, gibbous moon shining in through the window. Jaddamiah fumbled for the matchbox on the desk and pulled out its drawer, he struck it and lit the wick of one candle. He held it up and gave a deep groan, for there, low and behold, every sconce had a candle in it. The wall that divided his 'lohavara' and the hallway supported 3 sconce candle holders which were grandly sculptured of yellow oak. Female effigies were attached to oblong, curvaceous bases which were surrounded with flower arrangements and they held long tubes with curved ends, in their hands. The top was the candle holder. The yellow oak was embellished in bronze.

The silent hours crept by and a dog could be heard barking in the distance and Stari could be heard giving a boisterous moo. Stari's moo was a sign or knell from her, that it was either very late or early, depending on how one looked at it. Stari gave another moo. It was a vocalisation of her anticipation that it would be sunrise soon.

Jaddamiah dropped everything that he was doing; gave a powerful blow at each candle and went to his bedroom.

Part 3

Jaddamiah was up and about within 3 hours of having gone to bed. He rushed to the back of the house after breakfast. Outside at the barn; there were 6 stables for the horses. The Jabberwockies also had a sounder of pigs with one drove and chickens (from the Underhills) which provided the tastiest, biggest eggs (free for the taking, except that another item of food had to be exchanged for the eggs). In that way, the exchanges ensured that the gastronomic needs of every family in Béth-Élam was taken care of.

To his surprise all the horses were out. He was in too good a mood to be upset. He stood there with his hands on his hips, warming his face in the morning sun and breathed in deeply, lifting his nose towards the weald across the river. He was content. In 3 days he would set out on foot to the Plains of Hros to get a good horse that would carry him to the town of Weir. First he needed to ask his wife whether she knew of anyone that could assist him with the slight windfall, for her people lived there and he had not been to the Hrosvyras in ages.

That evening when some of the family members were sitting outside on the back porch by the hearth that overlooked the river, Hrosmægden slipped away quietly, went to the Jaddamiah's writing desk and made notes for the whole family. Some of the men were at Döppievölle Inn so, there weren't any adults in their bedrooms. She wrote in her neat handwriting on small pieces of paper, taking care to address them to her various children. She folded the papers over and made her way down the hallway and towards the corridor to the bedrooms. The bedroom doors were opposite each other and painted in various colours, of their owners' liking. Many picture frames hung on the corridor walls. She stopped and looked at one photo of her and her husband, the photo was tinted sepia, she thought for a moment; 'That photo was taken so long ago. It was time perhaps to have a new one taken'. She studied the photo but then her thoughts strayed to her husband's new 'hobby', namely dragon slaying. He was not one to give up easily. It did not sit altogether well with her. A deep furrow formed on her wrinkle-free forehead but when she realized that she was frowning, she ironed out the creases with the back of her hand. She took one or two steps and looked at all the other Jabberwocky males, each one being quite handsome, from each generation. There were lots of photographs.

She was thinking those thoughts as she walked towards the colourful doors, some closed and others ajar. The grandchildren's rooms were opposite their parents'. She entered each door on the left, those rooms got the midday to afternoon Sun, they belonged to the adults. She went through the slips of folded paper and placed it on each mantel piece. As she walked from room to room, she found herself enjoying the quietness of it all. Afterwards when all was done, she decided to have an early night to bed.

Part 4

The following morning Hrosmægden found him at his favourite spot. He was sitting in the rocking chair looking out of the window over the garden from his library. She was dressed in an elegant, light blue peplo. A light mauve peshtemal was coiled just under her bosom, while the rest of it was draped over her hips and fell from a knot between her thighs. Hrosmægden also wore a garland in her hair. Jaddamiah was glad to see her as she casually walked over to him. He wrapped his arms around her waist and nestled his head in the soft folds of her dress, so he could feel the warmth of her skin.

Children streamed in from play, through the kitchen door and their bright faces showed signs of expectation. Several licked their lips and saliva formed at the corners of their mouths. After much play, they were as famished as little 'sparrows'. Other younger children arrived from elsewhere in the house, already having had their baths. Those who came from the outside, crowded at one of several stone sinks, to wash their dusty hands.

Shouts and 'excuse me's' rang rampant, they were shuffling and bustling and jostling like young lambs at their ewe's teats.

The grown-ups were all present at supper that evening. Those who were absent at times or late for reasons beyond their control, were present that evening; word had been sent the previous night, that Grandsire Jabberwocky had an important announcement to make.

Everyone sensed it, for it began the day Jaddamiah received that letter, his first in a very long time.

The large kitchen had two, long oak tables which stood parallel; one for the grown-ups and the other for the children.

Jaddamiah stood up and tapped the empty glass in his hand with the polished, silver spoon. On seeing that, some of the littler ones got excited because they always got something special or something special was to be announced and . . . it usually had to do with eating, partying or some celebration.

"Spoom! Spoom! Spoom! Spoom!" a trio shouted. Jaddamiah looked their way and smiled warmly at his enthusiastic grandchildren.

The laughter and excitement began to simmer down. When all was quiet, he put the glass and 'spoom' down; his head was tilted, and his long hair obscured his face. He pushed it back, ran his open fingers through the ebony mass, and looked at his wife at the other end of the long table. She looked at him and smiled, she then winked at him; then blew him a kiss, a weak but acceptable approval. He spoke; "Children of children!" he looked to his left then down his own table, "Children of my wife's loins and all extensions by marriage whom, with some *effort*, I adore. . .

I. . . am. . . going on an ad-ven-ture! I am going on a quest! No!" then he said emphatically. "Perhaps those are not the correct words to use. I am going to Weir. Some of you no doubt may never have heard of it. There are wolves there, in those regions, who are shape-shifters. . ."

Great-grandsire Jabbamiah was not impressed and looked over his fingers; they were locked just under his eyes as he rested his elbows on the table. A great grandparent sat at opposite ends of the table where the children were seated.

Laughter broke out at the table, alarm and screams at the other.

"Father! Sire! Grandsire! Jaddamiah Jabberwocky, mind yourself!"

Complaints and reprimands came from either side. Jaddamiah laughed at the top of his voice, posted his head upward and looked at the ceiling, his hands inward and rested on his hips. When the joke was had, his wife said in her usual, plummy voice; "Many a thing said in jest is meant?"

"All-right, alright, all-*right* everybody! My apologies, I am going to slay the dragon. . ."

He paused, waited for another commotion but, there was none. All except Hrosmægden were nonplussed. They were all silent, looked up and down the table at one another, but mostly at Hrosmægden.

She nodded her head in a demure manner. The two tables broke out into a cacophony which was hard to quell.

Jaddamiah sat down and looked over to his beautiful wife, she smiled at him and it was like sunlight to him. She said that she loved him as he read her red, flushed lips from across the table. He started dishing his food and fell into silent ruminations. From its depths he heard his son Hrosfrēogan expletive; "Drats! That drack letter!"

The arguing and protestations carried on for nearly an hour, when they realized that they were very hungry. All began to jump into the supper with gusto. Then the myriad questions began;

"How big is the dragon?

What is its name?

It is really a dragon – How far is Weir?

Are you going alone?

Are you able to fight?

Have you got a lance?

Aren't you too old?

Why are you going?

Aren't you afraid?

Aren't you afraid of dying?"

And between those questions came a child's clear innocent shout; "Grandsire is my hero!"

The questions stopped as only forks and knives, spoons and teaspoons could be heard scraping against pewter and porcelain. Then some remarks;

"What do you know!

Shht!

Be silent! You're only a child!

What a silly thing to say!

Don't encourage father!"

Then some speculations followed;

"The dragon must be sleeping on a huge mountain of gold. Oh! We'll be wealthy then.

The reward must be a fortune.

Many Hrosvyra warriors will go with Grandsire.

The king, the mayor, the Prime Minister will court father."

A little child's voice was heard again, it was the youngest grandchild, her name was Geongmerkā. She came and sat on her grandsire's lap, holding a succulent, chicken drumstick in her left hand.

"Grand-sire!" she said, gently holding her little head down into the clavicle of her delicate shoulder. "When are you leaving?"

"Tomorrow my dearest Geongmerkā," he warmly replied.

For the second time a cacophony, the sound of an orchestra gone brabble, commenced.

Jaddamiah silently slid his chair back and away from the table and placed Geongmerkā on his hip. Hrosmægden slid her chair back, and they walked hand in hand down the long hallway towards the lounge room. They plonked themselves down onto the soft, green sofa in the large, oval room.

Part 5

H rosmægden told Jaddamiah that he should make his way to her uncle, for he was a man with a kind heart and he tended many horses. Sometimes horses suffered injuries on long journeys or in skirmishes, and he would he heal those that the Hrosvyras no long deemed fast enough. Hrosvyras saddled nothing but excellence, and so it was that her Uncle Gedymdeith (jedda-myth) saved those horses from further dis-ease or death. His hand was a tender one with those creatures, that most thought only good enough if they ran fast or carried heavy burdens but, he had other ideas. He believed that horses had great understanding, and some called him a 'horse whisperer'. Hrosmægden told Jaddamiah that her uncle Gedymdeith's homestead stood four miles from the main town, just after the bridge over the Afon Wen. It stood there for two reasons, Gedymdeith preferred a quiet life, away from the town and secondly, his two sons were guardians of the bridge. It fell to his family to protect the bridge as it was the first, formal entrance from the East, to the Plains of Hros. The river which ran under the bridge connecting the Hamsa Hrada to Laghu Hamsa Hrada, had many willows along its rich banks. Those weeping willows along the Vale of Tears were planted in commemoration of the great battle that took place in that area, and for all the lives of the Hrosvyras, in defending the bridge on the Plains of Hros. The bridge was named 'Wenhrosbont', a direct translation of what it actually meant, and in the common tongue would mean the 'silver horse bridge' or as some said 'bridge of silver horses'.

All was settled then, Uncle Gedymdeith was expecting him the following day.

The Journey to Weir

Part 1

The children came in ones and twos to apologize for their behaviour while others went straight to bed. At around eight, there was a knock at the front door, a rather loud one, which they knew could be none other than Mrs Underhill. Geongmerkā was still on her grandsires lap. She was fast asleep so Jaddamiah refused to go to the door. The other children whispered amongst themselves asking how on earth Mrs Underhill could have known anything of the 'draconian ad-ven-ture'. Again, the loud knock was heard.

"Jabberwocky!" came the shout. "I know you are dare. You canna fool this Underhill and besides I ken-heer yah all."

So Hrosmægden got up and went to answer the door, after all, she got on well with Mrs Underhill. There, a step lower and in front of the door, stood Mrs Underhill, her usual gleeful self. She wore her bonnet and wooden clogs, that's to say, that's what she always wore.

She pushed her way up and gave Hrosmægden a grand hug and said, "susvapnah!" Hrosmægden invited her in and closed the door. She then led her into the living room, after Mrs Underhill removed her clogs and left them at the door.

Mrs Underhill stood in the door with her hands resting on her hips, the family noticed that she was carrying something small wrapped in a rich, blue velvet cloth. "Jaddamiah!" she exclaimed. "May I remind you?" she pointed at him with her left index finger. "that nothing passes my eears and nouse. Well! Don't be alarmed. Although your idea is absolutely redeculous, *I* have come oh-verr to hand you a gift." She walked over to him, bent her knees and folded her dress underneath her and sat down, pushing herself between one of the children and Jaddamiah. Mrs Underhill looked around at those present, all eyes were on her by then and proceeded saying; "There are too many of yah and the hour is late, so pardon my impudence but susvapnah to yah all."

She turned to Jaddamiah and continued, "When attempting to slay a drahgoon Mr Jabberwocky, one needs a little more than courage, one needs something strong, something charming. . ." she said that without looking up and continued to unwrap the gift from its hiding place in the beautiful, velvet cloth. She did so as if she were fondling something very rare. All was quiet in the room, everyone eager to see what it was that she had brought, and deemed that important to give their father. Jaddamiah pushed his head back with neck and chin down and looked on dubiously. He frowned as that was something he could not hide when upset about something or with someone.

Hrosmægden tried to get his attention, to signal to him to stop with that look of disapproval. It was to no avail as he was too focussed on that mysterious gift which Mrs Underhill brought at that late hour.

". . .I know you're nort a man of arms, so here it is." Mrs Underhill held the gift in the air, between her pale fingers and in the light, was a beautifully kræfted phial of pale, apple-white hue. In it, blushed a wonderful, absinthian liquid.

"There it is!" she exclaimed with a twinkle in her hazel eyes.

She gave that to him but, he was reluctant to take it.

"Go-on Jabberwocky. Some courageous men never run out of courage but in the end, every courageous man runs out of stamina. This is for you, when you battle the Meline Drahgoon." She said it emphatically as if she meant every word which of course, she did.

"I am *not* going anywhere. Where did you hear such nonsense, and there will be no dragon slaying woman!"

Jaddamiah denied everything there and then. He continued to believe that she did not know that it was true, and that it was a wild guess of hers.

"Well then," she said getting up. "I was going to tell you what the drahgoon's name was but your insolence is unbecoming."

Mrs Underhill bowed her head to everyone, then went over to kiss Hrosmægden on the lips and said her goodnights. While leaving the living room, she gave Jaddamiah an indignant glance. When his wife returned, she was furious. It showed on her beautiful face. Some of the children joined in the reprimand because they thought that he treated Mrs Underhill improperly.

"How could she know of my business?" he complained vehemently.

"Well, that is of no consequence. Maybe one of the children told her so. Everyone in the room looked at one another apologetically, none feeling that they had done something of that nature. "Perhaps it was Jabbastille but even so, your behaviour was rude, and if it were one of the children or grandchildren that's all the same," said Hrosmægden.

"Before you leave you will apologize." Her voice was raised but her tone was not harsh. She wasn't a harsh woman even though, a daughter of a Hrosvyra. It was well before dawn when everyone vacated the warmth of the living room.

The following morning, Jaddamiah had great difficulty in getting up as he spoke with his children till the wee hours of that morning and Mrs Underhill's visit was unsolicited. Also, his wife demanded that he got enough rest as the best decision would be to then leave closest to sunset, advice which he took reluctantly at first. In the late of the afternoon when Jaddamiah was packed and ready, when he was certain that everything that was required was acquired, he stood in his bedroom looking at himself in the large, gilded mirror which hung over the bed. He turned his head to look at stray grey hairs, not too many…

Some marks were beginning to show on his face but that was quite normal for a man of his age, people always told him that he had too few for his age and he took that as a huge compliment.

He then walked out of the room but suddenly hurried back. Something that he thought would bring him great luck, had slipped his mind. The gift from his wife, the grand pashmina from the weaver in the high Drakensberg mountain range. He opened the wardrobe where he kept it, pulled it out hurriedly and left, leaving the wardrobe door ajar.

He fiddled in the corner at the front door before exiting, his mayll lay at his feet while doing that. At the door was a round, polished, bronze tin about two feet deep. In it were various trekking poles, shillelagh, pilgrim's staffs and other walking paraphernalia for, he was a bit of an ambulist. He fiddled and fiddled and turned them round and round, then decided to take the one made of Hazelwood; it was nearly as tall as he was. The top was covered in silver and came down an inch or so and, 3 inches below that were two silver bands. Below the bands, a diamond pastern crafted from a white resin with colourful crystal dust, ran on both sides, down the entire stick, so that the points of the diamonds kissed. "Yes" he thought, "this is the correct one".

He picked his mayll up and flung it over his shoulder, opened the door and walked down the garden path. He looked from left to right as the path wound its way to the gate, as if taking a last glance.

At the front gate stood Hrosmægden, the rest of the children and grandchildren, Mrs Underhill and many of the villagers. They were all 'well-wishers' and the children stood around telling them of the story before it began. Others were giving advice but, Mrs Underhill stood quietly with her hands on her hips.

Jaddamiah pulled himself away and moved to where she was standing and did namaste, after which he apologized for his impudence. She smiled and accepted his apology, then asked if he had packed it in. Jaddamiah knew he did not pack the phial so he blushed, blood filled his face with embarrassment but, his wife was near enough to save his bacon. "Sure he has it," came the liberator's reply. As she said that, she opened his tweed jacket to the pocket on the inside. She patted the bulge of the phial with her flat hand. Jaddamiah could feel it against his chest. He smiled, then sighed, he was relieved that he did not have to lie to Mrs Underhill. Mrs Underhill gave a laugh, the way teachers do when discovering someone had been saved from a faux pas, and fisted him gently against the chest, then gave a nudge to the cheeks as if he were only a little boy.

When at last he turned to his wife, Béth-Élam was already in the gloam of the mountain. The bright New Moon had started to climb high over Old Man Bllömpotvölle's cottage. The two stood a little step away from others. Hrosmægden held her husband's face in her right hand and looked deeply into his eyes and said affectionately, "May the stars shine and may their light fall upon your path, till you, who journey over hill and dale, moss for pillow, come home again." As she said those words, a tear rolled over her tender cheeks and at that moment, she looked down to wipe it away as it trailed down to the corner of her mouth. Something extraordinary then happened; Jaddamiah's face reflected in the gem on her ring. Hrosmægden was not the only one who saw that. Mrs Underhill and several of the children saw the gleam. The subsequent smile on Hrosmægden's face was wider than a mile, for that gem was held in high regard and there was an ancient Alkanina saying that went; "to escape evil and attain good fortune, one must see the reflection of the new moon either on the face of a friend, or on a turquoise gem." She did not tell him of it but whispered to him, "My heart is at peace; go now on your journey."

Part 2

addamiah Jabberwocky set off and took his first steps towards Weir on the 27th of September 8816. 'I go now. I do not know at which door my feet may fall' those words were on his mind or that's what he thought he said but, no audible words fell from his lips! Jaddamiah did not look back at the crowd that had congregated outside his house. When he passed number 31415, he heard a soft, husky voice call out to him. It was Hyperion at her gate. Jaddamiah stopped and retraced his steps back to her. She simply smiled and handed him a small, round pie made of gnomegold apples. Jaddamiah could smell the aroma issuing from it; it was still warm in his hand. He was glad that she said goodbye in that way and said, "Gratitude!"

Very quickly he was on his way again. At the last house on the left of Lamas Street, stood two figures. It was Semjase and her husband. While lighting his pipe, her husband shouted from beneath the flame and smoke, "Shall I harness some dwhëels, Jabberwocky?"

"That sounds like a plan Lemayian but, all journeys must first start on foot. Gratitude all the same!" and with that, he waved his walking staff at Lemayian.

Lemayian turned around and walked with his hands in his pockets, looking here and there at his garden, for he was not a sentimental man. Jaddamiah pulled up his nose to take in the sweet aroma of the tobacco. He looked back and saw that Semjase held a small, tin box in her hands. She slowly turned it sideways and upright so that the moonlight gave it an eerie glow. She smiled as she teased him, and he came galloping back. "One such as yourself should never leave without a little 'heat'". Semjase held the tin box close to her face and juddered the tin before his out stretched hand. When Jaddamiah took it from her she said, "It is a gift from Lemayian. Use it well."

"I will! I will dearest Semjase. You shouldn't have." He looked at the label on the top side and recognized from the red lettering and the name, that it was the finest tobacco from Alkana.

It was 'heat' or 'Purple Dell', that was the common name but, many just called it 'dhumra-tapas' or 'dhumra'. Dhumra-tapas simply meant 'purple tabac'.

"When you smoke it, think of us Jabberwocky!" came the voice of Lemayian from between the garden growth.

Jaddamiah looked into Semjase's eyes, took her hand and kissed it gently, then called back, "I will think of Semjase!" and gave a deep, mischievous laugh as he walked away.

Part 3

he ancient dwarve clock was passed and Jaddamiah walked up the two mile stretch to where Bllömpotvölle's cottage stood. As he walked between the beautiful hedges, the light from the Moon cast so much light that he could see the green of the leaves and the silver, dappled light on the leaves of the tall poplars which stood behind the hedges. He could smell the evening dampness on the grass in the middle of the double track, and his thoughts fell back to the dhumra and the gnomegold apple pie in his mayll. He giggled to himself. He giggled proudly at the thought that so many villagers thought him important enough to come out, farewell him and give him gifts.

The evening was still. The breeze had subsided by then and as he progressed up the hillside, it did not take him long to reach the old cottage of Bllömpotvölle. When Jaddamiah passed the cottage, he noticed that the lamp at the front gate was burning, which was something very rare to see. He stopped for a moment but when no one came forth, Jaddamiah continued somewhat disappointed, for he thought to himself that it would have been wonderful to have some words of cheer from that *ancient*.

After a mile, he felt compelled to look around one more time, for it was such a long time since he had set out on a long journey. To his surprise he noticed that in the distance, no lamp light was to be seen burning. As he cast his eyes on the moonlit road ahead, the grass had a silver-blue sheen *from* it. He gave that strange anomaly some thought for a few seconds and wandered why the light had been on in the first place, and now it was off. Although the moon was out to its full influence, he saw that the rumours were true after all. He could no longer see the weald line of trees, it was as if it were hidden from view. This unsettled his thoughts for a while. As he continued, it felt to him that he was alone, to his left and right shoulder were the wide, open spaces of Lyte Hros and then he looked upward. The sky was clear and dotted with bright, blue-silver lights – the stars. He could now see in the distance. The lights of Dystiġ, a little village of 50 people, came into view and that shook him from his uninhabited thoughts. He could feel the light gravel crunch beneath his feet and it was to that rhythm that he kept and was about to pass straight through Dystiġ. Unlike its neighbour Béth-Élam, Dystiġ had 20 homesteads. When he entered Dystig, some yards ahead of him, was a solitary figure dragging his feet in the dust, and little plumes rose around it in the moonlight. Jaddamiah knew there could only be one staggering drunk, all alone in the street, 'it must be Wasseling Broadbottle' he thought, as he picked his pace up to catch up to him. 'There is no Inn at Dystiġ, so either he's just come from some neighbour or, he's been ahead of me all along and stumbled from Döppievölle Inn' Jaddamiah continued thinking to himself.

When he caught up to him, he greeted him heartily but, he should not have done that because Wasseling got such a fright that he tripped over his own feet. He lay there on his side at an angle, dust in his face, his red tongue darting out like some accursed serpent trying to lick the dust from his lips.

Jaddamiah tried to help him up, but if you've ever tried helping a drunk to his feet, it is a rather precarious affair! You normally end up on the ground with them because it's like dragging some legless thing. Or they hold so tight onto your neck as if to choke you to death.

"errrr-gurrrrrrr- A Jam Hided- A Jam Hided! It's you. I knoooooo it i-sss yooooo," slurred the drunk.

"No silly-billy, I did *not* steal any jam and it's Jaddamiah. Ja-dda-miah!" Jaddamiah managed to straighten Wasseling Broadbottle onto his feet but, from the waist up, he was as limp as a ragdoll; a sight all the funnier when watched from a certain vantage point…

"Mead Jihad- Mead Jihad!" continued Wasseling whilst drooling over Jaddamiah's hands, who was not impressed at all. Jaddamiah succeeded in dragging the limp 'ragdoll' to the nearest lamp-light and tried to stand Wasseling up against the pole.

"Dullard Broadbottle!" exclaimed Jaddamiah. "And there will be no wars on ale either."

"Jaded Am Hi- Jaded Am Hi." Wasseling stumbled forward and grabbed the lamp post for support, then used his forefinger to point at Jaddamiah and continued, "Jaddamiah. Jaddamiah Jabberwocky is what I meant to say."

"Well, you certainly went about it the long way Wasseling Broadbottle," replied Jaddamiah as he picked his walking stick up and secured his mayll. "Now you've caused me delay Mr Broadbottle."

Wasseling Broadbottle clung to the pole, floppy-jawed and wilting over for some time before he said, "You can leave me here Jaddamiah and continue your moonlight stroll."

There were several kinds of drunk people, quiet, crazy, angry, talkative but, Wasseling Broadbottle was none of those so, the meeting with Jaddamiah would certainly be remembered.

Wasseling grinned and displayed his ale-washed teeth as Jaddamiah bid him farewell. "I'm going bo ted now! Wanna come?"

"That is a good idea Wasseling Broadbottle, go straight to bed."

Jaddamiah walked further and looked back constantly to the dusty, Broad Street, only to find Wasseling still leaning against the lamp pole. A dog barked in the stillness, as the upright figure of Jaddamiah disappeared out of sight, past the last cover of light that the village provided.

Shortly after that, the lone figure of Jaddamiah came to a cutting in the Wen Pen Mountain range and crossed the Pontigam, a bent, stone-arched bridge that linked the two Hros Plains.

He crossed over quickly, did a namaste, just in case any trolls that slept under the bridge woke up. Jaddamiah could smell the freshness from the flowing Afon Wen and the silence was broken by singing frogs and barking toads. It was strange that the bridge caused him to be flighty and he found that the hairs on his nape were standing on end and he had goose bumps. All of that because he had heard a sound like two pebbles being tapped together but, it was no one, just a little bit of silliness on his part. It was in fact, the sound of a cricket frog joining the amphibian chorus.

There was also a pleasant fragrance in the air, a sweet smell of honey, he could not place the smell exactly. The Afon Wen accompanied him to his right, at the feet of the mountains that towered upward like dark phantoms. Jaddamiah started to hum, perhaps it was the frogs that put that idea into his head. Soon he was singing the words, it was no walking song but, he liked it very much. He knew that it was something about travelling and farewells and leave-takings.

I've said good-bye
to you once before
while standing in an
open Duir.
But now it closes
for the night is falling.

The bells are ringing in
Steeples sheer and bright.
The lyra and harp is
fawning under
finger of Na Daoine Maithe.
The Ælves are waiting!
The Dwarves with revelries;
For I may not stay here
anymore.
I've laboured long in settled hours
and bid farewell to the Dryads leaving their bowers.
So too, now I must follow as
birds are emptied from every hollow.

While the Beles of men bring
cloud and shadow
I bid fare-well to family and fellow.

The time is spent for sighing and dreaming
And it was a marvellous time spent here with you.
So for me it is time to
say fare-well.
and it is better said in the evening so
I can leave the shimmering stars with you.

I return to Ælven-Home;
To the consciousness of Imladris,
under the warmth of Endürel
on Elysian Fields – Land of Trees.
To the Tree Kindred!
and to the gloaming Tree of Agniir,
to these I go faring.

All mortal harrows forsaking,
star-speed and light-year making.
Come now!
Come now all you Children!
For we have heeded the call.

Farewell and fare-thee-well.
No mortal ship will pass
through those waters.
East of East I go!
And now our lays
here have come to ending.

As he finished the song, Jaddamiah did not know it at the time but, that song was portentous, it was a presage. After such beautiful words his heart was settled, so was his spirit, for the words put him in a good mood. He continued, as he had about eight miles, as the crows flew, to walk before arriving at the home of his wife's uncle.

As the road curved away from the mountains, more light seemed to spread ahead of him as the mountain's shadow withdrew. At around midnight, he could see, scattered like fire flies on both sides of the river, lights from the Plains of Hros, which heralded the ending of this night's journey. He was happy for, he needed sleep. He felt some fine droplets on his skin and the freshness co-mingled with the profusion of scent from the parsley fields. Jaddamiah found it delightful or, as the Hrosvyra called it 'daase pietersielie velde'. It would rain so, he hastened his pace somewhat but, was soon brought to a halt as out of the darkness, or so it seemed, two horsemen appeared behind him.

"Who goes there? State your business!" came the command.

Jaddamiah stopped in his tracks and made an about turn. The horsemen came closer, so that he could see them clearly. They towered above him, each horse blocking his way back or forward. The two riders wore helmets made of silver, behind the eyes it had a beautiful, sinuous curve which ended on the cheek bones. At the back of the head, it curved up high like a horse's tail and on the crown was a long, sharp point. The front of the helmet had a floral embellishment of a four-leafed shamrock that ended with a single horse head above it. They looked like men not to be trifled with, so Jaddamiah answered, "I am Jaddamiah Jabberwocky of Béth-Élam, husband of Hrosmægden, youngest daughter of the House of Hrosweard."

He decided that he would not be intimidated and said it matter-of-factly when he looked up at them. The two Hrosvyras laughed and the one with strands of long, black hair that fell from his helmet replied, "That was a mouthful Jaddamiah, my cousin's husband. Rather proper of you. We bid you welcome to the Plains of Hros. I am Tigma and this is. . ." he was interrupted by Jaddamiah as he made a sweeping gesture with his arm, trying to introduce the second rider.

"Tigma?" asked Jaddamiah puzzled.

Tigma smiled and looked at his brother; who gave a pleasant laugh.

"Yes Jaddamiah, I am Tigma and it means 'fiery'. My sire gave me an ancient name for he is old fashioned but, enough of this mudra, the rains are coming. This is my youngest brother Ealadha, we apologize for the impolite greeting but, this responsibility befalls us for we are the Mergwarch." His voice was modulated; it was controlled and pleasant to listen to yet, he spoke with authority.

Ealadha smiled but said nothing and studied Jaddamiah. He then swung his horse around, it trotted for a moment and Ealadha slid down the saddle so that his body disappeared over the girth of his horse. He grabbed something in the dark, obscuring the view of Jaddamiah and returned and handed him a beautiful, green trefoil. Ealadha smiled but said nothing. Jaddamiah took it and thanked him. Big water droplets started to fall. "Make haste Jaddamiah our sire is expecting you, just another half mile," said Tigma. "Well, thank you very much gentlemen and I hope to meet you again." came Jaddamiah's reply.

With that he walked on briskly and when he looked around again, the Mergwarch were out of sight. Crossing over the bridge called 'Wen Hros Bont' left only a few paces to the homestead of Gedymdeith. Jaddamiah was excited to be there because the Hrosvyras were reputed to have beautiful homes that were sculpted out of the earth.

Even at night under the moonlight, the beauty of Gedymdeith's homestead could be seen. Gedymdeith's house was something to behold from the outside as Jaddamiah walked over the soft, wet, green, manicured grass. The Hrosvyras erected no walls or fences.

Mounds sprung up all over the Plains, and the one at Gedymdeith's homestead pushed out of the earth at a gentle angle. To the far side of that 30m incline, protruded a tall, thick arch of masonry, beautifully rendered from clay that was found in the river that ran through the Vale of Tears. Under the slender, domed roof in a niche in the arch, was a tall, maple door. Despite the rain, Jaddamiah stood for a moment to admire it before he entered. He wondered why his wife left the Hrosweard lifestyle to live with him in Béth-Élam. He was lost in admiration of Hrosvyras architecture, under the gentle, falling rain.

The angle of the sloped grass only went up halfway besides the entrance arch and another incline could be seen. On that section slanted, glass panels glowed blue under the moonlight.

Jaddamiah ran in under the arch and rang the silver bell that was suspended by a thin chain from the ceiling. The sound could be heard softly peeling through the interior. He further admired the door with a perfectly sculpted horse with a long stem in its mouth, where at the end of it was a four-leaf shamrock. The whole sculpture was in relief. As he waited, Jaddamiah ran his wet fingers over the wood because it was so. . . touchable, 'I suppose that *was* the whole objective behind it' he thought to himself.

Then the door opened wide. Jaddamiah heard no footsteps and light from within coursed out over him. In the doorway stood a tall man of noble bearing. His long, dark, honey-coloured hair was almost black, and it fell in smooth waves to his chest. His hairline was far back and revealed a long, sloped forehead which was burned dark from torrid afternoons on horseback. He had no facial hair except for a long goatee at the end of his chin and his face appeared kind and gentle.

He was second in line to the chiefdom, not the sons of his eldest brother, no. They fell third in line after Gedymdeith. Only chiefs of the Hros grew facial hair, and it was for that reason that he groomed his goatee. Over the centuries they came to be known by the moniker, 'the goatees' and over time, all Hrosvyra males came to be known as the 'Long-Goths' but, they also had the habit of wearing long, red leather coats. Whether it was because of the long chin hair or the long red leather coats, no one could tell because they continued to be known as the 'Long-Goths'.

Deep furrows pushed back his high, brown-orange cheekbones from the alar groove of his hooked nose. Between his lower lip and the round curved chin were furrow lines, that spread like eagle's wings. When he smiled, those furrows ironed out and his clear, light, yellowish-green eyes spoke to you.

He stood with both his arms raised, ready to embrace.

"Sus-vapnah! Sus-vapnah my dear Jabberwocky. Welcome! Welcome! Do come in immediately." He took Jaddamiah in one arm, with the other he closed the heavy door and walked with Jaddamiah down the slender hallway saying, "I am Gedymdeith Hrosweard, the uncle of your beloved wife." As they walked down the hallway, Jaddamiah noticed that on both sides, on long slender tables that ran the length of the wall, geometrical glass boxes were neatly placed. Some were round, and others were square shaped.

In them an array of butterflies lay suspended on pins that were made of wood. Gedymdeith noticed his interest and stopped so Jaddamiah could admire them. In a long, single sentence he said, "Have you noticed Jaddamiah, for I see you have an interest in my fifaldara, that everywhere you go where the profane practice the harmful ritual of burying lifeless bodies under the ground, thus polluting the beautiful Dhara with putrefaction, in those cities littered with those sites of burial grounds, have you ever noticed there in those great metropolises or in nature herself, one will hardly find these creatures lying about?" Jaddamiah thought for a moment, speechless. He was captivated by the melodious, soft tones with which Gedymdeith spoke, not dissimilar to his wife's plummy voice or way of speaking. It was typical of the Hrosvyras yet, Gedymdeith had a less prominent side to his voice for, the Hrosvyras were a proud people. He came out of his brief enthrallment then answered thoughtfully saying, "Yes, you are quite correct, rarely so."

"This collection has therefore taken me a life-time for none of my fifaldara were killed by my hands nor for my pleasure. These creatures don't litter the weald or meadow floors easily, one might think their disappearance quite accursed. Entomology and philology also taught me that the word 'boterschijte' is used in some tongues. The conclusion formed because 'butterfly', the common term, excrement may have been thought to resemble butter, hence giving the name 'butter-bumption' then 'butter-fly'. In Ninfa they are called 'SomerFaegegele', 'the magick bird of summer.'" There was a pause, a moment of silence; Jaddamiah was utterly captivated by all that talk, talk, talk. In fact, the only sound that broke it, was the falling rain on the slanted glass windows further in the interior.

"In any case, lets proceed to a more comfortable locus," Gedymdeith went on showing the way with the sweep of his arm.

The common name for the homesteads of the Hrosvyras was 'Pit House' but that interior did not fit such a rudimentary name.

Multiple branch-like columns supported the cedar floors while a spiral staircase situated in the central area of the house acted as dominant element. The spiral staircase snaked its way up toward two more floors around a large, erect, 700year old deodar tree. The branches on the ground floor were clipped and the bark peeled back and Jaddamiah could not understand how, after so many years, the wonderful, spicy aroma of its wood remained strongly fragrant. He breathed in deeply. On the first floor, the wooden floor was traced out to give the branches space to live. That style was repeated on the second floor and eventually it sped up out through a well-crafted hole in the ceiling, through which no rain fell at all. Gedymdeith leaned against the trunk and closed his eyes, and while doing that. called out the words reverentially, "Devadāru! Devadāru! Devadāru!" Gedymdeith led Jaddamiah into a small room, a library, one that led off from the spiral staircase. The two men lit their pipes and a hot pot of spicebush tea with passionflower fruit was brought in. Jaddamiah spoke and told his story, after which, Gedymdeith rolled out a large map and drew Jaddamiah's attention to it. "Jaddamiah!" exclaimed Gedymdeith in a now gravelly voice. He oscillated between that gravelly voice and a suave voice, a real story teller's voice. He continued, "You could easily have sailed from the river port of Albtraum along a 114mile section of the river to Skallagrimmr, some 13miles from Weir or right to Weir itself because they have a small staithe. But that 114mile stretch is not called Afon Wen, it is called the River Næddre, and for generations it is believed that a water serpent lives in that stretch of the river, hence the name. At the beginning of the River Næddre stands a tall walled city, impregnable. No-one leaves, no-one enters because it is the home of the Paladins. There is a river port with some households surrounding it; they are the custodians of the port."

At that point, Jaddamiah interjected and spoke using his hands and waving his long, slender, right index finger. "Those Paladins? I have heard of them but have never seen or met them."

"Aah! Ahah!" exclaimed Gedymdeith while turning his goatee around his finger. He pulled his head back and dropped his square jaw. "I suspect you have Jaddamiah, husband of my niece, I *suspect* you *have*. Is there not such a one called Ğägna in your village?"

Jaddamiah thought for a moment, his finger was on his lips as his green eyes rolled around in their sockets. After a few seconds of contemplation, he shook his head from side to side. "So? There is no one of that name that you know? There is no stranger at Béth-Élam?"

A thought came to him; "Yes! Yer—sss, yes," he said as he ran his fingers through his hair again. His back was arched as he sat forward on the chair, his legs crossed at the knees.

"There is such a person, people speak poorly of him and he comes and goes at ill begotten hours and the under cloak of darkness. A very tall fellow I imagine, if he slouched less." Jaddamiah said that sympathetically as he looked at Gedymdeith. Gedymdeith smiled in acknowledgement and then went on with his story.

"He *is* the Paladin." He sat quietly for a moment then looked up to the vaulted ceiling and its awe-inspiring equine friezes. He looked at Jaddamiah again and continued as if something new came to mind. "It is a strange thing to me; this Ğägna in Béth-Élam, for Béth-Élam is a sleepy, little hamlet and there would be no reason for any Paladin to be stationed there. Has there been a recent row in your village? Or anything out of the commonplace, perchance, a happenstance?"

Jaddamiah couldn't think of anything. He then wished that he had spent more time with Mrs Underhill, perhaps it would have ensured that he knew *of* something. Gedymdeith followed his expressions but, continued without waiting for a reply. "At any rate Jaddamiah, when then did he arrive?" "We do not know. After 451 was burned down, one morning, we saw that fellow building and fixing only one little room of the house on the first floor. We thought he was peculiar, cracked he was . . . or so some thought. He came one other time to Döppievölle Inn and no one's seen him since."

Jaddamiah could not understand why all that had any relevance but, his thoughts were soon interrupted when Gedymdeith asked a favour of him. "Will you keep me abreast as soon as he returns?" Jaddamiah willingly shook his head. "Now let us continue. I won't keep you any longer from your sleep. Would you like some ale, perhaps some more tea?"

"Some more tea please," replied Jaddamiah as he held his empty mug forward. "Now where have I laid off?" asked Gedymdeith.

"You were telling of the River Næddre and the river serpent," replied Jaddamiah attentively. "You are a good listener Jaddamiah. Yes, that is exactly where I left off the tale. That 114 mile stretch is also believed to be under *liminal time* for the ancient legends tell that the wealds along that stretch, are possessed of Horwolves and there Maelgwn. . ."

Jaddamiah's eyes became big as marbles and he sat ramrod straight in the chair.

"You've heard of Horwolves, have you not?"

"But of course Gedymdeith but, my thoughts were that they were only legends."

"Legends you say Mr Jabberwocky, *legends*? Let me tell you about legends. There is a special word which describes it well, the word is luminary; a *leading light*, guiding light. *Inspiration* Jaddamiah!"

Gedymdeith laughed, stroking his goatee, like someone who knew a secret. "Things to be read, family of my niece, things to be read," he reiterated. "To be read like Stars, like the weald, like horses dear boy, to augur! Great horn spoon! The staithe at the other end of the 114mile stretch have only one family living at it and though no one speaks of it, I believe they are horwolves who amble around the weald of Vani (Vana) Zarvari. The River Næddre flows between that mighty weald. Now from Öoragörks to Ælfenna; it seems to me Mr Jabberwocky, that you will be on foot and horse, I shall gladly give you one and there is something else. . ." with that, Gedymdeith pushed himself up from the sofa. "Come with me. I have something marvellous for you."

Gedymdeith led him into a long, slender room that had many candles burning in sconces of a wonderful, leafy-green colour. The light and shadows swam on the walls and reflected from the highly polished, clay floor. An ignorant person would easily have mistaken it for marble flooring. The room was warm and welcoming and above the large, stone hearth from where a fire was crackling, hung the House of Hrosweard pennon, varying only slightly in each Hrosweard family. Along the left wall, starting at the entrance and running the distance of the wall, was a slender ledge of a greenish wood and on it were various helmets. Gedymdeith walked to more-or-less the middle to where one of the helmets was slightly raised on a single spike of wood. As he walked, he ran his finger gently over the smoothness of the wood. "This one is my favourite, it was given me by the Ælves, the *Ælves* you know," Gedymdeith emphasized in his mellifluous voice. Jaddamiah came to his side and looked at the beautiful helmet. It looked more like a work of art than something used in battle. Gedymdeith took it from its stand and said, handing it to Jaddamiah, "go ahead. . . it is not enough to look at such wonder, you must feel it in your hands, it's made of white pewter, very hard to find."

Jaddamiah took it cautiously; all over the helmet ran golden leaf filigree with golden, sculpted wings on the sides. On the crest was a raised Blue Dragon, fashioned with it wings slightly raised.

"Is pewter tough enough to protect the head?" asked Jaddamiah.

"Ha ha ha ha ha ha hah! You are correct, very right indeed, it is softer than other metals but also easy to mould in wondrous fashion however, can a mortal give a mortal wound to an Ælve when the helmets are charmed?" laughed Gedymdeith, taking the helmet from Jaddamiah and returning it to its place.

Two solid pillars stood, just a few meters from the wall, at the end of each room. On those pillars hung various blades, daggers, heirloom swords and a beautifully crafted anlaas, with an emerant hilt. Gedymdeith walked to the furthest pillar and took an elegant sword from its hanging place. He held it over both his open palms and smiled. His face lit up as if remembering some past conquest. He turned on his heel and held it there, for Jaddamiah. Jaddamiah looked at the blade. He had never seen one of such magnificence. "Here! Go ahead and take it. You are now its custodian. Be careful, for she is invidious to the wrong individual. When it was gifted to me, it came with a name. . . 'Mordēre'. . . the blade is called Mordēre for, she bites! In the ancient tongue. . ." and he said *that* with his head gently swaying from side to side, as if proud to announce it, ". . .it is called 'Vidazati' which means 'bite to pieces'".

Jaddamiah took it and stroked it like the mane of a great horse. The steel was cool, very cool but, its hilt was warm to the touch. The sword, kræfted by the Ælves, was long and curved like an outstretched 'S'. It seemed that the blade and hilt made of hazel wood, was a single object. Near the hilt the blade was slightly perforated, and the blade was made of lilūlium steel. In the hilt, the steel spiralled through the wood till its steel end. From that, attached to a ring, a glimmering, silver chain extended for about five inches and ended with another ring. There the chain split into two parts and at one end hung a four-leafed shamrock made of lilūlium steel and on the other, a small dragon's head of an unknown, blue stone.

Jaddamiah spread his legs, gripped the sword with both hands, placed his feet firmly on the ground and swung the sword to the left of his shoulder then to the right. The blade sang as it cut through the warm air in the room. Gedymdeith stepped forward and stayed Jaddamiah's hand. "Remember Jaddamiah, not to grip the sword but, hold it firm yet lightly, like a child's toy. That of course, is easier said than done," said Gedymdeith in a pedagogue fashion, lowering his voice.

He then stood thinking for a moment.

"It is a pity!" exclaimed Jaddamiah. "An extra day would have been helpful to have some training from experienced hands."

"Perhaps Jaddamiah but, let us not talk of pity for, pity comes from misfortune."

Jaddamiah listened and ran his fingers on the top edge of the blade all the way down near the tip. When he did that, a razor- sharp horn jumped out of the paper-thin blade and cut his long finger badly. Blood ran down the blade and to his utter amazement, fiery blue script began to form and run its way toward the hilt.

Gedymdeith jumped in and took the sword from him, the sharp horn disappeared back into the blade and the fiery, blue script vanished. Jaddamiah held his hand, Gedymdeith placed the sword on a round half-pillar that was covered with green, velvet cloth.

"Bairrfhionn! Bairrfhionn!" called Gedymdeith; he did not raise his voice much but almost instantly a tall, lissom, fair, long-haired maiden responded to the call.

"You have called me father, what is it?"

"Mordēre has cut Jaddamiah, please tend to his wound."

Gedymdeith lightly pushed Jaddamiah on the back to follow his daughter.

Part 4

The night passed like a dream as his sleep was sweet, and when Jaddamiah woke in the morning, he felt refreshed. He stretched himself under the sheet, spread star-fish and yawned.

Afterwards, he sat up in the bed with his arms spread behind him to support his weight.

The rain had stopped during the early hours of the morning and after breakfast, Jaddamiah stood drinking his tea on the well-manicured lawns and surveyed the land from the grass roof of Gedymdeith's home. The early morning sun warmed his skin and he felt invigorated, while inhaling the fresh air. The stars showed their blue faces and he felt that Béth-Élam was already a thousand miles away. Just before Gedymdeith was to take Jaddamiah to the stables, Jaddamiah removed the tart which Hyperion had baked, from his mayll and he neatly cut two triangular slices from it. The men enjoyed it with their morning tea. Afterwards Gedymdeith said, "I intend that someday I will meet the maiden who baked so fine an apple tart." and picked the remnants from the plate.

Part 5

The stables were no hash-mash affair. They were no different to the main house in that no material nor comfort for the horses was spared, and they had plenty of pietersielie for feed. The stables were like the homesteads, under the earth.

Gedymdeith and Jaddamiah walked down a grassy decline, a trodden-out path with an opening about twelve meters wide, emerged from a well-lit interior. Next to it were retainer walls of stone, that helped support the mouth of the stables.

Inside the fresh smell of straw laid out thick in places on the smooth surface could be smelled. Grooms were busy grooming, stable hands were washing and preparing horses but, beside one ornately sculptured wooden pillar, stout and thick, overlaid in bronze motifs, stood a beautiful horse on its 3 legs. A young man held the foot of the forth leg between his knees as nippers, hoof knife and rasp lay strewn at his feet on the ground, the young man's long black hair covered his head and face so that he was unrecognizable. When Jaddamiah stroked its face, the horse took an immediate liking to him. Gedymdeith held the opposite side of her head and said, "Good morning my lovely, how are you today Fágan? Tell Jaddamiah your name!" exclaimed Gedymdeith, as if speaking to a little child and encouraging it to say its name. "She is called Fágan, Mr Jabberwocky because of her dappled back and hind quarters." The young man busying himself at the coronet did not say a word.

The mare was exceptionally beautiful. She was pitch black, her left front foot and rear right foot had pure white stockings and from her mid back, rear and hump was white, with black, dappled spots. When the young man was satisfied and straightened his tall form, Jaddamiah recognized him, it was Ealadha.

"I must get back to my post father; she is right as rain Mr Jabberwocky. Fare thee well," he said in a gentle voice and walked to where a groom was waiting with his horse.

He handed over a tool to the groom, mounted his horse and sped off. The pawing of his horse's hooves could be heard on the hard surface, then the heavy thuds as it ran up the grassy incline and disappeared over the ridge. Jaddamiah mounted, took the reins in his hands; the seat was worn-in and felt very comfortable.

Jaddamiah smiled widely, for the Jabberwockies were fond of those lovable creatures. Gedymdeith stood looking up to him but only slightly, as he was *very* tall. He stood there with his fists resting on his hips.

"Well, husband of my niece, I have said all that I could say to you and though your stay was short, happy have we met, now happy let us part. The journey home is never too long, so giddy-up! Come back soon!" with that, he slapped Fágan on the rump, and she went off. "Steady Fágan! Steady my sweet! Take care of the Jabberwocky!" he called out aloud after the man and beast.

Part 6

There were no garden paths nor fences, for the Hrosvyras had none so, Fágan cantered over the first few hundred meters as Jaddamiah steered her to the road. Folk were already moving about as the Plains of Hros were busy. The Hrosvyra were an industrious people and went about their own business, unless summoned by greater powers, then they would respond accordingly. Some greeted, even though they did not recognize the stranger on the horse, they certainly knew the horse and who her Bele was.

As the two made their way to the eastern road proper, they made for the Eang Bont. The air was cool, for Summer was fast fading and many maidens could be seen along the road, some with stacks of folded washing on their heads, others herding cattle so Jaddamiah had to slow Fágan down, although she was a clever beast and did so almost of her own accord.

When he pushed through this bovine jam, they cantered off again, crossing over the Eang Bont. Jaddamiah noticed that the Afon Wen was flowing quite fast as it was filled from the night's rain. Fágan followed the bend in the road and there, standing on both sides of the road, no longer littered over the grass plains but all together, were thousands of mounds which popped up from the earth with all its myriad doors. He then saw how the population could be 18000 of which 6000, were the Mergwarch and 313, were the Teyrngwarch (the kings guard). Some doors were painted in various colours and those not painted, had grand sculptures and motifs on them. Those mounds stood in neat rows and for the four miles that followed, the road was neatly paved with cobble stones that shone silver from the rain that had fallen on them overnight. The pawing of Fagan's hooves joined the cacophony of sound from many horses and wagons that passed up and down. Stallions flared their nostrils, vapour rose in the cool morning air as Fágan passed; they cocked their heads left and right, the whites of their eyes enough to excite little children.

His progress was hampered somewhat again, as the early morning congestion continued but, that allowed him the time to study the large entrance to the House of Hrosweard, where the ruler and chief of all the Hrosvyras, Aherin Hrosweard, his father-in-law and the elder brother to Gedymdeith, resided. There were only 3 mounds before his, perhaps to show off his rank and title. Jaddamiah wondered what it looked like inside if the entrance was so ostentatious. Two tall flag poles stood at either end of the entrance, one with the personal escutcheon, the other of the Hrosvyras. Jaddamiah took that in, as he hoped that he would give it more personal attention at another time.

He came to a round-about in the road, where a vast, spherical shaped sculpture, crafted only from horse shoes, each shoe was rusty from the weather-beaten years, lay in the centre of it. It was an equine wonder, for it must have taken much time and care to construct it. Then Jaddamiah saw a structure that out-towered everything else. The 'Ina Nirmana' was called by such a name because the Alkaninas helped to build it. It was initially built because of a dispute between the two races over whose horses were better suited for riding. The structure itself was sunken but, two tall towers stood on the outside at either end. One faced north, 'nörtýrris' the other south, 'suðtýrris'. Those structures could be seen from many miles away, and they were the only structures of the Hrosvyras that were built above ground.

Once Jaddamiah passed the last row of homestead mounds, he came to a chicane in the road, at the end of it stood two Mergwarch mounds, one on either side of the road. One of the men on watch was Tigma.

"Many happy returns Jaddamiah!" he called out as he leaned against the arch of the door. Jaddamiah raised his right hand and smiled. He feathered the reins and gently spurred Fágan, then squeezed with his calves to encourage the horse forward and said, "sâa! sâa!"

Fágan understood him and immediately started to canter. Jaddamiah never quite understood it but, Lemayian had taught him that and it meant 'to go'. He said it didn't matter if you got on a horse for the first time or that you were a stranger to it, if you were on it and said those words, the horse would do exactly what you wanted.

Part 7

As Jaddamiah sat on his horse with his thoughts set on Weir, he suddenly remembered that when he reached Weir, it would be the first time in his life that he saw it. Many years prior, when he set out to Weir for the first time, he never reached it because he had an accident after the Pontigam; where his future wife found him and saved him from sure death. 'How strange?' he thought, 'that no matter what, destiny and fate could never be thwarted'.

Scattered over the lush green plains of Hros, the entrances of isolated dwellings with cattle or sheep grazing on the hillsides, could still be seen. A gentle tail wind had come up from the east which increased the pace a bit. Travellers on the road were few and scarce and Jaddamiah and Fágan found themselves to be the only company. Trees were scattered, and the weald could not be seen, as it lay far away at the feet of great mountains on the horizon. Bird sounds were few, if any, and only the wind played with blades of grass, like lissom fingers over lyre strings, sighing noiselessly and yet, the grass bent in acquiescence. With no sign of life, Jaddamiah breathed in the fragrance of the grass and he liked it for he knew it. It was respiration and inspiration. The beating of his heart, the sound of Fágan's hoofs on the hard ground, and the gentle vibration reaching through the pastern, through the hock and up the leg, along the thighs, over Fágan's back and through his own spine, and in turn interpreted in his head as sensations, were an at-onement few were conscious of but, it was there nonetheless.

The east wind was gentle, perhaps it was the chasubles of Vespyr that held Perun in check. . .

All was poetry for, whether it was the fingers of the wind writing it on the vanes of grass, or the fingers of the poet writing on leaves of paper, it all flowed from Nature's fanes and it was sacred. Jaddamiah once again inhaled a honey fragrance that he couldn't identify the night before. He then saw that the roadside and the fields were littered with tall spires of red, purple, white, blue, orange and mostly yellow, Candle Flowers. The sight was rainbowrific.

A sudden sound cut through the silence and caused Jaddamiah to sit erect. He cocked his head upward and he realized that it was five crows passing overhead. He watched them till all became one small black fleck in the distance, which fused into the ever-blue. He ran his eyes towards the east and saw that fluffy, grey clouds with large, round rumps had come up, and were being poked by the tops of the ragged mountain peaks.

His thoughts returned to the present, and as he felt the strong body of Fágan beneath him, he leaned forward and reached out with his right hand to caress her cheeks. She dropped her head and pushed gently against his hand, accepting that gesture. They both inherently knew that if they were to reach their destination, they would have to have a strong bond and not be separated from each other by more than a few hundred yards.

By late afternoon, the clouds that Jaddamiah had observed much earlier in the day, were looming dark on the horizon and the mountains drew nearer. It was almost time for him to rest and he wasn't prepared to take his horse any further. They had covered 25miles over roads consisting of hard-packed dirt or dirt-gravel mix, and though the roads were in a relatively decent condition, it was time to look for cover for the night.

All signs of the plains were now behind and the road started an incline, as Jaddamiah brought Fágan to a trot. It began begun with a long drag between two small hills no higher than 100ft. The hills were covered with long, green grass and trees lined its ridge. Jaddamiah turned back in the saddle and could see no one coming up behind them. He considered that he would see if there were some place to stay the night, over the hillock.

When on the other side, he noticed that it was much higher than the side from where they came. He could see the valley beneath them from the top of the hillock. The road was lined with tall pines and took a twist and turn upon itself. He was certain that he would find a resting place quickly.

After four miles, he saw to his left, a large set of grey rocks covered by grey-green moss. The pines had receded some distance from the road and an open field could be seen. As he came to halt the horse near the rocks, he saw that it made a kind-of triangular cave, the space under it receded for about two metres.

"Yes! This is the place we will camp for the night Fágan." he said as he dismounted. He patted her face as she bent her neck to nibble on the lush, long grass. Jaddamiah untied his mayll and blankets from her back and allowed her to walk about and graze.

He looked up to the sky as the clouds began to move faster overhead. He smelled rain and thought to himself; 'I'd better hurry up and get the fire going'. On the opposite side of the road was an old, wooden sign post which he hadn't noticed before. He smiled and thought aloud; 'I must be tired!'

The sign read; 'The Windy Piny Pass' and the distance was printed at the bottom of the now faded, bold letters; '4 miles to the top'. Jaddamiah inhaled deeply and caught the sweet, pine fragrance which drifted overhead.

After he explored the interior of the cave-let and was satisfied that it was mostly soft sea-sand, he made a bed for himself by gathering pine needles to rest his blanket on top of. He thought of an easy way to start the fire and gathered an armful of pine cones as they were in abundance. The fire roared and it was close to twilight, when Jaddamiah was treated to a magnificent aerial display of migrating starlings. They projected themselves from some nearby trees into the quiet, evening air. That dazzling display of nature was a sure sign that winter was approaching. Their swoops and dives formed dark, shape-shifting clouds in the sky that resembled giant whales, birds, seals and fish. He rose from his rocky seat and gazed upward, thankful that he wasn't alone after all. After their plumy show, they settled in the trees, too much complaining and jostling. 'What a mysterious murmuration' thought Jaddamiah to himself, as even Fágan had lifted her head to watch the commotion.

He walked over to his mayll and dug into it. Out came a fistful of grains that he handed to Fágan. She was happy and nuzzled him in 'gratitude' on his shoulder. When Jaddamiah turned to walk back to his cave-let, she nuzzled his buttocks. He smiled because he knew that the horse was content.

It wasn't long after that the rains came pouring down and Jaddamiah smiled to himself, for he was safe and the first *real* day of his journey had come to an end.

Strange Vergence

J t was a strange thing that a dragon found itself in Weir. No dragon had been seen before that time. That fact that the dragon manifested, ought to have been the result from great thoughtform but, Weir wasn't capable of such thoughtform. It was a town of 6,300 people and for the most part, a peaceful place, and not enough disresonance festered there to have such a manifestation.

It started with a shadow. It started quietly, like rain during the night, that one woke to discover by morning was turning to a storm. The rain lashed out from the dark sky. It pelted in grey jets, illuminated blue by sporadic flashes of lightning. There was no thunder and Jaddamiah knew nothing of its strength as its intensity increased. How sympathetic is man's witlessness of a future yet to be perceived. For the past, the present and the future are in one giant circle where-in only a few abide at its core. In the ancient tongue it was called the 'Kendra'.

Kendra was without time. It was a single trice and it was for the rulers of the Universe to stand there, to guard its portals, its duirs. It was a sorrow when Perfection struggled to see egregiousness commencing, because they are good. The Paladins had not yet foreseen the shadow for, their eyes were turned on other felicities. But Bhelaribhus, the Primary of the Keepers of Palador, had felt a vergence in the aethyrs.

He felt it flowing around his form and he could distinguish the tone and vibration of it. He saw and understood its glyphs that displayed against his consciousness. Dancing like Fáerië over a Laksmi Kuvela, though somewhat weaker, despite the fact that it flowed less freely away from Palador, it was still a wellspring of Virya and he could harness all its power.

The River Næddre flowed languidly and some hundred meters away in a retired spot, half shrouded in trees, stood a small hovel of the rudest construction. Its roof was of turf, and its walls were blotched with lichen. The garden to the cot was country idyll, and in the 8ft emerant, Sandarac hedges, the only entrance was a circle in it with a large, wooden door. As the hovel was far from any road and was only reached by a path over moorland and through weald or over mountain, it was seldom visited. The couple who lived there, were not the type to make many friends. The man, Lycurgus, was a sombre, melancholy-looking fellow, who walked in a stooping attitude, and whose pale face and deep-set, golden eyes under a pair of coarse brown, bushy brows, which met across the forehead, were ample to deter any one in search of his confrère. Lycurgus seldom spoke, and when he did, it was in the broadest patois of Ælves, of wolves or perhaps gardening. His long, grey beard and retiring habits, procured for him the name of the 'Hermit of Palador', though no one attributed to him any extraordinary enigmas. It was to that cottage that Bhelaribhus ran. He moved light-footed across the long grasses and wore a soft, long hood and cape that changed colours, varying according to his surroundings, so that he was difficult to detect or follow.

It was called 'Enu-Sillu' which roughly translates as 'changing shades'. The language was not of that Pradeza for, it was gifted to him by someone from Jinbōchō.

From where he stood, it appeared that a great, predominantly blue aureole, spiralled around the cottage. The aureole was dappled with colours of beautiful orange, black and purple. On closer inspection, one could see that the aureole consisted of hundreds of resplendent butterflies.

A tall, auburn Wulvlinga stood at the hedge, close to the door. Lolling at his feet a beautiful, silverish wolf lay sleeping. The wolf opened one eye, bright and cerulean and wiggled its glossy black nose, then it went back to its lolling. He was in fact, a gift from the one that was approaching. The Wulvlinga looked eastward then westward and tilted his snout to catch the breeze. Its long, curved, pointed ears moved in each direction as the eyes glanced. He was a tall Wulvlinga that stood at 6ft on all fours (on two legs he was about 12ft tall) but, he did not see Bhelaribhus who stood right beside him. Beside the Wulvlinga or rather, holding onto its right leg like a little knave to his father's leg, stood a beautiful Hobgoblin, sucking its thumb.

"Vinrúlfr!" called Bhelaribhus in a melodious, disembodied voice for this was his name when in Wulvlinga shape.

The Wulvlinga was startled, ground its teeth and jumped towards Bhelaribhus as he came into vision, and grazed him on the hand.

The Wulvlinga whimpered and instantly shape-shifted and in front of Bhelaribhus stood Lycurgus.

The Hobgoblin vanished, and it wasn't because it was afraid of Bhelaribhus. It was widely known that Hobgoblins had a fondness for all woodland spirits, especially wolves. The old folklores told that Hobgoblins and wolves had a perennial union and understanding. The Wulvlingas being loyal in nature, called Hobgoblins kindred, and they would often be seen haunting the wilds together. That type of friendship, of such collaborative governance had no beginning. Such friendships had no end. They were older than his-story and bittersweet as memories. . .

While the winds blow and the rivers flow,
The Seamróg turns sweet in the meadow,
The Hobgoblins play, the Wolvlingas do haunt,
Going about in perfect traunt.

"Bele Bhelaribhus, my humble apologies, I am so sorry, I did not know it was you!" exclaimed Lycurgus in an apologetic, gruff voice. He took the cold hand of Bhelaribhus into his warm big hands. Bhelaribhus pulled away, raised his hand to his lips, and licked it.

"There is no need to apologize old friend." he replied and watched as the cut in his pale, blue flesh disappeared and healed as if his hand had never been bitten. "It is strange to find you here Bele Bhelaribhus. I was not expecting you."

"Yes, neither was I Wulvlinga." 'Wulvlinga' was a term of endearment for the WeirWulfs which meant 'those connected with wolves', and the Ælves and Paladins referred to them as such.

They did not believe that 'WeirWulfs' was a fitting name for those disenfranchised creatures because their origins were stooped in pain and degradation.

"Come in! Come in!" invited Lycurgus as he opened the door. The large door made of elder wood, swung open lazily even with the strength of Lycurgus's push.

Bhelaribhus followed him and entered the beautiful garden filled with many wild flowers. It seemed to grow without care but if one observed carefully, one would notice that a hand was regularly nurturing it.

"Why did you tarry outside your door Lycurgus?" enquired the Paladin Bele.

Lycurgus stopped on the stone path, turned around and looked up at the tall Paladin. "Lately, it has become my custom" As Lycurgus spoke, Bhelaribhus noticed traces of disquiet on his face.

"I smell something strange on the aethyrs. That is *not* all.

I often contemplate on happier days that were spent with my scions, and the distance that now lies between us. How can I not keep guard?

How slow Time moves, in heavy hours,

As makes one wae and weary!

Then come ye glinting by

When I am but a feeble yett.

Several days ago, Ulfhamr spied two Waelwulfas along the Afon Wen, only a few miles from Albtraum."

"Was it not Varkazana?" asked the Paladin as if Time was something to forget.

"Yes, it is the month of the Wolf-Men," replied Lycurgus ruefully.

"Then my misgivings are initiated in wisdom, there *is* a fracas. For I have come here today to you Lycurgus! You are the oldest and the wisest of the Wolvlingas and stronger still than the Waelwulfas."

"Fracas you say? Well, it is in the watches of the night that the wise slumber." Lycurgus said that as a passing thought. He didn't mean for it to be spoken out loud. The Paladin looked at him sternly but did not reply.

He pushed his hood back so that it lay on his shoulders. His purple eyes were glistering in the sunlight. They held their own light so that Bhelaribhus appeared altogether lovely. He stood contemplating for a moment, as was his manner. Lycurgus then continued, "there is something else Bele Bhelaribhus"

"Yes? What is it Lycurgus!" replied Bhelaribhus firmly.

"I do not want to trouble the Paladins but, I must confess both Lyadalagapē and I are worried. It has been many days and neither Ulfheðin nor Ulfhamr have come around. They usually visit every day and when they cannot come, they send a syven. What's more, I cannot get their scent. We last saw them on the twenty forths."

Bhelaribhus stood there poker-faced; it belied his thoughts, for that was ill news. "Then I must leave at once and look into this matter." His words were emphatic. The Paladin drew his hood over his head and turned to leave but stopped. "Although this is ill news, let us intend that this is not a fell deed."

"There is one more thing. . ." Lycurgus paused for a long time and the Paladin did not prompt him. He waited for Lycurgus to say what was on his mind. ". . . Bleddyn has gone to search for them. . .I could not convince her to stay."

Bhelaribhus didn't answer, for he knew what that meant, especially that Lycurgus used the name Bleddyn instead of Lyadalagapē.

Lycurgus was not a man for entertaining guests but, he would have preferred that the Paladin came in to eat with him but, Bhelaribhus left through the door and was gone. Lycurgus stooped down to pat the wolf. As always, Aethelwulf was by his side.

Strange Spheres and Shears

When Jaddamiah woke and peered, sleepy eyed over his blankets, he saw that next to his makeshift bed, against the foot of the wall of the cave-let, a stream of water had formed.

He sat up and rubbed his eyes. Fágan was nowhere to be seen and the long grasses glittered with silver, luminous droplets. Some shone with striking orange and green in them, as the rising sun peeped over the tall pines. The dampness of the wood could be smelt, and smoke still rose from his burned-out fire.

He could swear that it was an ammil for the air felt chilly.

He reasoned that a storm must have ensued through the night and got up immediately, not knowing whether the mare had run away to look for shelter or ran back to her master. As he stood outside stretching his somnolent limbs and yawned. He clearly heard fast- flowing water. What he didn't know was that the Afon Wen made a huge, sweeping bend not far from the road in the weald. Jaddamiah grabbed his two water canteens and waded through the long grasses. He didn't walk far when he stood stock still, for he heard a faint sound around his head but couldn't see anything in the bright, morning light. When he stopped the sound would stop, when he started walking, the faint sound would follow.

"Fágan! Fágan!" he called out, but there was no response. As Jaddamiah got closer to the tree line where the light changed, it became clearer to him that the faint sound that he was hearing, came from a crescent shaped light next to him. At first he tried to shoo the thing away, he used the canteen in his right hand to swat it away but, the crescent dodged his efforts, like a bee or a fly. He quickly gave up on that. The sound that emanated from it was sweet, a beautiful unearthly strain and vaguely melancholic. When he went under the cover of the trees, where it was much darker, he could clearly see that it was a strange sphere of great brilliance. He stood still in complete and utter amazement. The sphere had stopped moving. It had its own light but, Jaddamiah couldn't see the source of it. It was perfect in its geometry and it was paper thin. He then realized that in its centre, a colourful gammadion rotated. It resembled a barber pole with its colours and shape but, instead of white and red it was red and green. In the ancient tongue it was called 'Svastika'.

When it moved forward, he followed it in a wonder and it zig-zagged between the trees till it stopped and hovered; it made no mechanical sound. Jaddamiah stood in awe. His mouth gaped at the spectacle. Fágan lifted her head in recognition and then pointed her head in the direction of the water. Jaddamiah heard a sound from a large, rocky isthmus in the river, and it was the water splashed against it, that made the sound.

Other than those obstacles, the Afon Wen was completely navigable as the water flowed in a large mass around the isthmus. Jaddamiah ran to Fágan and put his arms around her. When he patted her, he realised that she was bone dry. *How* she managed *that* in the storm he did not know, but he was glad that they were reunited again. After drinking water and filling his canteens, he washed himself in the cool water as it was the only bath he could take for a while. The two walked back to their campsite and the sphere accompanied them.

Jaddamiah rekindled the fire and placed his pan on it. He recited an egg recipe, which his grandmother had taught him long before, aloud; "When the pan has been well oiled with good butter, put into it as many eggs as it would hold, that each yolk may be whole. When the egg whites become slightly hard, stir and add a piece of butter, pepper and salt. When done, the yolks should be separate from the whites although stirred together. Serve on hot buttered toast with fish sauce (of which he had none), potted meat (he had caught no Coney), cheese, or fish (he had managed to grab one from the river. It was luck for he was no fisherman) spread over it first. The eggs should be of the consistency of butter. Time, five minutes."

Jaddamiah was very fond of jumble eggs so he expected that, before he reached Weir, he would run out of them.

He thought himself very clever for having used the end of his sword to make his toast. After breakfast, it was time to saddle up and pack what little belongings he had. He soon recommenced his journey. He felt a cool breeze on his face when he set Fágan trotting.

After the night's storm, the road had dried out quickly and Fágan didn't have to deal with heavy mud. Jaddamiah looked at the sphere that floated next to his shoulder and wondered if it was a Fǣge. He had heard that in that part of the world the Fáerië often took that appearance. He hadn't actually met a person who had reported being accompanied by such a wonder because it was said that the Fáerië had moved out in 'The Last March' of December 8000.

The road took Jaddamiah in a southerly direction. He noticed that on either side of the road colourful hythes, heathers and low bush lie sculpted in amazing topiary; colours of lilac Foxhollow Wanderer, lilac-rose Fáerië Queen, Spring Torch in mauve, Alba in wonderful, white bells and several other varieties that he did not recognize. They grew in profusion as if the seasons did not seem to matter. Jaddamiah didn't know that the stretch of the road was called '5 Mile Hythe'.

Suddenly Fágan and the sphere stopped. Try as he would, Jaddamiah could get nothing out of Fágan. Jaddamiah huffed and puffed, then tried speaking to the sphere but no words were forthcoming.

The sphere bobbed around a few times and that made Jaddamiah look up. There sashaying over the hythe, over the heather, was a blue-green haze. He sat up in his saddle and cupped his hand over his eyes so that he could see what it was. The blue-green haze came closer to the side of the road, then with a sudden swoosh, the sphere dashed towards it, making circles around the colourful haze. It was diaphanous but clearly visible. What followed nearly caused Jaddamiah to tip over the side of the horse. A pair of bright- yellow shears was trimming the hythe!

Blue butterflies fluttered over the heathers, bees could be heard filling the air with their music. He raised himself and Fágan sighed, drew in a deep breath then let it out slowly and audibly through her nostrils. The sigh seemed to express relief (like an aaaaah! when removing a pair of tight boots). If truth were told, she was extremely happy!

The shears snipped and clipped in circles but Jaddamiah could see no hands. It was acrobatic topiary at its best. Jaddamiah cocked his head left and right, up and down, this way and that, following the direction that the shears jumped and flung. What was even more amazing, was that the blue-green haze and the bright, yellow shears began to sing;

> *"Clip! Snip! Clip Snip!*
> *Clip, snip, nick!*
> *Prune, cut, crop and clip,*
> *Here at 5 Mile Hythe.*
> *I have a voice, I have a mind*
> *I'm fast, cheerful, kind.*
> *I speed with thought, I make with hands*
> *and cross the many lands.*
> *I clear the day from rain with Fáerië light;*
> *But love it when I go to bed at night.*
> *I materialize or sing to simple folks*
> *and run away from querulous okes.*
> *I find my peace in hythe and heather,*
> *Nature and I in league together.*
> *Though some have found me in paint or type,*
> *Be careful! Much that is tripe*
> *will leave you disenchanted or empty breasted,*
> *for ill things will get your brain arrested.*
> *Though some may think this is a foolish dream,*
> *Be advised! It's never kind to be mean.*
> *These quondam delights*
> *are simply Fáerië rites.*

It's an attitude atmospheric, it makes the spirit soar!
Can anyone ask for more?
So many men quibble, quarrel, grumble, grouse.

Such behaviour cannot be said to be a puerile douse.
on what simply is sublime,
to wander through a bygone time.
We shudder at the thoughts of such men,
Me wonders if they'll ever fall in love again?
Clip! Snip! Clip Snip!
Clip, snip, nick!
Prune, cut, crop and clip
Here at 5 Mile Hythe

As Jaddamiah listened to the song, the voice waned over the floriated mounds with butterflies and bees following behind. The blue-green haze faded out of sight and the yellow shears simply fell to the ground some hundred meters down the road.

Jaddamiah pulled Fágan by the reins and walked briskly towards the spot where the shears had fallen. He picked it up and examined it carefully by running his fingers over the bright, yellow painted wood. He could not tell that under the paint, the wood was Nilanaga wood. The blades were sharp and there was no residue to indicate that so much clipping had been done. Jaddamiah fiddled with his mayll and carefully secured and stored the shears deep inside of it. "Well, well, well!" exclaimed Jaddamiah to himself or actually to Fágan and the Sphere. "This has been a strange morning and I *think* I might say that it is becoming a real *adventure*. I need to get on with things now, and hope there won't be any more strange happenings till we've covered enough ground Fágan. Sâa! sâa!" He called out and the mare cantered off.

Great blue mountains, like an illustrious, purpureal stage, loomed at his shoulders. Fluffy white clouds hung from the blue sky, like scenes from a child's picture book. As the road turned east, Jaddamiah noticed that ahead of them, the road was forced between two stretches of mountains and it disappeared between those great works of Eridu. The midday light in the mountain valley, was so vibrant, golden and violet in appearance that even at that time of year, it was like a 'pretend summertime' and Jaddamiah had never seen it before. He felt dwarfed amongst those immensities and the silence was oppressive. The mountainous regions of Eridu were only for a few, those acquainted with solitude and isolation, those who loved quietude. As before, the quietude was broken but that time for a different reason. Barking dogs and the tinkle of bells could be heard coming up from behind. Not more than a quarter mile behind, a Malbon-Maldon wagon was gaining on him. The wagon was pulled by a team of eight, Malbon draft horses.

As the wagon drew closer, Jaddamiah could hear the call, "Dragan! Dragan! Dragan! Slow down!" The owner of the wagon was Pádraigmór Fíngin and he was a zythepsarist.

It was at the voice of a young boy, that Jaddamiah slowed his horse and moved to the side of the road. He sat in his saddle with his hand on his knee when the wagon stopped next to him.

The draft horses were recognisable by their height and muscular build. Jaddamiah was the first to say something; "Sus-vapnah! Sus-vapnah!" he greeted. "Those are great, bay shires you have stranger. The biggest I've ever seen."

The man who sat next to the boy, was a bit of a jollux with a red face and blonde hair. Jaddamiah noticed a long scabbard hung from a strong, thick leather belt around the man's waist. He lifted his hat from his head and replied. "Aaaah! Sus-vapnah stranger. You must be from deep heart of Ériu, I ken by yah greetin. Mesa heppy to met yah. Desa my seun, Pádraigóg and I am Pádraigmór."

The man was correct, his son was a carbon copy of himself only thinner with strawberry hair. The boy was very polite. He jumped from his seat and walked over to Jaddamiah, looked him straight in the eye and stretched out his hand to introduce himself.

"Mesa heppy to met yah an say to yah Sus-vapnah . . . in yah oon speech." Jaddamiah smiled warmly and bent down to greet the cheerful chap. Pádraigóg then disappeared between the horses which dwarfed him, and fiddled with their reins and straps. Pádraigmór pointed to the tall, shire horse and said, "Thetta one is Mammoth, he was born in 8720, stends at 21.2 hends high, end his peak weight is estimated et 3,300 lb. The bleck one is called Dragan which means to pull."

Jaddamiah sat aghast, for it was the biggest draft horse he had ever seen. "Your horses are beautiful. When I tell my son of this, he would be hard pressed to believe the tale I tell him."

Pádraigmór laughed heartily.

"Forgive my rude behaviour; I have not given my name. I am Jaddamiah, son of Jabbamiah Jabberwocky of Béth-Élam."

Pádraigmór scratched his head and crinkled his button nose, then answered in his adenoidal voice, "Aaaaaah! Béth-Élam! Wherall der children play carefree as e-butterfly on espring afternoon." He thought again, somewhat puzzled then went on, "Noooo, kent say mesa heard thet name before, Jabberwocky! But we betta getta along before der darkie, Malbon is jissa ovar de Malbon-Silff en yah doona wanna be caught crossing dare in der darkie."

"Then let's not waste any more time Pádraigmór. Your kindness, is it a ken of your kin?"

Pádraigmór laughed heartily again then, while pointing at Jaddamiah replied, "Yoosa learning fast! It is jist so es yah says. . . mesa kin are kind." Pádraigóg jumped up beside his father and Pádraigmór gave the vocal signal to Mammoth. The draft horses began pulling their burden with equine enthusiasm. Fágan trotted next to the seat of the 'Malbon-Maldon' wagon. Jaddamiah studied the Malbon-Maldon wagon for it was built with its floor curved upward to prevent the beer barrels from tipping and shifting. There were 24 being carried with 6 more between the base of the wheels. On average, the Malbon-Maldon wagon was 18 feet long, 11 feet high and 4 feet wide. It could carry up to 12,000 pounds of goods. The seams in the body of the wagon were stuffed with pitch to protect it from leaking while crossing rivers. Also, for protection against bad weather, stretched across the wagon was a tough, white sailcloth cover. Water barrels painted in bright yellow and blue, were built on the side of the wagon. Jaddamiah also noticed a pine toolbox that held tools for repairs.

The road inclined quickly and became more gravely. A double track of pressed rock, from years of wagon plodding, could be seen and felt. All signs of tree and leaf suddenly fell away and the mountain rose out of the earth on their left shoulder, creating a 5m path that dropped away steeply on the right.

Jaddamiah also noticed 3 tall peaks, which pyramidal tips were capped with snow, not too far away.

"Those snow-capped peaks over yonder remind me of the zaqaru of Alkana," said Jaddamiah as he pointed towards the peaks.

"Those?" added Pádraigmór proudly, "Those mighty peaks are der wealth of Maldon and Malbon. In days of yore, men mineded phosphate under dos mountains, today we get oowa salt from dem. It is called Mount Kalisalz but, wear jiste call dem Monte Kali for short. In actual fect the salt on yah table, is Salt of Maldon."

The squeaking and clattering of the wagon, and the sound of 36 hooves continued, and no one spoke for a while. Pádraigmór was concentrating because he didn't want his precious cargo to topple over the Malbon-Silff. Pádraigóg had jumped off again and walked beside the horses on the silff end, which Jaddamiah found quite nerve racking but, the boy was obviously used to it. Jaddamiah suddenly realized that the Sphere wasn't with them. He turned in his saddle but, there was no sign of it.

After some time, the rumbling stopped and the hard, grey stone track eased out. The verge grew wider and safer as turf spread beneath horse and wagon. Pádraigmór got back on.

The road tilted downward while both sides of the tall mountains still accompanied them. Soon, the glimmer of town lights could be seen and blue smoke twirled from chimney stacks. The weald thickened on their left shoulder and the right of the mountain tightly embraced the road.

Pines, ash and oak stood shoulder-to-shoulder and at equal heights. They arrived at a T-junction that had signboards that looked like they were freshly painted.

Jaddamiah brought his mare to a standstill and to ease his numbness, lifted his caboose from the saddle. He read the signs fixedly. The one sign read; 'Weir 300 miles', the second sign read; 'Malbon 1 mile' and the third; 'Maldon 38 miles'. The rest, written in a neat handwriting, referred to the Windy Piny Pass. "Common paradezya!" shouted Pádraigmór to Jaddamiah. "Or doo yah preffer travailen?" Jaddamiah turned and looked up the incline of the road. There was a sign next to it that simply read 'Saline Highway'. The boy stood under it, legs apart and hands on his side, and shouted, "Mesa vader says yusa come horm weeth us. Come! Come! Yusa sliepe with us." Jaddamiah sighed a sigh of relief, and trotted Fágan up, behind the wagon. The boy ran after his father's wagon and jumped on, a thing he seemed to love doing. So, as the lights came on in Malbon at twilight, the end of the third day of Jaddamiah Jabberwocky's journey to Weir drew to a close.

Provender and Howling Wolves

Malbon was a walled town with a population of 10,930 people.

The Saline Highway was neatly cobbled; it made its way up the incline to the ridge where the two mountains joined by a shoulder. At the top of it, they went underneath a tall, clock tower that also served as the Night Watchman's tower. The watchman was a jovial fellow of strong build and was stoking the lamps on the exterior of the tower walls. "Better late then never Pádraigmór!" he called out.

"No time for tellin a cutta-witty-life tale this evenin. Mesa hever e guestess from Béth-Élam toonight," replied Pádraigmór.

"Aaaaah! Béth-Élam. Mesa wonder if yah knoo Dheya?" asked the guardsman in a voice like a foghorn. "Dheya? How small the world is. He's my neighbour!" replied Jaddamiah. "Hisse fetchin feller dasa Dheya!" called the guard from behind them.

Jaddamiah was already feeling at home when he entered Malbon and as the Night Watchman closed the large, intimidating iron doors behind them. It was amazing as the lights came on, like a set of glowing dominoes. His eyes wondered on the peripheries of the beefy walls, then ran under the mighty trees behind the walls.

They dawdled pass the town fountain, flanked by characteristic, half-timbered buildings. Loaded wagons were surrounded by workmen who chatted about the long day's journey while others kindled 'heat' set in the chambers of their pipes. He saw through wide, open doors that some were filled with grain and corn. Farm animals were being driven to their resting places by a boisterous, young wagon trainer. Tourists and townsfolk were walking up and down the busy sidewalks and shop windows came alive. There was 5000 years of history between those cobbles, and a quiet mind could hear echoes retelling many tales and legends between the turrets and its clock towers.

Eventually, when a path was cleared through the early evening's hubbub, they moved forward and Jaddamiah was shaken out of his bewonderment. They continued downhill and when the road started to flatten out, they passed an interesting 600-year-old 'castle-ette' that belonged to Malbon's Azapala. It was located between two, large Ash and looked like a four-story tree house. Again, Jaddamiah's eyes drank in that queer town, which he had never visited nor heard of before. The 'Mynd Unman' could be heard flowing strongly past the Azapala's 'castle-ette'; it was actually a creek, fed by the Woolmer river. It was called 'Mynd Unman' because it went nowhere in particular. The big Woolmer, 'Wolves pool' in the common tongue, fed it constantly.

The town's people had built a large, red water mill and catchment area where that river wash immobilized. From that, the water was directed to every household in Malbon via a quiet, ingenious, copper piping system. The system was since used in Alkana and Ninfa. In Malbon, when the sun climbed the sky in the morning or late afternoon, when it started on its eastward ho, the copper pipes shone like a strange gold, and it was quite magical to look at. Those copper pipes were maintained by the 'koper seuns' – orphaned boys from many different Pradezas. It was customary that local boys born in Malbon and Maldon, regardless of lineage or class, had to spend at least 3 months doing that task.

When they arrived up at dead end, in a quiet street that the locals simply called 'bottom of de seck (sack)', they were greeted by a field filled with bright mangel-wurzels, a type of turnip. The Mynd Unman flowed right through it so that they had to cross a shallow, walled, stone bridge. The land belonged to Pádraigmór. A quaint, timber-framed, weald hall house, stood next to the bridge. Blue smoke mounted from the chimney and the surrounding lights in the neighbourhood, cast a soft, amber light on its peg tiles.

The huge wagon and its weary horses came to an abrupt halt. The father and son jumped from their high perch and Pádraigóg rushed up a few stone steps through the gate, set in a well-manicured hedge. Pádraigmór stood with his hands on his hips and waited on Jaddamiah. It seemed he walked into a wonderland.

Groomsmen and attendants came skipping out. Some greeted the horses like they were their own children and one came up to Fágan and immediately took a liking to her. "Doon't woory bout yah belongins, all tekken care off Mr Jabberwocky," assured Pádraigmór. He then took Jaddamiah through the gate and gently held his arm. When they passed through, Pádraigmór stopped and said to Jaddamiah, "Mesa dear wife made this gate, it is made of secred hazel end she beleeves once yah steppe ovar it yoosa be safe end protected by magic. Soo! es not too alarm yah let mesa say, welcome too our humble abode!"

"I feel very welcome Pádraigmór," Jaddamiah assured and brought his right arm over Pádraigmór's shoulder. "You have not alarmed me for my wife," and with those words he held his arm across his chest. "She has the wicca-eye so, I am acquainted with glaumerie too."

"Then yoosa will getta-long fine wiith mesa wife." replied Pádraigmór.

The black and white vertical timber gave the house a wonderful appeal, as all along the middle of the construction, separating the ground floor from the one above, creeped ivy. Flowers gave a most intoxicating scent when one entered the house. It was a homely one and though attendants could be seen gliding out of view through open doors, there was a calmness that carried through, it started as you entered the gates.

A young lady dressed neatly in a golden, yellow kirtle with a white shirt beneath, introduced herself as Verchsaer, and immediately asked Jaddamiah to follow her. She led him up a flight of stairs to a room where fresh towels hung and a steaming, shining, steel bath rested on a clean, pine floor. Everything was neat, and the fragrance of lavender permeated the room. She shyly made genuflection and left, closing the door behind her.

Jaddamiah wasted no time because the ready-made bath filled with soapy bubbles, was a treat. He soaked for a while and when the water felt as if it was cooling down, he opened the brass tap to let more warm water in. When he was done, he found neatly folded trousers, a shirt and waist jacket on a chair close by. He didn't know when it arrived or whether he fell asleep and then it arrived, neither did he know how his hostess knew his size but, at that moment he didn't care. He was on his way to do something queer and had the strangest day to say the least. So, what more could possibly happen that could be any stranger than what he had already experienced?

He walked down the way he was shown and found himself standing in the cross passage all by himself but, that only lasted a moment as suddenly, a very jovial voice came from behind him. It was Pádraigmór; looking fresh as ever. He was shaven and dressed in his fluffy, green nightgown, slippers to match and a soft green, woollen, tasselled night cap. "Come! Come friend! Feel mostest welcome in our home." Pádraigmór led Jaddamiah to the parlour and they sat down on a soft sofa. "Let us blow some heat, it will ease oura weiting for mesa starvin. En I hope yah are too." Jaddamiah shook his head and tried not to appear desperate. Pádraigmór took a quirky, bright glass stash jar, from the deep pockets of his nightgown. There was a green frog on it, and the jar was hand-made from premium quality, borosilicate glass. Its golden contents glowed inside as Pádraigmór popped the cork cap and set it aside on the little table between them. He took out his pipe, knocked the contents from its bowl into the fire and then started to fill the chamber, and then handed it to Jaddamiah. Pádraigmór sank into his soft, wing-back and sighed deeply after taking a puff from his pipe. It was a short-stemmed pipe and when Jaddamiah took out his long 'lesepfeife', he smiled, for the long ones were his favourite. The pipe was called a 'Dandin' because it was 16 inches long, hand made and purchased in Alkana. The *real* Dandin, kept watch and guarded valuables and important citadels, so you couldn't expect them to go all night without a smoke. It was for that reason that they had pipes that were made with exceptionally long stems, so the smoke and the pipe wouldn't be in their line of sight as they kept watch.

The 'lesepfeife' was a gift from Jaddamiah's father in law, and it was so called by the Hrosvyras, so generally people called it by that name, although in Alkana it was called 'tatinagavamzi', 'vamzi' for short.

"Whettegwan Jaddamiah, yoosa gunna hit up de heat tenite? Mesa likeh yoosa vamzi! Aaaaaah!" said Pádraigmór with wild enthusiasm. Just then a tall, middle aged woman with long, dark auburn hair came in through the door. Jaddamiah held the pipe behind his back and got up immediately, as a courtesy to the lady of the house. "I am Féhmiaælfwine and I see that your new clothes fit well," she said in deep and strong, pleasant voice. She extended her strong hand, tilting her head slightly, in a coy manner, to the side.

Jaddamiah pinched the lapel of his waist jacket and replied, "It is an honour to make your acquaintance Féhmiaælfwine. Thank you for having me in your lovely home and gratitude for the fine clothing."

"I am certain you two gentlemen are ravishing. Do come along!" she commanded without coercion. Jaddamiah noticed that Féhmiaælfwine used a different dialect from her son and husband; her vowels were more conservative, and she spoke clearly like someone from another region. He watched her as she walked ahead of him. She walked as if gliding over the floor, and she betrayed an air of mysticism with her silver hair light and gleaming. He thought that Féhmiaælfwine and Pádraigmór were an odd match but, he could not have been further from the truth. As they gathered around the table, Jaddamiah was happy for meeting Pádraigmór for if he hadn't, he would have gone right by Malbon and would have slept in the wilds. As he watched Féhmiaælfwine set the last bits on the table, a long, clear howl could be heard from the darkness outside. Pádraigóg who stood next to his mother, dropped the jug of water and clung to his mother's skirt. He caressed both his ears with an upward motion and exclaimed, "By jas!" then said again, "Mesa hedda gra…ate fright! Mother, Mesa pologize for der mess-a-make."

"Careful my son!" his mother answered in her clear, fruity voice.

"Whetta ails yah now?" Pádraigmór retorted.

"Mesa think I heard a Waelwulfas!" replied Pádraigóg

"Pádraigóg! Yah lupin fancies mekka foes of nothin," said his father as he clicked his teeth. "Besides, wolves only come to der Woolmer to slakeka deir thirst," he went on.

"Mesa said Waelwulfas! Waelwulfas Vader." replied the boy, as he corrected his father. Pádraigmór grew red in the face and replied again, trying to maintain his composure; "It *is* oonly wolves. Perheps even owls end der Waelwulfas don't walk as in Vinrúlfr days, not here in Malbon. No one's seen or heard Vinrúlfr for over a 1000 years. Nooo-one!" Just then an owl hooted.

"Ets oonly en owl," he assured again in a calmer voice, that time feeling more satisfied, that is was indeed an owl.

All the food was on the table, the fire roared close by and Jaddamiah listened intently to what was being said and heard, out in the dark wilds. His thoughts went back to the Sphere and those mysterious shears. Féhmiaælfwine stood at the table as the 3 males took their seats. She patiently waited, then in her fruity voice, said as she looked from father to son. "An ill-boding. Owls may hoot but, you are quite right my son, that was Waelwulfas." and with that, she elegantly slid into her seat.

Pádraigmór shook his head and in a diffident voice replied to his wife, "wylfenne geðohtas! wylfenne geðohtas me loovlee one."

She signalled with her hands for Jaddamiah to dish his food but, he was caught off-guard, as he was still listening to Féhmiaælfwine. She had already stopped talking but he was still intrigued by her manner and looks. She had full, thick blood-flushed lips with an upturned nose, and her clear, green eyes were awash in a balance of yellow and pale-blue that evened out to a brilliant, pale green and was set evenly under her hawk-winged, dark eyebrows. "You first!" she exclaimed softly, and that brought Jaddamiah out of his musings. The table was laden with good bread, mature cheeses; there was pickled mangel-wurzel and warm potato soup, still steaming in the bowl. "So! If yoosa don't mend mesa asking where are yah off too?" asked Pádraigmór.

"Erm. . . believe it or not Pádraigmór, I am off to Weir."

When he mentioned the name Weir, Féhmiaælfwine and her son glanced at each other, without Jaddamiah noticing.

"Weir yoosa say?" asked Pádraigmór rhetorically. "Mesa read in de 'paper' theysa looking for dragoon slayers."

Pádraigmór thought for a moment after stating that, his spoon filled with soup caught mid-air, between plate and lip. He shook his shoulders and shuddered. "Waelwulfas! Dragoons! No! say noothin further. Letsa talk bout faira theengs."

"Do you have a wife and children Jaddamiah?" asked Féhmiaælfwine, changing the subject to something familial.

Pádraigóg's ears were lupine as he sat quietly listening to the adults. His mother knew that later when it was time for him to go to bed, he would ask her plenty of questions about dragons and wolves and such Elemental powers, to him, she was a compendium.

The evening passed by quietly. The house was still. After the meal, while the men smoked their pipes and enjoyed a glass of cold, mangel-wurzel beer, they listened to Pádraigóg's recital of 'Songs from the Woodwind Choir':

The sky is dark though the night is young
The Firs they bend as the North Wind comes
Zephyr leans against the green old Ash
And clouds cross the moon as the Woodwind sings;
"Tis time to sleep, Tis time to dream,
Pan plays his pipe, and happy sings the Wind."
In the village there is silence
as lamp lights cling to the dark
No soul is moving, curtains are drawn
but only I can hear them sing;
"Tis time to sleep, Tis time to dream,
We sing for you, these songs for you."

> *The mortal listens to the din of frivolity*
> *and sets his eyes to brutal pantomimes*
> *The trees hold onto Freya so tight.*
> *But I can hear the Woodwind sing;*
> *"Tis time to sleep, Tis time to dream,*
> *We sing for you, these songs for you,*
>
> *For soon young child we will come for you.*

That lovely, poetic recital, tore Jaddamiah's mind to thoughts of his children and grandchildren who were miles and miles away. Afterwards, he asked Pádraigóg if he would give him a copy of that poem to which he willingly agreed for, the boy was a budding rhymester. Later but not so late, everyone turned to bed.

Through the Wild

J addamiah managed to get up quite early the following morning. He had a quick breakfast with Féhmiaælfwine and Pádraigóg.

Pádraigmór had left before dawn because he had business to tend to. He passed well wishes via his wife to Jaddamiah, and apologized for his rudeness as host, but nonetheless, left Jaddamiah a grand gift which consisted of a smart, glass jar of red 'heat'; filled to the cork and with the fancy frog of the same colour, attached to the jar. He also left him a fine, wooden box of Maldon salt flakes. Féhmiaælfwine gave Jaddamiah the recipe for pickled mangel-wurzel and mangel-wurzel beer.

The recipes went as follows;

Pickled Mangel-wurzel
In a stew-pan over the fire:
One cup of vinegar and water combined,
one tablespoonful of sugar,
one teaspoonful of Maldon salt,
a dust of pepper.

Wash the mangle-wurzel (allow about an inch of top to remain when preparing to cook) and place in a stew-pan with boiling water, cook until tender. Skin the mangel-wurzel, slice and pour over the heated vinegar mixture. Stand aside till cold then serve. Or serve hot like buttered beets. PS. *'exceed spinach', and the stems and stalks of the larger leaves 'eat like asparagus'*

Mangel-wurzel beer
For a ten-gallon cask.

Boil in fourteen gallons of water 6ty pounds of mangel-wurzel, which has been well washed and sliced across, putting some kind of weight on the roots to keep them under water; having boiled an hour and a half, they may be taken out, well broken, and all the liquor pressed from the roots; put it, and that in which they were boiled, on again to boil, with four ounces of hops;

let them boil about an hour and a half, then cool the liquor, as quickly as possible, to 70° Fahrenheit; strain it through a thick cloth laid over a sieve or drainer;

put it into the vat with about 6 ounces of good yeast, stir it well, cover it, and let it stand twenty-four hours;

If the yeast has then well risen, skim it off, and barrel the beer, keeping back the thick sediment. While the fermentation goes on in the cask, it may be filled up the beer left over, or any other kind at hand; when the fermentation ceases, which may be in two or 3 days, the cask must be bunged up, and in a few days more, the beer may be used from the cask, or bottled.

PS: but the beer will be better made in larger quantities; and its strength may be increased by adding a greater proportion of mangel-wurzel.

It is thus that he set off, Fágan was just as well looked after. The two slowly walked down the cobbled street and over the bridge. At the big fountain spurting its tall watery spire a hundred meters up into the cold morning air, Jaddamiah and Fágan turned up the Saline Highway toward the town gates. Although it was daytime and he saw everything in a different light, it had not lost its Fáerië-like splendour. The Saline was busier than the previous evening. Many wagons, empty and loaded, were waiting in tow to get out of Malbon. On the opposite side, other wagons and travellers were heading towards Maldon.

To Jaddamiah, it felt like the winds of time polished the half-timbered gables and blew through the grooves of centuries of horse carts and wagons. Without Jaddamiah knowing it, young Pádraigóg was sitting in a mossy niche in the clock tower. When it finally came for Jaddamiah to pass under the tower, he gave one last glance back down the road. Meanwhile, Pádraigóg sat fingering the ancient stonework; he had already waited for a full 20 minutes for Jaddamiah and Fágan to pass underneath, all the while, he caressed the flight feathers of the arrow in his crossbow.

Quietly he whispered to his friend who sat and watched next to him, "Mesa em the arrow, mesa em the bow, mesa em the wind." Then he released it with all the power of an abled-bodied 11year old, the arrow left its eyrie. As Jaddamiah was about to pass a solitary, tall Phuradorn tree that stood at the side of the road, the arrow swooshed past his ear and stung the glass-smooth trunk of the tree. He looked back and Pádraigóg stood up from his eyrie and shouted at the top of his voice, "Fare-well" and waved frantically then disappeared as only young boys do. Jaddamiah smiled and dismounted his horse. There was a note on the shaft of the arrow. He removed the arrow with some difficulty, then removed the note with care. He stood and read it quietly, 'Songs from the WoodWind Choir'.

A lump grew in his throat but, he held back the tears. He was moved by the kindness that family had showed him. His mayll was now too small for everything, so he had received another bag which he could carry on his back; in that were all his new goodies.

Afterwards, he put the palm of his hand against the tree, he had never seen one like that before. The smooth trunk gleamed silver in the morning sun as he looked around but found no other tree similar to it. The morning sunlight caused its purple leaves to glow a lilac hue. He also smelled a specific fragrance descending on him but, he couldn't place it.

When he reached the T-junction, he turned to the right and looked back. For only a moment, a blue, diaphanous light surrounded the tree. For the following few miles, it was all he thought about. He knew that he saw that phenomena times before but, could just not remember when. He sat in silence and didn't pay attention to his surroundings because he was caught up in thought. Suddenly he broke out in laughter as he recalled. It was the Vēḏu Vīrü between Béth-Élam and Élles that the same phenomena occurred from time to time; that area was guarded by the Ælves.

He didn't take Fágan to a canter as, there were two wagons slightly ahead of them, and he thought that they would be good company on the road that he hardly knew. After some time, the two wagons allowed Jaddamiah to take Fágan up to a canter. They did that for an hour so that the convoy gained ground on the good terrain. Beautiful, lush woodlands spread on either side of the road and the air was fresh from the rain. All the while the Kuavarg was on their right flank, like hobnailed wings some 30 miles away and to the left at some 6 miles, like a barrier of spears, lay the Kurtidāgh; both ranges met eventually. They were connected to The Drakensberg and the road lay like discarded string in the Vargdarreh. Kurtidāgh although named such, was actually part of The Drakensberg, and it boasted the thirteen highest peaks in all of Eridu. There was a legend amongst the towns and villages, that at times during Samhain or Beltane, beautiful children could be seen wandering in the mountains during twilight, their skins were almost diaphanous and exuded wondrous light, no one had ever really spoken to one and they were called 'The Children of Naron'. The tallest peak stood at 42650.9ft and was called 'Gamahare' or 'Spirits of the Dead'. The lowest peak was at a height of 28,251ft and was called 'Kalema' which meant 'springtide'. When arriving from the east, Gamahare was the first peak one saw. It was also the first point that the sun touched each morning in all of Midhe. The snows hardly touched it, except for a brief 3-week period in mid-winter.

When Jaddamiah's eyes were tearing at the caruncles from staring at those great peaks, he cast his eyes to lowlier vernal things. Bursting forth in splendour, in patches on both sides of the road in the woodland, the Erica (heaths/heathers) with its vertical plumes of dazzling blossoms, grew. Its delicate fragrance was quite refreshing and Jaddamiah wished he could take a handful and give it to his wife as a floral garland. The sky wasn't perfectly clear as rain clouds drifted by from time to time but, the smears of blue made for a very pleasant day.

When the day was fading in the west, Jaddamiah had been eating in-saddle all day so, he picked the pace up to speak to one of the drivers of the wagons ahead of him. The first wagon, directly in front of him, was a closed wagon that had a white canvas cover. He also noticed a symbol that covered the middle of the canvas cover. The emblem was a time piece with two cracks and it was split in two by a sword that rested in the cracks. All of that was in a silver circle.

How odd thought Jaddamiah, for he had never seen such a symbol before. Jaddamiah didn't know what the cargo was because generally, only food cargo was covered but, he surmised by the sound and the rattling, that perhaps it were planks. The wagon in the very front was transporting 100 bags of salt.

"Say there, Mr 'Branwen', how far are you going this evening?" asked Jaddamiah as he came alongside the rear seat. A middle-aged man with full beard and moustache removed the pipe between his thin lips and answered in a burly voice, "You'd better speak to the car lady at the front stranger. I'm just a carter. My name's Fuhrmann by the way," he went on in a friendly tone.

"I am Jaddamiah Jabberwocky of Béth-Élam, pleased to make your acquaintance."

"You're a long way from home Mr Jabberwocky, but do speak to the lady, mind you, she's a bit strong so don't be taken aback."

Jaddamiah noticed that Mr Fuhrmann didn't speak in the same dialect of Pádraigmór, and wondered what exactly he meant by 'strong lady'.

On the front seat sat a pale-skinned woman by herself. Although the sun had nearly completely fallen behind the western horizon, Jaddamiah could clearly see the blue veins rivering across her bosom and around her pale, alabaster neck.

A silver chain hung around her neck, and at the end of it hung the same symbol as the one on the white, canvas covering.

Her hair was loose and wild. Long, red tendrils hung to her waist. When she turned her head towards Jaddamiah, her wide, green set eyes seemed to penetrate him. Her eyes were as deep in colour as the deepest emerants. She had heard every word spoken between Jaddamiah and Mr Fuhrmann. "So, you are called Jaddamiah!" she said; and it wasn't a question.

"Yes. Jaddamiah Jabberwocky" he replied

"I am Morkaél" She spoke matter-of-factly, and Jaddamiah felt slightly uncomfortable for, although the tone was pleasant, she had a commanding voice. Jaddamiah got to the point quickly. "I am travelling to Weir and appreciate the company because I don't know the area. How far will you go tonight before resting?"

Morkaél looked at him for a moment, her face showed no emotion. Then a trace, just a smidgen of a smile started, she had a full upper lip and as she relented to the smidgen, her face lit up. "Men fear nothingness. . . so they populate it with phantoms in their madness. The road to Weir is filled with phantoms, so are these lands." as she said *that*, she left the reins with her right hand and made a sweeping gesture.

"You should not travel alone. Lace your horse to the back and come sit up-front with Morkaél. We journey another 20 miles, then may stop." With those words she stopped her horses and put 3 fingers between her fleshy lips and gave a howling kind of whistle. The wagon leading the way slowed down instantly. Mr Fuhrmann was already up from his seat when Jaddamiah led Fágan to the back of the wagon. He had lit two lanterns at the rear, one on either side. Mr Fuhrmann seemed to be in a great hurry as he carefully took the reins and did as his mistress instructed. "You may go up front Mr Jabberwocky. I'll take good care of your mare, what is her name?" asked Mr Fuhrmann

"Her name is Fágan." replied Jaddamiah

"That is a beautiful name for a mare." nodded Mr Fuhrmann

Jaddamiah felt the wagon pulling away so, he ran forward to Morkaél and jumped up next to her. She had wrapped a beautiful, dark shawl over her sky-blue dress and Jaddamiah noticed a dagger glinting in the pale moonlight. "My retainers await their goods." she announced. . .

Jaddamiah felt the chill, he thought that he had not dressed warm enough. He couldn't understand how Morkaél was dressed in the manner that she was. The seat was a tight fit so, he could feel her body next to his and it was then that he understood; her body was as if on fire.

Some silence followed after that, but Jaddamiah needed to know why only 20 miles, and so he asked, "May I ask ma-lady why we are specifically journeying on for only 20 miles?" She didn't bother to look in his direction but answered, "The men are afraid to travel to the 'Crossing of the Amura Val' and rest there so, we will make camp at the end of 20 miles." Nothing else was discussed for the rest of the journey. Sometime later, Jaddamiah noticed that the clouds had completely enveloped the sky and hid the moon from sight. There was blackness in that land that belied the absence of the moon, and if the wagon ahead of them hadn't had two lanterns burning, it would not have been visible. Something in the south eastern sky had grabbed the attention of Morkaél, something which Jaddamiah also tried to follow. It was a great light that seemed to float across the sky and it didn't quiver, like other objects normally did; even a meteor had a slight quiver when moving across the arc of the sky.

After a few minutes, it became dim. It was extremely high in the sky; although the sky was cloudy, one could see that it looked like wild fire.

"I lost it," he found himself thinking aloud. Morkaél had heard him and when the clouds parted she said to him, "No! It is still there." Jaddamiah could see nothing, for an object of such brightness should be seen against a sky now parted from clouds. She kept looking for a while and he noticed that her eyes appeared as if without pupil or iris. Her eyes glittered in the dark. Only after watching for a long time, did she say more of a thought to herself in passing, than telling him, "It has passed. Dazottara. Dazottara," she whispered under her breath. She had spoken in soft tones as if confused. Jaddamiah didn't understand what she was saying but, didn't bother to enquire any further.

The clouds came and went, and the moon flew by; chasing or running away as always, never following the course that was set for her, not like the sun. . .

Samsara

$\mathcal{T}$he village of Béth-Élam, although small, made up for its size in many other ways. The village folk were simple folk, who enjoyed being left alone in their corner of the world. They enjoyed eating and revelries had two loves which forged their reputation and put the name of their village 'on the map', in all of Eridu, so to speak. They loved travelling and gardening. . .

Jaddamiah, on his journey to Weir, now added to that inclination but, there were always those before him who in their turn, travelled far and near. Two such people were Dheya Illyrian and Lemayian Abathwa. Those two were neighbours and close friend because they laboured together. Lemayian owned eight sets of dwhëel coaches; which were a very fast way, also a very smooth way, of transporting people. The dwhëels were much faster than horses and that way of earning a living, was proving to be more sustainable.

Dheya and Lemayian were 'brother whips', 'conductor and branwen' all-in-one. Whether they were alone or together, they did many things together, and never quarrelled. There were other that travelled now and again, like Mr Underhill.

So, folk traverse over Earthmother's skin, a samsara, some to misery, some to pain and thus it was that the latter, met with Jaddamiah at the place of weariness 'Llewerig'.

Jaddamiah noticed that the woodland had given way to an open space of shorn green grass. He also saw several large fires blazing, and seated around those fires, in circles, were dark, shadowed figures. He could smell roast mutton; he could smell 'heat'. Single horses were foraging close to the fires, and other which were still harnessed to their wagons, foraged where they were parked. A wagon with handsome horses was slowly approaching them on the opposite side of the road. Jaddamiah immediately recognised the man at the reins. He called out, "Underhill! Underhill! Great horn spoons! I never thought I'd find you along this road."

"Mr Jabberwocky! Sus-vapnah, Sus-vapnah!" came the reply and Mr Underhill pulled to the side of the road onto the grass, bringing his horses to an immediate halt.

Morkaél and Mr Fuhrmann wasted no time; they hoisted two one-man tents, one for Mr Fuhrmann and one for Jaddamiah. She also made a fire between the two tents.

Jaddamiah was chatting to Mr Underhill. He told of his journey and the wonderful folk he had met, omitting the more fanciful bits. Mr Underhill as always, was wearing his apron and waist jacket but, he donned a dark, blue coat over that for warmth.

Jaddamiah and Mr Underhill walked to where the fire was kindled and where Mr Fuhrmann was preparing to make tea. Jaddamiah wanted him to meet the folk that had been so kind to him.

Morkaél was standing close to the fire near her wagon, she was sliding her arms into a dark, green cape and cowl, and Jaddamiah on seeing that, did not think that was for warmth or comfort, rather that it was for concealment.

"Morkaél ma-lady, please forgive my sluggishness but, to see my compeer so far from home is most heart-warming," said Jaddamiah apologetically.

"The partisans who watch the stage of life, despise the sluggard in the strife, but I see no sluggards here tonight, only friends re-uniting. No need for apologies Jaddamiah."

"Forsooth, you speak rightly. This is my compeer Mr Underhill, an old friend. And this, Mr Underhill, is Morkaél and her carter Mr Fuhrmann," replied Jaddamiah.

Mr Underhill held out his hand and removed his hat, but Morkaél did not remove her cape.

"Pleased to make your acquaintance," said Mr Underhill.

"Underhill?" replied Morkaél, in a questioning tone, as if the name revived some memory.

"Yes ma-lady," he replied with a broad smile.

"Mr Underhill, are you held or taken?"

He was overcome by her beauty as the flames of the fire illumed her alabaster skin so, didn't answer immediately. Also, he was wondering what she meant. "Parfay ma-lady, that depends on the oath," he then replied wittingly as she released his hand. He then presented his hand to Mr Fuhrmann. Mr Fuhrmann gave him a sturdy hand shake.

"An oath broken is a life taken." she said in her matter-of-fact way. She dropped her head slightly and walked off, out of the fire light. She blended into the darkness, so that one could only see a shadow standing at the road side. She stood watch there till the following morning.

"You are most welcome to sit with us Mr Underhill, unless you prefer your own company," said Mr Fuhrmann in his burly voice. "Tea is almost ready."

"I will gladly accept your invitation for, I will not well away in this land, alone in the dark," Mr Underhill replied and sat down on a wooden seat that Mr Fuhrmann had taken off the wagon.

"What sorrows could a man like you possibly have Mr Underhill?" asked Jaddamiah.

Mr Underhill laughed and replied, "I have no evil sorrow but, I do lament the absence of my family because I miss them dearly. I am not often on the road."

"As long as it doesn't fester to become a teen," replied Mr Fuhrmann while pouring the tea from mug to mug a few times, then filling them properly.

While sipping his tea, Jaddamiah crawled into his tent and scratched around like a dog in a kennel.

He returned momentarily with a medium sized parcel neatly wrapped in a skilfully woven tea-towel. He sat next to Mr Underhill and unwrapped it. Mr Underhill watched him and smelled the aroma, it was still very fresh.

"Blades-son!" he exclaimed. "You tease me dear friend."

Jaddamiah laughed heartily as Mr Fuhrmann looked at the two.

"Would you each like a slice, gentlemen? It was given to me, as a journey gift, by a very beautiful woman."

Jaddamiah sent the dish around as each in turn removed a wedge from the gnome apple pie. Mr Underhill's slice immediately went to his mouth, as it entered his mouth, he closed his dark eyes to savour its flavour.

"Where against shall I measure such culinary delights?" asked Mr Fuhrmann as he dunked his into his mug of tea.

Mr Underhill laughed a laugh of satisfaction, and replied, "I know the baker and I will tell Mrs Hyperion Illyrian that you were 'food-charmed' by her baking."

"Gramercy! Gramercy!" replied Mr Fuhrmann again while stroking his beard.

"Yes, I'm thankful Mr Fuhrmann, that you two weren't the first whom I've shared this with but, I think this lovely pie has come to its journey's end, have some more."

The men eagerly took another wedge out of the pie, only one remained. Jaddamiah got up and walked to his horse for she was standing close by, sleeping. He removed his canteen and washed the pie dish, dried it with a tea towel and brought it back, asking if Mr Underhill would be so kind to return it to its owner. "In our Béth-Élam we say 'gratitude' Mr Underhill but, I think we should take the word 'gramercy' back to it for, it sounds good and rolls off the tongue mighty smooth!"

"Yes. I have not heard it before," he replied with 'fed up' enthusiasm.

"Well, please return this to our wonderful friend. Tell her from me, that I have shared it with several, new friends. There is just one piece that will journey further with me. I only wish that I could have returned it with a gift of my own."

"Certes, certes old friend. She will be pleased."

"And I shall make an ode; someday I will come by Béth-Élam to have a greater portion," added Mr Fuhrmann.

"I shall tell her," replied both men simultaneously, after which all 3 joined in laughter. They then realized that it was still over the camp, fires were burning but, men were sleeping, either next to them or in their wagons or tents.

At that moment Jaddamiah removed his pipe and a stash of 'Purple Dell' that Lemayian had given him. He filled his pipe and started to smoke it.

"Under normal circumstance I. . ." and he dragged out the 'I', "I would carry two pipes but, I am afraid you will have to get your own for this is 'Purple Dell', which Lemayian gave me before leaving."

"You are carrying fine gifts Mr Jabberwocky," said Mr Underhill as he dug into his inner pocket and pulled out his lesepfeife. It was a fine-looking pipe. "I think it's time to turn in for I've had a long day gentlemen!" said Mr Fuhrmann as they noticed the stillness of the night. "Good-night" then he left the two compeers by themselves. As he walked away, Mr Underhill said to Jaddamiah, "Why does the lady not join us? She stands alone in the shadow?"

Mr Fuhrmann overheard and replied as he entered his tent.

"Foul things move in these parts Mr Underhill, and the men are afraid." At that very moment, a strange howl could be heard, not nearly wolfish enough for there was an anthropomorphic sound to it. "Gardyloo!" came a soft, deep exclamation.

The two men at the fire instantly turned around, Mr Underhill's hand was on his dagger. There, towering behind them, stood Morkaél. "You make phantoms out of the dark ma' lady," said Mr Underhill a little annoyed for, he did not like being startled to grasp his dagger, for nothing.

"You are mistaken stranger, for that truly was a warning cry," assured Morkaél in such sweet tones, so as to make a demon a believer. "I have heard of these lands ma' lady but, we are far away from the Amura Val," replied another stranger as he drew closer to the fire. "You are a compeer Mr Underhill, and I have only known this lady Morkaél a few hours but, I can assure you this land is enchanted. . . wholly so." said Jaddamiah earnestly.

"If it wasn't for the warning in my heart, I would have said my entire two days have been a dream but, my eyes are not yet grown feeble." "You are a wise man Jaddamiah. . . Mr Jabberwocky," replied Morkaél as she poured some hot tea for herself.

"Twixt meeting you 3, I started to think this night wanion," replied Mr Underhill, trying to make light the moment.

"No ill luck here Mr Underhill, there is only Fate or Destiny in these lands!" replied Morkaél emphatically.

"Then why stand guard alone fair lady. Why do these men sleep deeply and behave recklessly?" asked Mr Underhill concernedly.

She didn't reply and after slaking her thirst, she walked Ælve-footed to where she stood before.

"She's a strange one Jaddamiah." Said Mr Underhill.

"Ay, but fair and brave," replied Jaddamiah softly.

"Is she Ælve-kind?" Mr Underhill found himself asking.

"I have never seen the Ælves my friend, and though her face seems obscured at times, she certainly behaves like one. I will tell you a strange tale. It happened just as we were travelling here from Malbon. We saw a strange sight passing through the sky. No, perhaps that is the incorrect thing to say for, it was so high that it would have to be said that it passed above the sky. Although it was very cloudy, we could see the bright light very vividly. Eftsoons I lost it or perhaps it wasn't soon but, in any case, she could still see it after I had long stopped seeing it. Then a strange thing happened to her eyes, it was as if they changed, so that the whole eye became one colour of deep, deep green." "Dazottara. Dazottara," whispered Mr Underhill to himself. My dear Hertia speaks of those Elvysshe things often.

"Great horn spoon!" exclaimed Jaddamiah, nearly waking up the whole camp. "Those were the exact words she uttered under her breath. . . the way you are doing now."

"Halálseren! That is what some call it. All that I know of it my Hertia taught me but, she spoke of it in a hushed voice and I think, if what you say is true, *that* brings ill omen. You are my friend Jaddamiah but, these last days I have learned things that make my heart uneasy."

"I didn't mean for it to be so friend,' replied Jaddamiah in a compassionate tone.

Mr Underhill said in slow, calm tones, "At first I thought this was a chance meeting but, perhaps Fate and Destiny do rule this land." Then he turned suddenly to Jaddamiah, he turned up the collar of his coat. His chestnut, soaked eyes were burning with a copper glow. His lips were flushed red and he crinkled the corners of his eyes, wrinkling his wide nose; a strange question arose in his mind for only then, did it dawn on him, that it was strange to see Jaddamiah travelling so far east.

"Jaddamiah!" he called out. "What brings you to these parts and where does your journey take you too?"

"Drat! I wish now you hadn't asked me that. Only because the night already has been so strange, I journey to Weir" Jaddamiah paused.

"And, go on?" encouraged Mr Underhill sitting up on the seat. "ToslaytheMelineDragon." He said those last words rapidly, without taking a breath. Mr Underhill's eyes widened, and he could not believe what he was hearing.

"Jaddamiah Jabberwocky, son of Jabbamiah Jabberwocky! I behave foolish at times, so says my Hertia but, what you tell me sounds preposterous besides, there hasn't been a dragon in Éridu for. . .for. . .for." then he stopped. "There has *never* been a dragon in Éridu and the last dragon in Midhe was seen in the 2nd Age" resumed Mr Underhill in complaintive voice but, before Jaddamiah could reply, he added matter-of-factly, "conceivably in Damāvand!"

"That may be so for, I am not well versed in *dragons but* . . . the citizens of Weir have asked me to help them, and we are not short of help in this world yet," Jaddamiah replied firmly.

"Besides! There is a *substantial* reward."

As Mr Underhill emptied the contents of his tea into the fire, and the sparks shot up into the dark causing a spangle, he replied, "I think I need some strong ale now, the ones I pour for the Dwarves."

"Döppievölle Inn is miles away, so perhaps you should go to sleep and besides, you pour strong ale but don't drink it. I certainly do" retorted Jaddamiah.

"Beforetime yes but, now the occasion calls for it!" replied Mr Underhill again. "Does your wife know of this matter?"

Jaddamiah clicked his teeth and replied, "Everyone in Béth-Élam *knows* and by now all those on the Plains of Hros." Mr Underhill shook his head from side to side and looked into his empty mug, then to the fire. "I think its suits me best to visit Meena once in a blue moon." Jaddamiah laughed softly and Mr Underhill laughed in a low voice and nudged Jaddamiah in the ribs.

They got up and walked their separate ways, Jaddamiah to his tent and Mr Underhill to his wagon. Mr Underhill returned shortly with a peshtemal and he lay down besides the log, covered himself, and went to sleep. Jaddamiah didn't do the same. He hurriedly took a thick, blue leather book from his sack and undid the broad leather strap over it. The strap had a button hole in it and the button was a large, silver star. He ran his hand over the roughish paper. He still saw some flakes of wood and it smelled wonderful. The empty pages were made from Ninfan handcrafted paper. He took out his ink pot, opened it, dipped the staff pen into it, and touched the corner of the first page, Jaddamiah was satisfied that didn't bleed. This was not his usual staff pen with which he wrote at home, this was a simpler one, a bit of a pinchbeck. He held the top of his pen between his mouth in deep thought; "What shall I call it?" he asked himself under the candle light.

"What shall I call the book? All good books have a good title, one cannot commence without it."

He spoke in that manner and held the staff pen to his lips. "Ahha!" Jaddamiah called out for he had a thought, a name, two names. He spoke out the words so that he could get a 'feel' for the title, 'The Book of Drycræft'. He thought for a moment again, and twirled his staff pen between his fingers. "dry. . .cræft. It means 'skilled in magick' and there was an awful lot of magick going around. Hmmmmm, I wonder. Perhaps 'Dombec, Book of Lore'. Yes, I prefer 'Dombec, The *Book* of *Lore*'"

So, he penned the title of his book on the first page.

When Jaddamiah was done writing, telling Hrosmægden all that he could, a certain poem came to mind, one that once, long before Hyperion received as a child when she met the Queen of Ninfa, it was called 'The Ink Pot';

The ink pot dries up
as words gently fade
softly gently falling
like crisp golden leaves

Who cares for words
rending hearts all broken
violent syllables
crumble to floors as the sound
of silence magnifies my dreams.
As shadows creep swiftly

into every city
words begin to fail me
as my dreams begin to take
their Celestial flight.

New words begin to form
inside this vestibule of thought
words that can't be spoken
on ill feigned shards of wood.

Voices call me
as earthly seasons roll on
into one tempestuous storm
and mortal begins to see all
his deeds in raindrops on finite shores.

Moment after moment
words become a struggle
as every tree and leaf
every star and sun
every crystal dewdrop
calls my name to the Shore-less Seas.

Far beyond where mortal can reach
way beyond the jacinth orb
long past the moonlight
further still than Idyll
there is home for me.

The following morning, the cloud cover had lifted but, it was cool. Mr Underhill found that Morkaél was sitting on the seat opposite him, in front of a fire that was going strong. The light of the sun was only partially throwing its streaks skyward over the tips of the mountains, like thanes holding a temporary crown.

He sat up immediately with his back against a log and rubbed his eyes. He looked over his shoulder and saw two tall, robust men walk from the spot he last saw her standing on.

Mr Fuhrmann had already prepared a good breakfast over a separate portion of coals. It smelled like fresh jumbled eggs, buttered bread and tea. "Rise at five, dine at 9, up at five, to bed at 9, makes man live ten times 9" teased Morkaél.

"But some of us aren't men are we?" asked Mr Underhill.

"Perhaps not" she replied.

Jaddamiah filled ten pages with writing and in between, drew some sketches as best as he could remember. He was the last to put his head through the tent. Mr Fuhrmann had fed the horses and breakfast was a quick affair because Morkaél was itching to go. The place was stirring with men calling orders, others reining horses, still others checking their loads. It was a wagon and coach jam as everyone tried to set off in opposite directions.

Mr Underhill walked up to the front of Morkaél's wagon and thought he would push for an answer concerning her load. He was curious. "You seem eager to leave ma'lady, what is your load?"

She looked down at him and smiled and humoured him, "Glæmboom! I transport Glæmboom to the Ælves of the Zarvari Vana."

Mr Underhill thought for a moment, for he was an average-travelled man, he also knew much about lore but, as he stretched his mind, he couldn't remember anything connected to a place called Zarvari Vana.

"I'm sorry ma' lady but, I know the name to mean the 'Twilight Weald' in common speech but, I have never heard of such a place", he said puzzled.

She smiled and replied, "The Zarvari Vana is an ancient weald and the City of Palador is in it. It is a city that no mortal can enter."

"Ma'lady Morkaél, if you don't mind me speaking my mind, you are an enigma, the likes I've never met afore but, the loveliest nonetheless, and who knows if our paths will ever cross but, now we must say farewell."

"You have a sweet tongue stranger and I accept your compliment," replied Morkaél, who wasn't easily flattered. She looked down at him as if to say something, her eyes swam with a mysterious light. Mr Underhill looked up at her expectantly. "I knew your wife once, Mr Underhill. . .but that was long ago" she said, in a melancholic tone. Mr Underhill did not reply and did not know why. Mr Underhill looked at Mr Fuhrmann and said, "Gramercy! Your hospitality shall be repaid if ever you pass by Béth-Élam or if our paths cross again." Morkaél gave the reins a tug and the horses set off immediately. Mr Underhill then turned to Jaddamiah and said in a serious voice, "My dear friend, do you have any news I can carry to your family?" "Oh yes!" Jaddamiah replied and took a pale, yellow envelope from his inner, waste jacket pocket. He handed it to Mr Underhill. He took the envelope and looked at it, it had the name of Jaddamiah's wife on it; 'Hrosmægden'.

Mr Underhill gently tapped the envelope in the palm of his hand and said in mild fashion, "Lackaday, lackaday old friend! I would rather that you should turn around and follow me home, than to trek to Weir. I can see that you are resolute, and no amount of friendship will turn you away from your quest so, do what you must, and may we meet again." "By jas Shabeen!" replied Jaddamiah, touched by his compassion. "By jas!" replied Mr Underhill and walked away. Then he suddenly realised that he wanted to ask Jaddamiah about the prophecy of Dheya but didn't. He wanted to get home quickly. He wanted to see if Dheya had arrived home. He scratched his head and thought of Hertia, she would certainly know. Mr Underhill made sure his hat was snug on his head, licked his lips, and walked on in silence.

Mr Underhill turned into Lamas Street on the 5th of October 8816, drove straight to his front gate, locked the handbrake of his wagon and dashed off to No 31415. When he arrived at their front door he banged loudly, something he never did. He impatiently turned the brim of his hat between his fingers until the door opened. There stood Gromel, her warmth, the tenderness in her bright eyes and a face that never seemed to age. The name that had stuck over the years, one that Hyperion had given her when she was but young. The bluish-steel right eye like a midwinter sky and the left eye, black-flecked with deep, brown-like-pecan-shell lashes, that winked when she was happiest. Those uncanny, dark limbal rings broke his spell of impatience, that he near forgot what he went for. For a moment, he simply looked into her eyes, and they stared back with a smile, as if giving life to his weary, travelled soul. "Greetings dear Gromel!" he exclaimed out of breath. Gromel gave him a big hug and kissed him on both cheeks.

"Do come in! Do come in!" she exclaimed. "For it feels that we are passing through tremendous hours. . ." With those words Mr Underhill fell silent, pensive, for it was as déjà vu, almost like he had heard it somewhere on his journey. He shook from this reverie and said, "What-ever do you mean dear Gromel?"

She closed the door behind him and led him into the kitchen, as was her custom. While she made him coffee, she spoke in tender tones, "Folk are coming and going Shabeen, and some are not returning. . .and if you have come for anyone in this home, they are as lost flakes of snow. All are gone. . ." she stopped abruptly, bit her lip and sat in silence. She had just set down cookies and coffee for Mr Underhill. He didn't interrupt her and was certain that those words were not intended for him to hear. It appeared that she was lost in thought; travelling beyond the fields of men but, she momentarily came out from it and went on, "No! That is some distant event. The girls are off playing, Hyperion had rushed out and didn't say a word to anyone and hasn't returned, and Dheya is overdue, and I see the worst."

Mr Underhill took her hands in his, and replied hurriedly, "Yes! Yes! Yes! That was just the thing I meant to tell you. . .to ask you. On my way to Boondock a strange man from Maldon came to me and told me to remind Dheya of a strange prophecy. It took me a while to recall *what* prophecy he was talking about, albeit vague to me now. I was longing for home and my mind was to go straight to Hertia. She is versed in lore and such things but, it bothered me so much, that I had to personally to see if Dheya was home. . .but, but now I see, it *is* as I feared. . ."

He released her hands and put his fist under his chin, in a contemplative manner. "Certainly," replied Gromel. "It's always the same in Béth-Élam. Folks forget the little things and little things have great beginnings like, the leaving of Talib, the scrying of Grandsire Cinaed, the arrival of Semjase. . .many forgettings. Those who are commissioned to remember and then don't, that is an ill omen. *That* prophecy has meaning, and your meeting the stranger comes as a warning but, it is forfeit, because the father of this home is lost, and my daughter goes to look for him." Mr Underhill started to sweat. He wiped his brow with the back of his hand but sat quietly because he had nothing to say. The unearthly silence was disturbed by the arrival of Hertia as she came calling down the passage; "Wet the tae! Wet the tae, wet the tae!". When she entered the kitchen, surprised that Hyperion was absent and seeing her husband and Gromel she said, "I knocked and knocked! Are you two in a dream?" she complained in her usual manner yet, smiled for she was so happy to see her husband but, that smile quickly faded because she knew something was amiss. She delayed her kiss and hug for she knew, she always knew, that Hyperion was not at home. She sat down immediately because what happened to Hyperion, had happened once before, to the very woman sitting beside her. They spent the afternoon sitting quietly, then talking, then questioning . . .Mr Underhill eventually went home, exhausted.

Hertia and Gromel remained there till the following morning. . .

❖

Jaddamiah and his horse took to the road immediately. Llewerig was now only a grassy, clearing with wet wood and smoke stole upwards. Fágan galloped for a short while before catching up with Morkaél's wagon. She was at the front of four other wagons travelling towards the Crossing of Amura Val.

When Jaddamiah came beside her, she glanced at him, her bright eyes glittered in the morning light. He smiled at her; even though she didn't talk much, he enjoyed her company. The Great Eastern Road was now being pushed right up to the foot of The Kurtidāgh. Its slopes reached upwards like imposing spires of granite, rock and stone. Despite it being late in the season, there was a magickal luminosity about that valley and its two mountain ranges. The mid-morning sun threw its light onto the Kuavarg and it gave its unfriendly slopes a most beautiful colouration of gold and shadows of ochre. In some places, a strange, blue, vaporous haze lingered in clefts. Tall pines stood as dark sentinels. It was an utterly, beautiful scene; enough to intoxicate the senses with cerulean languor. Behind those, billowed enormous chalky clouds against an azure sky that was filled with twinkling, morning stars. On some crevasses and pinnacles, the light of day cast shadows of tawny orange and purple. Far away from the road on the right flank, closer to the Kuavarg, the woodland floor glowed lilac, purple and orange and moulded the low trees in a rusty, black-brown shadow. Where the trees touched one another tightly, it became an immense weald where some tall, tall trees rose out like green campaniles. The trunks of those trees glimmered. Jaddamiah was spellbound. He raised his arm and pointed in their direction and asked Morkaél what those beautiful trees were called. "Glæmboom" she replied and looked in the direction that Jaddamiah was pointing. "Some folk call those trees 'Ælve-gleam' and in the ancient speech, they were sometimes called 'Bhurga' which meant a 'tree whose bark is used to write upon'. When we arrive at the Crossing of Amura Vel Jaddamiah, you will see what I mean, for there, at the crossing on the road running north, are two Glæmboom on either side of the road."

The caravan was then only a mile or two from the Amura Vel and just like the previous night, a strange howl was heard, that time much louder.

"Gardyloo!" Morkaél called out softly.

"Why is it a warning? Is it for us?" asked Jaddamiah trying to understand its cause.

"No," she replied emphatically. "It is not for us, it is for themselves. They are communicating with each other. We are being watched." She spoke in an elusive manner, and there was no specificity so, Jaddamiah couldn't understand what she meant so, he asked, "Who are they? Who do you speak of?"

"The Ælves! The Wolvlingas! Jaddamiah, must you folk always persist?" she said that with a smidgeon of frustration.

"By Wolvlingas, do you mean Waelwulfas?"

"No Jaddamiah, you mean to say Waelwulfas but, I meant Wolvlingas. The Waelwulfas are totally different. They are a malicious lot, evil denizens of the Dark One." Jaddamiah thought about what she said for some moments, then he started talking again without looking at her. He sat in his saddle with one hand on the reins and the other on his knee. "I was recently a guest of some really nice folk in Malbon. The man of the house was a zythepsarist, and in the evening of my arrival, while we were having supper, the wife and the son expressed similar words to what you are using now. In fact, there was a howling that evening and it caused a bit of consternation on the part of the father, as if he did not want the name of the howling creature mentioned. It seemed to me that they knew something of those creatures you speak of."

"By creature, do you mean animal-kind Jaddamiah?"

Her eyes flashed as she posed the question, but Jaddamiah could see where she was going with it and didn't answer her. He dropped his head. "It would be best you keep in mind Jaddamiah that words are a war when spoken incorrectly, an enchantment when spoken beautifully, and powerful when understood. But a *correct name* Jaddamiah, you will soon learn, is everything."

Her voice quivered as she spoke. She cocked her head to the side, and combed her long hair with her fingers, so that her exquisite profile could be seen. In sunlight, her complexion was like a pale rose and the neat, pale blue canopy, shaded her from the sun and rain. Her beauty drew his gaze, drew him in. Jaddamiah also noticed that her ears were slightly pointy, like that of the Ælfenna. They stopped briefly to eat, then set off again. By late afternoon they eventually reached the Crossing of the Amura Val. The ground was sodden, and he could smell that fresh rain had fallen there earlier. A large spider web caught Morkaél's eye. It glittered in the late afternoon sun and was filled with a million silver drops of water, beaded like some onnian necklace.

The web was so large that even Jaddamiah noticed it and wondered at that arachnid tapestry. Morkaél brought the wagon and horses to a standstill to the right of the road, under the tall Glæmboom. The front wagons turned southwards and one continued east. Jaddamiah was curious and wanted to see the Ælves. He had read about them in tales and legends but, never actually saw them. Besides, he thought to himself, 'You do not save any time by working too fast; hurrying will cause you to make mistakes, and you will have to take extra time to do the job over again.' So, he dismounted Fágan and she was happy to dig her nose into the grass and nibble. It seemed that her master had cut the day's journey shorter than the previous one. Mr Fuhrmann ensured that all the horses got fresh water. He checked their feet, even did Jaddamiah the favour of checking on Fágan's shoes. Jaddamiah stared at the tall Glæmboom. He thought that they looked similar to birch but, birch grew taller and didn't have a silver gleam on their smooth bark. Despite the waning day, they seemed to have a glow within, and of themselves. He looked southward and the wagons were gone. The western road was empty and the wagon that had proceeded eastward, was fading out of sight. The sign that pointed north simply said 'Amura Vel', and Jaddamiah knew that it translated as 'Daemon Veil'. He was suddenly overcome with a feeling of intense loneliness. A cold breeze had started, and as he looked toward the Amura Val, it seemed to him that the road disappeared, as if it didn't exist, not because of feeble sight but, it simply seemed as if the road vanished, even from the short distance where he was standing.

'The other wagons certainly wasted no time. They sped off as soon as possible and displayed great celerity. They didn't thank us nor wave good-bye. Very ominous,' thought Jaddamiah.

He walked closer to the tree where Morkaél was scrutinising the web. She had instructed Mr Fuhrmann to bring the step ladder.

Jaddamiah looked for markings or messages on the bark but couldn't see any. He was a tad disappointed and thought that perhaps Morkaél had embellished her description of the trees. He looked up as she climbed the ladder. "Do you see it Jaddamiah?" she asked with a smile. "See what ma-lady? The web?" Morkaél laughed for the first time since he had met her, and it was infectious because he found himself laughing too. She gently shook her head from side to side. "No mortal!" She exclaimed. She pointed, as close as possible to the web, not to break its silver threads. A large spider sat in the middle of the web. It was hairy, dark blue with big, green eyes and the ends of its long hairs were bright, orange-red. Its legs were at least 12 inches long.

"Don't you see the arachniform? Come up!" she called and waved her arm. "The ladder will not hold both of us,' Jaddamiah replied in trepidation. "Come on, Jaddamiah!" she commanded. He went up immediately and was surprised that the ladder was quite firm under their weight. He felt the unnatural warmth of her body again, and it felt comforting to him. He hadn't felt that when touching others. "Look!" she exclaimed and cocked her head forward. She took her long hair in her hands and pulled it to the side, so that he could have a clearer view. Jaddamiah narrowed his eyes. The westering light created worlds of kaleidoscopic wander in the onnian orbs. He clearly then saw a strange script, similar to a cursive hand writing that he could not understand nor recall from any book or Pradeza. If anyone were to pass by at that moment, they would never have guessed that it was a script. He didn't believe what he saw, and he rubbed his eyes. At the bottom of the ladder, Mr Fuhrmann walked away and laughed softly to himself.

"Yes ma-lady, I see it now. Look!" he called out.

"Look how blue it twinkles. Who wrote it, what does it mean?"

"It is normally only for me to see, and its meaning, is meant only for me but, today I shall share it with you. The message is quite simple, and it was left by the Ælves. 'We are coming.' That is its translation." The large spider moved, and it cantered down one of the silver threads. Morkaél held out her pale hands and it crawled into it, smothering her palms. Jaddamiah sprinted down the ladder and stood looking up with his hands on his hips.

"She is called 'Kaladamza' Jaddamiah. 'Kala-damza'. It is such a beautiful name. It means 'the dark blue sting' but, of course, the common speech doesn't do the meaning justice. Common words merely refer to a creature with four pairs of legs and a body with two segments, belonging to a large class that includes spiders, scorpions and mites, of which she is not!" As she said those words, she caressed the fur of the spider but, there was no sting to her pale, slender hands. "Aroint! Aroint!" she said softly to the spider. The big, blue spider crawled onto the ladder, scurried down it, and ran and disappeared somewhere in the long grasses.

Jaddamiah jumped aside but he was too slow, for if Kaladamza wanted too, he would have been a corpse already. As Morkaél descended the ladder, Jaddamiah saw a new phenomenon. Runes became visible all over the trunk, and feint, ringing of bells were heard approaching from somewhere up the road. Jaddamiah looked up the road and Morkaél stood next him. She put her hair up for the first time and twirled it into a neat bun above her head. She wiped her torso, priming herself up as if expecting some important person. The sound came closer but, nothing came into view. The sound of galloping horses could also be heard, and the ground trembled beneath them. Then suddenly, sight and sound burst forth as if a veil was torn. Rider on horse appeared, and Jaddamiah beheld a wondrous sight, that he would speak of for years to come.

Jaddamiah Jabberwocky

Jaddamiah's eyes were like saucers as he turned in circles and nearly lost his balance, as 6 horses danced around them. Morkaél of course, stood dead still. A peaceful smile ran across her face and she rested her arms, with her fingers lightly locked, in front of her body. She was the epitome of contentment. Mr Fuhrmann had come closer and stood on the outside of that display. It was obvious that he was used to it. He removed his hat in a reverential display. The white horses calmed down, and a tall, waiflike figure that rode without bridle, headstall or reins, dismounted. One rider, on a pitch-black steed, still pranced about. The figure looked stern, and his long, flowing white hair fluttered in the breeze. His eyes were like blazing coals of fire and if Morkaél's eyes were a pre-curser to that, hers paled in comparison. There was no pupil, no sclera and only the irides burned blue-white. The Ælves who surrounded Morkaél and Jaddamiah were the same. Some had blue eyes, others blood orange like the eyes of owls. If it were dark, those eyes would have sent the fear of Mesa-sum-na, the 'Son of Death' into someone. "Who is this *mortal* who accompanies you, *maiden* loved by the Ælves?" His voice was clear and thick with emotion yet, his composure was completely devoid of any mortal passion. After emphasising the word 'maiden', his voice became dulcet and inviting. "He is called Jaddamiah Jabberwocky, from Béth-Élam, my Bele. He is a sojourner though, I did not ask where he was going. He asked for our company and I paid him kindness," answered Morkaél as she looked down slightly. Her voice was clear and firm but melodious. Jaddamiah stood very still. He was filled with both wonder and dread, and it felt like the world around him had fallen away. It felt as if time and tide had ceased. He understood that though the Ælve spoke sternly, there was no guile, no malice in his being. The Ælve on the horse, although no Ælve, stilled his fiery horse and dismounted. He smiled, then broke into laughter. He walked over to Morkaél, put a hand on each shoulder and said, "There is no evil thing that you can do Morkaél. With you, we are well pleased." The other Ælves, all tall in stature, even taller than Morkaél, started transferring the wagon load of Glæmboom planks to their horseless wagon. Its large wheels were made of solid gold and small, crafted blue bells made of lilūlium steel, hung all round it, on scarlet cords. There was no part of it that was untidy or weatherworn. The Paladin turned to Jaddamiah. Jaddamiah, who was also a tall man, had to look up to him for, he was 9ft tall and by no means the tallest Paladin. He extended his hand to Jaddamiah and said, "I am Bealdorsuhles, the Bele of Light." Jaddamiah didn't reply as he held the firm hand of the Paladin. He looked up and marvelled. When he finally fell out of his swoon, he said in a timid voice, "You do not look like the other Ælves but, you act like one." Jaddamiah found it hard to articulate what he meant. What he was trying to say, was that the Paladin, though having Ælven ears, his skin seemed to be made of steel, blue alloy. His hand didn't feel hard like steel but, felt like a strange, cool liquid and as the last rays of the sun filtered through the weald trees, the Paladin's face glittered with a million, pin-point slivers of silver and blue. "It is because I am no Ælve Jaddamiah, I *am* a Paladin." The others broke into child-like laughter at hearing that. Jaddamiah spoke again with a little more confidence. He looked around at the Ælves and noticed that their eyes had subsided and were as normal as his own. Some were dark green. Some were hazel-brown and others, blue. "You do not now appear as you arrived and though I am filled with dread, there is also wonder in me for having such a privilege. Each moment that passes, it seems that you are changing in appearance yet, you are not."

Bealdorsuhles replied in tender voice, "We are never the same with others as when we are alone. We are different even when we are in the dark with them." Jaddamiah was somewhat confused yet, marvelled at those words. He believed that he knew and understood. A sudden, chilly wind came up, icy cold. The Ælves ears pricked like those of a cat that was at heightened awareness.

They looked around with sudden changed awareness, some even looked up towards the sky. Then there was the strange howl, the same that Jaddamiah had heard previously. There appeared to be a commotion in the weald, and it was approaching. It sounded like many leaves were shaking in a terrible wind. Jaddamiah saw that the tree tops were stirring, and the ground rumbled as if it were under the currents of a wave. Their eyes returned to their former glory, and one of the others spoke for the first time, his voice was guttural, yet clear and penetrating. "We must go, there is a vergence!" Bealdorsuhles took both Jaddamiah's hands into his one hand and said looking at the Ælve that spoke; "Yes Dalethdir, open the duir for us." Dalethdir roughly meant 'the Ælve that is the doorkeeper'. He had the most beautiful complexion. It was like the interior of an azure sea shell; palest shades of celeste, pays bleu, sky blue, powder blue, pink, mauve, honeydew, flash white and old lace. His skin was like a paduasoy, and around his long, copper-cinnamon hair, was a thin, golden band. Engraved on the front-centre, was an eagle called 'Meriearndir' of the North Sea. The golden band sported a tall, turquoise feather which curved over like a spring, crescent moon. Underneath his long, deep-blue cape, his body was covered with what looked like shells of lesser blue, made of lilūlium steel. It seemed 3 dimensional but was in fact, the elaborate kræftwork of his kin. His shoes were made of pure gold, and it fitted the heel like a glove. The arch was open, and gold encased his toes. The shoe curved upwards at the toes, and formed a thin thread back towards the ankle, making a slender loop. Gold, considered to be as hard as diamonds yet, those were as flexible as bamboo. It was called 'skeumier'.

Jaddamiah nearly toppled over and leaned against Morkaél to maintain his balance. Out of the weald came two, mammoth creatures and Jaddamiah exclaimed, "Great horn spoon! Are those trolls?"

Morkaél replied, slightly annoyed, "Jaddamiah! Can trolls be so dapper, so graceful?" Indeed, they were dapper, and there were two of them, and they swayed like stately poplars, in the west wind. They wore long, blue, high waisted, fustian trousers with white braces, that had images of trees on them. Over their dark, linen shirts, they wore soft, dark grey, woollen, waist jackets and on their feet, brown leather boots. Their soft, cuddly, teddy-bear faces, had long, Ælvish ears. Their faces were smooth like babies' bottoms. Their big, round, black eyes blinked rapidly but, those Þursar were not to be trifled with, and often accompanied the Ælves. They looked down on the group some 29ft below. The slightly taller one, with the silver-grey waist jacket, started talking in a silvery voice, "I am Gimlillÿs, son of Gimvöllekaas and I bring a message from our Master, to *you* Jaddamiah." Gimlillÿs gave Jaddamiah 3 purple anemones (he was too stunned to say anything) then paused and rested one hand on top of the other on his silver walking cane. He went on again, "Not all jars that are empty should be discarded, not all jars that are full are useful, look deeply and you may discover the jewels that are hidden."

It was Gimvöllekaas's turn to speak, "My name is Gimvöllekaas but, my message is for the Ælves. My Master, Peridir, bid you return and make haste for, there has been a vergence on the aethyrs, and there is a wrinkle in the flow of Irfan."

The wagon was the first to take off, then all the Ælves mounted their horses and sped off. Bealdorsuhles swept Morkaél up and was gone. So, they disappeared, as they appeared.

In Memoriam

᛫᛫᛫

What is to be read next was told by an enigma, for no one knew much about his whereabouts, only the report that he chose to reveal. He was from the most eastern tip of the southern Pradeza called the 'Pradeza of South-Ta-merri'. It was said that 'Ponkie', for that was his name, was a hermit and lived an honourable life amongst his people, and because of that, the Ælves espoused him, and translocated Ponkie to Midhe and legend went, many eyes saw him wandering here or there, like some Magi or Wizard, whenever the Ælves were about. There was an old proverb;

'if Elqamar (Ponkie) rises the Ælves are in tide'

Ponkie was a handsome man, well built and of an umber complexion, as most Ondervelden were. An outstanding attribute were his clear, kind, bright, green eyes. They held a light in them that attracted strangers to him. Some folks said; 'kind eyes could look on anyone and find them beautiful'. It was through Ponkie, that people learned about events at Palador for, no one really knew, and no one had ever set foot inside the great fortress, except Ponkie.

The Paladorians and the Ælves never addressed Ponkie by that name. When they were alone with him, they called him 'Elqamar', 'the Ælve Moon'. The Ælves loved the stars but, something else they loved dearly, and that was the moon, the 'Teller-of-Time'. They loved her and her light more than the sun. If any word, in any Ælven tongue, described what love meant, it was 'Elqamar' or 'Alqamar', the literal word being just 'moon'. They called the sun 'Elsalah' which meant, 'Ælve-peace'.

The great yew slept some 300m from the narrow, woodland path, and Lycurgus led the way. After only a few meters or so, he stopped again and said, "Do you smell that. . .hmmmmm?" and inhaled deeply. When they found the large trunk of the yew, there was Ponkie, lying on his back, long grass straw between his lips; and besides him was a blazing, crackling fire. He got up hastily and hugged Lycurgus. He then vigorously shook Gwalather's hand because they knew each other well. Ponkie looked at Hyperion, Gul and Göbel-Malu. "My folk call me Ponkie, but they are long lost to me. The Ælvefolk call me Elqamar, you can call me what your spirit feels best to call me." He genuflected and smiled warmly, his green eyes darted. Hyperion and the others smiled back at him. Gul and Göbel-Malu said, "We shall call you as the Ælves do." Hyperion was speechless because she didn't feel a stranger to him.

In fact, she especially took a liking to him, for there was a warmth to his presence that she could not isolate. She also noticed that there was a 'glow' about him, visibly so, something she had never seen with anyone else before.

The rest of the Hobgoblins who did not drive off with the wild horses, wandered about while Gwalather stood alert and stared at the failing light. Lycurgus then drew Ponkie aside and explained all that had transpired but, whether the Ælves would give Hyperion an audience; of that he was dubiously optimistic. "There is no need to be dubious Master Wulf for, if your concern is warranted, I would not be standing before you. The circles of the turning world are peculiar, and Fate is Lady over most. . ." replied Ponkie. "You speak un-precisely like the Ælves," interjected Lycurgus, making a long, drawn out sigh, and standing with his hands on his hips.

"Speak plainly Elqamar," said Lycurgus again, in a stern voice.

Ponkie was unmoved, the glow in his eyes became clearer and he replied in a soft, modulated voice, "The Ælves will see her but, first she must journey to the Ninduglilene. . ."

Lycurgus interjected, this time displaying some annoyance, "Grrrrrrrrrrrrrrrrrr! Eee—egad!" his eyes changed from calm hazel to greenish-gold. The yew shook her branches as if some great storm passed through her underskirts. She dropped scores of needles over Lycurgus's face and instantly he knew his place. Those about, became unsettled, but Elqamar was poised and certain.

"So, it is, dear Ponkie," returned Lycurgus with a more subdued voice. "I beg your pardon for acting so inappropriately. It would seem, that the Ælves. . .would send us. . .to the Ælfenne."

"Be not dismayed Lycurgus," replied Ponkie, rubbing the upper arm of Lycurgus, which for him was a bit of a stretch. Lycurgus shoved his hands into his pockets and turned to the rising moon, to contemplate. "Sit down on the earth my lady," said Ponkie to Hyperion, in a trustworthy tone while, he quickly fiddled in his mayll which hung from a low branch. He pulled out a smudge of sage, separated it and pushed the rest back. He lit one in the fire and as Hyperion sat poised in front of the fire with her legs crossed, he walked around her, circling her with the smoking sage. Hyperion lifted her chin, took a deep breath and closed her heavy eyelids. When the sage had burned out, Ponkie crushed the ash with his thumb. "Allow me my lady," he charmingly said to Hyperion while he carefully held the back of her head, and pressed gently between her eyes, staining her skin with the ash. Gul and Gamba looked on curiously while Lycurgus bent down, close to the fire and was already asleep, his back leaned against the wise, old yew. His thick moustache twitched, it was not an easy sleep. "There!" said he warmly satisfied. "Now I. . .<u>can</u>. . .see you." This custom was strange to her but, she felt in a homely place, willingly allowing Ponkie to continue.

He took her strong, slender hands into his and rubbed the tops of her hand with his thumbs and said,

"I hold it truth, with They who Rule
Though he be gone, those who live never die.
Clasp not grief but let it fly
Treasure now your new borne jewel!

For the Fates who forecast the years
Have sent in loss a grander match
And though we are not fit to catch
The grief of your falling tears;

May my words be a portend
That plucked the plumes from darkness ravens gloss
And count me as friend in your season of loss,
That I may be the handsel ere our end.

That our after years should be
The long result of love and friendships affection.
Behold! You the maiden that lost and reclaims perfection;
Through the Waters of Time are set free. . ."

Hyperion rose-cheeked and bashful that she was called a maiden, lowered her head so that her glorious copper-coloured hair partially veiled her face. Since the Hobgoblin horde had redeemed her from the water, she felt renewed.

". . .And if thou feelest human and divine
Of highest maidenhood, accept it now.
Your will is Theirs. We know not how.
Their ways are sweet, so compline.

Your man; I knew him once,
He was loved. You are just;
So you are loved by a Higher Trust.
All of Nature, your name announce!

Old Yew, speaks from its silent, woody Rings,
Yew, Oak and Ash, Ring bearers most supreme.
Your unborn knave, diehm!
Their roots know him before the names of many earthly kings.

The Ninduglilene brings the flower again,
And brings you this, barnälvor.
Hark this ælvweard! Before
You grow weary and complain,
Ere the Teller of Time beats out
The petty lives of men;
A 1000 years and then,
You shall know no doubt.

Of Falhordur, we must taste,
To seek ælfrēd from that high place.
Not for thee will we seek their grace,
Though your charm is beyond chaste.

We go there as an avenue to High Palador.
But first we rest under high blue star
And wait for the Sun to break the dark
Lest we make haste like fools unto locked door.

My words though wind never trips,
Rather they engirdle from the cold
I am here placed, to help your grief unfold.
All these whispers come from un-lying lips."

Thus, ended the sweet and melodic, soliloquy of Elqamar; that Hyperion reached out and embraced him. She shed tears of sorrow over russet cheeks, for glee and gratitude; that such dulcet words could carry such credence and calm and warmth.

But as always, there were those disturbers of the peace, and so the still, quiet night was burdened with harsher words and requests.

"Master Wulf?"

"Mhoooo?"

"Master Wulf!"

"Mhooo. . . what is it!" shouted Lycurgus.

Lycurgus opened one eye and looked at Gwalather sheepishly.

"I thought we had to hustle. . ."

"The Ælves know not Time. . .Ponkie? Well Ponkie. . .he is Elqamar." And with that, Lycurgus went back to sleep, in fact, he then snored.

The search for Dheya was now over. Hyperion knew it as she lay with her hands folded under her cheek, upon the soft, tweed jacket that Ponkie rolled over, to make a pillow. The fire was roaring as Gwalather kept watch, not winking an eye. Gamba scouted the area for almost 3 miles away. The rest of the other horde returned long after midnight, and it was their low voices, regaling their time with the band of horses, how far they went who could tell, for Hobgoblins could cover many miles over vast distances at night. Hyperion was awoken by the drone of their voices but, was soon off again because their whispers, was soothing to hear. . .or rather, their *attempts* to whisper…

At daybreak, Ponkie was back. He didn't sleep because he had a close relationship with those who frequented the haunts of the moon and also, he loved the dark. He took forty winks to regain his strength and by the time breakfast was laid out, everyone knew why he had slipped away in the night. 3 maidens arrived from nowhere it seemed, shoulders heavy laden with all kinds of sweets and treats for hungry tummies. Sleeping under the fair-roof had contributed to their hunger and they were grateful for the feast.

The Council of Palador

The tower was called Artunis and it meant 'truth and accurate'. The space was commodious, and about 20feet in front of two very tall doors of about 90ft high, stood a dogged guard with his arms crossed. He wore a golden band with a Frawahr symbol on his forehead. His cape and cowl were of an orangey-red and green. Hanging from his waist, in two scabbards laced together with thick red-brown leather and studded with precious jewels, were two large swords. One was a long, broad sword called 'Gladdon', and the other a slender sword that had no guard for the hand and fingers and was called 'Tiraspala'.

Beside each pillar, which was much taller than the doors, stood two more guards and they held golden spears.

Ponkie walked towards the doors which dwarfed him. those pillars had a large, round base 12ft tall and 6m wide. Standing shoulder to shoulder in gold relief were images of the Guardian Ælves. The pillars were fluted and rose upward and; the doors were made of oak, as were all the interior doors. On each door were 12 circles, coloured consecutively in gold and copper. In each circle was a rune followed by the name 'Artunis', in purple. (Artunis was the name of that tower and the rune cast on the door, was for knowledge, protection and right speech). It was sometimes also used by an Ælve, Vala, Talaith of Wisdom for giving a personal or secret message. The two guardians stood like brazen statues. Ponkie didn't say a word to them and they made no sign of acknowledging him, although they were very familiar with him. They simply came out of their brazen states and opened the gigantic, tall doors for him to enter, then returned to their positions.

Inside, the walls were stark, without ornamentation or accoutrements. From the doors, a passage ran between two, triangular walls with 6 sconce candle holders on each side. the candles which burned in them were at least 30cm thick and illuminated the dark walls. Those walls supported a semi-amphitheatre where those who listened in on important matters sat but, most times were not allowed to take part in the discourse on hand. In the centre of the cobalt blue floor, stood a grand, round table that seated twelve. The table was made of rowan wood and engraved in the centre was a large tormentilla. The air was permeated with fresh rowan wood and tormentilla. Dulcet sweetness was smelt everywhere, and the quietness belied those who moved inside, for several Ælves were seated on the flanks of the table. One very tall Ælve dressed in soft, black draperies, stood with his elbow against the wall as if looking out of the tall window but, there was no window. Each of the ornate seats with their high backs, were kræfted out of the 9 sacred trees bearing a rich jewel at the top of each head rest. Beyond the far end of the table, over the floor space on each side upon a dais, stood two large, white, carved chairs. One was made of pure white sandstone and the other of grey rock. The seats were empty but, like an ergonomic space, one could clearly see the indentation made by whomever had sat upon them. At the foot of the dais, in front of the great, white, throne-like seat, was another very large, wooden seat. It had a very soft, blue silk pillow upon it and seemed quite elementary compared to the one above it. On its head rest and carved in an embellished circle; was the following inscription, 'Prince of Wolves'.

Several Ælve faces lit up on seeing Ponkie. They waved him over towards them and Ponkie obliged. He climbed the steps up to where they were seated in a deferential fashion. Ponkie had only been seated for a while and listened to the Ælves when a strange, diaphanous light began to form on the grey seat. After only moments, a plumed form took shape and sat on the grand, throne-like edifice. It was an Ælve of exceptional beauty. In Palador they said the words, 'Shyam Varna' for such exceptional beauty. His composure was as silent and serene as his appearance. His garb was voluminous and plumed and was as white as snow. He wore a skull cap made of a single, white pearl and in the centre of it, between his eyes, was a black eastlea inlay, trimmed with gold. His eyes were amber, and it seemed to be aflame. That Ælve was not from that Pradeza, neither any on Dhara. The Himyar Ælves were an unrevealing kindred, from very deep in the galaxy, and they never bothered with the affairs of men but, sometimes when there were great councils on Dhara, they would arrive and sit to observe. The seated Ælves stood up. The contemplative Ælve who stared as if through a window, turned around, joined everyone in genuflection, and sat down again. Ponkie did the same. The first of those to sit around the table arrived. He was a strange looking Paladin, and didn't fit the normal description, for he was much shorter than the rest. He hobbled in, dressed in old, weatherworn clothes; his face wore the scars of age and his hand was firmly placed on the hilt of his sword. He walked around the tormentilla and sat at the head of one end of the table. The table seated five on either side with one chair at each end. Before he sat down, he said to all present in a soft voice as not to disturb some great fane, "Elsaharsa kindred". The others held their hands up, their fore and index fingers pressed together, kissed their fingers, then continued in their silent chatter. That greeting was called 'Sandhana'. Ponkie sat quietly.

A few times the tall doors opened, and other times without the doors opening, a Palador materialized, until each seat around the table was taken. Eventually, only two places needed taking, the 'wolf' seat and the white seat. After some time, the great doors swung open as the two guards pushed upon them. Two hefty figures stood in the entrance. They were the þursar and around them stood the Ælves which were summoned and Morkaél. They entered boisterously. Morkaél decided to sit next to Elqamar. She walked to where he sat and made 'Elsaharsa' for; it seemed an age that they had last met. Another half hour passed, when the tall doors flung open again. Two, tall figures stood side by side and entered. Everyone arose, except for the Himyar Ælve upon his fair, grey sovereignty. The tall figures strode toward their appointed places. The one, a tall Paladin, was completely naked and stood at 12ft tall. His body was brilliantly gleaming, green-like Peridot and his eyes were flaming white. There was no separation of sclera, pupil or iris, just a flaming, white cauldron. The other, walked in as a tall man but, his stooping attitude belied that. He was dressed modestly except for the scabbard which rested in his broad hands and hung from his belt.

It was the only thing that was flamboyant about him. It was obvious that he had tried to neaten his long, honey coloured hair for the occasion. He took the seat below the dais.

The Paladorian seated on the white, started talking without getting up. His strong left arm rested in the niche of the white sandstone, and he held the other up, finger pointed.

"Ælves of old, those who have come to listen at this Council, Elqamar our blessed friend, and our Celestial guest," with that, he indicated to the Himyar Ælve who bowed his head. "Paladins seated around tormentilla, we shall now commence." After that, the great doors closed, the lock and key echoed in the vast hall of Artunis.

A new fragrance could be smelled, it was myrrh. The Paladin continued, "Before I set foot and mind in Artunis, you all knew me as Bhelaribhus. At *this* council, I am only Peridir," As he said that, his eyes flashed, and his strong body glittered because it was entirely made of Peridot. In that state he did not need any weapons, neither any garments because he was then 'the Gem of the Sun' and had the power of ten thousand suns. He spoke as all Paladins did, with power and authority. "Though many are gathered here, only Paladins seated around tormentilla may speak, or those who are called upon to speak, may do so. This shall be called 'The First Council'." When the rest heard those last words, there was some brief chatter. "Let us begin.' he ended.

Following his introduction, everyone spoke in their normal way and some laughter was heard. Lycurgus got up from his seat because he was eager to speak with Elqamar, they were old friends. A broad smile appeared on Peridir's face as he spoke telepathically with the Himyar Ælve who was seated at the opposite end of the long table. Those great Ælve Beles, the Immortals, that Prince of Wolves, spoke of flowers, of trees and of the growing things in Nature. They were not ashamed that they spoke so fondly of lowlier things. They cared deeply for flowers and trees and spoke freely of them even amongst their weightiest affairs. After a while, what perhaps seemed like ages, each took his place and Peridir spoke again. The Moon and Stars, the Sun and the stones of the Dhara, pricked their fiery, silent ears as the Bele Peridir spoke.

"There feels to me that several disturbances in the Irfan or Eolas have manifested. In my sylvan indolence I came upon Vinrúlfr in the Zarvari Vana and my feelings have been just. I now call upon Lycurgus to speak." Lycurgus got up from his chair and tried to elongate himself, make himself as tall as possible. He stood still for a moment as if uncertain which course he should follow, then he looked over the great hall and started speaking.

"Elsaharsa to all of you! I will not form-shift here today, for we have a most distinguished guest," Lycurgus spoke softly, and bowed his head towards the Himyar Ælve on his grand seat. The Himyar Ælve made no sign nor movement. There was no trace of emotion on his face but, his eyes were filled with life, the very presence of Universal Waters was displayed in them. Lycurgus continued for he was accustomed to the ways of many Ælves. "We do not want to alarm the Ælves," he went on in his dry humour. Those present broke out in quiet laughter so, Lycurgus paused and waited for them to finish. "Yes, I jest but there is a spirit in me today that has become uneasy. We formwandlers are not easily moved by trivial, mortal anxiety or consternations but, when Bele Peridir summoned me here, I then knew that what had transpired in my Lycoven, was weightier than my life. Some of you know my sons well, and that they wonder about in the wilds daily but, always no matter how far they stray, they would return home to tell us of their where-abouts, no matter how secret. It has been our custom always. . ." There Peridir interjected. "Bid me speak Lycurgus!" he exclaimed. "Go ahead Bele."

"Tell it to them just as you conveyed the news to me Lycurgus."

Lycurgus nodded while twirling his thumbs.

"When Bele Peridir found me in the Twilight Weald, it had already been several days that Ulfheðin and Ulfhamr spied two Waelwulfas along the Afon Wen, only a few miles from Albtraum. As I confessed to Bele Peredir, it had been days that Ulfheðin and Ulfhamr had not returned home. Usually they would visit daily and when they could not make it, they would send a message. What's more, I could not pick up their scent, and as we currently speak, Merthblaidd-ddyn still searches in the wilds. We last saw them on the twenty forths. Bele Peridir overheard my thoughts whilst we spoke that day, and these words fell from my lips, 'it is in the watches of the night that the wise slumber'. We very well know that Ælve-time is not like any other but, I would urge you all to commence the *hands of time*." Lycurgus then sat down quietly with his head cast downward in his large hand. Some chatter broke out around tormentilla. Bealdorsuhles held his hand to his mouth and whispered to the Paladin seated next to him. The Paladin at the head of the table remained silent. At the other end of the long table sat another Paladin, he had a constitution similar to Peridir only, he was of purest gold.

He sat bare-chested and from his waist hung a long, golden skirt, shaped like a leaf. That Paladin raised his hand and the chatter stopped. Peredir continued, "I call Morkaél to speak, for if there is an ear to the ground, it is her who could share the ill that fall from men's lips." Morkaél stood up and begun to speak, "Sus-vapnah to all my kindred. It is as Bele Peredir has said, ill does fall from the lips of men for, I met a kind man while sojourning. Proud and ignorant but, kind nonetheless. He was Jaddamiah Jabberwocky of Béth-Élam. I heard him tell that while staying at Malbon, there were cries from the Waelwulfas. Also, the strangest tale he told. . ." Morkaél paused and ran her slender fingers through her hair before continuing. "He journeys to Weir, to fight a Meline Dragon," Again she paused, then went on thoughtfully. "There was no guile in him Bele Peredir." It was then that the tall, golden Ælve stood up and spoke, as Morkaél sat down. He kept his long arm still, while pointing to those around tormentilla. He called them out by name. First, he called out the Paladin at opposite end of the table, "Nirdhanin, Andhrimnir, Bealdorsuhles, Eriol, Hafgan" so he went through all eleven Paladin then, he continued, "And I, Elrukmavaksas, we have walked the night and scratched out holes in the wilds to sleep when men have turned us away. We have walked all corners of Dhara yet, none of the twelve, bear news of Meline Dragons, howling Waelwulfas, fracas in the Akasas and now this ill news," he pointed to Lycurgus and continued in his musical voice. "The loss of two Wolvlingas, how could this be? How have we squandered time? How is it that the red-haired maiden brings us such summary?" He fell back into his seat, his eyes glowed for the flame that burned in them, was wrath. Peridir got up for the first time and spoke again, "Still your-self Elrukmavaksas! Let us not fashion eidolon in the dark like the Moha. Let me tell you a short tale. The age in which mortals call the future, many thousands of years hence, I was journeying from star to star when I came upon the Duir that leads to Dhara, and there standing before it, I overheard two Igigi saying, 'Unhappy, ill-fated, while they live, the idea of ceasing to be is, nevertheless, a horror to them. They look not for solace in annihilation; it does not even bring them the promise of rest. In their madness, they even look upon nothingness with terror. They have peopled it with phantoms. Look you at these pediments, these towers and domes and spires that pierce the mist and rear on high their glittering symbols. Mortals bow in adoration before demiurge, after demiurge who has given them a life that is worse than death and a death that is worse than life'. Let all know present today that it is that moment we must avoid. Though all seated around tormentilla have changed constitution for the evils of Dhara, we are all Ælve. We are the rulers of *the universe*. Let us be so now."

"Then what do you propose be our action henceforth Bele Peridir?" asked Andhrimnir, speaking for the first time.

Peridir sat and replied, "Set a watch in every weald, in every land, we shall not be caught dreaming again. Alert the Ælves on Vel Domas and Vel Samoda and find Ulfheðin and Ulfhamr. I will go North to Jinbōchō to seek counsel."

"Those kindred care not for the affairs of men Bele Peridir," the tall Dalethdir called out as he rose to his feet.

"Forgive me, I mean not to speak out of turn at The First Council but, are you to use my Le Badhaprapta to reach there with java?"

"It is not our place to *care* for the affairs of *men* but, for the love of Dhara – Janana, though you have not spoken out of turn dear Dalethdir, because that is your jurisdiction. I will not use swift Duirs. I will travel like mortals do, for I need to hear what the birds sing, and listen to the wind whisper, to the trees and the gossip of river rat and beaver. In that way I will learn much. I will use the duirs of the ash and oak for cover."

"Well, I will take your offer swift Dalethdir, for there is rumour that the tables of Jinbōchō are laden with all manner of magickal provender!" Andhrimnir called out.

The hall broke out in laughter; there was even a slight trace, a smile started at the corners of the Himyar Ælve's mouth, as he sat in his splendour, poised and regal. Peridir held his hand up and the laughter settled down. He spoke again, "Let it be known, the 1st Council of Palador will take conference alone now."

Elqamar, Morkaél and all the rest, got up and filed out, chatting amongst themselves.

Andhrimnir led the way for he was taking them to have the dinner which he had prepared. There was no need for him to be physically present while the Paladins continued for, he was able to listen from any location within the halls of Palador.

When the great doors were shut, Peredir commenced the discourse. He turned to Elrukmavaksas and said, "It is my impression that this Jaddamiah Jabberwocky of Béth-Élam has some part to play in this *fate,* if fate indeed it is. So Elrukmavaksas, you must journey to Weir and observe, but you do not have my permission to intervene." Elrukmavaksas sat forward in his adorned chair. His forefinger was at his lips but, he sank back again and didn't speak. Eriol sat quietly as always, but was startled when Peridir spoke to him, "Eriol! Leave your dreaming and take my heed. You *must* accompany Lycurgus and find his beloved sons. Do not return without them. Do you understand?" Peridir's voice was strong and stern. Eriol looked up towards the dais and replied, "Yes my Bele, I will do as you bid me." He spoke in a sad, melancholic voice as if his thoughts were on some distant shore.

"Let it be known that the 1st Council of Palador, 1st October 8817 has now ended, those of you whom I have individually instructed, go in peace. The rest of you know my thoughts, for it is not hidden. So, it is done! So, let it be written!"

Bhelaribhus

Bhelaribhus stood in a part of the garden of Palador known as 'Yanagola'. Thirteen, tall junipers stood in a large circle. The interior of the circle was paved in glittering, white sand stone, inlaid with fine, clear quartz. He looked up towards the starry sky and at the glowing, third star of Haasil. It was called 'Nastaloka' for it shone over Palador and it meant: 'that which is lost to human sight'. No mortal eye could see Nastaloka. He pondered for a moment, then covered his head with his perse cape and set off into the night. For some hours he walked slowly, carefully, so not to disturb any grasses or wild flowers. He also did that to ensure that no one was following. He decided to walk in a north-easterly direction first, into the thickest part of the weald. He then crossed the River Næddre, where a profusion of vertical trees stood soldiering. When he was certain that he was alone, he discarded his mortal veil and slowly faded out of sight, between the dark of the trees and the night, and became Peridir again. Although he was cautious, he wasn't overly careful and so started whistling the tune of an ancient song, so that a high, far priyagitah responded to his tune. The words of the tune were arcane and peculiar. At length, Peridir came upon Lake Vadana in Zarvari Vana; it was called that because it was in the shape of a woman's face, and it seemed that the water was running from her lips. The water made up 3 chutes that became one, then divided again into 6, all feeding into River Næddre. He was very fond of that lake so, took the detour past it.

Nature and The Hours

❧

Alone pelican sailed through the water, the ducks and geese had already left the lake for warmer climes. He listened clearly and heard the quails whisper that they too would be off soon.

There was coolness to the air that was uncanny, as if he were by the seaside. Some said that one could catch the smell of the sea far inland, and it was so for Peridir. The flowers stood quietly in their Florien splendour and sang with profound pulsation.

The measure of those flowers were like an immortal; tall, like an effigy standing in a forgotten Ninfian village square; silent, yet speaking a thousand nameless joys. Standing amongst those unspoken worlds, crescendoed to a fever pitch unlike any other.

A Monarch butterfly alighted on bright, cherry-pink snapdragons. Peridir stood silently and contemplated. . .

'Even now, amongst these flowers, while a flock of honey-eaters complain and protest in the nearby trees, hidden from view but not from my bright eyes, yet even now, while Willie-wagtail flutters in the branches of tall trees, going joyously on without a care it seems, I feel the presence of decay. It was even in the air that flowed through Peridir. Not contemplating on it would only be folly. The decay sets in on the world at the end of 26 000 years. While bee and butterfly, while Sidhe and Fáerië, Gnome and Dwarf, Dryad and Nymph, Sprite and Sylph and all the other Devas, slowly leave the world. The green things, the growing things remain alone. The trees stand alone, and their shadows are bent. Those thousands of Beings, those millions of things, those innumerable lives have escaped mans' care. Across the demilunes, plenilunes, the cycles of the Sun, the aeons, the ages, the months, days and hours; they fill all these moments with scorching beauty, together with the birds, weaving garlands of complete Magick. All these moments are lost in time like fresh morning dew is wasted on the desert. The race of man comes to these days for he has not cared, and those who did care, did not do so enough, or else we would not be here. And on some days when it is balmy, while I stand before the fragrant flowers in the wilderness listening to the invisible hours, those days when I am thinking of how it was in Bældæg's day. Then Time seemed insignificant; as insignificant as the vanished clepsydra is to the child with her sun-dial in her garden. Like sunflowers always turning to the

Sun, we force away the frowns of unhappy moments hoping they'd go away forever. But the Fates heed all things, and what has been dealt out to Nature has returned at last for, the unstoppable phenomena of Karma is dealing out its darkest hand. So Igreen stands between the glorious shores of fragrant Spring and icy Winter. And only we know whether to Spring or wither to Winter. But now I will dream of Spring and Summer; the season of peace; where I will walk upon a new shore, and where indolence and delight have no gates, not measured by hours or days. I will now enjoy these moments of solitude and walk, Bhelaribhus will not drink them as ordinary, he will look at each day with a nobler measure. Peradventure! Perchance he will not look to dates and times for maybe in the darkest hour, a cleft will appear between the Worlds. An aurulent light will push through, and it will envelope a few, perhaps one, and that one shall be in Realm Eternal.'

It was time to go but, his contemplation was discontinued by 3 beautiful swans. Peridir admired that mystery and then his countenance enlivened for he believed that at first, he was deceived, for in reality, as he gazed he could see they were no swans at all. Their leader, a blue Swan, spoke first in melodious intimations, "We salute you Great Bele of the host of Palador."

Peridir gave way and Bhelaribhus manifested and replied, "What jurisprudence is given to this Swan Maiden to lay eyes on a Paladorian while he bides here in the fane of Neter?" The 3 swans were filled with light; one was blue with large wings that spanned 3 meters. Its under-downs were pale blue and white. The second swan was white with a swarthy neck and the third was dark as night. They held their wings turned upward and settled in the shallow waters of the lake that lapped on the shore. The 3 swans walked out of the waters as maidens, shedding their plumes. Each wore a single diaphanous garment of sheer muslin, it clung to their bodies as light danced over the reliefs of their supernal forms. The maidens were not the only Therians. . .

The light wasn't coming from the Moon but, rather that it emanated from within or through their being. The first swan maiden spoke saying, "No other Jurisprudence moreover they who are pure, setting eyes upon he who is uncorrupted. We come in haste, we ask for a boon," replied the second maiden, all 3 genuflecting.

Bhelaribhus pushed back his hood, his countenance still aglow and blazing from transformation. "Such grace, such splendour makes heedless genuflection," he replied smiling. "If it is a boon you seek that I can give, I am mystified, for your bearing tells me you have travelled from Men-Nefer of the Khemitians."

"My Bele Bhelaribhus! Think not modestly of thy proficiency for we have come on behalf of the Marsh King's daughter, she who has vaulted from the progeny of the Sidhe and is ill with death and is drawn down to Loki's realm. We, though fair, are not allowed to go unto that nameless city that men call Jinbōchō. . ." At that point, he interposed their flowery speech and asked, "This is a great risk, for no foe knows I journey to those High Ælves. And all under dome of Palador is secret." He spoke with a loud voice, regal and powerful yet, not louder so weald spies would hear.

The 3 maidens bowed their heads, one slowly lifted her eyes and implored gently, "Our fate is bound to this knowing for, wither you grant our boon or no we shall all perish with the Marsh King's daughter for it was told that no mortal or other can live knowing thus. We seek council from one higher than ourselves and he with the Emerant eye sees all things and none is hidden from his sable brow."

"I will not ask more than I have asked, for there are those who are supernal but loftier than I. If I am the one who is destined to furnish your boon then, let your fate be annulled."

"We seek only one petal from the healing flower called "The Old Are Young Again" and she will be raised unto life." Their words were final, and they did not speak further.

Bhelaribhus was silent for that name was sacred, that flower and no part of its root or otherwise ever left that land for, it was forbidden. A crumple came over his brow, then he sighed and added, "I was not to make haste for seldom can one such as who, loves the solitudes of the wilderness leave so soon but, I will make haste for your request and fit to foot my sky shoes." After the exquisite Therians had flown, Peridir stood still for a moment; and had a fleeting thought, [1]'Ye living ones, ye are fools indeed who do not know the ways of the wind and the unseen forces that govern the processes of Life'.

Then a strange thing happened. Around his feet an azuline glow started to form. He slowly walked on that and lifted a foot from the ground. Zoomorphic patterns of the same colour and glowing brightly, started encircling his body. Within moments, he had been lifted high above the trees. From his feet, 3 long, crimped, glowing lines, sped ahead of him and formed a zoomorphic arch in the sky, through which he passed. The light in the dark sky collapsed on itself and he was gone as if the darkness had seized him. The Ælves called that 'Aferian Nibala'.

---

[1] The Spoon River Anthology - Edgar Lee Maste

Riddles and Games, Play it in the Dark

Some 70 miles from where Bhelaribhus had departed, just beyond the Anana Zarvari or The Mouth of Dämmerung, two gnomes and a Dwarve were playing a game in the dark. They had met on a peculiar note for the Dwarve Belides, was looking for an Elferingewort which he knew was in the area. The two gnomes, Goombah and Goombahllum, were sitting on the outside of the Elferingewort and about to pluck them, as they were travelling on their way to Okana and in need of a tincture. The Dwarve was happy to find the circle of Daeges Eage, and on seeing that raucous, he became furious that the two gnomes were desecrating his quickest way home. The quarrel was quickly quelled by Goombah and Goombahllum when they suggested a fortune-telling rhyme, as they believed that the fun would result in wise direction.

They soon forgot their quarrel because Belides had made a fire without wood, and it burned brightly about 3 feet off the grass. Gnomes made fires that way because they didn't want the fire to scorch the grass. The obliging grasses, wet with evening dew, quickly thought of an idea to repay the trio so asked the Daeges Eage to open their eyes so that they could sing some sylvan lullabies. The Daeges Eage happily obliged because they were in an Elferingewort.

The gnomes spoke sonorously, and the Dwarve had a sweet, adenoidal voice but, they spoke quietly despite their excitement.

"I'd say we must begin with riddles first!" exclaimed Belides.

"And we would like to begin with fortune-telling rhymes!" exclaimed Goombah in return.

"Very well then!" replied the Dwarve. "After all, you have the numbers. I am solo. Let's begin."

"Yes, yes, yes! Dwarve Belides but, if you fail to complete a rhyme, then you will have to cook us a meal," insisted Goombah, as his father listened to the dark, as if something unusual was about. The dwarve's ears pricked backward but he was more interested in the food part, so he replied again, "Very well Master Goombah but, the same applies to you." So, they started with Belides;

Ones scrumping ones a feef

Belides   "Daisy, daisy, who shall pass?
                Who shall it be who will see the glass?
                Rock or stone,
                Flower and bone
                All are the same
                When the dwarves proclaim"

Goombah   "Gnomes know poems
                And ancient tomes
                Letters and numbers
                The keys to unlock such puzzling jumbles
                We don't need eyes to see the glass
                For *we* know the ways of the whispering grass"

Belides   "Fief or feef
                King or peasant
                Bird or bee
                Light or sound
                Mortal or God
                Who moves fastest? Ælve or Sidhe?"

Goombahllum   "The dead travel fastest
                The flowers outlastest
                The snag of the ghetto
                Can be uncleaved by a hoe
                Duirs and portals
                Encumbering to mortals"

Belides   "There is no death that eternal lives
                And by aeons, life death outlives
                It is a secret to say all things die
                But it is a lie to say all things live.
                By Weregild death by drops is flowing
                All unobserved, Eolas fiercely glowing.
                Which word means live
                But sounds like die?"

| Goombah | "I know this!
Though I don't know much;
The Ælves move fastest!
Speed and flight are their province.
Life or death is a sweeping question
They live not, neither do they die.
They chomp not,
They waste nothing!" |

| Belides | "Don't fade away
Leaves morning
Comes evening,
Yet never ever leaves. It rules the world
And binds them,
But always sets them free." |

| Goombah | "What bell alerts the Ælve
Kræfted by those who deeply delve,
Sweetly sings yet never rings,
Yet it does unlock Fates Wings?" |

"Goombah! Goombah! The rules are ancient, that is no reimfor but a riddle. Pah! You've changed the game and the cadence," Belides complained vehemently.

"Yes, yes! But you must admit, it's a pretty good one and it so dearly fell on me to say it," Goombah replied apologetically.

"Well then! Here is the answer,"

| Belides | "Elsimtumsbell alerts the Ælves
The Dwarves are they who deeply delve,
8 Beles of Avern guard it well,
Even the Dark this truth would tell." |

This went on for at least 3 hours with neither giving in to the other. Eventually, one of the gnomes floundered but, wanted another chance, for they were hungry and desired the flavour of Dwarve food. Dwarves were excellent cooks. Again, there was that strange, distant sound, almost inaudible, a kind of whistle, distant, high pitched and silvery. Goombah and Belides were so involved in their game that they did not notice it. Goombahllum on the other hand, listened closely and sat still, clutching the shoulder tags of his jacket.

For some time after that, there was nothing from that mysterious sound that bothered Goombahllum. Belides walked through the Elferingewort and returned shortly with pockets oozing, shoulder slung, and arm filled with food and drink fit for a king. As they sat down to that midnight feast, some birds were heard chirping somewhere in the trees, perhaps a restless chick snuggling up to its parent. A dark shadow with outstretched wings passed over without the rush of wing or chirp. It was a flying fox and there were several species of wild fruit trees around them.

"Hmmmm Master Dwarve!" said Goombahllum. "The breast is tastier than grapefruit." "Yes, Master Goombahllum, but of course! We dwarves love our fish and meat, especially our fish! As you gnomes love your fruit and veg," replied the Dwarve sarcastically.

"That's because we do not eat the things we love," replied Goombah. "But do you drink blood because it looks like wine?" said Belides mockingly.

"You are being quite silly now Master Dwarve."

"No! I am *not*!"

"Well, you are suggesting we eat meat because quite a few *look* like vegetables or fruit."

"But everyone knows gnomes won't eat the growing things, so to compensate, they eat meat and plenty of it. What we dwarves love about the Ælves is that they *do* eat vegetables and fruit and leave all the fish and meat for us. Especially the fish! They do it as a point of principal whereas I find gnomes on the point of eating somewhat hypocritical," replied the Dwarve, starting to homilize, crunching into the juicy, yellow, buttery corn.

The corners of his mouth and cheeks were filled with left over yellow spots and there was blue gleam from the butter on his face.

"You are being too strict in your opinion Master Dwarve. Those gnomes who live under the earth, the 'Amana', for extended periods of time, do not eat meat nor vegetables. Are they not better than both we Wynebau gnomes and you dwarves?"

Belides thought for a second, holding his potato, skewered through his knife. "I cannot say who is better of the 3 but, what I can say is 3 covers all!" Then the trio broke into laughter and continued till every morsel and drip was utterly ravished.

They sat quietly in the long grasses, under the homely fire, when Goombah said something random with a big burp.

"Walnut does look like a brain and celery like bone," this was followed by a long burp that disturbed the stillness of the night. Even the rebellious crickets were asleep.

There was a strange howl, like some animal or creature was in great pain. Goombahllum jumped to his feet, his sword drawn, he stood in bent body stance, and turned slowly as his keen eyes pierced the dark.

Goombah and Belides didn't waste any time and were up on their feet because, that time they heard it too. The 3 circled the fire with their backs toward it. The sound had gone but there was an uneasiness amongst the once carefree campers.

"Perhaps we should use Master Dwarve's Elferingewort!" exclaimed Goombahllum hastily.

"We shall do no such thing until we find out what that menacing sound is," replied the Dwarve sharply. "Hmmmm, perhaps on second thought, you are correct Belides. No use in dragging foul things into stately homes."

"Aye! Gnome Goombahllum, you have read my thoughts. Let's set a watch for the night. I shall go first."

"We would be better served if we were in the 'Tweenlight' now," complained Goombah glumly. "Oooooh! Goombah son of Goombahllum, Levende ord! You speak a safe truth."

Belides took the first watch; by magick he dimmed the flames of the fire somewhat, so they were less observable, while the gnomes slept. Belides stood like a brazen statue for an hour but, nothing happened. He looked over his shoulder, the gnomes were sound asleep so, he decided to walk a little way, trying to pry the dark open with his sharp eyes. He came upon a clearing. It wasn't very wide, and long grass grew there.

He walked over to it because he knew of that weald but, had never been there before. In the centre of that clearing were large rocks that stuck out of the ground in a semi-circle. The rocks were covered in soft, vibrant, green moss. It was so well disguised that, if one were to stand a little way off, one would never know it was there. There was an opening in the ground where the circles of rocks were not completely closed. It appeared unused. It was just big enough for a small person to pass through comfortably, a large person would have had trouble passing through it. When he knelt to inspect it, he noticed that there were steps made of the same rock, and that it led down somewhere.

The Dwarve looked around and suddenly all was quiet around him, even the insect sounds were gone, and the air felt oppressive and ancient. It came from the entrance. He looked around to see whether he was being spied upon but, that area was so isolated that the thought was sheer madness. He had left his walking stick with the gnomes and wished that he had taken it because it was made of red cedar and had a huge, uncut piece of Aqua Aura Quartz, set at the top end, and it could have provided light in the darkness. He stood pondering briefly in the dark but, drew away from the hole because a foul odour came from it. He then rushed back to wake the gnomes. When he arrived at the camp, he shook them vigorously, "Is it already such a time Master Dwarve? You shake us like those who set watchmen on the walls of great cities in times of despair," said Goombahllum, still half asleep.

"There is no despair, only more strangeness. Have you woken up yet Goombahllum? Goombah!" he shouted towards the other gnome who was still lying down. Belides set up the fire quickly and put the kettle onto it for some strong, warm drink that could wake the gnomes from their slumberous state.

Afterwards, when they sat up and sipped on the warm coffee, Belides relayed what he had discovered. The gnomes displayed no sign of fear and with their swords drawn, they set off to the spot that the Dwarve had come upon earlier. With sword drawn in one hand, and his lit staff in the other, he held the light into the entrance but, at that moment some menacing sound, as if someone was in great pain, came from its depths.

The trio sprang back, clutching onto each other. "Master Dwarve, you should lead the way," said Goombah with trepidation.

"Why must I lead the way now that we hear offending sounds? I suggest fir fer, let's play the illumination game in-ging-goga."

"I agree! That sounds fair," replied Goombah because that was a good game to establish who would go first.

They started by standing close, and Belides started as he was the one who suggested it.

"In-ging-goga – I-figi-noga-I-figi-anyone - In-ging-goga. Out!" said Belides to Goombahllum. He was very happy that he was kicked out of the game. He stood by and looked down into the darkness and listened for any further sounds that emanated from what seemed like a bottomless pit. In the end, it was Belides who had to go ahead of the two anyway. He pushed his way through. He didn't bother with the stick because the crystal set at the top of it might get damaged, and he loved it dearly. He descended the steps, and the other two followed close behind. Goombahllum being the eldest, walked last and kept looking behind him. They were careful because it was slippery and after a while, the steps descended into water, where they could not pass. Belides was unhappy about that because such a secret with such mystery, was hindered by water. He stood there with only a feint view of things as there was hardly any light. He shouted to hear for an echo but, that which returned, was pure evil mixed with calls for help.

He stood pondering for a moment, then spoke under his breath, "There are no fair things here, whatever was, is gone. Those calls are strange because I recognize the voice."

"Whose voice is it Master Dwarve?" asked Goombahllum.

The Dwarve would not answer so, Goombah asked in a more demanding voice, "Master Dwarve! Does some evil have your tongue?"

Belides cleared his throat and replied, "To me it sounded like Ulfheðin, and Ulfheðin never wandered without his brother, Ulfhamr. Although those two wander many places, they would never stumble in here without good purpose. The warning in my heart tells me that some evil has been done to them."

The older gnome scratched his head and said, "Hmmmm, I know those names, they are the mighty sons of Vinrúlfr, the most famousest of the Goombahlupes," (that was what the gnomes called the Wolvlingas).

"But Baba, what might such mighty formwandlers be doing down there?" asked Goombah. The Dwarve interjected for he had no time for idle talk and was certain that evil was about. "Goombahllum, who is the fastest of us, for we must warn the Paladins, it is imperative?"

"I dare say it is you Master Dwarve. For you know more secret duirs than we gnomes do."

"But you gnomes can move through the earth," replied the Dwarve quickly.

"Well said! Well said, Master Dwarve," replied Goombahllum contemplatively, as he rubbed his hair on his head, with one hand at a time.

"Then perhaps we shall call it even," added Goombah jokingly.

"Master Dwarve!" said Goombahllum forcefully.

"Who has boats and chariots but do not ride them?

Who has armour and weaponry but never display them?

They eat food that is sweet but, one never sees it.

They are from this Universe but not in it. Who Master Dwarve?

Riddle me that Master Belides?"

Belides sat down on a step and thought for a while. He felt that the gnome was a bit unfair to jump the riddle on him without warning but, he did not complain. After some time, the gnome became impatient. "Master Dwarve, one cannot take so long to answer. It is not part of the rules of the ancient game. Do you give up? And if so, you must stay and we will go,"

"There will be no such thing Goombahllum, just give me, give me a second!" Belides ran through the list in his head quietly. He knew that somewhere he had heard that one before but, it was a long time ago. He then started to name them out aloud, counting them off on his fingers.

"The Noldor,

The Sons of El,

The Woodland Ælves,

The Grey Ælves,

The Kayadir,

The Moriquendi,

The Paladins. . ."

There the gnome interjected, "The Paladins are no Ælves Master Dwarve, *you* know this. Please play the game fairly."

"Now you've spoilt my concentration. Will Alambana do?" he asked sarcastically. "There are no Alambana on Eridu Belides," replied Goombahllum emphatically. The Dwarve became agitated and continued, "If we continue this way we will be here all night gnome Goombahllum."

He started again;

"The Morpheuns,

The Aguane,

The Noldor,

The Woodland Ælves,

The Grey Ælves,

The Kayadir,

The Moriquendi,

The DevaDrana,

The Alambana,

The Aahlaelvi. . ." Then he stopped.

Then he shouted, "The Ælves of 1,000 000 Years! Yes! Yes! That is the answer."

"My, my, Master Dwarve, that took *you* nearly a million years," said Goombahllum. "Let's hope the next one goes quicker."

"Yes, so be it but now it's my turn!" exclaimed Belides.

"Round she is, yet flat as a board

Chantry of the Lupine Beles.

Jewel on black velvet, Pearl in the sea

Unchanged but ever changing, eternally."

"The moon!" replied Goombahllum deepening his voice, then continued; "What flies in the sky but has no wings?

What perches on the mountain tops but has no talons?

What flies forever and never settles down?

Riddle me that Master Belides?"

"Clouds!" replied the Dwarve quickly.

"A harvest sown and reaped on the same day

In an unploughed field,

Which increases without growing,

Remains whole though it is eaten

Within and without,

Is useless and yet the staple of mortals."

"A war!" replied Goombahllum sadly and went on;

"Many lives have I.

Kind enough to warm the skin,

Light enough to caress the sky,

Far enough to instil longing,

Hot enough to crack Mountains."

"Fire." said Belides

"Wings have we, we are no birds,

Fire within, stronger than volcanoes,

Wise are we, ancient of days,

We are not creations, created we have,

What are we?"

Goombahllum thought for a moment, for it was the first time that Belides asked such a difficult one. Goombah chimed in and shouted, "Let me answer Baba! After all we are father and son, it should count as one voice."

"I will show kindness to the gnomes," replied Belides.

"Go ahead Goombah," encouraged Goombahllum for he still did not know the answer. "But it's obvious father, Dragons."

Goombahllum broke out in laughter and jumped straight into the next riddle.

"Touching one, yet holding two, it is a one-link chain binding those who keep words true,'til death rent it in twain. What is it?" Belides quickly replied: "A nuptial ring."

"One tooth to bite,
he's the foe of trees.
One tooth to fight,
as all dwarves know.
What is it?"
"An axe," replied Goombahllum with a smile.

"What knocks at your door but has no hands?
What dances in the wind and sings but has no voice?
Is quiet when the wind is asleep but still delights?"
Riddle me this Master Dwarve?"

Belides sat with his chin resting on his fingers and thought, his face a caricature of expression. The Dwarve was aware that if he got that one wrong, that he would stay. He preferred it but, he believed he would be more vigilant than the gnomes. On the other hand, if he got all 3 correct it would probably be okay because the Ælves would act quicker if a Dwarve was the messenger. He wanted to get to the answer for pride's sake, for riddle's sake, for the sake of the ancient game.

'But that is a hard one' he thought to himself and shook his head.

"I give up Master Gnome. Aye, it was a hard one, and my ken was tested." "All's right Master Dwarve, the answer is a chime. A chime! A wind chai-ime," replied the gnome, content with himself as he pushed his thumbs behind his breeches.

So Belides had to stay behind and keep watch while the gnomes set out towards Palador. The gnomes went by a secret way only known to them, as gnomes didn't tell in tales of those pursuits but, soon Goombahllum and his son popped out from a Sidhe that was one too soon as, they found themselves not at Palador but surrounded by Lycurgus and Eriol, with their sharp, shining blades bearing down on them. "What are you doing in these parts, wandering in the dark?" asked Lycurgus in a gruff voice. Lycurgus and Eriol appeared so suddenly that the gnomes were at first at a loss for words and stood there shuddering. "Speak gnomes! Or state your names?"

urged the Ælve. Then the two spoke simultaneously, "I-I am-am Goombah-Goombahllum, son, father of Goombahllum-Goombah." Eriol moved in closer, stood towering before them, and said in a deepened voice, "Which is it? Father or son, Goombah or Goombahllum?" He stood with his arms folded and waited for a reply. "Well, I am Goombahllum and this here be my son Goombah, we are sent with an urgent message to Palador, to bring it to the great Ælve Bele and the great Vinrúlfr, the most famousest of the Goombahghwers."

"What is your business with the great Goombahlupes, Goombahllum?" asked the Ælve even sterner. His form seemed to get taller as awesome light lit up the weald around them. "I'm so fragile that when you say my name you may break me," replied the elder gnome.

"This gnome speaks in riddles my Bele," said Vinrúlfr.

"Yes, perhaps he refers to silence or perhaps he keeps company with dwarves. Is it not Goombahllum? Tell us the truth of the matter now, or things will end dire for you."

"The Dwarve Belides sent us; we also come of our own accord for a terrible thing we think has befallen the two brothers. . ."

Goombahllum did not have time to complete his tale for immediately it felt like the earth beneath them shook and the trees cowered and the long, green grassed bent as Lycurgus skin-changed into a great angry Werewolve. So great was his anger that he appeared taller than usual, which was already very large.

"Do not waste our time, lead us to the Dwarve!"

Immediately 3 more Ælves appeared out of the dark; Furhōdir, who was a lissom Ælfennes with a face fair as the stars, and besides her stood El Elion and Hudōrdir.

Furhōdir led them away quickly, for she knew the secret ways of the weald and was swift as a Hazelwitch and gentle like the dander from an Ancient Lime.

Belides became impatient; he heard more groans and pangs of agony ascending from the dark depths so, he proceeded slowly downwards. When he reached the water, he knew for sure he could not go further. He had no choice but to use the light from the crystal on his staff; he whispered some dwarvish over the Eastlea; "Lu laraak, lu teema nuru, lu koru," a bright, sparkling blue and gold chatoyance played over the stone that spiralled down the staff to his hand; *that* cast light even further. The water before him stretched on for miles and miles or so it seemed in the gloaming light. He would have to swim across or find a coracle but there was none floating around. He spoke in his head to himself and wondered how such a place could exist, as he was only about 600 or 700 meters below the surface where he had entered. After all, he was a Dwarve, and dwarves should know about such places in the deeps of Dhara. He did not recognize the smell of the place either, for dwarves and gnomes could remember any smell and could locate any forgotten place by it alone. In any case, he had become hungry from all the excitement, so he sat on the steps and took out some left overs from their meal and peered out across the water. In the low light, the silence was unnerving, and he could feel that place was old, very old. As he looked in the distance and across the water, he thought that he had seen a light-green glow just beneath the surface. As he sat there, a certain riddle came to mind; 'The more that there is, the less that you see. Squint all you wish when surrounded by me.' Belides jumped up afterwards and drew his sword for, he heard the shuffling of feet behind him. He quickly returned it to its sheath and laughed, most relieved, for it was the Ælves. Lycurgus was himself again because if he were in the Werewolve shape, he would not fit through the narrow entrance. Again, the sounds were heard coming from across the water, and that time it was louder. Amongst the Wolvlingas came a familiar sense.

"They are in great pain Bele Eriol, we must go, but how shall we cross the waters, they seem foul to me."

"No need to worry 'formwandler', it is no obstacle," replied Hudōrdir, "I have been sent for a purpose" his voice was smooth, soft and melodious, for his name meant 'Ælve of the water' and he had perfect equilibrium with it. He pushed forward and bent down, caressing the surface of the dark water with his pale, slender fingers, a path opened ahead of them. "Those who have certitude follow me," he said softly and led the way. The Dwarve walked next to him because he carried the light. As Hudōrdir walked next to Belides, he noticed some yellow dust on the Dwarve's shoulders and said softly in a mischievous tone, "Have you still been gathering fair-cheeked Flōra's yellow daisies?" The Dwarve looked up at the Ælve, his eyes danced, and he replied, "Yes! Tis true, it is how the two gnomes and I stumbled into each other." The gnomes were walking directly behind Eriol and listened to the conversation.

"We have aways to go, do regale the tale Belides," encouraged Hudōrdir. Furhōdir and El Elion walked side by side; their eyes pierced the dark, for the dark to Ælves was as bright as daylight. Walking directly behind them came Vinrúlfr, anxious but vigilant. He had changed again into Werewolve shape but, done so quietly that time as not to arouse the enemy of their approach. It was much more spacious now than before. So, the Dwarve began by retelling in whispered tones, all the events that led up to the arrival of the company of Ælves, while he sat on the dank steps. "It is a good thing you Ælves are so graithly," ended Belides rather cheerfully. "And this place Master Dwarve is very dowly, your light makes the passage more bearable," replied Hudōrdir. As they proceeded, Hudōrdir drew the water closer with his gaze, for he had 'the streaming light from his eyes'. As they proceeded forward the water parted before them. He thought that was a safer option so, he also closed the path behind them, so that the group moved in a clear, continuous, circular space, devoid of any water. The walls of water were not so tall as to impede their view of what was going on ahead or behind them.

After Hudōrdir had done that, the streaming from his eyes diminished, that was called 'Ažididan'. To the gnomes, the whole affair was somewhat overwhelming for, they were not use to so much water around them. They were of the earth, or from under it, after all. Hudōrdir noticed that a light was approaching in the water. The light seemed to draw closer and closer. The Dwarve had noticed it before and said to Hudōrdir, "I have seen it too, before you lot came upon me. Is it friend or foe? You Ælves have a keen sense on these matters." The Ælve did not reply as he was deep in thought, and his eyes looked straight ahead. Belides thought that the Ælve was up to something in his head, for some of the Ælve-kind could be in one place in body but, simultaneously in another place 'spirit body'. His curiosity overtook the slight trepidation, and he reminded himself; 'this could be a magickal creature, it may even be some Deva from the deeps.'

Eventually, when the light reached them, it grew brighter, and there beneath the surface was something that looked like a great, flying creature with large wings. "It must be the size of a house!" thought the Dwarve aloud. Each one heard a voice saying; "I am Iuvare." It was soft, like a thought, and it was in their heads. The creature stayed only for a moment then it returned from where it came. Hudōrdir suddenly stopped in his tracks, something was wrong. He spoke without looking around, "Furhōdir and El Elion you must return. Alert those at Vel Samoda and Vel Domas, take the gnomes with you." His voice was still soft but now, there was a tone of authority as he spoke. Furhōdir came beside him, "Why should we go back? Send the gnomes or the Dwarve. We are better warriors and you sense something is amiss. I *know* it, for the water told you so."

"I think it best that you go to warn the others," replied Hudōrdir. Furhōdir's beautiful, long hair was suspended in the air around her head as if in some place devoid of gravity, it moved hypnotically up and down, up and down in waves, and a pale, blue light glowed about them. When she looked at Hudōrdir, her eyes gave off a heated vapour, for she was angry.

"Shall I make prabartanā over you?" she asked him with a stern deep voice. "Let Bele Eriol make the decision, after all, he is the leader of this company," replied Hudōrdir standing aside.

"There will be no need for prabartanā my lady Furhōdir," he said in a commanding voice. Vinrúlfr had become restless; the others knew that if he wanted to in his current state, he could very well swim the distance even if it meant the end of his life, the Dwarve and the two gnomes spoke to each other in grumbling tones. Eriol spoke again, now in a more soothing voice, "Furhōdir go with Hudōrdir. Go and observe then come back, do nothing untoward no matter what you find." He touched Vinrúlfr on the shoulder and said, "Vinrúlfr! Remain here with the others; I shall go to warn those at Vel Samoda and Vel Domas, for I am quickest. This matter is settled."

"You only command thus for you already know the outcome," grumbled Vinrúlfr in his deep, growling voice. "I wish that I had more time with my sons," he went on. "Time?" asked Eriol as if it were of no consequence. "The only reason for time in this world is so that everything doesn't happen at once, and mortal wits don't trickle from their auricles."

"Easy for an Ælve to say," replied one of the gnomes under his breath but Eriol heard what he said. "To us, time is a stream but, for the Ælves time is an ocean, all happening in a single moment," said Vinrúlfr again.

"Orr purhaps hramsa," replied the Dwarve sarcastically.

"Master Dwarve means unions, doesn't he Baba?" said Goombah.

"Yes, tis a union to Ælves," came the soft reply from Furhōdir.

"Enough of these words," replied the Ælve as he opened a further passage through the waters with the touch of his slender fingers.

Furhōdir led the way as Hudōrdir followed; Eriol closed the way again between them and the two Ælves. In a moment, Eriol had gone too, slipped as it were, through the cracks of matter and time.

Eriol stood in the rain and looked up at the Moon overpassed by clouds. He covered his head of long hair with his hood and thought only for a moment to himself; 'I have heard rumours of war, I have seen Dazottara pass in every age and now we go to war again. How great a matter a little fire kindleth?'

As he strode off into the dark, he cast a 'sphere field' around him so the rain had no effect on him. He had only stridden for half a mile when he came to a bowl of which the entire interior and the rim was surrounded by young oak trees. It was called the 'Wood of the Lark' or as the Paladins called it 'Dar Chakavak'. He swiftly descended it, as if by a strange glide over the wet grasses, yet still the damp nits responded. At the bottom the dell it opened into a narrow slit, enough only for a person stepping sideways to pass. He moved quickly and nimbly like a dove in flight, until he reached a larger chamber with walls of graceful sandstone which seemed to have been swept into marvellous, sinuous chambers through the ages. There were two reliefs cut into the sandstone of oak trees so that they created a duir. One was silver, the other red. He approached it graciously, removed his hood and placed his hands on either side of the duir on each oak and spoke, "Silver oak and red oak! Derrybawn and Dair Dearg open now the way." The trees illuminated and glittered beautifully in red and silver, like the scintillations of pearls. They seemed to come forth out of the sandstone wall so that a Le Badhaprapta formed. To the Eldiĕni eye it would have seemed like an interminable eldritch dark, but to the eyes of the Ælve, its illumination was 10 000 times brighter than a Sun and like planturous rhapsodies.

Then came gentle replies in unison from the trees;

"When the rains fall on Eriol's cloak,
And the oaks illume best,
The Wulfmaer shall perish. The Black Scucca
Shall not quail before their deaths

> *But when gnome and warve comes riddling,*
> *And Dazottara dwines on the waned west*
> *The oaks shall part on Eriol's request,*
> *And the lark sings in its high nyth. . ."*

"Enter Mhor-Righ!" so Eriol entered. As Eriol entered and the darkness shut behind him, he heard the call of the lark under the falling rain. Eriol emerged an instant later, on the slopes of Vel Samoda through 9 great, interlinked arches. The colours on the interior remain vivid despite the many ages that had passed. The golden background was pierced with streaks of spring green, ivory, azure blue and red, and the pillars are made of Lapis Lazuli. The overlapping, curved, coffered ceilings were of Azurite, with golden mosaics of the woodlands, and ball flowers in the shape of tulips. He only looked at those briefly then stepped out. Its exterior was laden with heavy moss. It was raining and the slopes were covered in oak, ash, alder, birch, elm, hazel, hawthorn, willow and yew. They stood in rows, spread out from each arch. Larger oaks stood tall. They grew for eons and it was said that they could not be scorched and that the larger oaks come from the Realm of Daurtearmann; of which Eriol hailed. As he walked past one of those oaks, he pinched off a glittering, golden acorn, and slipped it between his lips. Eventually that acorn would melt. For an instant as the acorn melted on his tongue, he dreamt of the Elysian Fields on Hesperus, where a central Great Oak resided. It was said that the Great Oak bore 9 hundred bushels of acorns thrice a year, as well as large, red apples that were sweet as honey.

Deep in the underground places of the world, where the dank and wet slithered, and where the foul, throated frogs quawrked and Xul-Kappu scrithered and flew. A large arch was lit by bright light; shadow and flame could be seen cavorting on the inner walls and on the outer arch on either side, clung two Wezadrachs above two burning torches. They were on guard. Grey slime dripped from their outstretched wings. One of the Wezadrachs cocked its thorny, hairy head, and its pitch-black eyes looked in the direction of the two approaching Ælves. It made some screeching sound, inaudible to human ear but the Ælves heard every thought. The second one looked up immediately, and stood up on its legs, talons curled, mouth foaming for, of all the dark creatures spawned by the thoughts of billions, no creature was more vexing than a Wezadrach. It fed on anger and ambition was its gallish nourishment. They are altogether malevolent creatures. One skittered for they had sensed light, and above all things, the Ælves were light. One took to the air towards Furhōdir and Hudōrdir but, Hudōrdir had set himself and the Ælfennes in their separate Vesi-viittas. Cold below what any creature could endure, or the vision of the Wezadrachs to penetrate. The Wezadrachs had excellent sight but couldn't see through Vesi-viittas. The twisted creature hovered around the sphere at a safe distance, as cold evaporated from the surface of the watery sphere and tried to ascertain what it was. Those creatures hated the cold. Soon afterward, the Wezadrach that skittered away came fluttering back with two, armed Mush-dagur. The Ælves simply called them 'Enealal or Alal' meaning 'destroyers'. Those Alal stood eight feet tall, broad hipped and broad shouldered, with a mass of contorted muscle, and were armed with erlance. There was only one way that they could have obtained the erlance. they stole it from Lycurgus's sons. Their heads were round and scaley, with broad noses to take in plenty of oxygen. Their apparel was a type of fustanella or kilt around the waist, and the sides and hems were in strands. The strands were not of cloth, no, they were living, cavorting, thick serpents, that hissed and spat. The Alal strode forward looking left and right. They saw the Vesi-viittas but, they were uncertain what it was they were looking at. The scales on their torsos were smooth and that indicated that they were young Mush-dagur. The serpents that cavorted and gambolled, were on edge, their heads were cocked backwards so that their hoods were opened wide and redolent. Even they had more sense than those Mush-dagur. "Nomm-Os! Nomm-Os!" which meant, 'I am OS' they called out toward the veiled Ælves and demanded that the Ælves introduce themselves. Furhōdir's vesi-viitta glided forwarded towards them. A slender, pale blue, plasmic tendril extended forward past the Alal and through the arched entrance. What Furhōdir saw inside caused her to recoil, for Ulfheðin and Ulfhamr were impaled through the ankles and wrists; they were in their wolv form but, they were near death. A metallic, electrical noose hung around their necks and caused great shock to their beings, and standing before them was a tall Melchizedeck. The Melchizedeck, a highly intelligent being was not blind to the veil of the Ælves, so it spun around, startled by the magnetic energy of the Ælves. The wing talons at the end of its great wings pierced the flesh of the two brothers, impaling them further through the heart. There was a great cry of anguish and the Melchizedeck spoke clearly and said, "You are too late!" but there was no physical response from the Ælves. This angered the Wezadrachs. The Alal moved forward to strike because they were then well aware that their enemy was present but, Furhōdir and Hudōrdir were already gone. The vesi-viitta collapsed with a horrible splash and put out the terrible, roaring fire and the lot of virulence, were left in darkness. The Melchizedeck pressed a strange, square block in the stone wall and it slid open, through it he dragged his heavy form, his minions following and as the heavy wall slid closed with a thud, it crushed one of the Wezadrachs. A heavy, foul, impregnable stench filled the chamber.

Ulfhamr the elder of the two brothers, turned to his sibling, who had already exhaled his last breath and said, "Sometimes those who endure are hopeless but, you have not endured my brother, you pass now out of the Halls of Thēríon and to Avrek you Ascend."

Not nearly an instant had passed when Furhōdir and Hudōrdir returned with Ulfhamr, the gnomes and Belides. El Elion did not follow, he remained on guard. Ulfhamr was still breathing. Quickly Hudōrdir set Belides to work to unchain and uncuff Ulfhamr. Vinrúlfr was angry, he was vexed at the sight of his son. and let out a great growl, which shook the walls of the cavern. Dust dropped from the ceiling. He settled down again for he knew better. For a moment the Ælves allowed him to vent, and beside him, the gnomes wept. The Dwarve was quick, Ulfhamr was unchained and Vinrúlfr took his son into his great, strong arms and laid him on the cold floor. Furhōdir hailed El Elion so that he could provide light. In a clear voice he softly said, "Avra k'davra. Avra k'davra. Avra k'davra!". Four spheres of light manifested in the corners of the cavern, so that they could have pure light, the stench of the Wezadrach vanished. Vinrúlfr shapeshifted back as Lycurgus and looked down at his son, breathing in agony. Ulfhamr could not shapeshift while he was suffering. Lycurgus did not ask after Ulfheðin, for he knew that he had passed forward to Avrek and that pleased him well. He did not think in his heart that he would pass to the Dim World.

Belides was tampering at the door that the Melchizedeck had used, while the two Ælves had suspended Ulfhamr's body on a bed of soft, glittering oak leaves, that they had eljured.

"Belides!" called Furhōdir. "Don't mind yourself about reptilian duirs. They shall receive their fate." Belides stamped the wall in anger and pulled himself away. Already the Ælves and Lycurgus were passing through a duir that Eriol had eljured for, her connection to the Realm of Trees was enormous.

The gnomes waited till Belides came to it, and followed after him. so as they departed, the Ælve lights continued to burn and it would never go out, the dark dank places of the world once again left alone by itself to slumber in the pleasant light of the Ælves that forever kindles.

Vel Samoda

—※—

Vel Samoda was the furthest of the two watch towers of Palador and stood close to Skallagrimmr. The tower was perched on top of a hill (1,150feet(350 m)) and on top of the hill, stood a tree with a height of 4000ft (1219.2m) and a diameter of 500m. It was the highest natural structure on Eridu other than mountains. The tree calcified over millennia from when the First Ones arrived on Eridu. Ravished by the passage of time, it no longer had branches. From the base, a circular staircase etched into the rock gripped the outer walls and went around in 6 spirals. Up on that staircase were 12 dwellings. The spiral staircase ran through each abode. It was a wonder of the world.

The hill on which Vel Samoda stood had no dwellings on it and it was made of solid rock and covered in thick moss. From that soft, thick wonderment grew myriads of harlequin flowers, also known as 'Wandflower'. They stood tall and had open star-shaped white, orange, lavender, yellow or red flowers, often centred with contrasting, symmetrical patterns. Like the spiral staircase, those flowers circled the mound in the same way, beginning with white and ending in red profusion around the base of the calcified tower. It was told in places where strangers had met Ponkie that each 1st of Earrach, many swarms of bees come to the harlequin flowers on some Elvysshe air, and feasted there for the day. Before twilight, the bees entered the large, arched entrance to drink from the River Purat that flowed through the Ayvān, and then departed. After having slaked their thirst, the waters of the Purat remained sweet for 9 months of the year.

One could only access the tower from within the mound. Eriol walked to the entrance where twelve guards changed shifts every hour. There were two guards at the arched entrance at all times, while the other ten marched night and day, around the entire mound. It created a circle of sparkling light as colourful as the harlequin flowers growing on the mound, only more splendid to the eye. That was called the 'Path of Olwen'. At night, one could see the path which their effortless footfall had created over time.

An Ælfennes of Vel Samoda

He entered the large arch into the Ayvān, a hall where the Ælves received guests. It was largely an empty space as far as appearances went, except for 'the great stream' for, that was what Purat meant. From the inside, steps led out and up to the first dwelling; there were twelve of those set upon that spiral staircase called the 'Stairway of Tiemugara' and it was enough to make one giddy. The stairs normally went up to the front door of each dwelling, sometimes 3 stories and other times two or one. Some dwellings were tall and narrow, while others were tiered.

The stairs escaped onward out of the back door, higher and higher, passing through each dwelling. Why the Ælves climbed every step, (from bottom to top, a count of plus minus 3470.35 stairs) to whatever address they were heading to, no one knew, for it would have been easier for them to fly up, or pertessered upward as was their custom. Perhaps that was their way of doing things 'normal'. Few, if any mortals came there, Kings usually, and Princes making application for protection. Every visitor had to be escorted by the Ælves, so then no one really knew how to get to Vel Samoda by themselves except Ponkie. If anyone tried to force the information out of Ponkie, it would have been futile, because he seldom travelled alone. Though he appeared alone to the mortal eye, it was a grave error if anyone tried to harm him. Most of those who visited for official business on rare occasions, feared for their lives when they ascended the narrow, spiral staircase without any balustrades or hand rails. Ofcourse, what did the Ælves need hand rails for?

The place was a phenomenon with its Gutþiuda architecture, long lace eau-de-nil lichens hung like wraiths from the staircase, and from underneath the hulkish corbels. Four hand-built arches supported the structure, and always appeared in atmospheric, seasonal garb. Impressive gargoyles perched along the roofs, and battlements of the buildings formed of Lilūgur or commonly called 'Fáerië Wand Quartz'. Their glittering eyes set with red jasper looked down on passers-by, enough to give the ignorant the 'heebie-jeebies'. Each door was set in a pointed arch, flying buttress were made of ancient marble and ornate, vaulted ceilings supported Gutþiuda window frames. The homes felt light and airy.

When Bele Eriol arrived at the 3rd Kuhmaskan on the Tiemugara, he took a wooden plinth from a round, wooden holder with a fire Rune engraved into the wood. He blew over the tip and a little flame started at its end. With that, he lit a Napa-Tu which slid from a beautiful Dodecagon spinel. Each time someone touched it, one of the Napa-Tu would slide onto the suspended thread that hung under the eaves of the Kuhmaskan. The Napa-Tu started burning and bobbed its way along the filament. That fire crystal was heavy and very flammable, and about 3inches long and a centimetre in diameter.

It was beautiful to behold, it was so very, very Ælvish. The Napa-Tu did not just burn one colour but varying hues, dependent on which Ælve lit it, so that under the eaves there were always those Fáerië lights bobbing and burning. That custom was always performed at Kuhmaskan 3, 6 and 9. Bele Eriol inhaled the fragrance and tranquillity of the Andemarian Ælves. At one of its windows was a dark and furtive Ælfennes, looking upward toward her distant realm, in the sea of stars. At the 6th Kuhmaskan, Eriol passed several Embarah; beautiful they were, brave and lissom Elfenna warriors who knew nothing of fear and who took instruction from Hyperion. They softly acknowledged him with their irisian eyes but did not say a word, a kind of gesture that said, 'we are above temporalities'. Round and round, pass the 9th Kuhmaskan, where some Norlündir resided when visiting Eridu. Tall, long, bleak-haired, with their opal complexions, unadorned except for the fragrance of the North Sea of Hesperus, for the Norlündir were the gem of that sea.

Up he climbed the crystal stairs, still, quiet, gliding through the doors and over the floors of the Kuhmaskans. And in some Kuhmaskans the only sound that could be heard, were like soft sighs of great, passing stars.

At last, the dark figure came to the 12th Kuhmaskan. He remained outside its door and listened to a distant nightingale. He listened closely for that was called 'Hazār-āvā', 'singing a thousand songs'. He looked far down below at the glittering Path of Olwen, for Ælves could see it best. He entered the Kuhmaskan; it was a slender four-story edifice. Eriol ascended the spiral staircase within the interior. There was a door unlike the others, facing east towards the rising Sun. Out that door, the staircase continued to the adjacent building's roof which was further connected to another set of stairs. There one entered the door of the castle. Its ancient ramparts boasted two tall turrets, one was especially peculiar, for above it was a large nest which looked very elmy for, it did not seem to be constructed of old twigs and branches but, of live Wych Elm, vibrant and green with foliage carefully kræfted round and round by the great eagle of the south named 'Silvaearn'. Huhuk came there also from time to time, from far, fabled lands with messages or presages. But Urinšeg never came. For a time, Eriol looked out at the dark night, then as if disturbed by a pressing thought, as a shadow passed over him, he raised his left arm. That was all that was required.

Several of the Chādor Tamaashaa Kardan marching on the ramparts were aware that Bele Eriol had arrived. At the precise moment that he set foot over the Path of Olwen, everyone at Vel Samoda, even those asleep, knew of his presence. With the raising of his arm, a long haunting and tuneful whistle could be heard from on top of the ramparts, more beautiful than a whistling Hursagga Thrush. A sudden gust of wind pressed down on the castle and rampart walls, for Silvaearn spread her great wings and rose up and up and up. A flood of waking, sleeping powers came forth from their couches, Ælve and Elfenna knew that it was no harbouring dream, but the roar of sacred Pinions, summoned by the whistle of Etana. Silvaearn kept ascending yet, her gaze never left the Amala Vartula, beautiful living beings in the shape of crystals, that radiated in dark-blue or green. Silvaearn ascended higher till she was out of sight. Her bright, golden eyes and her glittering lumes gave her elevated secret away, for the purpose of her ascension into the skies was thus; the glow of the Amala Vartula were caught in her eyes. In turn, it reflected over many miles, like a great prism of boreal light, right to Vel Domas, Zamm, Il-Kur-Ngis, from eastern and central Drakensberg to Nilam Hesperiis to Marga in Ninfa, even unto the crystalline vision of Urinšeg at Jinbōchō.

And so, in little taverns or busy streets, perhaps on a clear night while shepherds guided their flocks, or in serene rivers flowing to the palaces of the sea, a Nymph or sozzled vagabond, to the fluttering eyelashes of a dear in the weald, or the susurration of many swallows, all saw the many lights that beamed and crossed the skies. Many saw and few understood but, from that night onward, that day was known as the 'Night of the Spindle Lights' throughout Eridu. Over the following few weeks, those lights withdrew into the Ākāśa, and for the most part, were never seen again.

The 'Night of the Spindle Lights' was not called so by *those* who knew, to them that meant the 'Night of the 1st Watch' had come.

Döppievölle Inn

———❦———

O ne of the Ælvysshe qualities of those staying in Béth-Élam, was to be completely oblivious to anything going on around the world (of course no one troubled themselves to pay any attention to those people except the Eternal Powers, which was often!) but, for the strange fate that someone, there was always someone, strayed into or out of Döppievölle Inn, who could be jolted into sobriety by an anomaly, a divergence, an astrologic happenstance and, so by morning or evening, everyone in Béth-Élam knew about it and they would talk about it, for the following month until all faded away within their minds. . .

The Powers Supernal knew of the le Badhaprapta that lay in Béth-Élam but, that particular night, and for some contrary reason, Wasseling Broadbottle was sober. Not only was he sober but, he was walking under the myriad blinters of the stars and looked towards the heavens. He stopped opposite the gate of the No 31415, took his hands out of his pockets, supported one elbow in the palm of his left hand and rested his chin upon the other hand. He gazed in absolute amazement at the passing Spindle Lights. He did not move. Only his mouth was agog and the sound that came from it, sounded like, "Everyone! Everybody! Everywhen! Everywhen!"

Then, from sheer jubilation, he changed dialect and went on, "Pawb! Pawb!" but of course, it all meant the same thing. Folk came out of their homes in their nightgowns and nightcaps, and those folk who excreted from Döppievölle Inn with 'nightcap' in hand, even the lowly folk from the wonty-tumps peered up from the field in which Stari grazed. Mrs Underhill rushed out broomstick in hand. She cantered down the steps and out of the gate, and on seeing Wasseling Broadbottle she exclaimed, "Wasseling Broadbottle, smeug eow dagga?" She was very upset, and although that was a question, it did not sound like one. The situation was rare. Of course Wasseling Broadbottle was sober, as sober as the Endymion climate. He pointed up towards the canopy of heaven and in unison everyone said, "Aaaah!"

No one returned to bed that night. The children played as if it were day and the rest filled Döppievölle Inn. So bursting was it, that folk lined the walls, even those who didn't drink strong ale before twilight were there, and some from Élles arrived.

". . .an ill omen it is. . ." someone superstitious remarked "a happy limpidity me says," replied Ummia Blackbouredust.

Mrs Underhill came with eight pints of beer for the table and as she stomped them down, froth spilt over the sides of the glass, and she remarked, "Yes Ummia Blackbouredust! It is a limpidity but, it is also an omen for dark folk wandering about." She straightened her back, hand on her hips, looked around the place, then said again as she walked away, ". . .the tolling of bells — a terrible war is coming. . ."

"What was that she said?" asked Ummia. A Jabberwocky who sat at the table, an old man with long, grey hair, replied after removing his silver ear trumpet from his ear, exchanged it between his fingers for a long pipe and his was particularly long, two feet at least. The folk used a metonym for him, 'Long-pipe Jabberwocky', "The tolling of bells . . . a terrible war is coming!" he shouted.

"War! War! Wha-er?" asked a visitor from Élles. An older fellow, all crooked and croom, his face similar to that of a Magi. "I've been to Ninfa just recently and I heard no tales of war."

Ummia shook his head from side to side, took a deep, slow gulp of ale and ran his fingers through his thick, black hair.

"Sight before hearsay." He replied. 'Long-pipe Jabberwocky' puffed away. Ummia looked over his shoulder then added, "The testimony of one eyewitness is worth more than the hearsay of a hundred. And I dare-say, there is an eyewitness or two in Béth-Élam." He looked over his shoulder again then said, "I have been in Béth-Élam a long time and I still can't figure it out . . . who it is."

After that he didn't say another word till dawn. Instead, he chose to sing, for he had a choral voice and was a distinguished player of the Pezala;

> *Make me a harp of willow wood*
> *And I will sing a song serene*
> *Haloo'ed a stranger screamed*
> *In the dead of night.*
> *We saw the searing Ælvysshe beams*
> *Lilt of light pellucid streams*
> *It made for inns of babbling gossip*
> *Mellish eves for mortal cosset.*
>
> *The fire is roaring,*
> *Legends a'lore-ing*
> *The ale is flowing under hill,*
> *Klink and clank, kith of tapster fill.*
>
> *Hear us sing in the dead of night;*
> *Sing, sung songs tween reverberate hills,*
> *Cantons contend of love or life,*
> *Blithe children cleave to blintering stars.*

Dwarve and Ælve, Drover, Earer,
Fish Fag and Gabeler
Many strangers strut, Most come to rest
Between Béth-Élam and Evermore.

We are but simple folks
Though we 'skinner' and tell of Ælvish cloaks
We're just keepers of the garden gate
Perhaps there is one, peerless of late.
Some say it's a thing of omens clear,
Some say our world may disappear;
I put my fealty in a souvenir,
Our fates in the hand of the triumvir.

We lose ourselves in drink and cheer,
Friends and songs to quell our fear.
Far away from dungeons cold,
Blissful, without a quest for ill hoarded gold.

Make me a willow Skeppa at Béth-Élams gate,
Hawk and the thrush are never late.
Honey requites bitter futility
Seven Baile, all alike in dignity.

Make me a harp of Willow wood
And I will sing a song serene
Haloo'ed a stranger screamed
In the dead of night.

In Béth-Élam that night, other than the anomaly of the 'Spindle Lights' or that Wasseling Broadbottle was sober one night of 365 nights in 8816, the charm and wonder was that the whole village, man, woman and child, including Stari grazing in the field, were awake even unto the twitter light of the following day.

The Night of the Spindle Lights

M r Fuhrmann stood next to Jaddamiah and looked down the road, from the nothingness came gentle, echoing voices, "Fare-well! Fa. . .re. . .well! Farewell Jaddamiah!" It sounded so melodious that Jaddamiah fell, and sank down flat on the ground. He looked at the flowers and its fragrance permeated all around him.

"Well! That was some glaumerie. It makes me quite hungry. Alack! I cannot help myself, each time they disappear I feel sad. Alack."

Mr Fuhrmann touched Jaddamiah on the shoulder and said again, "Come friend. It's time for a hearty meal."

Jaddamiah tore himself from his earthy seat, and got up mumbling as he walked after Mr Fuhrmann, "Before this, I was blind, I was senseless. Now. . .have seen, but. . .my mind's memory. . .is feeble to recall . . . such splendour." he said that stuttering again. He noticed that it was the first time that he had stuttered since he had left home. He plonked himself beside the fire which Mr Fuhrmann had up and crackling in no time. Jaddamiah lay outstretched before the fire, with his long legs crossed over at the ankles. His hands were folded over his tummy and his head rested on a rock which he had turned into a pillow; something which Lemayian Abathwa had taught him.

He had found a squarish rock lying near their new camp sight, and knocked off some pieces with the hilt of his sword. He was smoking his vamzi and balanced the long stem between his lips. It was uncomfortable but, he was too cosy to hold it with his hand. His chest was wrapped up in his special pashmina. As he lay contemplating, the aroma of bacon wafted above the sweet smell of his vamzi. A verse came to mind called 'The Meat Song';

> *Please to meat you!*
> *Please to meat you!*
> *I ham stopping,*
> *I ham stopping,*
> *For a lupper or supper, when I'm weary or I'm hungry.*
> *We will fish for a recipe*

We will fish for the remedy
For the meat that we need
ease our taste buds with some mead.
How far will we go? Through the snow all and sundry.
*For the * Skeet from the Tweed*
is our dietary creed
We warn you with a sigh
that the steaks are very high
The Ooragnak lurk and loiter in the place of this comestible
We will use our brew of Figs
Just in case they want long pigs

You may say there are other fish
but we are pressed to change our dish
After all we are hue-mans, it takes a while to be adjustable
Plate up!
Plate up!
It's time to eat
all our meat.
Herbivores, carnivores, omnivores, Labradors and all-ivores
all must ingest
this is no jest!
Chuck the bones over your shoulder
There a dog a stakeholder
get up, stand up, clap your hands, sit down and turn around
Knife and fork,
bottle and cork
keep them fat never lean
tummies full, mouths are clean.
Now we are fed-up, can we get up from this set up? Marvellous!

Jaddamiah looked upward to the night sky, clear with its million, billion stars, and with it he smiled, generally satisfied with himself. Onion, leak and clove of garlic, rosemary and sweet potato with bacon and chestnut mushrooms, plum tomatoes and Mr Fuhrmann for posterity's sake, poured some ale in, from his mug. All broiling in a silver skittle, burned black from many

---

* <u>Tweed (the Tweed river is the only River that one finds Skeet Fish, in this area Hobgoblins and Oorigorks</u> <u>are found in profusion.</u>

a night under the starry, starry skies. One could not ask for better. The Coney's sat in a row like hungry school children, some rabbits stood upright on their hind-quarters, even an old, red fox came by. That was enough to cause confusion, or did they come for the warm glow of the fire-light? For a 'pig in the street is not the pig on the table' whereas the chicken is the same on the plate as in the farmyard. How Mr Fuhrmann did it, Jaddamiah didn't know, for he even had the nicest baked bread handy. The two sat silently eating. Only the sound of their forks scraping the bottom of their tin plates, broke the silence of the dark, sacred night.

Happy have We Met, Merry let Us Part

The next morning when the Sun was barely climbing up toward the morning from the eastern sky, Jaddamiah leant against the Glæmboom. He had walked to it because he noticed that he no longer saw any Runes on the bark. It seemed that the tree was charmed; even the Runes appeared at the will of the Ælves and disappeared at their command. It was with a heavy heart that he mounted Fágan. He dearly wanted to say his many thanks and goodbyes to Morkaél, but he knew he had drear business in Weir, and he had to set out early. Mr Fuhrmann stood with both hands deep in his trouser pockets in the middle of the road facing west, then turned slowly to face eastward, and that's the way Jaddamiah found him when he came besides him with Fágan. He lowered his hand and shook Mr Fuhrmann's. "Mr Fuhrmann!" he said in an earnest tone. "Gratitude! Gramercy! for the meals that you cooked for me. I will remember these days. . ." said Jaddamiah again thoughtfully, then continued. "of you, of fair Morkaél, of Kaladamza, of Gimlillÿs and Gimvöllekaas." Jaddamiah fell silent again, and looked towards where the road vanished through some dense trees. "Especially the Ælves . . . the Ælves." He gently nudged Fágan without saying another word to Mr Fuhrmann. After about 200m he simply raised his arm and waved without turning around. "It's fare-well then! Not good-bye!" shouted Mr Fuhrmann after him. Jaddamiah waved again and Mr Fuhrmann stood there till Jaddamiah and Fágan were completely blotted out by the shadows of the trees. Jaddamiah drove his horse on all day, and hardly took any respite. On the second day after leaving Mr Fuhrmann, Jaddamiah kept on in the same way with the large mountain close to his left shoulder, and the great weald on his right. It was getting dense with profusion of trees. It was quite cool, so horse and rider took liberties going further and faster. The days were quiet, nothing stirred, and Jaddamiah kept looking over his shoulder. There was a sense of urgency that was driving him on, that he didn't understand. On the third day, the mountains loomed on either side, as he drew ever to closer to the mountain crossing called 'Vakratuvakra'. In the northern common speech, it was called 'Pasio Wëych' or just 'Dro-Dro' which meant 'to turn'. It was at the foot of that pass that he made his camp. He stuck close to the road, only a little way off to the weald side, under a large oak. Twilight had already passed, and the weald looming so close to the imposing mountains made the place gloomy and dark. Jaddamiah, in his haste to make a fire against the cold and the wilds, omitted to see that the oak which he decided to camp at, was dead. It had no foliage; no green leaves but had plenty of gnarled branches. For an unknown reason, it was called 'Morsdarack' but, those from Palador called her 'Duirparina' which was 'Oak of deception'. At least there were plenty of juicy, green grasses around for Fágan, not that she didn't get her fair share of good horse feed from her master. Jaddamiah ensured that provisions were made for her on this journey but, it was slowly running out. They were tired, the road though flat with very minor undulations, had found them going faster and they had covered 83miles in just 3 days. Jaddamiah lay tossing and turning for some time and that, in the eldritch dark, felt like hours. Meanwhile, rain was pelting in his little village of Béth-Élam. Hrosmægden could not sleep either. She had just woken from a terrible dream. She swung her long legs off the bed and placed her warm feet on the soft rug. She could see serpentine rivulets running down the stained glass of the bedroom window. Several strikes of lightning coloured the still room with its blue light. She twirled her long, black hair on top of her head, then reached for her night gown, deciding to write the dream down. She first thought of making herself a caudle but decided that a glass of warm milk and honey with a pinch of nutmeg, would help her sleep better. Afterwards, she tip-toed down the stairs as softly as she could, walking down the hallway to the kitchen. She was well accustomed to walking in low light or moving through her house in the dark, a knack that most mothers seemed to master. She prepared the dreamy night-time drink and walked to her husband's study and lit a candle that had already burned halfway. She sunk into his chair and threw her left leg over the arm of the chair. The drink was very soothing as she took sips of it. Her mind was focussed on the dream that had woken her, which was most unusual. It disturbed her so, that she stole some decent paper from the desk drawer, and began writing a letter to him, instead of entering the dream into her journal. As she started writing with one of the lesser staff pens, she didn't bother to write her own address but, started by addressing her husband. He no doubt would be a little agitated, as the Jabberwockies prided themselves as good letter writers. After all, there were 3 generations of postman in the family!

Dearest Husband

I know that you will forgive me for using some of your favourite blue ink, as we all know you do not like black ink but, I intend that this letter will find you healthy and well as I think it will reach Weir not too long after you arrive.

I wish I knew where in the wilds you are tonight for it is raining terribly here in Béth-Élam. It is very late, sometime after two in the morning. I had a strange dream wake me up, here it is, just as I had it. I do not know why it is that I feel compelled to write it to you but, I do. Perhaps it is both far-sighted and symbolic. Remember dearest husband that I love you very much.

<u>Here is the dream:</u>

'Of the five women, one was named Nivara (it means unmarried girl or pristine - she is not mortal kind) This maiden opened a very tall door and said; "Can you pass through?" (The door is not mortal kind and Nivara is a symbolic name) "Make it work and it's yours." In the middle of the room there was a broken Pezala. A certain woman made it work (this Pezala is in Béth-Élam). The other four women sat at the Pezala and played The Requiem (This is an ill omen). Then Nivara said: "Tell me the story. You heard it so many times." "I need to hear it again" she demanded. You said "ok". A woman called Nanu (you will meet this woman, she speaks little but has fear, yet she has wisdom) came to you and gave you a translucent Hushas Tear-shaped stone. In the stone, there were many open books. The letters on the pages were so small that you couldn't read them. (you could not read the words for they too are not mortal kind - they are found in a great sacred place). She said: "you know what to do". So, you took a ship and sailed the seas. When you arrived at the palace, there was no one there except an empty throne. "Place the stone on the throne," you heard Nanu's voice say. So you did.

Suddenly a king was sitting on the throne. His clothes were dirty and torn to shreds. He was blind. On his left arm he had an insignia, "I am the ruler". (the king is symbolic of a mighty ruler, he is blind because he is all seeing and has no partiality)

Before the king there were two huge piles. One was fanciful food, and the other broken gadgets (This ruler walks both in our world and the spirit world). On his right side there were seated seven billion lepers. Each leper held a flag made of silk. On the flags there was an inscription: "We are the walking dead"

On his left side there was a man, eating rice soup with the fork from a bowl full of holes (this is also an ill omen). Then a crow flew in through the broken window and said; "Why don't you remember yourself?"

My dearest husband, this is what was revealed to me. The rest is veiled but I feel you have only started your journey.

Your longing wife
Hrosmægden Jabberwocky

PS – here is a verse for you:
Sing, sing
Softly, sing fading into lullabies
Of meadows and of Spring.
Lullabies of falling light in the weald
By afternoon's delight.
Sing, Sing!
How can you not sing?
Softly, tenderly
Wandering in the night
As every star above
Lights your path ahead.

Hrosmægden folded the pages in 3, slipped it into an envelope and addressed it to her husband but, she came to an impasse for she did not have of an address. She pondered on that for a moment, 'perhaps he will reside at a Tavern or Inn'. She tapped her slender fingers on the table, thinking, and then the candle went out. She was left in the dark. She sat in darkness for a while and sighed. A flash of blue light entered the room again, and there at the door for a moment, Hrosmægden thought she saw a little figure leaning against the door frame. She sat up straight and pierced the dark with her eyes. A second rapid flash came, and there the little figurine was again. This time it spoke in somewhat inaudible tones. "Grrrrra! Gran...Grrrra...

nnee!" Hrosmægden smiled in relief, for she thought for a moment she was seeing strange apparitions, but it was little Geongmerkā.

"What in the name of the Fáerië are you doing up so late my sweet? Come here my dear Geongmerkā!" The little girl walked over to her grandmother, stumbled over some things but made her way onto Hrosmægden's lap. She kissed her granddaughter and brushed her hair with her fingers. "I had a dream," she murmured and rubbed her hands over her eyes sleepily. "In the dream, you have a sister. . ."

Hrosmægden listened for more but, there was no more to tell, and the bearer of the dream was fast asleep against her grandmother's warm breast. Hrosmægden's mind drifted into a full ocean, a wide-open sea, one she had not sailed on for what seemed like lifetime ago. She remembered that she had a sister, a twin in fact, one long gone, one that carried sweet memories of childhood. Geongmerkā had the key; she had opened a drawer buried deep in the cavernous vaults of her grandmother's mind. In it, the dust lay thick as autumn leaves on a weald floor, cracked and brown, the gold, long disappeared over the fading years. Her eyes did not blink for she was deep in thought, tears formed in the corners of her eyes, like silver dew drops they trickled out and rolled over her soft cheeks, and only a great Seer would have been able to see Hrosmægden's past through her hoary teardrops.

'How could it be?' she thought. "that one could lose touch with one's own sister, to live such separate lives, countless miles apart. Had her children, and her children's children kept her busy all these decades? Of course, they did! No! That was just an excuse, a maternal excuse used by all the womenfolk over the ages. It is a strange, uncanny co-incidence,' she went on thinking; 'both she and I had fallen in love with men separate from our worlds. Before us, it was our mother too. Do these things not skip a generation? It seemed that fate and destiny are connected to every living thing. All objects inanimate and animate, seen and unseen, known and unknown. I *must* find her address! But Heavens to Betsy!' She didn't know where in Eridu her sister went to live. She would go, without announcing herself, to her father's house first thing in the morning. She smiled and rubbed the tears from her wet cheeks with the back of her hand, and suddenly felt cold. The rain had stopped, so she carried Geongmerkā and laid her down gently beside her, and the two slept soundly till morning.

The Wolvlingas return to Vel Samoda

———◈———

Bele Eriol walked up the 33 steps. On each step stood a guardian Ælve dressed in large robes of mazarine taffeta, splattered thick with aurulent stars. Their black hair demdema and spangled with gold, on their head coronets of stars, and their faces dusky. There they stood watching, ever watching. As Bele Eriol passed, a gentle echo could be heard. The hailing of his name was like a gentle murmur as he passed between the dusky Ælvish corridor, and entered into the tower of the Keep. The tower was 96ft tall and spacious inside. The ground floor had a solitary, ornate chair kræfted of a strange, lilac anbar, and filled with manyfold scintillations. In a circle around the seat was a ring of ever- burning fire. The towering, elegant Ælve, rose from his seat and walked through the flames, his arms open in a welcome gesture. "Come Bele Eriol. Death follows you, but you are most welcome at Vel Samoda," said he in a voice that sounded like a torrent.

Eriol walked toward him and embraced him, but mostly he laid his head on his host's breast and sighed. "You sigh like one of the Aleidhiath," he replied, stroking Eriol's hair.

"I do Elmerkar. One of those we love has been mortally wounded."

Elmerkar drew Eriol away and looked into his eyes. "Yes. That is so, they come as we speak." In a dirgeful voice Eriol replied, "We shall call that place 'Itimamitudagur', for there is no appropriate name in any other tongue." (In the years that followed, he drew many Melchizedecks, Wezadrachs and other sunless creatures unto that place and slew them. Bele Elmerkar had slayed a number more than any other Ælve. The true meaning of his name was unknown but, some said that it meant 'the hunter shrouded in light')

———◈———

Now here and there, a room on high or a passage below, or a precarious step where an Ælve sat to play a lyra or harp, their lissom fingers fell from their instruments. Vel Samoda fell silent, as silent as a stray shell on distant, desert sand.

When Hudōrdir and the company arrived, four Elfenna were waiting for Lycurgus and his son. Those Elfenna were called 'Tahharavigata' and they set Lycurgus on a palanquin trimmed with blue bells, for they forebode him to walk after his loss. Two bore Lycurgus and two bore Ulfhamr's body but, Ulfhamr's palanquin was covered with vimzinpuspa.

Light-footed, the Elfenna carried the two palanquins up Tiemugara, and the bells rang gently. Even unto Jinbōchō went the music as they ascended the spiral staircase. Belides looked down and saw great hordes of Hobgoblins appearing from the weald. They surrounded the mound of harlequin flowers and sat there in silence under the stars. They waited all night, making invocation;

> ". . . Sixty times the Water of Life
> Sixty times the Food of Life
> Sprinkle on the Ghobfrænd. . ."

Over and over they sang the invocation in their wondrous voices.

The company of Hudōrdir followed behind the palanquins, the Dwarve walked between Hudōrdir and Furhōdir, and the two gnomes followed behind El Elion. The Dwarve and Gnomes moaned that they had to climb so many steps; they asked Furhōdir why the Ælves didn't just pertessered as it would've make things easier and quicker. She smiled warmly at them and asked them to be still as she put her finger to her lips. It was not long after that, even before they arrived at the 2nd Kuhmaskan, that the gnomes moaned again about the giddy height, again Furhōdir asked them to be still. She held Goombah's hand and signalled El Elion to hold Goombahllum's.

So it was, and at least they could not complain about the darkness because at that time each night, light was cast on every step. It wasn't the kræft of any Dwarve or Ælve but, it was said that the Ælves summoned Pegasus and Okunoku from the starry heavens, and each took her Diamond Breath and blew over each step. Their breath pierced the hard, calcified tree, and made a shaft no larger than a wood stave; so that when the Sun rose in the east and set in the west, these hewn portals held the roseate, flavescent and orange light of the Sun till late in the night. On occasion, when the moon was overwhelmed by rain or cloud, lampyglowdia came out in their hundreds of thousands, and sailed in one long, spiralic line, thick as taffy, lighting up the staircase.

Such was the wonder of that coruscating event, that the Fratakara of Alkana once each year, came to see it. So, from the Wander flower Mound to the 3rd Kuhmaskan and to the 5th, to the 6th and to the 9th, till the topmost pinnacle – all was still as the company passed. When the company was received by Elmerkar and Bele Eriol, Lycurgus wept much, for he too, like all the Hobgoblins hoped that the Ælves would return at least one son back to life, but their word was final, and they would not return him to love's root again. Only then was there utter silence at Vel Samoda, for all the Hobgoblins returned into the wealds and their voices became only a distant murmur. Unto this day, even through the decay of time, when one passed through the Weald of Zarvari Vana or passed close to where Vel Samoda once stood, strangers would say that they could hear gentle Hobgoblins singing, sometimes soft lullabies, on the wind. Sometimes they would catch the words;

> "... *Sixty times the Water of Life*
> *Sixty times the Food of Life*
> *Sprinkle on the Ghobfrænd...*"

Over the years and centuries, those names were changed, some even believed that if they bathed in the waters, that they would achieve immortality or regeneration but, of those folk tales, no one could swear by.

Night passed to day, word was sent to Vel Domas, and while the Bele of the Paladins was received at Jinbōchō, the Ælves in Midhe were drawn into battle.

Erset la Tari

The night after the 1st Council of Palador; two Paladins and two Ælves set out toward Albtraum but, they were waylaid by the scent of Vargrs and they inevitably knew that the Vargrs were accompanied by Hal-ba Uruku. Hal-ba Uruku was sometimes referred to as 'Hal-ba' or 'Uruku'. They were monstrous, two-legged creatures, tall and dank, malignant and cold. Their sight was ghastly, their vibration enough to cause anyone to recoil. So repulsive were the Uruku's vibration that their body geometry caused the Eldiěni to go into freezing convulsion, paralysis, torsion and caused pudenda in maidens. Nirdhanin and Inca Illa, Dalethdir and Ælffeðra pursued the Vargrs and Uruku. They chased them all night through thicket and brier, through vale and wood. Then there was a splitting, the Vargrs went one way and the Uruku another. Ælffeðra had enough of running and chasing, so he took to the air; for his name meant 'Ælve with Wings' or 'Winged Ælve'. His wings beat so fast that there was no wing-flap sound from it, he could move them so fast till the vibration became so high, as to render him imperceptible. Ælffeðra remained just over the tops of the trees, and noticed in the distance, that the two Uruku, though having separated from the Vargrs, were actually heading in the same direction, due south past the Amura Vel. Those creatures adopted speed that belied their form or strength, and that ominous in nature. When the Ælves and Paladins regrouped, Dalethdir suggested that they had used some dark duir to pass out of sight. The four separated again at twilight, the Paladins kept off the road towards the Crossing of Amura Vel. At Llewerig they changed their form to mortal kind and tried to ascertain amongst the wayfarers of any questionable news but, none was forthcoming.

Ælffeðra and Dalethdir kept towards the forest, one below, one above as to draw as much energy from the trees as possible. They did that until they arrived at the foot of the great Vakratuvakra.

Close to evening, Ælffeðra descended onto Gamahare. The wide, purple wings curled round him while he crouched in the thick snow, his eyes searched and didn't blink.

He spotted in the distance, some 40 miles away, a lower set of peaks, awl shaped, so that at their feet lay a great plane.

The four had regrouped and headed to the Mouth of Masku.

Ælffeðra sat still, disturbed by that place. It wasn't long that he stopped thinking because he suddenly became aware that he wasn't alone up in the heights of the world. From the western peaks a very tall, titanic form came striding. The subtle form walked over the peaks and through the valleys towards him in its gangly fashion, playing idly with the snow-capped peaks, creating blenks as he passed. It was a tornado and his name was 'Tornadis'. Tornadis paused by the squatting Ælve and spoke, "Child of the Pavonian Dragon, I sense that we both are insensitive to that place." A twisty turn of cloud began to reach out and pointed towards the Mouth of Masku but, before the Ælve answered, Eorðdyn appeared in her slow, jaunting strut. She had slinked through a secret crevice in one of the nearby peaks. "Dearest companion," said Tornadis, "I am certain you share our disdain for that perl-lace-over-yonder. For long it lay in silence but look now, an Ælve it awakened."

"In truth we agree, even the Emmets they have destroyed. What of our Sylvan Fanes whose feet mingle with Fleur, her fragrant children have vanished from this disagreeable place," replied Eorðdyn.

"Shall we assist the Ælve and go down to destroy them, as in days of yore?" asked Tornadis with a mischievous smile but, Ælffeðra graciously declined saying, "I must dissuade your enthusiasm. It would be an unfair advantage. Perchance, someday we will meet again."

Eorðdyn had already returned from where she came and Tornadis fell away disenchanted. To Ælffeðra, it seemed more alarming, for one of the Vargrs had what looked like a female, slung over its back. How they had gotten so far, so quickly, he could not fathom. Ælffeðra's natural tendency was to pursue them but, he also had

Wisdom, so he returned to his kin for, if the Vargrs and Uruku were entering the Mouth of Masku, he knew with certainty, that they were heading towards Erset la Tari. Ælffeðra stopped for a moment and turned around. He looked deeper and there was a fierce flame in his eyes. He mounted the aethyrs with his wings racing faster than a falling star, towards those black gates.

Dynyansek

❦

The Vargrs ran full speed ahead, not once looking back, while the two Uruku followed closely behind. They didn't stop till they stood between the Towers of Nakālu for, there they felt safe and they feared the Ælves who pursued them. They had done a terrible deed.

The two Vargrs licked their flews in satisfaction, their long, black tongues swiped their noses and muzzles. They looked up at the Uruku for some insidious affirmation but, they received none only, "Bur hurkel!"

The Vargrs proceeded between the Towers of Nakālu and as they passed, from above on the ramparts, they heard many voices singing down to them;

Death to the living,
Death to the living,
Long life to the killers,
Success to hunter Vargrs
And ill luck to 'bocanáchs'!
And ill luck to 'bocanáchs'!

An entrance was cut into a hedge with two square towers either side made of moldavite. Each of the towers measured 43 ft (13.1 m) high. The sides measured 36.2 ft (11.03 m) by 42.2 ft (12.86 m). Arriving between those towers, made the innocent feel uneasy for, on both tower words were inscribed in relief of Lingam Stone;

Eli Baltuti Ima"Idu Mituti

The Vargrs held their heads up high; their long, unruly tails held up. They started trotting proudly away but, it is said that 'pride goeth before a fall'. The two Uruku only saw a glimmer of light pass but, all too late, as Ælffeðra plunged down from the heights and cut one of the Vargrs through his back and broke its spine, causing instant death as it lay in two halves. With his free hand he grasped the limp body of Lyadalagapē and left the second Vargr to whimper and growl.

The Uruku were already at its side but Ælffeðra was gone. The Uruku looked at each other dolefully, from the ramparts the guards fell silent, their Master would not look kindly on that failure. From the Towers of Nakālu to the edifice of Erset la Tari ran a straight road of cobbles, next to it running higgledy-piggledy was the river Drava, the only river in Eridu that ran north, and it did so fast. The road was well paved but other than that, there was nothing to be seen, no tree, no growing thing. After 6 miles another two towers stood, they were higher than the Towers of Nakālu. Those towers were 666ft high (202.997m) and shaped like a hexagram. Each point was sharp and made its top-most part look like a hideous crown. It was called the 'Tower of Izru' and 6 Necromancers lived there. It had 6 doors and those doors were made of Šapāku, a substance that fell from heaven as molten metal. After another 6 miles the 'Tower of Magulû' threatened over the previous two at a height of 866ft (263.957m), two more towers stood, each 6 miles apart and each higher than the other but, of the 3 aforesaid, they had the worst reputation. It was to that tower by a 6 dwhëeled conveyance, that one of the Uruku sped. The lesser of the two feared for its life and headed eastward towards Meueage (the lizard district) to find some food, for it was ravenous. From the 'Tower of Magulû' the Uruku could reach Dynyansek instantly, instead of running thirty miles.

Great torches were lit at regular intervals along the road. The torches were made of bundles of cane or bamboo strips, just rough and tumble. They used tinder at the end of the torches, beaten fine enough to catch alight easily.

Erset la Tari was a terrible place, a place of no return. It was also referred to as 'hell of the grave' for, it was an empty place and foreboding. In other languages, it was also called 'Malrolia' which meant, 'ill will'. In Midhe that place was called 'Larks-lees' or 'Leers' which meant 'neglected lands' but, the Midhe lived in peace for a long time and that name was no longer remembered. A great Lord lived in Leers, one that did not forget, he was handsome and filled with light. His name was Damasandra; for he was the Ælve Guardian of one of the four corners of Eridu. After darkness and shadow went into his heart, that jurisdiction was not replaced. The Melchizedecks were a most powerful race, and answered only to the Great Meline Dragon but, even they feared Damasandra, and obeyed his will. The Ælves called him 'Kašadom' which meant 'to overpower with doom'. The mighty Lord Damasandra ruled Erset la Tari. The region nestled between the mountains bore the name, but at its centre stood an edifice altogether more menacing, if not in design than in its symbology, It was a ferruginous structure and it always appeared like some putridation was leaking from its walls. Not far from its entrance grew two trees, all gnarled and barkly, and filled with innumerable purple berries, that had become melanic with age. A female, who had become a crone's bane, named 'Mussuku-Emētu' lived *in* the tree. Many years before the servant of Merodach-Baladan bound her, she was named 'Hyldeblomstdrik'. He bound her because she would not perish, for, once upon a time that was a barkley wood and those two Elders were set in the middle of the barkley wood.

The master architect of Damasandra cleared the land, burned the trees and pulled out their deep roots but, the two elders would not submit their matter and so, Bīnudhē was called. Bīnudhē tortured her and set curses and hexes upon her, for his name meant 'tree doom'. The Uruku strode towards the entrance but, first walked toward one of the trees and tore off a branch, the tree bled, and its blood trickled into the Drava. The Uruku then uttered customary words;

"Crones bane! I rent of thy wood and over and over will I rent
till all illerwood is rent."

Despite the torture, there were no painful shrieks from her, she was silent and then replied;

6 long strides shalt thou take,
Into Dynyansek thou must go,
This the last rent of my bough.

But the future thou canst not see,
King of Eridu Damasandra shalt not be.
Rise up Dryad and rise up Faun,
For Kašadom, he maun
Bend to the will of the Bee

And myself renewed, unsullied Illerwood Tree.

Twelve Paladins are standing by,
Their feet are the earth, and their eyes are the sky,
The knave will thrive wherever they be.
He <u>*shall*</u> *be born under a tree.*

The Uruku was vexed at that response, because trees had never previously made such utterances. He did not quite understand its meaning but, he remembered it, to tell it to his Master.

6 long strides he took then stopped, fear crept over him as he looked through the entrance and into the glowing, gloaming place.

Dynyansek was large. Its base was oval and some 3.72823 miles in diameter, it was named 'Banû'. The walls were 60ft thick and 60ft high and upon that, rising upward in a curved support, holding the edifice was something akin to the shape of a lamp but, not at all a lamp, the ferruginous colouration and the damp outer walls made it repugnant. So big it was, that it was said an entire Vimāna could enter it, yet, to have any Vimāna land on Eridu, was forbidden for many millennia.

An Ælve needed no craft nor cunning and needed no space-ships (Vimāna) to traverse the great distances of the Universes. The hordes under Ēl Elyōn (The Most-High God), the Meline Dragon and his subjects used space-ships to travel between worlds and stars and interfered with the affairs of others. The Ælves were completely aligned with the Universal Labyrinth and, as a result, could 'jump' telepathically between stars; for the Ælves, it was as easy as blinking an eye. That ferruginous-coloured lamp shape was a fallacy, a false fane, feigned in a weald once filled with beautiful trees. The walls on the oval base curved upward in one smooth sweep, and it grew outward then straight up again into a long, slender, cylinder-like spout that dripped all day, all night, never ending. Resting in the middle of the rimmed, disc-shaped structure that rose into the heavens, was a smooth, glutinous, cylindrical mass that reached a height of 3 miles. The rimmed, disc-shaped structure was named 'Nāṣiru' and had thick, wide, low walls with a wide aperture, so that 6 male guards walked abreast around it, and changed every 6 hours.

The 3mile-high, cylindrical mass was named 'Dimtu Ilimmu Shumsuene' and from the topmost part to the bottom, 666 times in egregious scrawl too despairing to say out loud, were 9 names written;

'Uggae' - God of death
'Mulla Xul' - Egregious devil
'Alal' - Destroyer
'Idimmu' - Demon
'Gidim Xul' - Egregious ghost
'Telal' - Warrior Demon
'Kashshaptu' - Witch
'Dingir Xul' - Egregious god
'Utuk Xul' - Egregious spirit

Those were the names that Kašadom inscribed with his own fingers. The highest part of it was reconstructed after thirteen legions of Ælves from Jinbōchō, had descended from the stars and destroyed the tower. It was destroyed so that it could not be built higher. That incident had not been recorded in any books, and was generally accepted, as happened long before the age of man.

The Uruku entered Banû and walked about 500 meters, and came to a platform. He gazed down for a moment, for that edifice sunk down into the earth. Below were many levels, some made of light, some of made matter and other levels made of quintessence.

Bēlu-Ēpišu, the master architect, took all the energy from the millions of trees and absorbed them into that medium.

There below was industry, malignant makings, armies great and small in their thousands being readied for battle, other darker creatures who had slept for an age, were being recalled from the vasty, black deeps and readied for unpleasant mischief. Ready to feed on man's fear and thoughtform.

The Uruku stepped back and smiled, he stood in the centre of the platform. 6 belts of square, dark light, stacked one on top the other surrounded him; the belts flipped over and under him until the platform became no more than an inanimate surface, then the belts of light changed and became four dimensional.

The Uruku's skin changed for he was no Uruku, but one of two egregious siblings, one more terrible in nature than the other, and his name was Búbkalu. Within moments, the inanimate surface lifted upward at a great speed. The lift stopped, as Búbkalu waited for the 'sliding light' to open, he straightened up, gently beat his hefty fist into his open hand, and held his head up high as a flame flickered between the tips of his curved, scarlet horns.

The 'sliding light' opened, he stepped out into a polygon space. At its centre was a dais with 14 steps on four sides that ascended to a seated Power; a Principality of utmost revolt. The throne was shadowed, while all round the polygon space, a soft, purple light was cast from some nameless source. In the gloom of the throne, two inflictious, bright flames burned, and the goldenrod flames from the eyes of that Principality, illuminated the hacele which covered the entire throne in a wrapt vogue. Zillions of tiny, golden scales were fashioned so that the flames from his eyes cast light that wickered and flickered here and there and appeared as a great dragon horde. Búbkalu walked forward and held his fist in his open hand. He knelt on the floor, head low, and said nothing; as was customary. All was silent and as the moments passed. Búbkalu became uneasy for it was not the custom for the 'Son of Death' to act that way. Then a mighty voice spoke which sounded like many, angry manifestations. It was filled with despair and said, "Why does 'the one, who makes those who run stand still' enter into the presence of Mesa-sum-na, nay Merodach-Baladan, without his sister and companion?". As he spoke those words, zillions of flames danced on each scale of his hacele. It illuminated the entire polygon-shaped throne-room. The flames danced like little serpents but, Búbkalu didn't raise his head, just yet. . .

At the foot of each flight of stairs stood four guards. Each were 9ft tall and 6ft wide. They had enormous feet which no shoe could fit so, all you saw were large, green, scaled feet and claws. Their hideous bodies were covered in elegant, soft clothes that were richly embroided as, they loved to conceal their scales with beautiful clothes. They secretly envied the soft skin of the Eldiěni women. "Speak!" commanded the mighty voice again.

"My Lord!" exclaimed Búbkalu, at last looking up at his master. "Greetings to you Merodach-Baladan. My news is one of half measures and thus only half of two have come to thee. . ."

Merodach-Baladan lifted his hand from the large, black orb that rested in its niche, at the end of the arm rest of the throne. Búbkalu arose and stood before his Lord and Master. Merodach-Baladan caressed the orb and as he did so electric charges crackled, flickered and flashed from the tips of his fingers over the orb. His right hand rested on the hilt of a tall, golden sword, and he lifted it and pointed the blade at Búbkalu and replied, "Know ye not that the Son of Death sees? It is a victory nonetheless that we have hurt them, and it will hurt them into *battle*!"

"Búbkalu smiled at the thought but, it quickly dissipated as he asked, "But how would the God Damasandra respond to this matter?" Merodach-Baladan raised his finger and set his sword down again and replied, "I will soothe his heart. Go! I will call upon you soon for another task."

Búbkalu genuflected and left the room but, before he reached the door, a voice crept up behind him and said, "Let Búbgaz know, this shall not be held against her. Do not return without her next time." Búbkalu stopped, turned and replied, "I vow, my Lord."

<hr>

Ælffeðra was overcome with compassion for he knew that Lycurgus would take that bitterly to heart. He looked down and saw Dalethdir between the trees, and so set himself down with Lyadalagapē in his arms.

Dalethdir was speechless at first; he leant against a large linden tree. He looked out of the tree line, where a black river issued around the place, while a wide, arched bridge suspended the river. A mile from that bridge was a hedge, it was thick and low (4ft high), at least 100 feet thick with gorse and thorns that were 9 inches long. He turned to Ælffeðra then knelt beside Lyadalagapē's body and said, "The beautiful wolf lover is no more with us. How could such a thing be? How did she find herself so far from Zarvari Vana? Tell me Ælffeðra, wings of light! Tell it all?"

Ælffeðra spoke, "I chased the Vargrs and the Uruku till I grew weary of playing. . .I ascended to the heights to the great Gamahare and spied them slinking into the Mouth of Masku, where they headed through Lytherenna," (So the Ælves called Nakālu. The Ælves abstained from using Dynyansek speech, although it was close to the speech of Jinbōchō but, Damasandra and Merodach-Baladan poisoned it to suit their desires.)

"I would not set wing nor foot in that cursed land but when I looked again, I spied the Vargrs carrying someone so, against wisdom, I went to see and thus slew one of the Vargrs."

"Your wisdom is not questioned here dearest Ælffeðra for this is an act of war. Long has it been foreseen. Soon the child, even the trees and the stars whisper of, will come. . ."

"Hush Dalethdir! You stride through too many duirs and thus hear too much. Be silent upon this known matter. . ." interjected Ælffeðra in his blithe voice, for so it always sounded.

Just then the two Paladins came upon them and their response was not so measured as the two Ælves. They needn't be regaled at what had transpired, they only needed to see the body of Lyadalagapē.

"What are we waiting for!" exclaimed Nirdhanin.

"Let's go and smite them!" replied Inca Illa hurriedly.

As he spoke those words, they shed their mortal facade and standing over Ælffeðra and

Dalethdir, were two beings akin to Ymirstuff, 20ft tall, bald, naked, their bodies made of some mysterious, metallic, interstellar amalgamation. Ælffeðra rose to his feet and replied in a still voice, "Nay! Tis not wisdom, we are but few?" "It is rash!" exclaimed Dalethdir softly.

"Rash? Rash!" asked the two paladins in unison, for they were of single thought. "Tis not rash kindred. Look! Look!" they replied with the sweep of the arm. "We are legion."

Now amongst them it appeared as every tree was Paladin, 12000 of them.

For the Slaying of Cubs

"**Y**ou have tempted us, Paladins, I shall find a secret duir to rest Lyadalagapē. Thereafter, we shall encircle fire and flame and set out in the morning."

It wasn't long after then, when Dalethdir returned from the weald and the four sat singing around the fire all night. In the morning of 3rd October 8817 they sprang to prosecution. Across the stone bridge he rushed, Ælffeðra took to the air. Nirdhanin leapt over the river, Inca Illa strode onto the bridge and crushed it to pebbles and the earth trembled. Inca Illa, was bright and shone, and smote the gorse hedge with fire and flame from ten thousand Suns that poured from his eyes.

Panic struck the Towers of Nakālu, drums began to beat, there were seven on each tower. On the left tower the seven drummers were led by a boy aged seven, named Nathan Futrell, his ankles were in stocks, on the other tower the 6 drummers were led by a slightly older boy named John Joseph Clem, his ankles were also in stocks and those were only two of the myriad children stolen from afar by minions of the Lords of Shadows. The drum-rolls could be heard everywhere as their dirty base line could be heard echoing louder, further up as each tower joined in. It was no music that little boys should be playing and instructing, neither of any delusion of storm approaching but, a violent call to arms. The two Paladins were nearly upon the towers, the drum-roll changed immediately, and the twelve voices started a chant against the oncoming legions;

"Death to the living,
Death to the living,
Long life to the killers,
Success to the hunter dark
And ill luck to Paladins!
And ill luck to Paladins!"

Faster and faster the zongagongos (war drums) beat, greater and greater the chants, darker and darker the spells came from the imp voices in 'victus' vocals;

"Adi la basi alaku,
Adi la basi alaku,
Adi la basi alaku!"

The Paladins rammed the towers but, it only shook and remained upright nonetheless. The legions gathered in formation of a long bow, while Nirdhanin and Inca Illa paused for a moment and smiled.

Dalethdir was beside them in a flash, he then stood still, he breathed in the aethyrs and opened his arms, palms facing downwards, and began to spin, heel to toes, toes to heels, dust kicked up as a great tornado. This was called 'Idin-Atu-Kata'; a duir was opened into the earth while the entire plain lifted upwards, so that it was suspended 300ft off the surface. The two Paladins entered, going beneath the foundations of the towers, lifting them up over their mighty shoulders, and flung them a mile away while rock and stones came crashing down. Several drums came crashing down over several flying Wezadrachs, with their wings stuck, they came tumbling to the ground.

Vargr and Uruku came forth. They came from the second set of towers that oozed out like pismire. As the Towers of Nakālu were about to hit the earth Ælffeðra shouted, "The knaves! The knaves!"

He netted Clem and Futrell in his vast wings. Ælffeðra fell to the ground, while the knaves were safe and sound. Ælffeðra didn't perish because he could die but, as the Lore of Law stated, 'a life for a life', that battle was not sanctioned, his body disintegrated into beautiful embers of myriad colours after which many butterfly wings flaked to the ground, until a huge pile of broken wings was formed. Clem and Futrell emerged from within the mound of wings, their faces smeared with glimmering colour. All was not lost for Ælffeðra, though he passed through the duirs of death, an Ælve had many bodies. The legion strode against the hordes, while those trapped above on the suspended plain could flee nowhere, except for jumping to their deaths or standing and fighting. The Paladins were filled with many hierarchies, some of fire, some of water, still others, of forces never seen and which could not be named, for they were unnameable in the tongues of men and so, were not found in the memory of man. Many winged Melchizedecks ascended to the suspended plane but, no sooner did they arrive than their wings were broken like the sea upon rocks for, such was the presence of Paladins, the battle was ill timed for the enemy. Dalethdir opened many duirs, his intention was to get to the utmost towers but the Duirs were shut by some higher power.

From his high tower Merodach-Baladan was vexed, as his looked upon the slaying of his hordes. He called upon Búbgaz the destroyer and Búbkalu and they obeyed gladly, because they always wanted to be at war. But Kašadom did not yet see from his high citadel what was below, for he was performing Algumes Māluku. So great was his desire to ensnare and keep an eye on the whole world, that he spied into the deepest depths of the future of Eridu, so far did he look until the name of Eridu was no more, and men gave it some other appellation. He wanted to see just how the Kwizir could be used against all men, even unto the littlest infant.

Búbkalu came out and ascended immediately to the suspended plain. The Paladins were below, and they drove the plain ever on through the air towards Dynyansek but, when they came as far as the Tower of Magulû, from below, canon shots were fired. They were mobilised by the dwhëels, wild carnivorous dwhëels. Those canons shot fire and molten, hot sulphur. With Búbgaz and Búbkalu they brought 1000 Mush-dagur to distract the Paladins. Búbkalu begun to weave his dark arts, also with them came Ṭēmubīšu. Ṭēmubīšu was a terrible creature, its body was covered with thick, silver-brown skin like that of the kharga or karkadann found in the deserts of Alkana. It was tall and walked on two legs, Ṭēmubīšu had more head than face.

Still the battle was not going as Merodach-Baladan would have it, so he did a dangerous thing, he personally went up to the abode of his Lord Damasandra, with him he took two Wezadrachs for they had silence and invisibility as their strength.

When the 3 approached their Lord and Master, Merodach-Baladan vanished from view and he and the two Wezadrachs tried hard to pry open one eye of their Lord, for some meters away was a great window without hindrance and they thought that if they could just open one of his eyes towards the battle below, while he turned about to walk back over the flaming algumes, that some advantage would come to them on the battle field but alas, their Master would not be disturbed, not even in so subtle a fashion.

Then Merodach-Baladan gave up, for he did not want to risk his Master waking to discover the cause of that precocious development. In the depths of his heart he called out to his father Meleḥasbu, 'the King of Darkness' for deliverance but, his father did not heed his call.

Before the Twi fold Coronet

The Bele of the Paladins entered a great entrance hall with a high nave, the aisle pillars were as high as the nave itself, beautifully and ornately arched. Peridir stood still for a moment as the black Phantom Quartz floor gleamed out before him for some 30m. It was a place enough even to take away the breath of Paladins, for it was named 'E-Barra', 'the Shining House'.

Each pillar was made from a different jewel or crystal. He heard many trees calling, so he walked onward. Eight flights of stairs there were, wide and illustrious. Down he strode, and down, for each flight had seventy-eight steps. Each landing more glorious than the former and increasing by 30m each time. Soft was the light that fell through the double cupolas on high; the first cupola was set between landings 4 and 5 and the second cupola between landings 6 and 7. The ceiling tiles were kræfted of Ahua Awer and Ellādunu respectively. The jewelled crystal floors and pillars reflected it back, up, down and across, so that Peridir passed through a medley of light. When Peridir reached the 4th landing, he stumbled as a great shadow came over him; after which, the four Elements as well as the four Guardians of Eridu encircled him. For a moment he saw them, then they disappeared. He then saw clearly that a terrible battle was taking place, he regained his composure and continued because he could not then turn from his task. When he had descended the long nave with its kaleidoscope of light, he came to a great door kræfted of Ilubit Tuklati (in Midhe it was called 'Firday's Stone'), the doors were ajar but only partially, just enough space for Peridir to pass through but, he didn't, he paused, for the light that drizzled out was blinding even to one such as he. He again took on the light of Bhelaribhus for, when sempiternal beings entered any realm or dimension other than their own, whether they were Ælve or Faege, Melchizedeck or Fáerië, Dwarve or Ala-Gibil, they were subject to its Lores, they were bound by what some called 'The Oath of the Hazel Rod' or 'Segaisslat'.

There stood a kingly Ælve; he was tall, his back was slightly bent as he peered into the eastlea floor. When Bhelaribhus walked in, he slowly lifted his head and straightened himself, his folded arms was behind his back. The kingly Ælve wore his long silver hair in a long pony tail, while two plaits encircled his head. Above his head turning slowly, was a suspended silver coronet, ablaze in blue flame, while between his eyes shone a star of special magnificence. It glowed in 9 dimensions and it was like silver adamant but as that colour receded, it glowed azuline, like a sea and when the azuline dissipated, the silver ascended out of it, like a throbbing heart. Below his thick, silver eyebrows, his eyes shone like stars yet, they were clear as day so that when one looked at them closely, it appeared that they were hollow orbs while living nebulas danced, swirled and twirled inside. The one who was brave enough to investigate them, desired to enter them like a gate into a further universe. But his skin? Aaah!

It was dark, so dark, that dark which was called midnight blue. Stars glittered in his face, dimming and glowing and glowing then dimming. His face was smooth as glass. His bearing was much greater, grander, it was orphic. The Ælve stood alone in that room, that fane, for it was vast. Few entered his presence, not even the dwarves of The Avern, albeit that they were light also. He abided alone in that vast hall, so that it alone on Eridu could contain his majesty, his awesome, terrible power. As Bhelaribhus entered he shaded his eyes with his hands. "I may listen!" exclaimed Enmendurana softly. "I will diminish for Bele Bhelaribhus. After all, the world steals *thy light* a while and diminishes so most wondrous a one." "You are most accommodating Shāhanshāh," replied Bhelaribhus bowing. "Do not bow before me. At Dur-an-ki no one is above the other." Bhelaribhus straightened himself and went forward saying, "yet your *light* proves you are above all others in Eridu and your twifold crown," said Bhelaribhus smiling warmly. The two embraced and all over Eridu, Multanaddassi could be seen, thus was their combined power, in a single embrace.

Ṭēmubīšu had more head than face; he was the preventer of fulfilment. All was xul about him, his face receded inwards, and his larynx was so large that it hid his hideous, small mouth. The large and grotesque larynx connected to his ears, a deformity that gave the appearances of olifant ears. The battle waged on, blood flowed, wrath waxed. Búbkalu reached for his lance, he spun it in the palm of his hand, a beam of dark light emerged from the black shaft. The light moved like a wave towards the Paladins, and only for a moment, they were immobilised, for the earth itself begun to break apart, like Eorðdyn running amok. Búbkalu had failed to make those who run stand still, for they moved the very earth beneath them. The sky had grown dark and ominous as nature started to shed her tears in torrents, hiding the Sun. Then Búbgaz saw that Dalethdir had started to open a new duir but, she was swift, and was upon him in an instant. Dalethdir drew Agsweran from his sheath. Agsweran blushed with light. Búbgaz stood tall, her body armour near impregnable. In each hand she had spinning blades. She did not hesitate; she flung both at the Ælve, her speed was uncanny. Dalethdir ducked, they whirred by turning in an arc, returning towards her instantly. Dalethdir side-stepped, lowered his body, his cape rustled, a low swishing . . . Búbgaz heard the slight rasping of torn fabric and drove forward with her lance. The Ælve countered with Agsweran. The spinning blades returned to their holsters and hung along the Destroyer's thighs.

With her lance constantly switching from hand to hand, she struck over and over and over, as the metallicity of celestial objects kissed passionately.

Then it happened. All over Eridu where the Sun was hiding and the Moon made night, even on the cloudy dark fields of battle in front of the Tower of Magulû, the frenzied gloom began to melt, a frenetic show of Multanaddassi plunged down. So great was the wonder, so unexpected, that many Kwizir fled in terror.

When Bhelaribhus drew back he looked Enmendurana over and smiled. He then looked at the twifold crown placed upon the throne of the dais. It was a wonder even to Bele of the Paladins. It was gold and silver with a strange glass, taken from the stars. At its front was the image of a tree and at its rear, a burning eight-fold star. Only two of those were in Eridu. Enmendurana exclaimed, "Thy coming is as doom, yet I heareth the fluttering of wings . . . A boon?" Bhelaribhus turned from his grasp and walked some paces away, then stopped, he replied with a solemn voice, "The Shāhanshāh Enmendurana of Duranki hears my thoughts even before I speak. Even so, I must entreat, and it is my duty to go to the city found in the tales of Eldiĕni, called Jinbōchō. . ."

"A moment," interjected Enmendurana elegantly raising his hand. "I sense — one of us has *fallen*."

Enmendurana lifted his slender, glittering hands upward, then the ceiling was illuminated with great and terrible vistas. Bhelaribhus was astounded for his mind was not lingering over the world, as to be in the presence of the Shāhanshāh meant all energy, all being had to be present, with the moment on hand. "Tá eolas agam ar an áit seo!" exclaimed Bhelarbhis in the old tongue of Midhe. In a single second all that had transpired was seen and experienced by Bhelarbhis and Enmendurana. In one mind they lifted their hands upward to the passing scene, they spread their fingers and atop each finger burned a flame of a different hue. The battle field was set a-light with Multanaddassi, their eyes cast up suddenly, saw a new wonderment but Dalethdir, Nirdhanin and Inca Illa felt it, as their forms started to fade away like grains of sand that fall through an hourglass. Búbgaz gave a vexated scream because she sorely wanted to destroy Dalethdir. And with the two Paladins went the legions. If anyone were present in the shadow of the trees, they would have seen the body of Lyadalagapē ascend towards the heights of the trees and vanish. Many bloodied bodies limped about, thousands of Kwizir lay slain, several of the legion had also fallen. By the power of Bhelaribhus and Enmendurana those 3 were called back for, that battle was not their bidding but, it was too late, as out of the forest charged five hundred

Wolvlingas and five hundred Waelwulfas for, all the days that Lyadalagapē was wondering alone in the wilds searching for her sons, she was also enlisting that army and a mighty veer they were.

It was said 'for the slaying of cubs breeds a mother's vexation', and so it was. Though named by the Ælves, Lyadalagapē, the beautiful wolf lover, she was also named 'Blaiddfamdis' when Lycurgus first found her. The five hundred Waelwulfas were named the 'Wirlonaa', from which place Blaiddfamdis raised them who could tell, for with that secret she went to her end. They never ventured out into the light of day, for the Wirlonaa were those Waelwulfas who could no longer change back to human form, they were cursed, for once long before, they chose to escape from the yolk of the dark forces and were cursed for it.

They were mighty "slaughter wolves" not to be trifled with.

Búbgaz 'The Destroyer' wasted no time, she rushed towards John Joseph Clem and Nathan Futrell, picked them up and swiftly transported them to one of the lesser towers. She shackled them and set them to zongagongos for a second time in that battle. At first, they refused, then she beat them with the feathered fletching of an arrow until they fell in line and started to drum, to beat, to drum again. And they were good at it; it was their forte, their metier. New voices joined the deathly zongagongos.

> *"Worse than the wolves they are!*
> *Curse their foster-makers,*
> *Pine for life made mortal.*
> *A stain on life, a mar!*
> *Curse the Oath-breakers,*
> *Marriage of grief and guilt of Myrtle"*

Soon after, that was sung 3 times over, invocations of a darker ilk were offered;

> *"Death to the living,*
> *Death to the living,*
> *Long life to the killers,*
> *Success to the Kwizir dark*
> *And ill luck to Elru'u!*
> *And ill luck to Elru'u!"*

. . .and later years they were called 'The Drums of Ħqêl Dmâ' which meant 'the field of blood'. With new voices went new curses, new spells against the Wirlonaa but, so accursed were they that it no longer mattered. Those curses could not quell their anger and regret for the 1000 rushed forward on all fours, like a mighty storm raging on the Hærn of Njǫrvasund.

The two veers rushed forward in two 'V' formations alongside each other. The well natured

Wolvlingas and the cursed 'slaughter wolves'; but their modification was only relative, they did not function as a pair of divergent pedigrees, expressed as two sorrows of severance over time, no, they were all one vekish wulvery. They had no armour, there was no need of them. They were not interested in any magical capture, all of one mind, seize, bind and destroy, this was their thought. So, as they rushed forward and kept their formation, they devoured and tore the Kwizir who were still fumbling about from earlier. A new flurry of arrows darkened the sky, while the remnants of Multanaddassi fell, and while Liulfr the leader of the Wirlonaa ran at the forefront, one could almost see a smile forming on his face, as a glint of a falling star was reflecting in his ravenous eyes. Liulfr was a pure and immeasurable Wulveplicity. The two veers were an invasion of Phantoms and the power of transfiguration. The flurry of arrows missed here and fell there, struck one, struck another, but no arrow could bring down a Wolvlingas, let alone one Wirlonaa. The Kwizir were commanded to stand and fight, their spears and tulwars ready in hand. The double 'V' onslaught pushed through that horde as their speed and power was a hammer against gravity. The two veers stood up and growled in unison, and one thousand voices shattered the shields of the Kwizir; shattered their eardrums so that they started to argue amongst themselves, failing to follow commands. From his high citadel Merodach-Baladan bore witness to another kind of justice, one of incomprehensible power. From Jinbōchō, Bhelaribhus and Enmendurana looked on at the cruelty and they felt unequalled pity. They saw that the untimely battle had become a machine of some other nature, something of a horrendous stepping stone, a vehicle.

Búbgaz and her brother Búbkalu had become weary of that raucous, and they called upon Ṭēmubīšu. That trinity led the strong of the Mush-dagur and went up against the Wulvlingas and the Waelwulfas.

When Búbgaz came upon the first Wulvlinga, she lifted and embraced it up in her strong arms, and crushed its spine, then brought it down over her knee. There was no whimper, no growl of anger only amputation, hacking, ripping and tearing, then death.

Hemming saw that, and turned towards the scene. She stormed towards Búbgaz. Hemming was larger than all the five hundred Wulvlingas, she was their leader for she held 'the Wolvs of the Paladins' dear. As she ran towards Búbgaz, a lone Kwizir came into her path, lance ready for piercing. She didn't stop. She was much faster. She simply took the glaive and ran it right through the Kwizir and pulled it through its back, while still running. She came upon Búbgaz without thought or pause, striking at once.

Búbgaz stepped back but, the blade left a bleeding cut over her pale breast. Even though her armour was near impregnable, it left her bosom exposed. "Mey Booie!" she exclaimed and brought her right hand over her bosom. She soaked her fingers in the blood and ran it over her tongue. "Kakkishu!" she called out to Hemming. "Though my skin is silken-soft my will is like rock." Hemming growled, she then stood on all fours, and was in a stance of attack, ready to leap. Búbgaz was also ready, with fire and a cold calmness, their eyes pinned on each other.

Hemming struck first. It was not a blow. She shape-shifted.

That caught Búbgaz off guard. She knew well that the Wirlonaa could do no such thing. "No!" she exclaimed. "It cannot be!"

Hemming dashed forward, Kwizir lance in hand, and used the hook of the lance to topple Búbgaz off her feet. It worked. Búbgaz fell backwards but was up again with the agility of a feline. She performed a kip-up. Suddenly, 3 Kwizir surrounded Hemming. She shape-shifted again and with one single blow of her large hands, her claws scraped the faces of the Kwizir and broke their necks clear off their shoulders. She was the only Wirlonaa who could shape-shift. Wulvlinga against Kwizir. Kwizir against Waelwulfas. Hemming against Búbgaz. Búbkalu and Ţēmubīšu against Liulfr.

Fate was upon the field. Without reason, consideration or excuse, life was being extinguished. Still it seemed that the two 'V' formations moved like a wedge in a mighty tree, driving forward till the battle came to an impasse about a half mile from Dynyansek. Trapped between the two poles of their might, reduced each to his own fury while the Fates paced up and down the sky unseen, waiting. No more light rained down from the sky, the Sun hid his face and the Moon, she would not rise. Driven by outspoken hate, the Kwizir fought on and on. Ţēmubīšu summoned the hordes of Wezadrachs, and they flew out from their lugubrious turrets, blackening the sky till all light had ceased. The high mountains groaned, and the earth was torn asunder, as Búbgaz and Búbkalu turned on the grim light of their eyes to look on the ghastly battle field. With each sweeping glance in search of their opponents, the ground was split. Wolvlingas and Waelwulfas needed no shadow of Moon or bright Sun to see, darkness was as daylight to them. Glaive split lance, metal burned metal, anger and hatred increased but, mostly blood flowed like rivers, until hordes lay slain from either side. The Son of Death looked on, he would not wake his Master, he thought in his heart that a master stroke had been played, because all would have to choose. The Ragnarök was crescendoing and soon Götterdämmerung was unavoidable.

Bele Bhelaribhus studied the mind of the Shāhanshāh and he understood. The Bele of the Paladins summoned Vala, and Vana used his 'Þulur'. He also summoned Andhrimnir and Andhrimnir, two sempiternal Ælves from the stars. They stood on high and asked Heimdall to see for them from where the call came but, he declined. He was impartial and replied with a voice like the sound of thunder and said, "Listen only to the strings of Vana and follow Þulur." They heard Þulur sounding through time and space yet, they were glad because she didn't reveal their secret names.

The two Ælves filled with glamour, spread their immense wings and all the avidity of all the eternities glittered in their wings as they came down to Eridu. While passing through the stars with the speed of a thought, they conflated and fell from the heavens like innumerable soot. Andhrimnir ascended to the aethyrs and joined them and the 3 conflated again, and became more innumerable, and they came down on the battle field as a wall between foe and foe, even between Hemming and Búbgaz and between Búbkalu and Ṯēmubīšu against Liulfr. Their power was terrible. Neither Wulvlinga nor Waelwulfas' eyes could penetrate the dark. The Son of Death drew back a pace from the window, for a glint of fear overcame him. If the unnamed Ælvish power wanted to, they could consume all before them to nothingness. And so, of a sudden 'He who Overpowers with Doom' woke up, for he felt a great supremacy not found on Eridu, come down to his domain.

Thousands lay slain and that battle, in after time, was named 'The Battle of Ħqêl Dmâ' which meant 'field of blood'.

Crown of Ebony

———✦———

Bhelaribhus and Enmendurana abided for a long time. While the two fell into speech, far away, much further away, 'He who Overpowers with Doom' woke up from Algumes Māluk. He was greatly disturbed.

He glided towards his balcony where he could look down at what lie waste before him. He cried out with a great voice and the earth shook, so that late on the 4th of October 8817 the first earthdin of that age in Midhe occurred, and it rend the earth from the flatlands of Dynyansek, passed and just missed the Mooring of Vakrapuri as far as the Principality of Gätker Yic. In Béth-Élam, it was the talk of the village for many days, as they were touched by a mere shaking, a couple of plates here and a glass or two there, fell from its shelving, but that was all. Lord Kašadom returned inside immediately and summoned his subordinates to council, though it wasn't a council, it was a warning. He saw that Dheya's death was a loss and not a gain to his kingdom, that the pursuit of Lyadalagapē rather than enticing the Realm of Ælves, did nothing but draw them out to open war. He now craved for revenge and since he did not have the One Ring yet, that 'ring of fire' that burned away all ignorance and illusion, Kašadom was desiring it more because he wanted that no one in Eridu should have illumination. Even at his coming out of the state of Algumes Māluku, Kašadom already foresaw a different plan to get the ring, a strategy more subtle. He coveted the second most powerful thing in Eridu, the star-like jewel of the Ice Queen, for she wore it in her crown, and it was close at hand in the Mountains of Vakratuvakra. Kašadom wanted to stretch his long arm and seize it. He appeared then in the Hall of Umsundulu and Hei for, once ages before, Damasandra reigned supreme in a most fertile land in the far South, a place now called 'Ta-merri'. There he was loved and impartial, and it was his custom at times, to use their dialect and speak their tongue. He remembered those times often because he wasn't entirely egregious. The Hall of Umsundulu and Hei was situated in the centre of Dimtu Ilimmu Shumsuene, and its walls had a strange construction. It wasn't a solid construction but some form that seemed, if touched, would twist to stone and assimilate it. Peculiar, irksome, stark, haggard, grief-stricken charismata, including emaciated statues, adorned the walls which were filled and littered with cavities of all shapes and lengths.

Sunlight fell through it and created ominous silhouettes, and the moonlight fell into it with a feeling of haunting at night.

Those emaciated statues were of creatures not found in the memory of man and neither did he want to meet them. The interior floor wasn't entirely flat; it had jaggered upturned parts and points; and was laid with Qamunite, Azagnite and Moldavite with only the centre being flat and of a polygon shape. The floor was filled with gaps that provided a view down into the catacombs below. Those catacombs were far from being underground, only Kašadom lingered there. If one were to inspect it, the whole thing was a hyperboloid structure of electric geometry, wholly opposed to any human form. It was there where he summoned his vassals to the centre most part, the only flat part around a square table. At the eastern side of the table that grew out of the floor itself, stood a dais. It was separate and raised, and where Kašadom sat. No one sat upon it even if they tried, for all around it, protruded many spears and spikes. One could not walk up to it and sit down; one had to appear in it. Kašadom did just that for, he was a phantom more than he was flesh. Like foxes on fire, tied tail to tail, burning and spreading fire through wheat fields, so the desire of his bidding was felt and heard, and for two days he waited in that seat for the arrival of his vassals. If they were unable to attend personally, their heads of state were to answer the call. At that point in time, he refused to give Merodach-Baladan an audience and so, Kašadom brooded. Those who could, arrived, and those who couldn't didn't, because their Lord and Master Kašadom would not have it so. They that couldn't, were in secret craft and were laying schemes always to ensnare, for something greater that he had foreseen. First came Merodach-Baladan after being allowed to do so, with him arrived Búbgaz for she could be in several places at once. Her brother Búbkalu accompanied her. Then came Krallen, slinking in, bag over shoulder, and sat apart from them but, Merodach-Baladan bid him come closer, for he was his master. Afterwards came Vidar, she had many legions under her command. Telemon, Grand Draconian, followed. Melpomene also arrived. She was large in form, so much so that the edifice could not contain her, and she had to diminish. She was extremely powerful. She was crimson in appearance, hairless and had aniridian eyes which glared brilliant, luminous green. Her large hacele seemed tattered and torn, as she held it to her breast with both hands clasped in powerful fists for, the hacele was all she wore. Her skin could be seen through the hacele; brilliant and luminous, ever in motion like great torrents of water and cloud for, Melpomene ruled the storms and great waters. Charybdis came with her; she ruled over and raised the Lemures at full Moon. Two others arrived, and they were lithe and phantom-like, their names were Avalon and Finnbeara (the Wind Draconian).

Jaggannath came but, he too had to diminish. He was ugly, grey and strange of form. No one present knew why he was summoned because for it was forbidden to land any Vimāna in Eridu yet, they knew, Halálseren continued to draw nearer. The leader of the Kwizir, the wing of the Wezadrachs and a representative of the Melchizedecks on Eridu, arrived after that. Lastly, arrived one feminine being, cloaked and veiled in soft cloth, folds draped and fell; it was white, without blemish and pinned to it were many ribbons of all hues, and for each there was dis-ease allied to lewdness; black, blue, brown, burgundy, cloud, copper, cream, grey, green, gold, jade, coloured, orange, peach, pearl, pink, purple, puzzle red, silver, teal, violet, white and yellow. When she arrived, all those that were present except Kašadom, stood up. When she was seated, they sat down again. She acted demurely and removed her veil and it revealed a radiant and beautiful face. She was silver- skinned and her long, flaxen hair was braided into many plaits, her statuesque form spoke of one with power.

She was Fescessenine and she was one all mortals feared, in sickness and in death, her arm stretched far. The fifteen sat around the table but, there were still many vacant seats.

Kašadom spoke to Fescessenine and asked, "From where cometh thou great lady?" She replied in dulcet tones, "My Lord!" bowing her head, "I have roamed the earth through every kingdom, city and town and have afflicted many in squalor, and obscenity they revel. So it was that I gave it to them in abundance. But the little villages and hamlets elude me for they care for the green and growing things and gracious Ariel have sway of their hearts. Yet there was one small place that holds a strange name, with a strange king in the North, where all are afflicted yet, I have no power over them. . ."

"Yes! I have seen that place and I have foreseen that it will be of worth soon," said her master. Fescessenine started singing, as that was her way at times. She had a beautiful voice but, what she sang of, could not be repeated. Her audience applauded and when she glanced at her Lord for approval, he was not on his dais. They turned their heads and saw that he was standing idly at the large, glass pavilion and they saw him there as only a flaming phantom. A quiver ran through their hearts for they knew full well, that he was vexed. He did not turn around; he only raised his hand and pointed to Merodach-Baladan and 'The Son of Death' knew his master's mind and replied, "I cannot answer for my failure Master, for you read the answers in my mind but, I shall go unto my father's citadel and we shall make this matter right. One thing I must confess is hidden from thee. . ."

The phantom was enraged, of a sudden a cloud of khthōnic flame floated in the air over Merodach-Baladan and several others. Damasandra then subdued Kašadom and an ebony crown could be seen emanating, and great, curved horns of flame, on The Master's head. His eye glinted with a light filled with despair. Some looked away but, Merodach-Baladan held his glance, he dared not look away.

"Nothing is hid from me!" exclaimed Damasandra. "Nothing. Though for the warning in me that speaks. . .speak Son of Death, I listen." Damasandra again appeared on his dais, that seat that was called 'Kurnugia Dúr.gar Zalmat-Qaqadi'.

When there was absolute silence, Merodach-Baladan spoke, "With permission Lord, I will let the siblings regale it to you, for it is they who brought it to me." Damasandra sat forward, for he greatly favoured Búbgaz and her brother Búbkalu.

The siblings stood but, it was Búbkalu that spoke, "Mussuku-Emētu has prophesied my King, though this has not happened for an age.

I have told it to my sister so she may speak, for her voice is sweeter." Damasandra then smiled for the first time, he kindly made a gesture with his hand, allowing Búbgaz to address him.

"Here are the words that Mussuku-Emētu uttered and may you understand them my King,

"6 long strides shalt thou take,
Into Dynyansek thou must go,
This the last rent of my bough.
But the future thou canst not see,
King of Eridu Damasandra shalt not be.
Rise up Dryad and rise up Faun,
For Kašadom, he maun
Bend to the will of the Bee
And myself renewed, unsullied Illerwood Tree.

Twelve Paladins are standing by,
Their feet are the earth, and their eyes are the sky,
The knave will thrive wherever they be.
He shall be born under a tree."

Before Búbgaz was done repeating the prophecy, oohs and aahs, and various phatic expressions were uttered amongst her hearers. An air of disbelief could be felt but, the one on the khthonic Zalmat-Qaqadi throne was silent. He raised his left arm and all fell silent. "Verily this has been hidden from me, it is a riddle as well as a prophecy, one that will be hard to augur. . .indeed my scotoma." He fell silent for some time then continued, "Be seated Búbgaz, you and your brother serve me well. A word afterwards. I will not linger here on a battle ill lost, but will turn my eye on the war to come. . .for *war* is coming."

His last words were as a hammer falling on an anvil, as if wielded by the god Thor himself. Suddenly, he appeared gliding over the large table and he said to his audience, "Behold!"

The table that seemed to grow out of the floor was in fact a grand diorama of Eridu. Great care had been taken to make an exact replica, all the seas, oceans were made of blue Moonstone, rivers were made of white ivory, the mountains and hills made of Picture Jasper and the cities, towns and villages of ebony wood.

The Ælvish citadels and locations were made of Oak, Ash, Deodar and Gold, well, at least those that he knew of. Real grass and trees, all in miniature form, were there also.

He told them of his campaigns, of his entanglements but, his obsession was to ensnare the Ring Bearer. His voice was grave and abysmal and as he spoke to his hearers, gusts of wind passed between the words. He pointed out a location where he thought the Ring Bearer would be born, and all sat assiduously listening. A beautiful, blue light appeared at the location, and then hovered over the table. It bobbed this way and that, like an Alkana-Landras. At times, it vanished and appeared elsewhere, so that those around the table, also Damasandra, didn't know where the child would arrive or not.

So, he sent Kwizir in their thousands to many cities, towns and villages to spy. He also sent Wezadrachs to inhabit many newborn children, and into the woods and wealds he employed all manner of creature, mammal or bird as spies. Damasandra also commanded that when the time came, that Búbgaz and her brother Búbkalu disguise themselves as children, to ensnare the Ring Bearer. They then appeared on the diorama as lesser lights, filled with white radiance, a radiance filled with electric geometry, undesirable, not benign. He spoke long, many-a-thing was uttered too stygian and morose or egregious to chronicle here now, for some things are better left unsaid for even such things have a power of their own for Tulpa.

Duirparina

———❧———

Jaddamiah got up on the morning of the 5th October and shook off the night in the cold, morning air. He had a great feeling of avidity and when he looked up at the naked oak, he wanted to leave that place quickly as, he could not understand the restless night that had transpired; with an oak that was the only tree for miles and miles standing naked, he thought the oak quite impudent. He walked over to his horse and embraced her. She was loyal, always there in the morning. He saddled and bridled, fed and ate as quickly as time would allow, and left the oak. They had only trotted a few meters from the oak when Jaddamiah clearly heard strange voices. It was soft, not boisterous but, sounded very menacing. He could hear that it was more than one voice, voices jeering and ludibrious. He turned his head suddenly but, saw nothing. The voices were almost hissing, so he jabbed Fágan in her side with the spur of which he felt bad for afterwards but, she cantered away and kept at it till they were well clear of Duirparina. When Jaddamiah thought that they were far enough away from the strange tree, he asked Fágan to slow down, and glanced back again but all was clear but not safe, for swooping overhead were two, white torraps, making an awful noise. He shaded his eyes and slanted his hands over them, looking up at the birds as they circled overhead, that time flying lower. 3 black crows with luxurious plumes that radiated in the Sunlight, emerged through the clouds and drove the torraps away. Jaddamiah and Fágan were again left alone on the road.

"The place is not good for imagination, and does not bring restful dreams at night," he said dubiously to Fágan.

The Menace of The Gra'ga'

Jaddamiah did not travel long, when ahead him a great, walled chasm unexpectedly showed its face through the trees. The trees stopped abruptly thereafter, and the road was squeezed as he came to Pasio Wëych. The sign post and the board were entwined with pretty, white flowers, and made the words barely visible to the traveller. The pass started to climb its way between the mountains and twisted and turned back on itself, so that it faced east then straightened out again, and ran north west then turned again to west, and eventually south; and flattening out of the Aravali region.

The Southern Aravali covered a distance of 90 miles. The mountain range was part of the Drakensberg but, also fell under the same name of Aravali. It had a triangular shape, the eastern part of the divide separated Aravali from Zarvari Vana but was in no way less perilous. It wasn't part of the Principality of Palador and the awl-shaped mountains excluded it perfectly. The interior of the Aravali was covered in a woodland with a lake in its centre; nearly growing right out of the lake was a beautiful, tree-drowned mountain or hill called Ælverhøj, though the Ælves called it 'Il-Kur-Ngis'.

When going along the Vakratuvakra one looked down on the myriad trees standing between those mighty mountains. There was no way Jaddamiah could cross Vakratuvakra in a day, so once again, he had to sleep in the wilds. To his right stood a tall peak covered in clouds, it took him some two hours to traverse that long sweep. Just after midday, the great, western Sun was at his back, the road tilted downward and became easier over a foggity patch. It seemed that it had rained earlier, the air was permeated with a most adorable fragrance from the tall, silver-blue fir trees that grew to a height of 12ft and stood in profusion for about 300 meters. Jaddamiah closed his eyes and took a deep breath for, there was something altogether charming when the Sunlight and rain released the fragrance from the Blue Ice tree. The road sank further into the weald and Jaddamiah's eyes bolted open, he pursed his upper lip, pulled it up so that it touched the tip of his nose. It was horrible, the stench overpowered that moment of olfactory bliss. It smelled of rancid butter, dog bog or barf stench. He turned back in his saddle and rested his free hand on Fágan's rump. He looked down but, she had made no 'go-bumptions'. He scanned the area as he sat on his saddle but could not identify the stench; neither had he ever before smelled such a vile odour.

He raised his speed to a trot, and didn't really know why but, the hairs on his back were standing on end. A few moments later he thought he heard some cracking of tree branches but, saw nothing. The stirring was faint to start off with and it always kept to the weald some meters away yet alongside of him. Fágan's ears were pricked, her nostrils flared and her eyes rolled as the white of the eyes became visible. Jaddamiah felt no trembling of her muscles so he was set at ease for he didn't want Fágan to be spooked by whatever they were sensing. He felt that impalpable spleen arise in him, an annoyance with his own senses, for he could not see the danger, neither having a word for it. But no weald or woodland yields herself to sight, and those who would not make acquaintance or placations before entering her fanes, were better left unentered. He heard it from time to time, and when they stopped, it stopped, when they sped up, it sped up. At that point, Jaddamiah's right hand was firmly placed on the hilt of his sword. 'Would I have to use Mordēre prematurely? Would this be my first test long before the reality?' Those questions irritated his mind, his chest was damp from nervous sweat. The invisible menace kept on well into the late afternoon, and Jaddamiah only realized it when eager growls had risen from his belly. They had carried on pass the midday-meal but, his eagerness to get to some form of safety drove him on. 'The weald is always silent when one needs her to be most cheerful! When one needs her to be most talkative she is without voice'. Those accumulating thoughts filled his mind. The creaking and cracking and brushing became louder and closer until in one, short moment, he saw a shadow cross the road ahead. They now had weald on either side and no mountain wall to protect them on the right, for the road had turned north east again. Only a few, still moments had passed when that menace could be heard on both sides of the road. Jaddamiah felt that it was not the spirit of the place but a vile offender, an intruder or intruders. Great Mountains of the world oppress or invoke great loneliness and oceans overpower, but places filled with millions of trees exercise a power altogether alien to the mortal, more foreboding to the profane. Jaddamiah was hungry to the point of fainting. He had hoped that he would simply climb out of the weald, for the road felt like it was ascending again. The stench was then too great to bear, and he knew that whomever it was, whatever it was, was very close. He gently dragged Mordēre out, then let it drom back in its scabbard. He had an idea and dismounted Fágan. He thought that if the menace proved real, it wouldn't attack the gift that Gedymdeith had given him. "Sâa! Sâa!" shouted Jaddamiah and Fágan stood up on her hind legs, blowing and snoring, she sped off, Jaddamiah shouted, "Run! Run to high ground Fágan!" Sunlight had perished behind the ragged teeth of the mountains and was hiding from sight, and gloom set in without and within. The stench started to growl. It was perhaps wise to lay down the lore of pragmatism regarding darkness and note, for in the gloom of things the dreads of mortals escalate exponentially, and the canopies of the witching hours magnify significantly to the eyes which are perhaps not ideal for seeing, turning every object in Nature to a pan-ic.

Suddenly, bursting forth out of the tree line along the road, from both sides, sprang two

Gra'ga's. Jaddamiah gripped Mordēre in his right hand as the first Gra'ga leapt through the air, its woeful mouth agape, claws extended, and its fangs dripping with wretched putrescent. Jaddamiah slashed the dark beast across the neck, dealing a galling blow. He stumbled forward, surprised at his own strength, lost his foothold and fell to the ground. The blow was clearly not deep enough to sever the Gra'ga's head, as it turned around and stood still only for a moment, ready to make the second strike. The Gra'ga growled with menace, hissing as the cold vapour steamed from between its spike-like teeth. Jaddamiah glanced down the road, then at the Gra'ga, and then down to his sword, for there were the beginnings of the dim, blue light appearing, it grew bright as the words began to form; 'अन एविल् देअथ् विल्ल् सेत फ़ोर्थ् व्होम् थे बलादे पिएर्चेस्'. The horn was extended, Jaddamiah smiled in relief, for as the second Gra'ga chased Fágan down the road, the first one began to call out in horrendous pain, whimpering, and to Jaddamiah's surprise its head fell from its body. The horrible beast fell over like an anchor dropping to the depths of the sea.

The thrill of his success did not last long as the second Gra'ga stopped in its tracks and lifted its head, although daylight was failing, Jaddamiah could clearly see its two, glittering blood-orange eyes. It made a long, wailing-howling call, and Jaddamiah did not need any glaumerie to interpret that! Almost instantly, eight more Gra'ga's jumped out from the tree line on either side. Four of them held ferocious wodfreca; two turned aside and set full speed after the second Gra'ga, while the rest sped towards Jaddamiah. Jaddamiah, foolish or brave who could tell, stood with his legs apart, held Mordēre with both hands, yet gently, for he remembered Gedymdeith's instruction. He felt his heart slowing down, the dead thud in his chest was beginning to calm, he could not understand, he also started hearing the soft, light tingling sound of bells, then out of the trees two large creatures crashed forth in thunderous roar. Jaddamiah stood in awe as two Þursar plucked several Gra'ga's and their riders from the road and catapulted them through the air.

"We come! We come! We come Mr Jabberwocky!" exclaimed one.

They were Gimlillÿs and Gimvöllekaas. The Gra'ga and the wodfreca tried in vain to put up a fight but, it was like using tooth picks to fight a great lion. A third Thurisaz burst out from the trees further up the road, completely jabberclotting those beasts which set after Fágan. A strange, long, dog whistle was heard, immediately all attack, all pursuit stopped as the Gra'ga's and their wodfreca scurried into the weald. All was still again. The 3 Þursar strode to Jaddamiah, who had wiped his blade of the green murky, slimy blood and sheathed his glaive. He stood with his hand on his hips, a smile wider than a mile, for he could not believe his luck. When the 3 Þursar came to Jaddamiah they straightened their habiliments and sat down beside him. The third held Fágan gently with his hand, and set her down, speaking some strange tongue to her. Fágan was very pleased to be reunited with her master and so was he. The third Thurisaz began to speak first, "It is a good evening Mr Jabberwocky. You can call me Flaine although the Ælve Beles don't like nicknames much," with that, he laughed so loud that the trees shook. He then reached for a lovely blanket that was strung to his back and sat down, covering his legs. "I am most happy to make your acquaintance," he spoke in a deep, bold voice and seemed older than the other two. He pulled Jaddamiah closer and set Jaddamiah on his knee. "But I am more happy for meeting you, for I say that was a spotta-bother and fie to those horrible creatures," exclaimed Jaddamiah.

"Aye! But have you forgotten us so hastily Mr Jaddamiah? We can be found in most spots of bother, to unbother those in a spot of bother," replied Gimvöllekaas.

The other two laughed to hearts content. Just then, 3 Ælves appeared from under the trees. They were on horseback but were hardly heard or seen, it was the tall Elrukmavaksas who spoke first, "And the Ælves chase the bother away, don't we Gimvöllekaas?" Jaddamiah looked back to see where those words came from, for the voice sounded regal and proud. For the second time Jaddamiah was in reverent awe as that Ælve dismounted his fair horse. Jaddamiah also noticed that none of the Ælves drove with the contraptions of saddle or rein. Elrukmavaksas had a beautiful light that surrounded his form. It was as if they were sitting in a late sunset for Jaddamiah had not seen such beauty before. His golden face burned bright, that it seemed there was no darkness around. Flaine took Jaddamiah off his knee as Elrukmavaksas walked forward. "Jaddamiah of Béth-Élam, I am called Elrukmavaksas and my Master bid me to pelisse you. Allow me to present you to our host for we are in *their* realm now."

The two Ælves that stood beside him were of slightly shorter stature but much leaner, lissom and capricious. The male had long, auburn hair that swept past leaf-like ears, set around a chiselled face. His eyes, like the Ælfennes who stood close by, were the colour of lime and were alluring and mysterious. The outer edge of their eyes had a vivid, black ring. When Jaddamiah looked at them he felt calm and at peace. They were clothed in weald green and grey, those two carried no visible weapons that Jaddamiah could see. He could not bring himself to break his gaze for, the colour of their skin was like driftwood. Looking upon those woodland Ælves, was pleasant in every way. Elrukmavaksas introduced the Ælfennes first, "My lady Lusinfiodh." She lifted her arm the way a leaf drifts down to the weald floor and laid her willowy hand on Jaddamiah's shoulder and said, "I am Lusinfiodh, light of the weald." She had a deep, clear voice. "And I am called Ulmus. It is not oft we have a sojourner of Béth-Élam passing through our Realm. We did not arrest the wodfreca but, we chased them out of harm's way and our kindred will do the rest further aweald." As Ulmus spoke those words in his sonorous voice, he held his hand on Jaddamiah's shoulder and looked down, long into his eyes. Then said again, "Their presence here is ill news, I hope we've set your heart at peace. Come!" he said to Jaddamiah, "Let us kindle a fire and rest."

Jaddamiah's stomach growled, the Ælves looked at him and smiled.

"Come!" exclaimed Lusinfiodh gently leading Jaddamiah away to the edge of the weald. "One such as yourself has not entered our Realm, not ever since the world began. Now you shall be the first to observe but, you shall not enter, for the privilege is held for the one who goes Enûma Eliš. I apologize but, there is no tongue that can reckon this. But come; let us replenish the matter in you that sustains."

Her voice was like a dream as she lifted her right hand; her index and middle finger held together and pointed upward while her pinkie and ring finger were held inward to the palm of her hand. Her thumb was held inward also but away from her hand.

"This is called Ṛbhú-Kata and this specific one is called Atu-Kata of which there are 100 thousand million variations. Atu-Kata inaccurately translated meant 'gatekeeper movement'. For each arboreta there are katas, this is how the Ælves commune with the trees. It is called 'Isukata'." Light streamed from her fingers. It became like a little, fiery, glistering tree at first, then as she held her hand up higher, the colours became like a starburst accompanied by the formation of a galactic jet. Jaddamiah was numb; he was also speechless when Lusinfiodh dragged him through the duir. Shortly afterwards, he found himself accompanied by Lusinfiodh, in a different location surrounded by eight Glæmbooms which created a short avenue and commenced from a large ava-llan. At the centre of the ava-llan grew a white hawthorn, covered in thick blossoms. No grass grew where the Hawthorne stood, but in its place was a circle of hard soil. There were two Ælves and two Elfenna sitting on the ground with their legs crossed, and playing a game. They were deeply involved or so it seemed, 3 golden lances and one of viridian green were planted in the grass beyond the sand circle. Lusinfiodh and Jaddamiah were in a sphere of light and hovered above the ground. As she walked forward the sphere moved forward too. She stopped where the Ælves were gaming and stepped out. Jaddamiah followed suit or rather attempted too but he found the gelatinous, paper-thin wall, prohibited any such action. "I come upon you *gaming*! There are foul creatures about in the weald. Care you not?" said the Ælfennes to the four but, they did not glance her way but instead replied, "Our weald is safe from harm. Look!" exclaimed one pointing to the ground. Jaddamiah could hear every word clearly, as if he sat right in their midst. He looked towards the ground and saw myriad marbles. At first, he thought that the bare ground was dull but, in that light neither day nor night; he found that it sparkled with crystals and mica, feldspar and amphiboles. On the ground the most amazing marbles were lying about; some were made from alabaster while others were made of the rarest glass, still others were made of rarer crystals. There were taws, mibs or ducks, also Bumblebees, Jaspers and Clambroths. "Annitu! Annitu! Beleti Immaru ak ina isu." Spoke one of the four but, Jaddamiah heard that it was all four who spoke in unison. He pushed his head against the gelatinous sides of the sphere, hoping to get a better view of things but in the process, the shape of his face became moulded against the sphere.

Several peewees were circling the other marbles, while many clear marbles parted and made a path. Those clear marbles had the shapes of trees within and they sparkled brilliantly. In the middle of the marbles with sylvan shapes, a 27mm cosmic vortex marble was moving gently through the path of clear, sylvan marbles.

In another circle behind the clear sylvan marbles, hundreds of cat eye marbles vibrated and bounced up and down like Pezala keys. Jaddamiah could not believe his eyes; his head swayed this way and that as he watched with childlike enthusiasm. The marbles changed continuously but always in circles, there was a calmness to all the movement. Then the outer circle and inner danced like stately poplars, as a row of 'Ancient Oxblood V-Green Swir' marbles, started forming a svastika. Again, one of the Ælves spoke, "Me ngíz-al ngishnugal golyó ene," he said in a powerful authoritative voice. The others in unison, "Nergal. . . nergal . . . nergal." Lusinfiodh smiled warmly and glided over them. With the sweep of her arm, Jaddamiah's sphere followed. She raised it up so that he was several hundred feet off the ground, from there he watched. He saw Lusinfiodh enter the Glæmboom avenue and as she passed underneath them, the trees began to glow, glister and spangle. She walked to the 9th set of Glæmboom and stood in front of it. Jaddamiah surveyed from his bird's eye view and what he saw was a splendoured thing. He saw splendid sights where great trees rose. Il-Kur-Ngis's crystal edifices displayed Labradorescence through the flora and sylva that clambered the heights; crags with its feral, antediluvian waters and streams soared downward, to many rivered paths that were guarded by a thousand tree tops.

Puttinghochs, weepy, teared dispassionately under ornate wooden foot-bridges while branching away now and then, were constricted pathways which snuggled into leaf-whelmed, primordial trees where legions of Elemental Spirits loitered in indolence. Sound was an abstract idea in Il-Kur-Ngis for all that came to fancy Jaddamiah's ears were the burbling, warbling, crafty trickling of Merlonnic waters from numberless, obscured fountains that kissed sylvan feet. Greened, turquoised coppered domes peeped niftily from their vernal linens, a scant revelation of built things.

The leaf-whelmed secret growth seemed to him to preserve mysteries of age-forgotten, rustic boustrophedons that were written on every leaf by hands that went from Heaven to Eridu, and mortal could never know.

The beauty of Il-Kur-Ngis was a place rarely found, only in deep, deep, sweet cavernous dreams; so it seemed to Jaddamiah.

There, time-touched things were waiting, as the group of Ælves clearly showed when Lusinfiodh approached at first with Jaddamiah. He saw no movement, or perhaps he did but, they were mere glints, flutters, from bright butterflies that sang of ancient purple things. The Ælves were still at their marbles. It was Lusinfiodh who showed any sign of movement for, as she busied herself by a Glæmboom, a bright, luminous insect came by and settled on the bark of the tree. It started to puncture the bark and large golden drops poured out; Lusinfiodh gathered those in the palms of her hands. She picked some leaves from the tree and created a little pouch, woven with strands of light. When she had placed all in that pouch, she returned to Jaddamiah. She gently took his hands into hers and placed the pouch in them saying; "Never shalt thou be of want if these be your ailment. Perchance someday your kind shall name this 'Manu' or 'Šekar' or 'Honey that falls from Glæmboom leaves'. Accept this, it is yours. It is our Illaliazu."

Jaddamiah opened the pouch, in it lay many glittering acorn-like objects, he brought one to his lips between his fingers but, Lusinfiodh stopped him from eating it in Il-Kur-Ngis. When Lusinfiodh and Jaddamiah reappeared from the forest, there, right in the middle of the road, the Woodland Ælves of the Kur Udor were kindling a large fire. A dome of pastel blue light was cast around them all, while two of the Þursar kept watch. Flaine walked off into the weald towards the east. Jaddamiah could not wait to eat though, having received such an Elvysshe gift he was no doubt filled with . . . with . . . with a certain desolation. The wonder that he had seen caused him to be like that, so, he sat quietly eating. In fact, he had four of the Illaliazu, taking the fifth deep in thought; he fell into a deep swoon. The Ælves giggled amongst themselves as Jaddamiah lay unconscious in front of the fire, and while he slept, they sang lullabies and recited verses. They left him that way until the 7th hour had passed, then Elrukmavaksas took him out of his swoon for, to pass beyond the 8th hour in *that* state, could prove fatal to one of the Eldiĕni.

When he awoke, he remembered that what he had consumed was soft, softer than Ninfa Harsa, but much tastier; like a swirl of juvenēscere with the scent of white heliotrope, called 'Samsum Emu' by those from Jinbōchō. Elrukmavaksas got up and shook Jaddamiah's hand and said, "You are in good hands Jaddamiah but, I must be off! My path leads westward. Perhaps our paths will cross again." He mounted his horse and trotted down the road and was soon lost in the darkness; his light faded with him like a star. It was half hour before midnight. Jaddamiah said quietly after having his share as the honey filled him up quite quickly. From time to time he looked up at Lusinfiodh, then dropped his gaze in blushing awkwardness, for he did not know what to say to such a noble being. Afterwards they sang while Jaddamiah drifted in and out of a lucid sleep, he caught some of the words from time to time;

> "...in the wild wood – in the wild wood
> Come what may for here you will find your childhood
> All the seasons fade
> And only Summer remains in this glade
> In the wild wood where the songs are sung
> You will find from the Trees, the Lore is hung
> By every flower
> You'll find the power
> That sustains the universe
> And we will teach it to you, verse by verse.

> *In the wild wood . . .in the wild wood*
> *come ga-ther. . .*

And so, the music became fainter and trailed off, until it was heard just above the sound of the wind that had started up from the west. Jaddamiah lay sleeping, he didn't know when he fell asleep but through his deep sleep, he heard those words again;

> *"... in the wild wood...*
> *Come gather...*
> *Gather round! You've been found*
> *In the circles of the weald..."*

He didn't know when he woke up again, for time seemed all jumbled up like many toys in a room after unthinking play, but those words he heard again;

> *"... in the circles of the forest*
> *I am king of the florists*
> *In the groves of the trees*
> *Only this lullaby shall please*
> *By every bower*
> *Where there is a flower*
> *Its fragrance shall be your breath*
> *For in this wild wood there is no death."*

Fágan stood before her master, her head bowed low; she snorted, then licked his face. Jaddamiah opened his eyes to a clear day, without a breeze or passing cloud. The mountains stood in their resplendent poise, the colours changed as the Sun climbed higher. There were no sign of any Ælves, neither any signs that a fire burned all night. He got to his feet, rubbed his belly with the palm of his hand, for it was strange to him that there was no morning hunger. Fágan nudged him forward with her nose and he knew that she wanted to get on with the journey. He mounted and she trotted off. The road climbed out of the woodland, and elevated to a height that he could see the Vidhu Hrada as it swam all alone, amongst the densely populated trees that lined its shores at the foot of Il-Kur-Ngis. They rode on into the night through to the next morning without incident, neither any water nor food passing over their lips. Jaddamiah and his loyal Fágan carried on through the next day and found that on the morning of the 9th of October the abra was behind them and it was the thirteenth day of his journey. At first, he didn't realize it but, hunger stopped him as the road lay facing west.

On their left, bathed in mid-autumn sunshine, was a beautiful glade. He saw clusters of tall lupins and Thor's mantle growing to a height of 3 meters. Beautiful, wild, yellow daisies contrasted with soft larkspur which created an enchanting haze of floral light over the shire. There were hundreds of those flowers, and one could imagine what it looked like in spring or mid-Summer.

Jaddamiah rubbed out his eyes, because he saw just about a 3/4mile ahead of him, from the opposite direction, a wagon approaching. As it came closer, he noticed that it was two wagons; one was heavy laden, the other was a hansom drawn only by one horse. When the travellers met up with him it seemed that they were quite hasty, flighty in fact, as Jaddamiah flagged them down. Mr Loopenval as he introduced himself, was a man in his early 50s, his hair curled about his head like branches of a red Loha tree from Alkana. His two sons were sitting on the wagon which he was driving, and at the back was the hansom in which his wife and daughter sat. His wife, Grace Loopenval, managed a smile but, Jaddamiah realized behind her graceful smile there was some anxiety. She was the epitome of the women of Weir. She had long, red hair of which 3 plaits were wound around her head, something that the people of the north or of Midhe had learned from the Elfenna. If that hair style was not worn, it simply meant that they had no dealings with the Ælves. The eldest son, an 18-year old who resembled his father, was called Trippin Loopenval, he sat next to his father with a long sword resting on his knees, it was an elegant sword, most likely a family heirloom.

"Where be you going Mr Jaddamiah, you are right far from your doorstep and you know what the old tales say about leaving your front door." his question was also an admonition, and Jaddamiah was to find out perhaps rightly so.

"Well, Mr Loopenval, I am going to Weir to fight the Dragon."

Mr Rush Loopenval turned white like an aspen. He nearly choked on his words but, they managed to come out nonetheless, "Drag-gon! Wee-iir! Mr Jabberwocky! It is exactly the place we're fleeing from. You should put all such foolduggeries aside and join us instantly to Maldon," he said that with great seriousness in his tone. He stuck his hand out and pointed in the opposite direction saying further, "If you say where you say you are from, then that's. . ." and Mr Rush Loopenval began to count on his one hand saying again, "13 days of travel to your door step." "Thirteen Days!" exclaimed Jaddamiah and went all hoary. He held his face in his hands and looked very upset. "My, Mr Jabberwocky, have I said something to offend you?" "He does not seem well my love!" exclaimed his wife in a sweet voice. Jaddamiah's legs felt lame, his head started spinning and he fell from his horse with a thud on the soft ground. Mr and Mrs Loopenval were immediately at his side and when Jaddamiah came to, he found himself looking up into the face of a beautiful, chartreuse-eyed maiden, his damp head resting in her lap. "Don't worry yourself Mr Jaddamiah," assured Grace "We've damped your head as you fell from your mare for no reason at all."

"My dear, pretty wife," said Rush. "He seems to be in need of a morning drink instead of breakfast."

The family stood peering over him except Trippin, for he was standing on the foot panel looking up and down the road, sword in hand. "Perhaps he needs gruel father? Or ale hoof, perhaps some ale-bree," said his daughter thoughtfully.

"Child hush! Let your mother decide," and for the first time, laughter broke out amongst them. "Though having said hush dear, Aineislis, the women of our north western parts Mr Jaddamiah, especially about Weir and Skallagrimmr, do 'tun the herbe ale hoove into their ale'." Grace's head disappeared for a moment. When she returned and filled the space with her fair countenance, Jaddamiah grabbed the bottle out of her grasp, opened the top and took a long gulp, then bolted up and sat with his hand behind his back and flat on the ground.

"You do take to excitement Mr Jabberwocky!" exclaimed Grace.

"Yes, I told you the ale would help," answered Rush with a proud smile.

"I do apologize for my behaviour although I don't like to admit it, I tend to agonize over triskaidekaphobia from time to time."

"Trick-ster-kaleidoscopia-what?" exclaimed Trippin from above his perch. "Please Mr Jabberwocky. . ."

"Please do call me Jaddamiah. After that ale we should be on a first name basis," interjected Jaddamiah comically.

"Indeed Jaddamiah! Please use less persuasive words, we are only simple folk and my dear Grace was not aiming to trick you with the ale sir," assured Rush.

Jaddamiah got up and steadied himself by holding on to the wagon.

He bowed to the young maiden and said, "You have made a soft pillow for my head dear Aineislis, I shall not forget it and for the hospitality of this family, I must make gramercy."

He turned to Rush and explained himself further, "What I meant to say dear fellow, was that by your right count you have brought me to the realization that today is the thirteenth day of my journey and I can no longer go further. Absolutely not! The number thirteen has proven to be bad for me."

"Father!" called Trippin, "We must make for the pass before nightfall, when shall we press on?" Rush scratched his head and stood with his cap in his hand. "Mr Jaddamiah Jabberwocky, ummm Jaddamiah, I can only say on behalf of my family, that we wish you slay the Dragon and free the town of our birth but, in one word I say to you, aroint! Our roads must part now."

"And I dear Jaddamiah, I commend you to your own content," said Grace in a kind tone yet, to Jaddamiah it felt ambiguous.

The two wagons were soon out of sight. Jaddamiah walked over the verge of the road and got down, laying on his side, legs crossed, he would not move an inch further. A small but distinctive blue butterfly began to flutter around him, then a melodious voice started singing yet, Jaddamiah could see no one;

Hello hello weary fellow
Hello hello silly callow
Your superstition is a polichinelle
Why don't yah cheer up, be like a flickering tallow
You have been moved 3 days hence
Who could make such recompense?
Only they of Ælven-kind

Why have yah been so very blind
Perhaps a gift, perhaps a consequence
Who cares, get up! Today always meetsyah sometime hence

Jaddamiah sat up; he stretched his neck to gain a clearer view for he recognized the merriment in the song, and the voice from the Windy Piny Pass and the magick scissors. He couldn't see anything except the butterflies that accompanied before. He reclined onto his back, locked his fingers and placed his hands behind his head. He plucked a blade of grass and sucked on it and smiled while he listened to the medley;

I am heartily glad I came hither to you
The Ælves have saved you a shoe or two
Be ever grateful
Be sprightful.
Come dance! Come sing! Can you hear my Tamborello?
It rings because Bllömpotvölle is a <u>merry</u> fellow!

Jaddamiah wasn't sure if he heard the name correctly, so he lifted himself onto his elbow, and listened if the name would be called out again.

Yes! You heard correctly!
So fly directly!
Nothing remains but that we kindle the child thither
The flowers of the wicca-hazel wither.
Make haste! Not like a fly and zither.
And hitherto doth fate on pride tend

But yours is not the end,
Another journey waits round the bend.

Whither would you have me?
Though better be, if I were with Princess Mea!
Some whither, some die!
But Nature speaks, never a lie,
To such ends I make amends
All fates and destinies now append.

One Mile Yew

$\mathcal{T}$he sun faded and the butterflies with it. Jaddamiah fell asleep in the long grasses between the fragrant and colourful flowers until he woke up; when the westering Sun started to make her way over the edge of the wide, wild world. Jaddamiah felt very much up in spirits, he remembered what Bllömpotvölle said in the medley, that he should not waste time in leaving but, he thought to himself that the day still had two hours or so of sunlight left, and he had not written in his journal for several days, and it was good-a time as any, so he took out his pen and paper. He didn't forget to write of Bllömpotvölle or what a silly Jabberwocky he had been for having voted against him for 3 years in a row; not to participate in the Spring Garden Festival. He made a note of apologizing and in brackets he wrote; 'that is to say that this Bllömpotvölle is indeed our Bllömpotvölle, I must eagerly apologize'.

When the butterflies were settled onto their perches on the underside of some comfortable leaf and petal; or perhaps crawled deep between blades of grass or into a crevice of a sunlit rock where cooler breezes had begun to descend over the shire, he was satisfied with his thoughts on paper. It was then that Jaddamiah mounted his horse, one hand gently on the reins while the other held his lesepfeife. Jaddamiah blew smoke from his pursed lips into the evening air. For the first time, he was doing the very thing which he had not done for decades, albeit the thirteenth day was already behind him. Jaddamiah found that he had to hold Fágan back somewhat for it seemed that not travelling for an entire day did her good, and it felt that she was well rested. He sat and pondered while enjoying his lesepfeife; just the simple pleasure of holding it in his hand was a great deal of comfort to him. Jaddamiah didn't know it yet but, the road ahead was quite flat with some undulations, but they were not enough to push Fágan to exhaustion and as he considered that, he reckoned that in 3 days, he would be in Weir. Although it was night-time, he could see well ahead that the road was a deeply, cloven track. Nightlife clamoured to a crescendo, and as he drew closer, the crickets, frogs, mice, kit foxes and hares stopped their chitter-chatter and gollywagger but as soon as he passed, the blethering started up again and sounded like a nocturnal ebb and flow. A hermit crab popped its head from a deep puddle of water and scurried back at the vibration of approaching hooves; a right, giantly sound when such a tall creature like Fágan passed. Near midnight, the road started rolling upward till they arrived at a ridge, from that vantage point Jaddamiah saw the light and dark shadows from the lay of the land. A lonely cottage could be seen in the distance, with its blue smoke lifting towards the sky. The crescent Moon was sleeping on her back, while the bright Ilandadur (Iludi 'Ælve-Dream' in the speech of Jinbōchō) kept a lofty eye. He thought that it was a good spot to have his midnight supper and realised that his stomach was growling. When he jumped off Fágan, he found the green grass was bountiful and broke off a handful, chewed on it for a moment and gave the rest to Fágan. At 1:30am, he gathered his belongings, watered down the fire that he had made and took advantage of the gentle downhill by taking Fágan for a brief trot. The road gave in after a mile from leaving the camp site to a tight lane of yews, a short while later they came to a fantastical tunnel. Jaddamiah brought Fágan to a standstill at the tunnel and dismounted, he reached for his lanthorn on her rump and lit the lamp. He led Fágan while holding the lanthorn up from an old, woven, green carry cord. He immediately recognized the trees and for the sport of it, wanted to see if he could spot a 'Golden Bow'. He was right glad that the full Moon was asleep, for its bright light cast imaginative phantoms, and he soon realized his light did the same thing. The flame coloured the ancient trees to a vibrant olive green from the moss on it, others it stained a strange purple near the very tops of the curling branches, while those standing in the middle were a reddish, motley, yellow. Jaddamiah didn't know that he was passing under what folks called 'One Mile Yew'. The tunnel was exactly a mile long and some believed those trees were up to 9 thousand years old. The passage was covered by its million, million needles and Jaddamiah heard it crunching under Fágan's hooves. If it had been daytime, Jaddamiah would have been able to see One Mile Yew from the very spot where he had his midnight supper. The hill was named 'Deva Daru Zaila'. Jaddamiah stood still and felt compelled to listen. He felt safe under the 'fairest of ancients'. From the little lore that he knew, he remembered that the yew's wood created great bows. He thought that he heard voices, many voices, softly, near the very edges of perceptibility but, as much as he tried, he could not interpret what he thought was speech. When he reached the end of the tunnel, he stopped again and sighed deeply. He put the lanthorn out, somewhat disappointed because, there was a bit of jape in his idea in looking for a 'golden bow'; he would have liked if it were true but, something of that nature hadn't been seen for over 3,000 years. He turned around, slid his foot into the stirrup, threw his right leg over his saddle, and continued his journey. About five hundred metres from the entrance of the One Mile Yew, he passed the hermit cottage that he had seen from a distance. On the outside, in the gloaming light, it seemed unwelcome so, he rode past and wondered to himself as to who could stay so far in the wilderness, from anything at all. When the sky began to show the first signs of sound passing through the air by the twittering of birds, Jaddamiah wanted to get off the road and sleep. On his right shoulder the land sloped upwards and was filled with thickets. Behind the thickets stood tall trees. The hill created a natural wall on his right so that it made a sort of 'cutting'. It then moved away from the side of the road, and his eyes caught a glimpse of a dark indentation. He put pressure on the right side of the reins and Fágan turned around. From the height that Jaddamiah sat, he saw that it was a sandy cave but, when he dismounted, he couldn't see it. He wanted to investigate further. Jaddamiah found that the cave was made of soft, white sand; big enough for four people to sleep or hide comfortably in.

Jaddamiah wasted no time undoing some of the burdens on Fágans back and let her loose to wander about on the grassy banks that grew on opposite sides of the stream. He swaddled himself in a blanket and soon fell into a deep sleep.

The Dwhëels Save the Day

It was customary to first send a request to the Chief when seeking council or favour or any other grievances. All subjects had to adhere to that law even his own household, except the king's wife.

Hrosmægden was in bed contemplating on that while Geongmerkā lay sleeping beside her. The early morning light was beginning to brighten up the room, only just. When Hrosmægden got up from bed trying not to disturb Geongmerkā, she had decided what to do. She would go straight to her father's house and ask him, quite directly, where exactly her sister lived, for she was certain that he knew, for after all he was the Chief, and chiefs and kings had spies. At breakfast she stated her intentions to the rest of the family, and no one objected for she merely informed them, not wanting nor needing their permission. That day Hrosmægden looked particularly lovely as she left the gate that led through her garden. Her elegant figure moved across the cobbles as she made her way to number 528. She hoped that the owner of the house would oblige by taking her to the Plains of Hros by using his dwhëels. She needed to hurry and the dwhëels were much faster than horses. Hrosmægden walked up the path that led to the egg-yolk, yellow door, over the paved sandstone hexagons that glittered in the sunlight. Before she knocked on the door, she took a long look at the garden for, who in Béth-Élam could pass up such a sight! When she had enough of that floral chalice, she turned around to knock on the door but, it was already wide open. She looked to the face of Semjase; the two women broke out in femoral laughter as Semjase bid her welcome. "Sus-vapnah Hrosmægden!" she greeted in her sotto voice. The women embraced as Semjase was an affectionate woman.

Semjase was dressed in a pastel blue chiton; around her waist was a purple band of the same material wrapped wide over her hips, and tied in a knot that hung between her thighs.

"To what do I owe this pleasant visit?" asked Semjase.

"I am in a spot of bother," replied Hrosmægden. "I need to go to my father's house and the horses will take too long. Do you suppose Lemayian would drive me there? I am terribly sorry that it's such short notice," she went on apologetically. "You must come in through, I sense you are hurried. Lemayian arrived late yesterday afternoon but, I will wake him from his repose."

"Oh! I did not know that he had travelled. Do not disturb him, there must be another..." Semjase interjected.

"I insist that you come inside, it is bad manners to keep a guest at the entrance hall no matter how brief. I will call Lemayian."

Hrosmægden's face lit up; she followed Semjase into the lounge room. As Hrosmægden followed behind Semjase, she once again admired her slight form for though Semjase looked quite young, she was in fact very, very old. Semjase offered Hrosmægden a seat and elegantly vanished through the arched doorway to call her husband. Hrosmægden admired the cool, green lounge; gentle, flower motifs ran in a line around the oval room. It was furnished simply with its black and white square, tiled floors. A wonderful floral fragrance permeated the air and Hrosmægden enjoyed the quietness of the place that belied her own home. She felt a strong sacredness in that space, the same feeling that always surrounded Semjase. When Semjase returned, she stood in the doorway with a well-crafted oak tray with two glasses filled with freshly made tea. Lemayian will be down shortly," she assured as she offered Hrosmægden the iced tea. Shortly thereafter, Lemayian stood towering over them. He was a tall, handsome man, dark skinned with chiselled features, his black facial hair neatly trimmed and not a man to be trifled with but, when he smiled, his dark eyes lit up any room and it was so, that he entered the lounge, smiling with warmth and friendliness; he set Hrosmægden immediately at ease.

She got up and Lemayian made mild genuflection, then kissed her hand and drew her into his arms as he hugged her, as was the fashion of the folk of Béth-Élam, and she buried her head in his flowing demdema. Semjase stood by, poised with her back arched, as she pulled up her long, light flaxen hair onto the crown of her head. She then left quietly without her husband or Hrosmægden really noticing her absence, this was her fashion. Hrosmægden sat down again on the soft sofa, leaving Lemayian standing.

"Why are you still seated dear woman, Semjase said you are off to your father's house. Hmmmmm," said Lemayian jovially, holding his square jaw in his hand and reflecting on his statement. "You have not been to see him in an age." Hrosmægden smiled and replied, "It is true Lemayian. You remember well but, now I must go and see him for I have a letter for Jadda..." Lemayian interjected kindly and said to her reassuringly, "No need to explain dear Hrosmægden. I will take you, let us make haste." Hrosmægden was glad and smiled for the kindness of the Abathwa family, that was generally their way. She also liked to hear Lemayian speak the way that he did, something which he found himself doing by having spent so many years married to Semjase; she spoke in an old-fashioned, conservative way, which even reflected in her writing style.

Time was not wasted by Lemayian. In no time the wagon and its dwhëels sped down Lamas Street and made its way around the round-a-bout and climbed the hill up towards Old Man Bllömpotvölle's cottage, and on towards the Plains of Hros.

The House of Hrosveard

*T*he Chief's house was no ordinary hole in the ground, nor as smart as his brother's or some of the other 'horse Beles'. No. While every household on the Plains of Hros were sunken; a Pit House or as the old folks called it, a 'Houguehūs', the Chief's stood entirely above ground though inside, one could access underground rooms via descending, palatial stairways.

The Chief of the Hrosvyra's abode was an 'other space', an edifice utterly different from, yet fundamentally connected to, the rest of the structures surrounding it.

Lemayian drove his dwhëels in through the large gates that were 'smithy crafted' in the insignia of the House of Hrosweard. It consisted of a large, purple circle with two, thin golden-brown circles within, inside of that on a silver background, was a winged horse that stood on its hind legs. Opposite a Rjóður and underneath the winged horse, stood a Hros warrior with his sword in hand.

The gates were ajar, so they could go right through as they were already questioned, looked over, so forth and so on, the very same way Jaddamiah had been many days before.

The long driveway was winged with sprawling, green lawns and two large water ponds, one each side with ducks on its waters. In the middle of the driveway was a long rill that ran from the Chiefs abode. There weren't flowers except several weeping willows that grew on the plains. Lemayian commanded his dwhëels to stop and they followed his commands willingly. They stopped in front of a wide, curved staircase, its steps made of smooth, river stones. At the foot of those steps were two, tall, totem poles with a horse-head sculpture at the end of each.

Lemayian opened the carriage door and asked Hrosmægden if she wanted him to accompany her. She replied with a mischievous smile saying, "You are most helpful as always Lemayian but, I think the regulars are out, I should be fine." Lemayian smiled and held her hand as she ascended the first two steps. When Hrosmægden got to the top of the stairs, two guards with tall glittering spears bowed. They did not have to open the doors as was their usual custom because that day was well chosen by Hrosmægden, the doors of the Chief remained open till noon for any family member or extended family member to visit freely and commune with the Chief. It was called 'Bhlo-to-Tag' supposing the Chief had blue blood with reference to his royal bloodline; that couldn't be further from the truth for the Hrosvyras, though a great people, none were descendants from any celestial throne. They were descendants from Hroshirdas and Ewehirdas; wanderers of the great shires, common folk who carved for themselves a people and a land that no one wanted; a people who professed to be of the land but, had long before discarded the true way of the earth. They were from those called 'Paynes', from a golden age but, had broken the ancient oaths and subsequently sought every drop of blood possible, that could join them to deathlessness. Lemayian sat on the footing step of his carriage and surveyed the area, as he had not been there for a while and had forgotten how it looked. He noticed a large, bald eagle circling high overhead. Lemayian cupped his hands over his eyes to have a better look for few avian sights were as splendored as watching an eagle soar above one's head. The air currents soon carried

253

it off and out of sight so Lemayian's thoughts returned to the citadel, as he continued to look upon its architecture. The Chief's abode stood elevated so that one could look over the other pit houses that neatly stood in rows and further on, scattered over the green fields and hills. Four, tall columns of stone rose up above the front entrance and the roof; two sloped beams connected the outer two columns and a straight crossbeam between the two centre pieces. Perched on the two outer columns were two bald eagles, one with out-stretched wings ready for flight, on the left the eagle's wings were opened upwards. On the centre columns were the head of a Rjóður and the head of a horse but, not just any horse head, it was a Brague or, in the ancient tongue, 'Vaja'. When Hrosmægden walked through the tall, wide open doors with its deep carvings, two trumpets sounded, a sign to the Chief that he had a visitor. Inside, the ceilings were high and crafted of curved yellow oak beams that supported a hammer-beam with a large main arch that sprung from the wall-piece with collar beams. The trusses were fluted and at the end of each hammer-beam, underneath the brace, were the heads of bald eagles, the third emblem of the Hrosvyras. Running down the centre of the floor was a fireplace 8m long by 1.50m wide, that never stopped burning. Suspended from the ceiling was a floating chimney stack made of hardwood, lined on the interior with fireproof stone tiles. As the smoked escaped, the smell of sage and kinnikinnick permeated the air. Hrosmægden thought to herself that her father might have been smoking or perhaps they had just cleansed the hall. The candles were burning brightly, and cast familiar, velvety shadows, strangely recreating the sense of security Hrosmægden had once known when she frequented those oak halls. Beyond the large fireplace running right and left, were long corridors with beautiful enfilades, each with an ornate door. She approached the throne. It was set upon a dais, on the edge of that large, square dais were effigies of about a foot high, each of the previous Chiefs. On either side of the stage were two, large, arched doors.

The throne itself could revolve, so that the Chief could face the opposite direction and simultaneously be in the Hall of Feasting. That was a novel idea, especially when the Chief had royal guests.

Chief Aherin rose from his seat, a dark, plain, wooden chair with Runes upon its back. The arm rests ended in the large claws of eagles. The seat was flanked by two others, one step lower than the Chief's. On the left sat his advisor and on the right, his wife usually sat. She didn't take that position often, reserving it for important occasions only.

Two armed men stood at the foot of the steps that led up to the throne, one stepped forward and she recognized him as her handsome nephew Ealadha. In his bardic voice he said; "Welcome my cousin, daughter of the Chief! Chief Aherin, Captain of the host of the Hrosvyras and Commander in Chief of the Mergwarch, I present to you, your daughter, Hrosmægden Dyddanwy Jabberwocky!"

Usually the two guards would then draw their swords, holding it with the blades facing down but, touching at the pointed tips. It meant that a person could speak with the Chief but, wasn't allowed to approach him any closer. By not drawing their swords meant that the Chief welcomed his guest onto the raised dais.

It was the Chief's turn to speak but, before he did, a large, bald eagle rushed past her and flew to the Chief's outstretched arm.

Hrosmægden was startled as its broad wings gently clipping her head as it flew past. Aherin stood tall, on one arm the eagle, in the other hand his pipe, then he smiled and said, "My daughter, I knew you were coming, for Huhuk brought me tidings late yesterday near the twilight hour." Chief Aherin lifted his arm slightly indicating to the regal bird, "You do remember Huhuk, don't you daughter?"

"Yes beloved father, I do," replied Hrosmægden in her plumy voice. The Chief let his arm drop, and Huhuk with one jump, set herself onto Chief Aherin's throne, on the top of the head rest.

"Come! Come closer Hrosmægden Dyddanwy (dee THAN wee), so I can look upon your delightful face." Hrosmægden went closer, her father held her at arm's length and rested his large hands around her upper arms and said,

"How long I have waited for you. . .
In the afternoon on the breeze
In the noontide at the sea
In the Autumn on the trail.

In the dream you showed your shadow
In her voice created longing
So the years went on by.

Then one day;
In the gloom of the morning
While the skies were all grey

When the trees were all dancing
And birds kept on chirping
In the twilit of my home
You came passing and showed
Yourself to me.

In the West where I sprung from
From there you have blown
In the West of west where I'm going
You have come to set my spirits dancing!

Zephyr in the sky
Yes!
Zephyr right with me
Zephyr from the West
What a day this is turning
Out to be.

Though that song is of the West Wind's daughter, I recite it for you, for our meeting is long overdue. Welcome! Welcome! Welcome to my home." Chief Aherin pulled her towards him and embraced his child, he could feel Hrosmægden's tense body ease up and become like her old self again, in the days when she came freely to her father's arms. He held her for a time until he felt her warm arms around him, then tenderly pulled away.

"Come," he said pointing to the seat to his right, sit in your mothers place and let's talk for a while, unless your urgent return comes with a surprise." He said that with a smile on his sun-drenched face. Unlike his brother, his long, black hair was parted and hugged his ears tightly. His hair hung over his chest in two, long, thick plaits that were interwoven with beautiful, blue feathers attached to leather. At the end of the ornate plaits hung beautiful, glittering, purple and blue Wampum beads, a gift from the Fratakara of Alkana, which had become customary for the Hrosvyras to wear. The Chief wore no crown on that day but, as soon as the eagle left his arm, the man seated on the left got up and took the pipe from the Chief and replaced it with a large, plumed sceptre, which was made from a thin, gold stick filled with many large, black and white feathers. The pointed end was gold and very sharp and the Chief could throw it with great accuracy, at anyone that vexed him, although that today, it was only a symbol of his power. The tunic over his shoulders had large, wide sleeves and was made of brown, dyed wool; layered over a similar green garment. On his chest hung a large, beaded leaf fastened to a round, golden broche with the face of a horse in it.

Around his waist were lame fabric in which colourful threads were interwoven with leather. The Chief wore a larrigan on his feet, customary of the males; a high, oil-tanned, leather boot or moccasin was worn. Izvira-ehir approached the father and daughter with an oak sensor in his hand. That he swung up and down, so that its sacred smoke surrounded them. It was customary to cleanse all bad spirits or bad blood that could've existed between the two coming together after a long time. The sacred smoke was a blend of kinnikinnick and white seamróg, bear berry leaves and candlewick plant. When the tall, thin, pale-skinned Izvira-ehir had finished, he disappeared, and returned shortly thereafter with an ornate pipe. The stummel was made of willow wood and the stem of pure gold. He went towards the throne and lit the pipe, then handed it to the Chief, holding his left wrist with his right hand as a mark of respect. Chief Aherin took it and said to his daughter, "Come smoke with me for just a moment." He said it so delicately, pleadingly, that Hrosmægden found herself obliging. The kinnikinic was used in that sacred pipe. The smoke was offered to the Ancestors. The pipe itself acted as the line to the Ancestors or Spirits, and the smoke, as it rose, carried the messages. Those who shared the pipe, and the smoke, shared the same breath. In that case, they shared the same bloodline.

When Hrosmægden had taken the first puff she coughed, her father laughed and she joined in. After a few more she got the hang of it. "Father!" she exclaimed tenderly. "I would stay on if our affection requires it and we could talk all night but first, I must urge you to tell me where my sister lives, for I must get a letter to her urgently."

The expression on his brow changed. He fell silent and in deep thought, then looked into her eyes and replied, "Hrosmægden Dyddanwy you have brought me one joy, that is yourself, but you now remind me of two sadness's and perhaps we must make recompense..." She interjected and said, "But father, surely you must have spies as sure as Huhuk told you about my arrival," there was some irritation and impatience in her tone. "I did not say that I did not know where she was, only that perhaps we must make recompense," he answered affectionately.

"Forgive my impudence father, I only mean to say that it is urgent and that I need it."

"Are my beloved daughters in trouble that I know not of child?"

"Father! Do me this favour and if you have the address give it instantly please for, I must send this letter as soon as possible." The chief obliged without further ado, for he could tell that the matter was urgent but, did not know why. "Apartment Seven, Wringer Street in Weir. The Ælves call it 'Avinirnaya' and whether you choose either or not, she will still get it."

He paused for a moment then continued mumbling to himself but loud enough to hear, "Lasher! Yes, some call Weir, Lasher."

Hrosmægden took a deep breath and held her hand to her lips, she was flabbergasted. She sat still for a moment, 'how could this be a co-incidence?' she thought. She reached out to her father's arm and touched it, "Father, may the man who brought me have 'face' with you, for he is both kind and a friend. I must send him back to Béth-Élam instantly."

"There is no need my daughter, for if you seek your sister's whereabouts then we can take it ourselves." "What do you mean father?" she asked surprised. "You have been away too long. The Hrosvyras take care of their own, you have no need of a post person. I will send my best messenger as far as Malbon. There he will pass it to their post person and your letter will be delivered safely." The Chief called to Izvira-ehir and did not have to repeat himself, for he had heard all that was spoken. The Chief was certain that his instructions would be followed to the letter...

Two More Days

Jaddamiah felt hungry. Twilight had already set in and in his sandy cave, a pale, blue haze had filtered in, created by the shadows and receding light. He got up quickly and walked over to his horse. He scratched in his belongings, scratched some more; some things fell to the ground, pots and pans made an awful noise as he threw them on a pile. His face was like a bundle of cracks and crevices as he contorted it in angered fear. He relented and rested his arm on Fágan's back. He stood there in the twilight, his worst fear for the journey had been realized, the food was finished. He ran his tongue over his dry lips and thought of the lovely tart that Hyperion had baked him, and suddenly became sad and wished that at that moment, that he was sitting in his cosy library or in the family lounge in front of the hearth. He rested his head on the side of Fágan's neck and ran his flat hand over her soft coat. "I hope I haven't been too hasty dear friend. . ." then he made a long sigh. ". . .running off to stranger parts that I've never been," he said aloud to the horse.

An idea came to mind. He listlessly picked up all that he had thrown on the ground and packed all his belongings away. He then led Fágan by the reins and walked back the way he came, in search of the mysterious house on the side of the road. When he finally came upon the house, he found a gammer in her garden, with her generous breech facing the sky. She was bent down and plucked something from the ground. Jaddamiah peered over the low hedge but said nothing, after which he heard a hoarse voice saying, "I've been expecting you stranger," with that, she turned around slowly, sighed, and looked at him. She had a hand full of mushrooms and a wooden ladle in the other hand.

"An if you don't come in righta way you'll be dropping over from the hunger laddie," she remarked with a friendly smile on her face. She bent down again and continued what she was doing, like a hen picking in the soil. When she did that, Jaddamiah was sure that her face was that of a very young maiden, and that her movement that time, had a touch of legerity. He shook his head and felt that perhaps it was his hunger pangs that made him imagine things. He tied Fágan to the thick pole that supported her front gate. He plucked up the courage to speak and as he opened the gate said, "Perhaps you also know that my dear companion is famished, do you have some draught to slake our thirst madam? Please," he added afterwards. When she stood up again, he saw that she was old, to his estimation at least going on 120. That time her hand was full of mushrooms and carrots. "Here is plenty of that and much more laddie. You are kind to call your horse 'companion', and me likes those who are kind to animalia." As Jaddamiah entered the gate he bumped his head, and fell over flat onto his back, alarmed. He lay there stretched out star-fish-like and wondered how that could have happened. Again, the young fair maiden appeared. Her long, fair, hair fell over his face as she helped him up. He dusted his clothes off and shook his head vigorously. It was then that he looked at the gate and instead of a number on it, there was a word all shone up in brass letters that read 'Zenzizenzizenzic'. 'How odd,' he thought. He looked up and the old lady was again standing in her garden and laughing aloud. "Oh laddie! Gardyloo, I should have said to you! I invited you in but was careless in not opening the Duir. Please forgive me, come right in." She dropped her produce and clapped her hands, then picked up her mushrooms and carrots again. Jaddamiah followed cautiously, and that time he did not bump his head. She took her things and led the way to her black door, where she turned on a shiny, brass doorknob and entered. Jaddamiah followed but not before seeing the same word at the top of her door again, 'Zenzizenzizenzic'. He shook his head from side to side because he was utterly confused.

"My name is Jaddamiah Jabberwocky madam," he said and offered his hand to her. She looked him up and down, her sorrel face alight with its pale grey eyes. She raised her finger at him and said, "You look like the Moha but you don't sound it. Sit down; I will prepare a meal for you. My name is Adhahloka but, I am not associated with fright or eternal sentence." She then walked off through an open arch that led from the enigmatic little room that Jaddamiah found himself seated in.

He didn't know what she had meant, 'but I am not associated with terror, timeless punishment or abnegation' so he ran the name over in his mind to see if there were some recollection of it, in the filing cabinets of his brainbox.

At that moment, he couldn't think of anything, so he combed the room with his eyes. The first thing that caught his attention was a large, black sphere that nestled in its hazel stand. The stand itself was a little hazel tree of 21cm high, its branches cupped the large, dark sphere. He recognized it as eastlea, and it was the size of a football. There was also an ornate, crafted wooden box next to it, with the Rune ᚹ, engraved upon it, overlaid with gold. On the left and right of it, was the Rune ᚣ, also overlaid in gold; and separating the 3 Runes were two, oblong Amethyst crystals, nestled in the wood. Jaddamiah got up from the soft sofa for the little room was filled with all manner of enigmatic and interesting little objects. He felt after sitting in it for the duration of the time, that a calm had come over him, and he had no thought of anything. An archaic map framed in an elementary way and stained brown by the passing of time, hung on the wall. Runes were used as a border to the map and Jaddamiah didn't recognize them at all, but of course he couldn't, it was a map of the Underworld! Adhahloka caught Jaddamiah with his hands behind his back like an inquisitive child, staring at the map. She brought in, on a wooden tray, a simple brown lentil stew, buttered bread and a large, wooden mug with the steam still rising from its contents. Jaddamiah thanked her. Adhahloka shook her head, wiped her hands on her soiled apron and vanished again through the long-beaded curtain, or so it seemed to Jaddamiah. In fact, the curtain were many little crystals strung together. When he put the first spoonful into his mouth, his palette stung and sung, for the flavours were delightful; sun-dried seeds of mustard, fennel, cumin and tamarind could be tasted, as it came alive in his mouth.

Jaddamiah let his molars do most of the work, while Adhahloka returned with her own plate and sat opposite him. "Don't waste my food! Eat your food!" she exclaimed. Jaddamiah blushed and spoke with his mouth full, "No my lady! I am just pausing; this, this food is lip-smacking, finger licking good!" he found himself expressing.

"Well it ought to be, I made it," she replied and began a small incantation;

Water from the sky
Fire from the Sun
Food from the Earth
The Gnomes to till the ground
And mouths to eat and confound

After that, she ate. Jaddamiah ate very slowly because many thoughts crossed his mind, and his eyes saw many things as if every sense within him came alive. There was peacefulness about that house that he had never experienced before.

"What is it called that I am eating, if you don't mind me asking? It is delicious and though I recognize some of the flavours, I am unfamiliar with others. I am from Béth-Élam and we do enjoy our food so." She looked at him from under her brow and only started talking when she was done chewing, "It is called khadi."

"And what is that smooth texture that I feel over my tongue?" asked Jaddamiah eagerly. "We eat much milk, except when it be made sour it is called yog," she merrily replied. Jaddamiah thought about what she said and replied, "We love milk too but, I have never tasted anything like yog before." "Condense or intensify!" she replied, and held her hand on her well-rounded hips, laughing again. "Hmmm, this yog in the khadi. . .hmmmm. . .if my wife could see me now, all of Béth-Élam would march all this way just to have a taste of such exotic fare." As he said that he closed his eyes to express himself. Jaddamiah noticed that Adhahloka ate with her fingers as if they were a fork and knife, and that she didn't make a mess, not once. She twirled the rice in her stumpy fingers and scooped up the khadi with it. She didn't touch her bread in all that time. Jaddamiah then, for the first time, drank from the mug beside him, after taking a gulp he coughed profusely.

"Ana! Ana! Ana!" she exclaimed. Jaddamiah spoke through his coughing and wheezing, "Thank you, urrrg!" he said clearing his throat. "It went down the wrong pipe, pardon me."

When his hostess was done eating, she neatly put the plate beside her on the little table. She then took the bread and broke it and sipped of her drink. Jaddamiah tried to follow suit but, his bread had already vanished down his gullet. The fragrance from it was overwhelming to the senses, the aroma was of roses, apples, mauca and ripe amra; it was smooth as he licked the creaminess from his lips, leaving traces of pink froth.

Adhahloka noticed his delight and said in a twitting tone, "A thunderbolt gives birth to a spring, a broken heart to floods, so the saying goes. It is said that when a man arrives home with the fragrance on his person, and froth stained lips from the woods, that he had been wooed by a Water Elfenna. We call that swill 'Pusparus'." Once again Jaddamiah thought that he had seen a beautiful maiden, of supernal beauty, in front of him; light and lithe with large, esmeraude eyes. He shook his head from side to side but, before him was only an old, jollux woman. He frowned, for he was upset with himself, angry that what he thought he saw was in fact not there. 'Perhaps she put something in my food or drink' he thought. 'Perhaps I have come too far and am weary' he thought again but deceived he was, for she did no such thing.

In the morning when Jaddamiah woke up and looked through his window, it was clouded from his warm breath for, a lamella of snow lay on the ground outside. Jaddamiah smiled, his heart was jubilant because the first snows started falling.

He got up and dressed, then noticed a strange object hanging on the wall; it was a round piece of wood beautifully finished with icovellavna on the edges and in a fresh, thick, green twining.

On the surface were many, many little gears, silver and gold, some all rusty but working in perfect machination with little sprockets and springs. The ticking and clicking of sound, was equally thrilling and peaceful. He stood before it, losing all sense of time. A gentle bell rang and that broke Jaddamiah from his spell. He made up the bed and rushed out of the room and found the cottage empty. On the little table in the room where he had his meal the previous night, was another breakfast. He ate it with zeal and afterwards went outside to look for Adhahloka but, she was nowhere to be found. He didn't know how long a time had elapsed from the time that he stood daydreaming in the bedroom to that minute. He walked to where his horse was. She was still tied to the gate, so he took out some paper, and wrote a note of gratitude to his hostess and placed it inside the letter box. He then found a neat bundle of things wrapped in a clean, tartan cloth. When he opened it, it was filled with little jars of jam, a dozen of sumptuous cep, half a dozen of eggs and four slices of freshly baked bread, and a small bottle of Pusparus. In it was also a note written in a thick font;

> 'Mr Jaddamiah
> May you travel safely to Lasher.
> PS. Nothing is as it seems, best wishes Adhahloka'

Jaddamiah also knew that his horse was fed and happy, for there was a playful, mischievous glint in her eyes, a knowing. . . eolas. Jaddamiah felt alive.

The First Snows

———※———

Jaddamiah led Fágan by the reins for a mile and passed his sleeping place of the previous night. He had taken out his walking stick for he was so delighted. He scratched his pate in puzzlement, for it was a most mysterious visit at Adhahloka's cottage. When all the glaumerie had worn off, he secured his walking stick, mounted his horse and encouraged Fágan to a canter, which she kept for a full 3 hours then, slowed down to a walk.

They came to an area called 'The Fells of Skallagrimmr'. They were not very high by the way things went in Eridu and stood at a height of 3559.712 feet in altitude. They rose sharply from the road. If Jaddamiah were to climb them and look across the Fells, he would've seen the land drop and see Vel Samoda. And since it was veiled, it was appropriately named 'The Fells of Skallagrimmr'. He passed by the rustling trees on either side and which grew tightly together to where the land began to make its rise. That carried on for another mile, till the area opened some more and passed along a passage where waves of long, green grasses bowed in the gentle wind. The Fells were wiped with some light snow, like sparse icing on a cake, and Jaddamiah realized that he had become part of a tangle wood tale. It was only then that he realized it. Summer's heart was finally broken, the first snows had fallen.

Making the Last Camp

As he rode on slowly, he thought that was as good-a-place as any to make camp for the night. There were plenty of vernal lodgings there and along the Fells it somehow felt safe. The two sojourners walked on into the late afternoon, thick grey clouds had gathered so he stopped immediately, for he could smell that snow would be coming in the night, and he needed to gather firewood to fend off the cold. He looked for a place for the night and saw, not far down the road, a grey upswing in the road. He quickly moved towards it and found that it was an ancient stone bridge. Jaddamiah left Fágan to feed on what she could find, and he walked to where the central keystone on the top of the arch rose two feet out of the bridge in a trefoil shape and read the inscription.

The Teimhil Bridge – 5055

He looked over the edge and saw a path which ran downward close to its walls, toward the fast-flowing stream with its dark waters and saw that a large set of rocks created a good place to rest for the night. Some heather grew above it which could make good cover from the cold. When he led Fágan down the sheltered path, he saw that the spot appeared to have been used some time before and perhaps others had done the same as he would. The space was larger than it seemed from the bridge for; there also was shelter under the springing of the bridge, along a narrow ledge which ran parallel with the abutment. Towards the stream there was ample soft grass for Fágan. He shook his head holding his chin and thought, 'this is a good spot'. He disappeared back up the path toward the road and looked for kindling which he found plentiful but, no big pieces. He returned with an arm full and started the fire. He glanced towards the springing under the bridge and found that there under it, was a large stack of evenly chopped wood, he could not believe it. He crouched under the bridge along the narrow ledge and supported himself with his hand held against the roof of the bridge and still, couldn't believe his luck. In the stone of the bridge above the pile, these words were inscribed:

Replenish what you Burn

He traced the letters with his fingers; he could tell that the inscription was as old as the bridge itself. He sat on his haunches and wondered at it, for it sounded more like a riddle of sorts. Nevertheless, he gathered some pieces and made his way back to the camping spot. As he got the fire going the smell of coming snow was again upon the air. He wriggled his nose and looked towards the grey, darkening sky. 'Strange' he thought, 'it's October, the first snows should only arrive at Samhain' but, he trusted his nose and the clouds did have a snowy look, and the evidence was also there some miles back and close to Adhahloka's cottage. As he busied himself preparing his meal, while the fire roared and red-orange sparks climbed with the smoke to the sky, he noticed Fágan had her nose buried deep into something, she used her shoes to kick up some dirt. Jaddamiah walked over to where all the excavating took place and reached under her nose, "What do we have here Fágan?" he asked while feeling at some fruity body and pulled out a black Lasher tufer. In the areas of Weir and Skallagrimmr they were also called 'Kartoffels'.

"Gramercy! Gramercy! My, you have some nose on you dear horse," he said praising Fágan. "This here be some fine tufers," he went on as he held it up in his fingers. Jaddamiah stood up, he looked around in the fading light and looked for a nearby hazel or oak, for there was none standing where Fágan had found the tufers.

He walked to the fire and scratched out a fire brand, held it in front of him and walked passed the rocky outcrop. He squeezed through on a very narrow path, and stepped on some cracking hazelnuts under his feet, then he knew that a hazel tree was nearby. He hoped that he would find more tufers under her feet. Jaddamiah heard water cascading, not loud enough to suppose that the drop was a long one. The source was close to a natural, stone wall on a path around the bend. There stood an old hazel tree with its roots fingering over the rocks, and a 3foot waterfall babbled into a pond. As he held the firebrand up in the darkness, next to the tree lying on its side, was a decaying log. Jaddamiah walked over to it and dug under it and found one more. He got up and walked back to where he set up camp. He held the tufer to his nose and closed his eyes, trying to recall the sweet, syrup flavour that they produced. Jaddamiah felt for crispy, golden, delicious, potato chips and jumbled eggs that night, so he set off as best he could with the little fish oil that he had in a jar and started by peeling potatoes. When the meal was ready, he took out his pocket knife and shaved some flesh from one of the tufers. He was being very thrifty as it was very rare to find such a delicacy in the wilds. After licking off the remnants of his hearty meal and savouring the flavours, he felt the air grow cooler as soft, white flakes started falling. He added more wood to the fire, and it made a right blaze before him, that even Fágan drew closer.

As the early Moon broke through the clouds at intervals, he wrapped himself in his blanket with only his hand sticking out, and courageously entered some new details of his journey into his journal. He found that he sat in contemplation more than he wrote, and wondered if it was the effects of the hazel that stood close by? In the morning when the Sun broke through the woods, he found that his book was lying on the ground, half covered in snow, and the large coals from the fire, still provided her lambent heat.

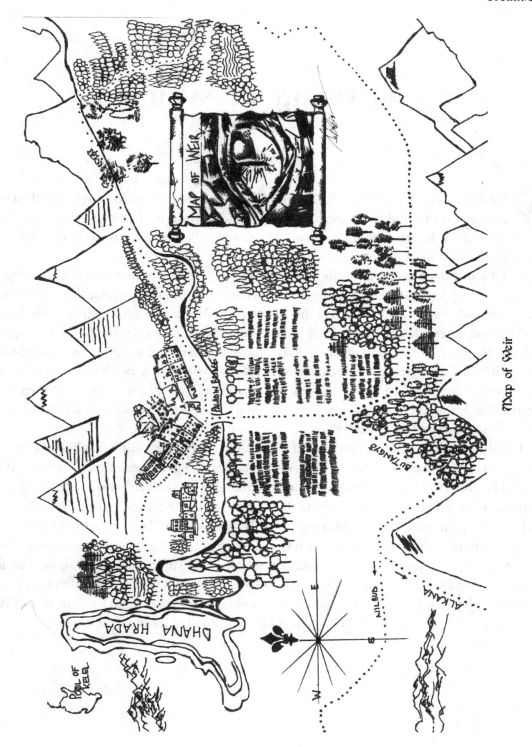

Map of Weir

Arriving at Weir

When Jaddamiah set off from the Teimhil Bridge and the narrow road was still filled with stranded mists, and the horse hooves made a clear imprint in the snow, he found that during the night, a lot had fallen. It was no longer a lamella but, after some two miles to his surprise, there was no snow on the ground at all.

After about fifteen miles, the Fells of Skallagrimmr gave way to more open land along the road, and many elms began to quail at the onset of winter's fingers and alongside those, grew many white pines. Oak leaves had also started their onset of golden leaves. Joining them in that payen treasury, stood stately hickory, their yellow leaves a sight against the expanse of faithful, evergreen, tall Pines. He wondered to himself whether any unseen Ælves were watching from some secret wood, or if Wolvlingas were close or even terrible Waelwulfas. At any rate he didn't feel strange, there were no hairs standing up on his back so Jaddamiah figured he was safe from their ills or cunning. The Sun was beginning to warm the day and amongst the bird sounds and the common sounds of the weald and woodland, the road bore them silently on to Lasher, to Weir.

Though the Sun was kissing earth, Jaddamiah could not help but think that he had answered a call from a clamant bell, and where then were the earthly kings to defend such a town as Weir? The road lay thin between the densely populated trees that lived on either side of it. Jaddamiah clearly saw the road take a curve up ahead, like a path separating thick, manicured hair.

He covered the mile quickly, making haste. It was as if an elastic band were stretching, pulling, hauling him in. When he arrived at the curve in the road, there were several well-placed signs upon a fork in the road. Jaddamiah dismounted and studied the road signs. The fork pointed backwards, the left road going back home, the right road pointing to Nilbud, Bútangyð and Alkana. One sign read Weir/Lasher one mile. Jaddamiah walked on in the direction of Weir and wondered if he would ever take the Great Western Road to its end. . .to the sea.

The Golden Breasted

***

Then came Elrukmavaksas, the 'Golden Breasted' through a Golden Wood. He had taken a shortcut. (That wood is not amongst the fields of men. Do not seek it, it will be in vain.)

His face had the delight of Ælfscýne, cinnamon, wheaten, titian, luteous and chrysochlorous. A sunburst shimmer was his countenance and his robe were adorned with Runes to ward off all divergence.

Yet that robe was the linen of simplicity, the colour like Emerant, not polished, not refined. To look upon Elrukmavaksas was to experience contentment. His countenance dimmed for he desired a lack of fear from those in the fields of men, though no man saw him come. He descended to Weir from the 'Lád of Ieldran', the road that no mortal could walk upon, close to Dhana Hrada. Far below he saw the maiden Inion, to her he was but a golden glow, like early morning dew upon a leaf. She stood transfixed, even though she could not see him clearly, it was that his aura impressed upon her, his light was filled with gladness, with the dance of life.

Jaddamiah Jabberwocky
Meets The Meline Dragon

❧

The Bridge was nestled into the woods that ran along the Afon Wen. The Palladian Bridge was the focal point as one entered Weir through the beautiful corn fields on either side of the road that led from the fork. The Afon Wen started wide and swept from its source, the Dhana Hrada. From the Dhana Hrada one could navigate the river all the way to where it joined the Lama Dupes and not encounter a waterfall or rapid.

To say that it was a 'meeting' is perhaps a human conundrum for after all, it's uncertain whether any Dragon wanted to meet a person. It was like asking if an emmit wanted to make acquaintance with an oliphantina. Dragons are not visible to humans but, humans are absolutely visible to Dragons. In fact, all creatures are visible to Dragons as it were; it is from Dragons that humans emanated after many millennia. . . The Dragon could not be seen, as Dragons do not exist on any human plains of perception.

As Jaddamiah was walking, he heard from afar, a soft voice come over the airs, just enough so he could hear it, ". . .Anusillu! Anusillu! Anusillu! . . .only a mooncalf enters where Ælves have yet to see the end. . ."

Jaddamiah then realized that he wouldn't be able to enter Weir from the 'Dragon Bridge'. (Some maps in the years that followed, would call it 'The Magpie Bridge' since many magpies were scorched in the conflict with the Dragon but, it was also called that, to stay men's fears as the term 'Dragons Bridge' brought back terrible memories.)

The Dragon lay sprawled across the road in front of the bridge which spanned over the River Wyvern, already so called before the arrival of Anusillu. The River Wyvern originated at the Palladian Bridge and ended at the Unnamed Road, from there onwards it became the Afon Wen again.

"As it often happens that the very face of a stranger showeth the mind; he comes walking a pilgrimage, is that wise? Not without some note of reproach. Vagrant feet, vagrant mind! Other folks may say to such a pilgrimage, 'A penny for your thought.' But I say, what is <u>pen</u>-ding? Gold coins for silver thoughts." Jabberwocky courageously replied with a question, "Is the term, a penny for your thoughts a play on words? For another word for coin is of course penny."

268

He ran his fingers through his long, black hair because it constantly fell in his face. Then he continued; "A penny. . .for your thoughts. . .as it were. . .?"

The Dragon laughed again in his deep, strong, pleasant way, then yawned. "I see what you mean little human, very phroneein indeed. You are becoming very wise in my company, an effect no doubt by being in our presence, for *good* or for *ill*. Take for example your balbutient speech; I know where it stems from. . . you will have a smooth tongue ere end. I can also tell that your long, lustrous hair is cause for much vanity, we will have to do something about *that*. Coming back to the subject of thoughts; this of course, as you very well know, is a fallacy. A fallacy of great trepidation. I like that word *trepidation*. It feels almost like thrice fearful..." Anusillu lifted his snout to the right, into the air away from the ground, and laughed once more in his fruity, honeyed tones. He continued; ". . .and then there is the rushing into part of the word like persons applying athleticism to things of the Spirit. Near the end they always pant, they lament with such exertion. 9 out of ten give up, always returning, dwindling back to trepid imbecility. A bit of anaphora that is, don't you think Mr . . .er, what—did you say your name was?" Jabberwocky sat against a beautiful, elegant larch some meters away, one of 3 already beginning to turn golden. The stench of stagnant blood blatters that had oozed out of decaying bodies lying about, was becoming unbearable. He breathed deeply and inhaled the fragrance from the tree. He had broken off some needles and crushed it between his hands, and when crushed it smelled of freshly cut grass with a hint of pine. As he shook the needles from his hand, he commenced his answer thoughtfully, for he was careful not to speak or think his name; "My name is Lucht Siúil. And I see several contradictions!"

"And what is it?" asked the Dragon in a tutorial voice. "Er. . .spirit and imbecility. . ." he said that while unconsciously counting on his fingers. The Dragon raised his diamond eyes. "Yes! Yes! Trypp. That's two but not more than 3."

The Dragon lifted its right front paw, and then curled his long lilūlium claws as if to pick his nails. He looked down at them pensively then continued. "I mean to say there are *not* several."

Jaddamiah's blood heated up and rose to his head, and he replied quickly, "Apologies Anusillu." Jaddamiah was by then exhausted from his journey, he was hungry and wasn't as alert as he needed to be. "Hmm. . .," replied the Dragon, ". . . one cannot be athletic and spirit at the same time. One is either wholly wicked or completely *spirit*. Half measures are such a wam-pum of the Moha. The Legion makes such beaches of them."

Jaddamiah sat wondering what the Dragon meant, he was frecking through his memories. He thought of the beaches of Ninfa, then of the Strönds of Many Coloured Sands, close to Alkana. Then like lightning, he snapped his thumb and index finger and shouted, "Wampum! Those are beads, they're made from shells. I get it! I get! I get it!"

"You get what?" asked the Dragon emphatically.

Jaddamiah pushed himself up against the trunk of the larch. He was then wide awake and sat with his back stiff like hemp, proud of his intellectual prowess. "You used the word wampum, then you said the Legion makes beaches of the Eldiĕni. Wampum are beads made from the beautiful shells lying on The Strönds of Many Coloured Sands; implying humans are brittle, boneless, feeble."

"All the same mister, coming back to the privacy of thoughts. . . There is no such thing! Thoughts compact crystal clear on the floors of the Akasas; to say that it is not so, is both fear and not private. We read thoughts like flames read wood. In your world wars, a Private is a soldier of the lowest rank, feudalized into service by noblemen. What is so private about war? What is so private about words put into thoughts? Words are a *war*! And no noble man ever goes to war. Bah!" Jabberwocky got up from his 'armchair' against the larch, and left his staff with the mayll leaning against it. He walked with his left hand stuck in his pocket and spoke with his right hand, waving it in the air like a celebrant. "I too, am averse to war Anusillu. It is such flag-waver cowardice." He stood with his hands in his pockets, looking up to the Dragon. "Be careful my Trypp. Don't trip yourself up, familiarity is suicidal." The Dragon said that for, he noticed that Jaddamiah had become quite comfortable with him but, Jaddamiah took no notice of that remark, as he was enjoying the discourse. "Flag-waver is not wam-pum! Wam-pum is at least vague concrete perception. No! Flag-wavers are like mist. No again! That is not the right thing to say. It is like clouds that rain and never gets you wet. Useless, without purpose but damaging even." "Ha...haaah...hah" laughed the Dragon. "Even if I benefit from it," he went on sniggering. "What is your meaning Anusillu?"

"Patriotism feeds me. It is useless to the Moha but, it feeds me. Here are two sides entreating that they both should be victorious when in fact there can never be two winners. The vanquished are the vanquishers of old. The vanquishers are the future vanquished." "Ouroboros is the word I believe," replied Jaddamiah, sarcastically. The Dragon smiled, revealing its myriad diamond teeth. It was often thought that Waiverns (Dragons) could not speak nor breathe fire, and that notion was perhaps correct but, this specific creature was a direct dream from a Superior Dragon, one of 6 Ancients, and one of two that were most powerful above all other Celestial Dragons. Those Dragons had not been known to take anthropomorphic form on Eridu though, throughout all antiquity they had always been the symbols of Immortality and Wisdom, of Esoteric Knowledge and of Eternity. The Sun was now setting in the west, and the sharp pillars of fangs gleamed and twinkled in their dark cavernous snare, like stars about to fall. "My, you are facetious after such a long journey gēaman. First and second place are both losers imprisoned by Fate. Third place is vantages as third time covers all, our wings are large." And with that statement the Meline Dragon, Anusillu, unfolded his pediments of Wearyan, those scales glittered in the twilight. As the Dragon spread his wings, Jaddamiah saw no weakness on its underside as, all the while whilst the Dragon held his discourse, Jaddamiah was looking for a weakness. The Dragon having showed himself off, was fully aware that those were Jaddamiah's thoughts. Jaddamiah was instantly despondent, as the wide, outstretched wings blotted out the last rays of the Sun. Weir was cast into darkness, no light; no flicker of flame could pierce and rekindle hope in such dark. Jaddamiah felt it; it was alive and clung to his being like lead, the darkness was aware of itself, it was conscious. The dogs didn't bark, the birds were silent, owls hooted, crows made a hullabaloo and for that moment, all were filled with dread, with despair, a rancour of hopelessness. It was only brief and when the Dragon had put his wings away, like a kindergarten at show-and- tell, twilight had entered, it was no longer day neither night.

"Now is the time! Now!" shouted Jaddamiah at the top of his voice, simultaneously unsheathing Mordēre from its scabbard. He lunged forward, the agility of his youth returning. The sharp, silver blade greedily struck, biting at the lower flank of the Dragon. The blade tore out of the hands of the precocious pretender, and fell mercilessly onto the flagstones, making a clangour. Its fall was like a comet from the heavens, for miles and miles a great, blue, purpureal light could be seen filling the sky like a transparent dome. People rushed out from villages far and near, fearful, thinking perhaps a great celestial event had expectantly Armageddoned upon them; which they omitted to prepare for. In future years that would be called 'Vargadrughni' and each year that sphere would appear at that location for 13 days and become a thing of beauty celebrated with great pomp and splendour; called 'The Rocana Parvan'. But then, at that moment, there were no thoughts of such revelries and celebrations.

The first casualty was Jaddamiah Jabberwocky, for he lay bruised and bleeding on the other side of the river, where there were curious and frightened bystanders, the hopeful people of Weir.

Those who had come from afar, those brave and unfortunates who had failed and abandoned the quest before it had begun, sank down sulking, most perhaps were relieved that they were not the only ones who failed. A woman and her son rushed to his side and helped him to his feet but, he was without his sword, Mordēre. His bruises were few and his wounds minor, one was a bloody eye but as always, his pride took a bite, a kind of ruthless irony as Mordēre meant 'to bite'. The biggest blow was that his hair, those long locks had become white as snow, brittle as old dog bones, and began to fall out like plumes scorched in flames. The Dragon laughed and looked over his shoulder while resting his formidable snout on the Palladian Bridge. "You are courageous and swift and alive. I will think well of you Trypp the traveller of Béth-Élam. I . . ." "Stop calling me Trypp!" shouted Jaddamiah. My name is Jaddamiah Jabberwocky!" The Dragon smiled slyly and went on, "I was going to say . . . shan't go there to punish your village for your impudence, for there is a great Geisha upon it. So, I will wait for you." Jaddamiah held his breath. His face turned many colours, for he had realized too late that it was a grave error. Something he had tried hard to prevent, but now Anusillu knew his name. The Dragon lifted its head proudly and opened its mouth, then with a colossal raw that sounded like sundering skies, exhaled into the early evening sky a torrent of flames and it lit Weir up. Rooms, billets, habitations that were dark, were floodlit bright as day, where candle and hearth light glowed was cast in shadow. The shadows crept over pediments and entablatures like a racing noonday Sun. It swept over Weir, then the Draconian flames dissipated, and the rains began to fall, as folks rushed back to their homes like rabbits rushing to their warrens. All was silent except for the falling rain. Dark clouds sailed by and if any had paid more attention, someone perhaps would have seen something enthralling. A little boy of only ten months young was sitting on the cobbles; his mother forgot that she had arrived with him. The little boy stood up, like a raggety toy, wobbling like a feeble, old person. He reached out into the air with his thin arms as if trying to catch something. He then fell backwards again, onto his padded bottom. Still he reached out for something zithering around his head. His tiny head cocked left then right, his innocent eyes darted like marbles in their soft, fleshy pockets. He was totally absorbed in that entomology. If anyone had paid attention, they would have seen that he was only millimetres from swatting it. The zithering fly underestimated the boy's zeal, that infant, that forgotten child. But alas, the drenched, slender figure with blond hair that stuck like rats' tails to her face, and her wet clothes carved out her epicurean form, came stalking on the sidewalk. Her white fingers spread out starfish against the walls of the homesteads along Wringer Street. The Ælves and the Dwarves called it 'Avinirnaya'. Her shadow hovered behind her over the walls across the street and skulked away down alley ways into the darkness only to resume its shape once she passed over a lane juncture. Her fear caused her to walk twisted over, so that her sleuth which followed behind her, appeared like a repugnant thing. Depending on light which stole out of window panes, it would follow her then jump ahead of her so that she almost strode upon it. She paced closer, step for step all alone; and her grey eyes were round like saucers, like a bewildered hound filled with fear. No one accompanied her; she was alone with the leviathan Dragon and her infant boy in the now, pelting rain. The stars were gone but lights flickered in scores of windows. Although those lights were burning, there was no one standing in them that she could call out to and her fear became oppressive. The sound of gurgling from rooftop gargoyles sounded like ludibrious laughter. A Wearyan lid any observer might have thought shut opened. From the Dragon's eye, light broke out as he looked in the direction of the boy infant; the little one gave up his pursuit of the fly. The fly gave up its zithering and was gone to search for safer stiffs.

The light that flowed from the Dragon's eye shone on the oblivious infant like an ophidian spotlight. His mother began to cry, to scream and shout; she could not move, she stood there frozen to the wall like a wet tree frog. Then the gurgling stopped. The rain stopped. In those moments the world seemed devoid, even from the sound of silence. Then a saviour! A winged creature on one of the stone pedestals, one of the stone gargoyles; began to snap loose from its Morpheun sepulchre. It broke free. Soft, blue light surrounded its contour, as its wings spread out; mortals called them effigies of stone but, the Ælves called them the 'Drumari'; 'The Dreamers'. The gargoyle swooped down swiftly, effortless without sound, and cradled the boy infant in her large hands and returned him to his mother. She accepted her child, kissed him violently and held him to her sodden, cold bosom. The gargoyle began to dissipate like blue plasma filled with many golden spangles. The mother fell to the ground; half her body leaned against the wall, with her infant held snug, she would still be there in the morning.

It was early in the morning the following day. She stood over him and through the slits of his eyes he saw her, but only as a haze. She held in her hands a bowl and a cup and slowly as he began to open his eyes wider, he realized that he felt no tiredness at all, the bright Sunlight filled the bedroom and the room was radiant like a yellow iris. He looked at the tall figure standing beside his bed, looking up to her, and her long, auburn hair gave way to strong, elegant facial lines that could be one person's only. . . Hrosmægden's! A fragrance came to him or perhaps fragrances, perfumed, of myrrh and khasambhava. He could smell the khasambhava on his own body but there were other notes too, of rose and sage. His mind raced back to the little library of Gedymdeith Hrosweard, for it was there where he smelt these fragrances in the same way.

Jaddamiah sat up suddenly and supported himself with his arms outstretched behind him, fingers spread open wide. He looked at the radiant face towering above him as the silence of the day thumped like a bee in the throat of a foxglove. "Hrosmægden, Hrosmægden, Hrosmægden!" whispered Jaddamiah. "How can this be?" he asked in wonder. The image shook her head, and replied in a silvery voice, "Not your wife, but her twin Eirmægden."

As she spoke those words, another female entered the room with a bow strung over her strong shoulders. She was younger, she came close to the older female and cupped her hands over the ear of the first, and whispered into it. Suddenly the older one gave the bowl and cup to the younger and left the room and hurried down the narrow flight of stairs. The younger one remained and sat herself next to Jaddamiah on the soft downs. He pulled himself up against the headboard and flung the soft, white pillows behind him. He rubbed the sleep from his eyes and looked into the clear eyes of the young woman. "It is time for you to eat and drink for it makes a man strong." Jaddamiah was about to ask a second question but, the young woman anticipated it or so it seemed, as she answered "Do not speak, save your Prana. Cintayate!" Jaddamiah assumed she meant that he be quiet, and so he contemplated on all that had happened. He could not help himself but found himself looking at the young woman. She spoke in a strange way, words he did not understand. Her speech was similar to that of his wife's but, there was an added parlance and the young woman spoke in a very regal way, she was certain of herself. Although her frame was slender, her shoulders were strong and her bare arms muscular, without being manly. One could see that the Sun loved her for the hue of her skin was as a Hindu desert and a light shone through her skin as if self-generated. Her aquiline nose was strong, yet her alar groove was fleshy and pronounced, this led the eye to her full pronounced upper lip, of a half pale, plum colour. The young woman's eyes were deep brown almost black and burning not from any negativity but a burning that reflected the wild places, the green and deep places of Dhara. From her well-shaped, oblong head hung long strands of brown, honey-coloured hair which reached to the nape of her back, parted with a distinctly in the middle. A thin, twined leather strip ran around her head. She then realized that she was being studied and looked Jaddamiah straight in the eye but, he was the first to look away. The young woman's eyes showed signs of the slightest smile, that he had been caught out. Jaddamiah then began to eat what was in his bowl. A sweet, spicy, pasty porridge, the colour of light beige. As he ate, he chewed on sweet black berries, he also tasted cinnamon. All was good, he smiled to himself in satisfaction, 'a good house where food is made well' he thought to himself. He had forgotten all about the Meline Dragon that was, until passing by the bedroom door was another female figure, holding onto the first woman's shoulder, barely being able to stand up. There was also an infant boy; he seemed hungry for he was crying. He heard the young woman mutter in delirium, "Dragon! Dragon! Gargoyle. . . light. . . light!". "Gaurjalakula!" exclaimed the young woman seated beside Jaddamiah and rushed out in the direction of the trio. Jaddamiah gently put his bowl of porridge aside, except the cup for whatever it was, he was drinking, was too tasty to put down and he tip-toed, bare feet to the next room. In that room was a large bed, twice or more the size of Jaddamiah's. There the mother and daughter were helping the new guest to settle down. Warm water, soap and basin were brought in, sage was lit and put into a censer and the daughter took the little infant in her arms, immediately he was quiet and smiled. They started to undress the young woman, removing her elegant black boots first. The young woman holding the child, looked at Jaddamiah, she cocked her head slightly and he knew it was a sign to leave, so he did. They were busy for a long time. Jaddamiah felt up in spirits, he had finished his meal, although meagre in appearance, he found that it made him full, fed up and not in need of more. He rubbed his stomach in circles with the palm of his hand and walked to the open window beside his bed.

'So, this is Weir by day' he thought as he looked over the roof tops of five and four-story buildings. Its houses of white and grey stone rose up in a spiral around the rock where the village was set, and the roofs were topped with terracotta tiles. He had a clear vantage point of Weir as his hostess's home seemed to be quite high up against the hillside. He cast his eyes here and there where beautiful old doorways, arcades and walls of flat stone made themselves visible. He also saw the grand Paladin Bridge and the Dragon still lying there. The streets usually busy with folk, coming and going, and getting on with life were mostly vacant that morning. Those who had anywhere to go did so, like mice running against the foot of a wall for fear of being spotted by a feral cat. Then he saw the Dragon rise, sitting on its mighty haunches, then spewing forth fire and flame and burning corpses that lie around and stunk. He burned them to a cinder so that only small piles of black ash remained of what was once some semblance of a mortal life. At that moment, Jaddamiah realized that it was not a dream and if it were, it could turn out to be a nightmare. The bright morning Sun, the ominous stillness and absence of a busy town was not rude reminder enough to him that he still had battle to make but, what came into his mind like a piercing lance, was a stern reminder that he dealt with no earthly or mortal foe, for the telepathic words impressed upon him was as follows; 'I burned them for you Mr Jabberwocky. For You! It was a tumaceous matter.' The words sung in his head, it burned, it wasn't pleasant. He pulled himself away from the window and turned on his heels instantly, finding himself face to face with his tall, elegant hostess. From the screeching sound of the voice in his head, to the face before him that was soft and feminine. She pulled him to herself and wrapped her long arms around him, pressing her body against his in a completely unselfconscious manner. She gently pulled herself away and said to the puzzled Jaddamiah. "I am Eirmægden. I am sure you have many questions, please forgive our frugal hospitality but it seems all our guests today are portentous, and we had to tend to an unexpected friend too or else, I would have paid more attention to you Jaddamiah, husband of my twin sister Hrosmægden. Come! Let us be more comfortable." And so, she led the way through the house. They descended a spiral, stone staircase covered in a red Alkanina rug runner to a lower floor. The place was quiet, a kind of peace permeated the place, the soft remains of incense could be smelled everywhere and he felt light-headed at times, more so then as he entered the sitting room, so that he found himself falling into the soft sofa rather than sitting in it. A girlish giggle ascended from an unnoticed corner, and his hostess apologized in her silvery voice by saying, "Don't be too concerned about your light headedness, it will pass. Our home is grounded and filled with crystals. The light headedness is felt by all who come in who are not grounded." Eirmægden lifted her pale, green peplo between her slender fingers and sat on the sofa with her right leg underneath her. She was barefoot indoors, as was the custom. She then took her long, jet black hair and raised it on her head into a chignon. From behind a light, silk fabric curtain where a suspended swing chair hung, came the person to which the giggle belonged, it was Iníon-Dé Danann, Eirmægden's daughter, whom Jaddamiah had already informally met upstairs. She had a book in her hand and in the other the sleeping infant, who now was a bundle of freshness and with a rosy blush on his cheeks, and he slept without a worry of his mother's recent joyless world. "I would embrace you if my arms were empty so forgive me, Ahamasmi, Iníon-Dé Danann" she introduced herself in the ancient tongue. "Iníon-Dé Danann, please use the common speech with our guest," reminded her mother. Iníon shot her mother a disapproving glance but, Jaddamiah gathered that she was introducing him to her name. Afterwards she retreated to her silk recess. Eirmægden sat with her elbow resting on the top of the sofa and with the fingers locked. She then unlocked them, indicating with her open palm that Jaddamiah should enjoy the finger snacks set on the low table before them. "I am most anxious. I have been with my wife for 60 years and have never heard of her twin sister, Eirmægden. Though your beauty and the slight manner that Iníon speaks with, tells me undoubtedly that you are Hrosvyra maidens. . ."

"Yes I was, but my daughter is not." Eirmægden corrected him.

"Oh! Forgive me but why is it so, the Hrosvyra are a proud people." Eirmægden cocked her head to the side, her silver earrings shaped like leaves, quivered at her earlobes. Her marionette lines became more pronounced as her full lips pulled over the white teeth as she smiled and said with a sigh, "I cannot tell you why it is that my sister never managed to tell you of her twin but, I know that she has told you that only twice have Hrosvyra married out of its kinfolk. It was her and it was I.

Our father grew fond of you but, my husband was not mortal kind that is why our daughter uses the ancient tongue and that is why her name is Iníon-Dé Danann, for it means 'Daughter of the People of the Goddess Dana'." Jaddamiah coughed as he choked on the wafer in his hand. Eirmægden allowed him to regain his composure then continued. Her light brown eyes were like a clear river bed, specs of olive green flickered in it, they seemed melancholic but not from any loss, yet they brightened her smooth skin, a trait from the women of her kind. She also had a wicca brow like her daughter but not as bony, a sign of wisdom it was said. "Soon after my sister moved to your village, I accompanied the father of Inion to Weir but that was long ago, and he has *Ascended*." Eirmægden paused again, she sighed while looking out of the window and listened to some twitter outside coming from the arbours.

Jaddamiah didn't understand what she meant. She could tell from the quizzical look on his face and the thoughtfulness carved out by frowning. "Bhavata etad na kartavyam amba!" came the reprimand from behind the silk veil. "It is no secret that I should keep daughter," replied Eirmægden in a stern voice. "When our daughter was only 9, he returned forward to the Fifth Age to fight the War of Ragnarök, in the ancient tongue it is called 'Avadhuya'. In it he was slain, and a slain Danann during Ragnarök becomes a Titan, and cannot return to Dhara. He cannot return to us. He now resides in Antarmada, as it is called in the Ancient Tongue but, in 'the tongue before the ages' it is 'Mul Lunergal', on his home world."

From behind the silk veil came groans and the clenching of teeth.

"Zantabhavena! You will wake the infant my 'cherry blossom'" replied Eirmægden with such tones of sweetness, that no sound was heard from that quarter again. Eirmægden sat quietly again, pensively. She then changed the subject. "It was I that intimated. . . you have come to Weir upon my instruction to the Town Council and the Azapala. Perhaps it was imprudent of me." She said, and dropped her head; her hair came cascading down over her face like an ebony curtain, and she pushed it back over her head.

"No. You were not imprudent." Jaddamiah assured her, drinking from the warm, mint tea. "I am convinced it was Fate that brought us together for last night I had this dream. In the dream there were five women. One of them was Nivara but, she also had another name which was strange. . . She opened a very tall door and said; 'Can you pass through? Make it work and it's yours.' In the middle of the room there was a broken Pezala. So, I made it work. The other four women sat at the Pezala and played the Requiem. Then Nivara said; 'tell me the story'. 'You heard it so many times'; I said. 'I need to hear it again', she demanded. 'Ok' I said. 'A woman called Nanu (which means 'I have nothing to say') came to me and gave me a translucent, Amerindian tear-shaped stone. In the stone there were many open books. The letters on the pages were so small that I couldn't read them. She said; 'you know what to do'.

So, I took a ship and sailed the seas. When I arrived at the palace there was no one there except an empty throne.

'Place the stone on the throne', I heard Nanu's voice. So I did.

Suddenly a king was sitting on the throne. His clothes were dirty and torn to shreds. He was blind. On his left arm he had insignia, 'I am the ruler'. Before the king, there were two, huge piles. One was fanciful food, and the other broken gadgets. On his right side there were seven billion lepers seated. Each leper held a flag made of silk. On the flags was an inscription; 'We are the walking dead'. On his left side there was a man, eating rice soup with the fork from a bowl full of holes. Then a crow flew in through the broken window and said: 'Why don't you remember Yourself?'"

Jaddamiah leaned forward. He had finished his tea and placed the empty yellow cup on the table. He then sat up, crossed his legs at the ankles and locked his fingers in each other, then said. "That was the dream. I know this dream means something but, I will wait some time to confirm its authenticity. Also, I know we have been united for a special purpose." Eirmægden ran her long, slender middle finger from the distinctly depressed area directly between her eyes, along the ridge of her nose to its tip; she traced it over her voluptuous lips and stopped at the beautiful, half-curved, squarish chin that gave the resemblance of a smooth river pebble. "Yes, we shall see if it is as you say. The young woman who I brought into our home, her name is Nanu, she is my friend. So, when she is feeling much better we can see how she has come to be in your dream. It is peculiar, for she is a woman of very few words, though I have never asked her the meaning of her name, as those entities are sacred." Jaddamiah could not believe what he was hearing, at the prospect of such a co-incidence he felt a quiver run up his spine. He wriggled in the soft chair he was sitting in, and for some reason his thoughts drifted to the Dragon. He twisted his face that many furrows appeared upon his face. That did not last long as his wiggled his nose like a hungry mouse smelling cheese. . . Eirmægden smiled, for she had an idea why his nose wiggled; the lavender fields had not been harvested, because the Meline Dragon blocked the way and it had overgrown. The midday Sun was then at its highest and the fragrance of the lavender was pleasant but strong to a new comer like Jaddamiah. She did not tell him the real reason why he wiggled his nose and kept that secret to herself. He raised his fingers to the wound next to his eye, he felt the scab but there was no pain. "What did you use to heal my wound, it has already scabbed, and I feel no pain?" he asked with disbelief and inquisition. "I used honey, red seamróg and lavender mixed to a paste," replied Eirmægden, for she was a herb magician. What she omitted to share with Jaddamiah was that it was a four leaf seamróg, and very hard to find. Jaddamiah looked around the room, cocked his head left and right and looked for a mirror but there was none. He saw a large disc made of silver against the wall, it had many sculpted rays surrounding it, it was the Sun. He got up running his fingers through his hair, and when his hand returned, a clump of brittle whiteness lay in it. Blood rushed to his head, his heart raced as he stumbled toward the solar disc hanging on the wall. He peered into it forgetting the wound next to his eye and gasped at what he saw; for the image was clear, his hair was white and withered, only a few black strands remained. He cowered back, bending his frame, recoiling backward and fell into the soft seat. "Why have you not told me! This is. . . worse. . . than the scar on my face," he cried as tears began to stream over his cheeks. Jaddamiah sobbed uncontrollably, the infant woke up but did not scream and Iníon who was also asleep came out of hibernation. At first Eirmægden did not get up from the sofa, she allowed Jaddamiah to express himself. Then she got up and floated away, that was her grace and demeanour. When she returned with a cup in her hand, she gave it to Jaddamiah to drink. Time had moved on, fast, yet not so fast as to exceed the minutes, the late afternoon had arrived and with it came anger, vengefulness was looming in Jaddamiah's head. Afterwards Jaddamiah made his way back to his room; he was standing in the bedroom, his hands were resting on the sill, arms spread apart as he looked out over the rooftops, when those words rung in his head; ". . . your long, lustrous hair is cause for much vanity, we will have to do something about *that*. . .your long, lustrous hair is cause for much vanity, we will have to do something about *that*. . .your long lustrous hair is cause for much vanity, we will have to do something about *that*. . ."

He reached for his head again and as he touched his hair, a second clump was left in his hand. The dream which he had was not in the forefront of his mind any longer. He was without his sword and all he knew was that he had to get it back. After sundown Jaddamiah sneaked out of the house and walked down Wringer Street. He tried his best not to be seen or people would follow him. He knew that it was impossible to go via the bridge as the Dragon was preventing it so, he silently passed by to the other side of Wringer Street, the part that ran in a north easterly direction. He was unaware that his hostess had anticipated that course of action and had sent her daughter Iníon to follow him. She followed Jaddamiah as he crossed the street, scurrying over a sloped, grassy bank and into the tree line that sentineled the river. There she could hide easier behind the trunks of trees, as Jaddamiah becreeped to the river's edge. He had no other option than to swim across the river to the other side. He sat right before the water, his socks and boots had already been removed. He sat with his knees against his chest, wiggling his toes as he pondered his next action. Jaddamiah thought too long, and as Iníon watched him from the shadows, she knew in her heart that he would not go through with it that night, a man of greater determination would already have been out the other side and up the opposite river bank. Besides, Jaddamiah had no weapon with which to defend himself so, she came emerged from her hiding place and walked with stealth towards Jaddamiah. She stood for moment behind him in silence; he didn't even know that she was there. He was deep in his own thoughts. She knew that she would startle him if she came from behind no matter how careful she was, so she took a step to the side and sat down as quietly as possible beside him. Jaddamiah had a fright nearly tumbled over into the river. Iníon reached out and caught him at the wrist, preventing his premature introduction to the Western Wyvern. She persuaded him to return home with her and to try retrieving his sword on another day, when he was more prepared. On their way back Iníon told Jaddamiah of an alternate plan to get his sword, although it would be a longer way than taking the short cut across the river and stood the risk of the Dragon seeing him. There was an old goat track behind Weir that hadn't been used for an age, except that it was used by the people of Weir who had no alternative. It was in fact how they got message to Jaddamiah in the first place but, since it was only a single goat track they could not get larger supplies easily into Weir. The town of Weir had been under siege by the Meline Dragon for two months. Food would soon become a demand. At any rate, going on that detour took one along the mountain for some 5 miles, at which point they had to cross the Afon Wen and trek another 5 miles through dense weald before arriving at the Great Western Road. A further 8 miles would get them back to the bridge.

Jaddamiah listened to her and worked the plan over in his head then looked at Iníon thoughtfully before saying, "I'm sure it would be much easier if such a cunning young maiden as yourself accompanied me." Iníon smiled then replied, "We will see what tomorrow holds for us. After all, a good sleep clears the mind of cob webs." "Well said young lady," replied Jaddamiah, feeling a bit up in spirits. They walked home in silence. Yet still he was anxious, anxious about Fágan. . . In the morning when Jaddamiah woke up, he turned over from his stomach onto his back, which he did most mornings to ponder but, something caught his attention on the little table beside his bed. The morning sunlight fell on the gold filigree just above the blade under the front bolster. He picked it up and marvelled at its workmanship. The blade was made of Surrā Hurasam inlaid with gold; the hilt was crafted of Abnu Zabarkizag with a horse head pommel, inlaid with gold and semi-precious stones. 'Only a horse maiden could bestow such a gift', those were his thoughts as he got out of bed and held it up to the light that poured through the bedroom window. When Jaddamiah arrived for breakfast and the aroma of 'black drink' drifted up the stairs, he was pleasantly surprised to see Nanu looking much healthier and sitting at the breakfast table. Iníon had the little one on her back, wrapped in a medium weight wrap with smooth texture and a nice softness that made it lovely to wrap little children in. It was made of 100% cotton as was the custom in those regions so, the little boy was very cheerful. Nanu sat quietly eating her food and when Jaddamiah asked how she felt that morning she answered, "I am feeling altogether marvellous but, let us not speak of past foolishness. Eirmægden told me that you have had a dream. This set me contemplating, so I have written these words down for you," she set the white page down on the table. "Perhaps Iníon should read it for my voice will not carry me, she has a more melodious voice." Iníon consented and read what Nanu had written down, "I have said all that I can say. I have said and told all that was allowed. Whatever has been omitted was done so for posterity and most things should not be uttered in the mortal speech. So here today, as I glance out, through my window to the lake that lies before me, without ripple in reflections of the sweetest greens and warmest earthy tones, rain clouds gather with promise of storms. The promises hold true like dreams clinging to the wings of Dragons. And the things we have not understood is not for lack of trying or that it has been kept from us, *but a forgetting*. This forgetfulness is pressed by memory soon to be known, and every moment that passes bring us closer to our masterpiece. If you have had disappointments let us not as fools view them so. Just like a storm passes over the sea to reveal the blessed sunshine, let your anger dissipate and command it not to return. For your command is not wishful thinking but a jurisdiction set in motion before the ages of Dhara, before the aeons of this world. Like an eagle in her eyrie, perched at the top of the world, nothing small goes unseen. Your dreams are known, your smallest intentions vibrate across time and space. While these last consonants and syllables fall on leaves of paper, before your eyes know that the Tao is at rest, and the Ælves themselves take command. All life is one and every seed that falls blossoms again."

The Unnamed Road

The people of Weir called it 'The Unnamed Road'. News spread quietly up and down the village and through it, for their lives now depended on its secrecy. Those who could not free themselves from the lacertilian talons of fear, used that road to leave Weir altogether, for they had no faith in their Dragon-slayer.

At night some 'gleaner girls' made a long journey so that they could gather what they could from the fields, as far away from the Dragon as possible. The warriors who were less hurt, accompanied them as if their protection could serve any purpose but, the girls were grateful for their chivalry. Five miles on along the River Wyvern was a narrow, old stone bridge, wild grass had found its way onto the bridge as it hadn't been used for decades. On the other side of the River Wyvern there was no track at all but, if towns-folk kept at it they would have an alternate route into Weir in no time, provided the Dragon didn't find out. So it happened, that Jaddamiah's letter arrived late in the afternoon on the 13th of October 8816 at the doorstep of his hostess.

Doppel Traum

❧

"It is better to dream while the others are waking for those that are waking are mostly asleep," an old Sage said once. When Jaddamiah opened the door, the womenfolk were all in the kitchen. It came both as a surprise and expectation when he read his name on the envelope. He could tell that it was Hrosmægden's hand writing, and it immediately put a smile on his face as he thanked the messenger. No sooner had he sat down on the sofa when the women noticed from the kitchen, that things were rather quiet in the sitting room, so they all went to see what the matter was.

He held the envelope up and the letter in his other hand, then said to them as they each took seat, Eirmægden remained standing.

"Doppel Traum! Doppel Traum!" Jaddamiah called out softly, most astounded that the dream was exact as he read it aloud to them.

"Then it is a confirmation Jaddamiah," said Eirmægden when he had finished reading the letter. "Yes, as we discussed Eirmægden. I will get my head around it as soon as the bridge is cleared of the Dragon," he replied with renewed vigour, stealing a glance at Iníon. "There is something else," he said again. "For goodness sake, what is it Jaddamiah?" pressed Iníon. "Is it for Mino?"

"From. . .her sister," replied Jaddamiah. Jaddamiah gave the letter to Eirmægden, her face reddened as nervousness arose in her that only family members could insight in one. She sat down next to Jaddamiah and read in silence. She noticed that the second page had the seal of the King of the Hrosvyras at the top, that surprised her. As she read it, her long hair fell to the sides of her face so that her face was hidden as she read. The letter was short and to the point, asking from her that the sisters be reunited in their father's home for the time was long overdue. The letter was signed by Hrosmægden and Chief Aherin, her father.

Tears fell from her face onto the page, smudging the names so that it seemed the bottom of the characters of the names themselves were overflowing with ink to the edge of the page. It is said, the orison of tears are alike to the hours not given in love, and whether it was for ill or good that she cried, Eirmægden realized that the years had so silently, so quickly glided away and it would be reckless to let more of them drop, forgotten towards the tomb.

Jaddamiah Reclaims his Mordēre

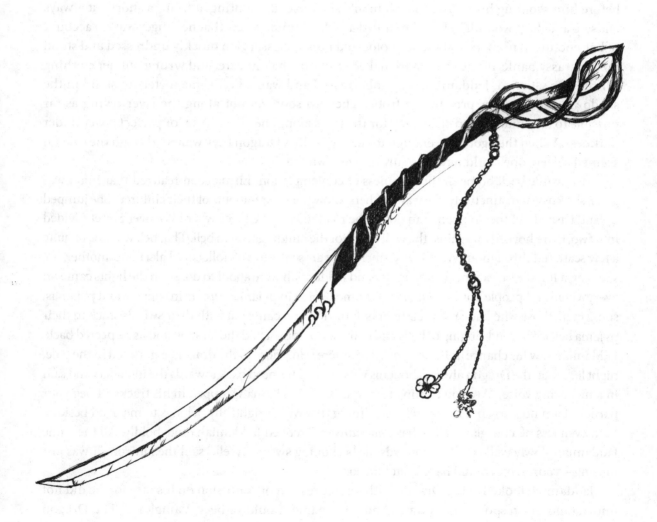

When Jaddamiah and Iníon had walked halfway along the River Wyvern by the 'Unnamed Road', he became impatient and threw caution to the wind, ran down the steep slope towards the quietly flowing river and dove in with a splash, testing the strong undercurrent. He thought that it was a waste of time to take so long a road just to come back to Weir. He decided that the short cut was best and though the undercurrent was strong, it seemed that the River Wyvern had been cautioned by the Fates for, Jaddamiah managed just fine and found himself standing on the opposite side of it shaking off his wetness while Iníon reluctant to get wet, dove in and following him. When she came out the other side, with the ease of a beaver, she stood before him scolding him, "You foolish man!" she scolded, pointing at him, "a short cut always ends up as a deep wound!" Then she smiled and Jaddamiah knew that her anger was on account of her nocturnal immersion but, he apologized nonetheless. Iníon quickly undressed and stood on the grassy banks of the river, stark naked with nonchalant care, and wrung out her clothing till she was satisfied. Jaddamiah was embarrassed and walked off some meters to stand in the shadows, allowing her private wardrobe. The two soon set out along the river trying as far possible to stay hidden and close to it, for the trees along the river made for perfect cover under darkness. When they got close enough to see the Meline Dragon they waited, though the dragon seemed asleep, one could never be sure, so they waited.

Meanwhile back home in the quietness of contemplation, Eirmægden realized that Iníon was gone, she knew it instinctively, the way mothers know the where-abouts of their children. She jumped up and rushed out the door. She ran down the road toward the place where Wringer Street divided into two, there hoisted up against the wall of one of the buildings, was a bell. That bell was one of quite a few scattered throughout Weir, if any emergency arose the town's folk could alert one another. So, she rang it for, she knew what her daughter and Jaddamiah were about to do. Soon the lights came on everywhere and people poured out of their homes, some in pyjamas, others in slippers and pyjamas, some men, those who had failed at attempts at the Dragon came out with their swords stuck in their pyjama belts. The loud ringing of bells and commotion distracted the Dragon and as he peered back, Jaddamiah saw his chance as Iníon spotted Mordēre lying close to the dragon, it glittered in the pale, night light but, the Dragon always about his wits, turned his head back towards the intruders and said in a menacing voice, "Are you coming to burglarate?" Jaddamiah stopped in his tracks. "I beg your pardon! I am no burglar. I am merely reclaiming that which rightfully belongs to me. And besides, I am even less of a burglar for you have *no mansion*," replied Jaddamiah quite boldly. All the while Jaddamiah slowly walked closer towards his beckoning sword. "Well," said the Dragon. "I was just musing – your name should have been Lofgeorn!"

Jaddamiah looked at the Dragon with an impression of confusion on his face for, he did not understand but responded anyway, "And your name should've been Vainglory." The Dragon raised his head and replied very seriously, "Oft sceall eorl monig anes willan wræc adreogan." But Jaddamiah was already heading for the sword; and was only a footfall away. The Dragon became enraged at his audacity and threw his neck backwards, its great body chafing the bridge and dislodging the scale completely that Jaddamiah had managed to slacken in the first encounter. Iníon, fleeting as an Ælfennes, rushed forward towards it and raised it as a shield as Jaddamiah cowered, for the flames were already being unleashed towards him but, Iníon was right beside him shielding them from the terrible blitzkrieg of fire. Over and over the flames teemed forth but to no avail for, as Iníon drew Jaddamiah backwards with her strong slender arms, the Dragon's own scale proved indestructible. Those who stood high enough in their windows or balconies saw what had happened. A great cheer came from the onlookers, people jeered at the Dragon and so he turned on them as Jaddamiah and Iníon fled along the river bank. Too slow were some of the booers and hecklers, for they were instantly flash-heated to death into lifelike poses. The heat blackened the walls behind, as many who stood against it, were also frozen in suspended action. Years later evidence would show the sudden muscle contractions, such as curled toes and bent fingers. Those contorted postures were not the consequences of a lingering anguish, but of the cadaveric spasm, a consequence of the heat from the Dragon's element. Others fled in terror and left the ghostly, frozen wraiths alone to endure the night. Some lodgings in the front line were ablaze; the bucket brigade braved the potential of another tally of flames from the Dragon but, came out nonetheless. Bells were ringing as those who fled in the opposite direction gave way to the 6-man-hand-pumped fire engine, powered by four red dwhëels. While they pumped and pumped and tried to put the fire out, the Dragon glanced over his shoulder and his laugh echoed through the pop, crackle and dance of the flames. It rang through the night; the dwhëels abandoned the engine and fled.

Suddenly Wringer Street was empty and silent, as only a few embers could be seen. Those in their houses put out their lights in the hope that darkness would save them, as Anusillu settled down to sleep. Jaddamiah swam back at the same point where he had crossed. Iníon, being infinitely wiser, used the Dragon scale as a kind of coracle, to row across to the other side. The two sat on the opposite banks of the Wyvern for a while catching their breath in silence for, if all be told, Jaddamiah had narrowly escaped death again.

❖

The sound of a beautiful poetic voice broke their bated silence;

"With his sword, the glowing Vidazati
Jaddamiah struck out the Dragons scale,
It sparkled and glittered in the dark,
Falling away from the mighty body,
The Fates for you have paved a prospect

But the wise say, take kindness with caution
Now this tale on the heights of the world will sound
While Ælves whisper it among the tremulous constellations.

They seized the new found golden jewel,
A shield gilded like a heavenly ember,
A maid surfed it over water,
Rocked it from shore to shore,
Virgin beauty, half Danann,
Gold skinned like a winter full Moon,
Bright eyed like the summer Sunshine,
Time without end you shall be remembered.

From the very hem of the Meline Dragon
A mortal plucked a thing of legends,
You have stirred a fire and ignited darkness,
Teased it like an infant's cradle,
You mistook pride for pearls
You mistook dreams for affirmations.
But where Dragons sleep Ælves are watching,
Where Dreams are dreamt Queen Medb is waiting.

Glide quietly to your ammë's homely house,
While perpetual night on some has fallen.
Death has thriven in the homes of Weir,
Even now Nature knows it,
Even now, the Stars can feel it.

Hide no more under leaf and wood beam,
I'll direct my spirit to the Gargoyles,
They will come with wings enswathe you.
Gargoyles came with varicoloured scintillations;
Took the virgin and the mortal,
She with 'Heavenly Ember' caught between her lissom arms
He content and mollified, Mordēre in his sheath again,
Iníon and Jaddamiah, to their home and nightly rest.
Oh, but Ælve why so hasty, said the maiden,
We don't even know your name,

Your words were kind and lordly. . .
And berate, seconded the mortal.
I am Elfara for I have intervened,
Though, My Bele told me nowise.
Thus he spake, this Elfara;
Go now maiden. Be gone mortal!
You have had a boon too many.

Off they went, the maiden and the mortal,
Leaving the Ælve alone in the shadows,
Too the night he gave his contemplations,
With his eyes made phantom observations,
And the Stars to give him solace,
Thus he faded into the darkness,

Becoming one again, with the dark sacred night-time,
Holding up the pillars of the gloom."

Through the night it had started to rain. When Jaddamiah got up and walked to the lavatory, the air was filled with petrichor. He looked out the window down into the backyards of the smaller houses; on their slated roofs and smokestacks, the sight was not a cheerful one, as he remembered the night before. Suddenly the wet roofs and rain made him miserable and he hoped that some good tea from the homely hand of his hostess would cheer him up. When the Sun had set and the town's people were at ease and the twilight had moved into night, and when the full Moon gave the shadows much flight, something strange happened. It was the second week that Jaddamiah attempted to slay the dragon. Fear creates blindness, but excitement has the same effect on the mind, for either Jaddamiah did not notice it at first, or it wasn't there to begin with, and therefore he didn't notice it at all but, then unbeknownst to him, it felt that he could not stay away from the Dragon. When the house was still and he thought no-one was watching he crept out, tip-toed with boots in his hands till he reached outside, slid them on and becreept toward the great Meline Dragon. Somehow, he had made a foefie slide from one tree to the other on the opposite side of the River Wyvern and quietly monkied across with hand and ankle, then crept up the bank, then for hours sat watching the Dragon. There was a strange seduction, he felt it even at a distance when in his bedroom chamber, and at times he felt the Dragon's voice in his head, gently murmuring to him.

Everything about the Dragon drew Jaddamiah towards it. What he did notice was that there was a certain smell, a perfume or whatever else it was, he could not tell; if it was in the air or floated around the Dragon, that was most intoxicating to him. He wondered as he sat under the dark of some trees and at a vantage point, if others smelled it too. The dragon turned its head in his direction, slowly, from where he was hiding, he clearly saw its golden, fiery eyes. It spoke to him, without voice or word like Lilith to Mr Vane. It was almost feminine in its gestures, and Jaddamiah felt himself moving from his place towards the creature but, before he could move an inch closer, Iníon was upon him, alighting from a thick branch above him, holding him back.

Still he could not bring himself to withdraw his gaze and as the Meline Dragon turned from its position, Jaddamiah and Iníon noticed that where the great paws of the Dragon had fallen, were no indentations from its colossal weight but, the ground was scorched, several scorch marks lying about from its feet.

The stillness of the night, the comfort of their veiling place made their skin crawl. "How joyous would it be, perchance we could float away on the river from the Dragon that watches us here," whispered Jaddamiah but, Iníon didn't reply.

On their way back, even while crossing the foefie slide, Jaddamiah could hear the dragon in his head; "Jaddamiah! Why, why do you persist with this action, do you not think of those you love? By those marks on your body and the loss of your hair, by the loss of your impediment, have you not learned? Must you writhe further in pain like a malcontent scoriated? To relish a love-song without triumph of the lover, to walk alone, like one that had the pestilence, to sigh, like a school-boy that had lost his A B C; to weep, like a young wench that had buried her lover, to fast like the pious that takes diet, to watch like one that fears robbing, to speak, puling, like a beggar at Requiem. . ."

Half Moon Rising while Fires Blazing

When they entered the quiet house as it usually was, Jaddamiah felt insatiably tired and he didn't know why. Iníon had a sense that his energy was drained by the Dragon or perhaps a psychic attack had occurred. He fell into the soft sofa while Iníon made him a strong cup of lemon and sage tea. Iníon, unlike her mother, left Jaddamiah to sleep on the sofa. The following morning he woke up to folk knocking on the door, outside in the street, people had gathered in anger, but most importantly, most fearful for their lives. Those who didn't take flight along the 'Unnamed Road' regretted it. In the dead of the night, the Meline Dragon lifted its large form off the ground, took to flight, having been struck by some thought that had crossed his mind. . .

It was most copious how a creature so large could take flight so easily, so effortlessly, but Dragons for all their largeness have a very, very light, skeletal system, though light, it was also strong, stronger than iron and lighter than wood, its density was just 3.5 pounds per cubic foot. Some nations had tried to harness its potential for building war machines and other objects of industry but, could never get hold of Dragon bone, for a peculiar thing occurred when Dragons were killed, of that a little later. Anusillu spread his large wings, overshadowing Weir. All were asleep even those that prided themselves with watching or protecting. He flew with a single purpose, flying silently despite his largeness, almost wilfully kept silent as if conspiring with the air. Along the river he wended and from its tri-rated stomach it begun, with the power of many furnaces up and through its mouth, the night and the mountain side were lit up as the Meline Dragon scorched the 'Unnamed Road' in its full length toward the bridge. Some last travellers who sneaked out over it, ran screaming backwards and forwards but, the creature of fire and flame could care less for their plight. It stooped downward towards a shrieking mule and violently cluthed it in its sharp talons, choking the breath from its lungs, and then climbing higher, gently turned back to Weir with the mule still kicking for dear life, as some of its cargo toppled towards the river and floated away to some distant place. Swooping over Weir, it was noiseless, no menacing shrieks to cause fear, and no moans of anger or growls to seize the listener's heart in paralytic hoarfrost. It was surprise and fear schemes so, when the citizens woke the following morning, all but fear had seized their hearts. The mule was dropped from on high and as it dropped, the Dragon set it on fire and its further incineration occurred as the mule dropped through the roof of the Inn where all the failed cavaliers and dragon-slayer pretenders were sweetly sleeping like innocent birds. Such innocence that was prone to act on compulsion and inclinations that had the dominion to bring themselves (and others) to ruin.

The crash and crackle awoke some; they set instantly to douse the flames while others slept on only to be teeming with fear and regret in the morning. That ruin occurred under a half Moon rising and a full Moon lurking.

Jaddamiah leapt from his sofa towards the front door, the women of the house joined him in close succession. The door bangers wanted him to take action, and for the first time the mob were led by the Azapala of Weir, who walked over in his long, soft plum-coloured gown. Half burnt candle, wooden spindle candlestick holder in hand and night-cap on his head, with an unbefitting dragon embroided onto it. He raised his hand so that the boisterous mob could calm down, then introduced himself to Jaddamiah by first asking in a brittle voice, "Mr Jabberwocky! Can you please come down from the step; I am *not* a tall man . . . as you can see." Jaddamiah looked clear over his balled pate, as he had by then taken off his night cap and stepped down off the door step, though still was taller than the Azapala. The Azapala stuck out his arm and hand like a metronome and introduced himself, "I am the Azapala of Weir, er . . . Obeseto Grando is my name. I apologize for only making my appearance to you now but, warm air rises and as you can see we've become very hot under the circumstances," as he spoke, he used his thick eyebrows to its full advantage to express himself, now and again he flung his arms out beside him and nearly into the faces of those standing too close, so that intermittently their shoulders waved in a kind of spiral swaying motion, till his arms came to rest beside him again. From his wrist dangled the emblem of Weir; a simply crafted, golden jewel in the shape of a bee and a water drop. His hand with the candle stick rested on his round, protruding potbelly, well hidden by his gown. Jaddamiah listened as he continued, for until then he had not had the opportunity to get any word in, "So now, anent … *the Dragon?* Anon, we must!" then he paused, then continued, "I beg your pardon, *you must* dispose of the Dragon! It is a menace, many lives have been lost this night, eke, you are the counselled one after all, albeit a *relative* procured the last word concerning your employment," he paused again, then broke out into foolish laughter and said, "Employment? Did I just say employment, no-one uses *that* word anymore, I meant to say your avocation Mr Jabberwocky, it is yours to see through," Obeseto Grando dropped his chin as he said those words, and stuck his index finger and his thumb of his free hand into his gown pocket, twiggling something round inside it.

In that brief pause, Jaddamiah immediately spoke, "I am pleased to make your acquaintance Mr Obeseto Grando, and as you rightly pointed out, it is my employment, I mean avocation, so the job will be done, I assure you," those were all the words Jaddamiah could afford so early in the morning as, behind him Iníon chuckled to herself. "So it is written, so let it be," replied Mr Obeseto Grando and turned towards the crowd and said loudly "You heard the Jabberwocky, he will get the job done. Now if you all will just let me be, to get back to my reading." He then preceded two steps and turned again to Jaddamiah and took out the thing he was twiddling in his pocket, it was a single, gold sovereign which he held between his fingers and said, "For you Mr Jaddamiah Jabberwocky! And there's more . . . if you see it all through, anon!" The Azapala paved a path through the mob, a red sea of angry faces. Jaddamiah slipped backwards through the door with the 3 women after him and, so his day started. When Jaddamiah sat down at the breakfast table, he realized that he was famished. Eirmægden had been brewing some wonderful Morgen rot-Bush tea. That morning the breakfast was much to Jaddamiah's liking as Eirmægden served slices of cold, pink ham, cheeses, jam, eggs, golden toasted bread, muffins and apple bread, of course Iníon ate no flesh at all, that was for the guests. Late that afternoon when he could not keep his mind away from the Dragon, he asked curmudgeonly if Iníon and her mother would accompany him to the Dhana Hrada. When the 3 figures walked along the sidewalk, the scene was strange. There was a stillness in the movement of folk, like some docile rabbit going by carefully not to disturb some great beast. When they had walked past the row of houses, they came to a square filled with flower stalls and other goods. Tomatoes smiled with red, fat faces, neatly packed in open wooden crates, great vats of oil, oranges and lemons could be had too. Garlic hung on strings next to the last of the charcuteries, adding much colour, and some old ladies dressed in black were selling large, sweet, white onions and wild herbs and lavender that grew on the slopes of the mountain overlooking the Dhana Hrada. It was market day and despite the vicious Dragon and the even more malicious attack of the previous night, the people of Weir were determined to carry on with life as best they could, albeit under town-arrest. The gleaner girls could no longer manage to harvest what was left of August, as Weir planted on 15 An Bhealtaine each year and harvested on 15 August, no such thing that year. . .on account of the Dragon. Children were playing about, and grown-ups were snacking and tasting charcuteries, for the spirit was much kinder than the morning's protestations.

Some called Jaddamiah over but, he was in no mood, so he shouted back thanking them and proceeded on his intended plan of action.

He felt like joining the men, smoking long, colourful lesepfeifies. He felt in the inside of his jacket pocket for his but, he had left it in his room. The wonder was not lost to him, neither to Iníon nor her mother at the cheek of it all, and that only pressed more on him to do the deed that he had set out to do when he departed from his doorstep, which seemed so long ago. When they had reached the outskirts of the town, they entered a narrow lane of tall poplars which stood either side of it. As they walked along the lane, white flecks of poplar seeds were drifting down upon them like flakes of snow, perhaps a foreboding of what was to come. Through the rustling leaves Jaddamiah thought he heard singing but, he couldn't tell where its source was but, in any case, he wiped it from his mind for it was not possible. Inion and her mother smiled to each other, for there, the singing started again, beautiful, sad, melodic defying the bright, blessed day. Jaddamiah stood stock still, his eyes pierced the green for any sign of the song bird, for it couldn't be; nightingales only appeared and sang at night! He looked at the two women with an expression of questioning on his face. Eirmægden shook her head with a smile starting over her lips. Inion looked at him and spoke in the ancient tongue, "Priyagitas Jaddamiah! Priyagitas! To see, one must get lost Jaddamiah, lost in Darsana"

They walked on in silence, all the while Jaddamiah's eyes were upward to the trees but he could not see them. They sat in the shadows, out of sight, for they only made themselves visible in the dark or under the Moon light.

The path twisted this way and that with tall foxgloves and mulleins growing alongside each other, as the tall poplars gave way to more light, filtered from the sky. The green shades of light changed as the sunlight played with many oaks that stood either side of the path that led off deeper into the weald. The path continued along a steep, wooded bank and before them laid the Dhana Hrada, a great stretch of water with large oaks billowing down to the water's edge. Suddenly they were alone, there was no-one around except them and Sun, sand, water, trees and wild flowers, with the gentle sounds of twittering. Jaddamiah found a large rock sticking out of the shallow water on the beach and went to sit on it. He bided time in thought while Eirmægden walked by herself, combing the contour of the lake. Inion found a secret cove and undressed, dipped into the cold water, something she was fond of doing throughout the year.

When the light fell behind the tall trees and the clouds had parted just enough so that a certain light filled the time of day, and the snow-capped mountains could be seen from that vantage point, the same light that shared Jaddamiah's journey to Weir; was cast over them in hues of gold then pink, and when that light slid down the mighty slopes, Jaddamiah watched Eirmægden and Inion approaching. Inion noticed a dark speck approaching from the eastern sky, and as it grew larger and closer, she pointed towards it so Jaddamiah saw that moments later, dark speck, that spot, was upon them. They then saw that is was a large flock of magpies, at least thirty or so, and when they got closer, they swooped down towards the water and turned to circle the trio on the lake shore. They did that 3 times, their plumes gleamed in the Sunlight, then they took off towards Weir. "It is uncommon to find magpies so late in the year," remarked Eirmægden in her silver voice.

"But did you notice emel!" exclaimed Inion, "There was a rainbow magpie with the flock." "A Rainbow Magpie? Hmmmm, most unusual, you have keen sight." On the way back they spoke about the Magpies, why they were around that time of year, why they circled around the 3 of them at the lake, what it all meant?

As they walked and talked, Iníon suddenly put out her arm and signalled them to stop, "Hush! Don't move! Be still, lest the earth tell the Ælves of our passing." She crouched and pointed upward, high along the mountain slope between the long grasses and the trees; Jaddamiah and Eirmægden ducked without realizing it, as if afraid to make some kind of irreverence, for Iníon spoke in whispered tones. As they looked up to where she was pointing, they noticed only a streak of silver light against the mountainside with faint, pale shadows, it was all their eyes could afford them. On the other hand, Iníon saw them clearly. The 3 held their positions for some time then, the scene passed and the silver light was gone. It was then that Jaddamiah realized how fortunate he was to have seen the Ælves on his way to Weir, but that pride was soon lost for Iníon gave the names of the Ælves she just saw. "Those are the Ravana Ælves from Haliath. They are smaller in stature if we had to compare them to other Ælves but, they are superior in every other way, if one could use such a phrase. They are often mistaken for Aerendgast but, of course, there are no such things as Aerendgast, it is only an old wives' tale of the *Eldiĕni.*" Iníon whispered as she spoke and was out of breath or so it seemed to the two listeners, who gave her all their attention. Though Jaddamiah had spent a brief time in the presence of some of the Ælves, his pride was touched as he listened to the young girl, for she knew the Ælves far better than he did. "I've often seen you slipping away from chores to go into the wild woodlands, now I know the reasons why . . ." her mother said thoughtfully. Iníon didn't reply but instead stood in deep thought before moving off again, as if she had been touched by a strange sadness. Jaddamiah noticed it and enquired why she seemed so melancholic then she asked him softly, "It is said that pain is joy once lost. Whenever I have glimpse of the Ælves passing in the woodlands or the wealds, I feel that I have lost a great joy."

Jaddamiah was silent after that, contemplating on her answer; no-one spoke after that as they walked home — each was trying to understand the nadirs of what had been uttered.

Battle of The Round Moon

———❖———

At night when the house was quiet, when Nana and Maredudd had returned to their own home and it was the beginning of the third week of the Draconian affair, as the days bled out, so the cold of Winter through Autumn glided into Weir. Jaddamiah thought that he would sit down to write into his journal of all that had happened thus far, and also to write his dear wife a letter and try to find anyone who was brave or foolish enough, travelling by way of Malbon to post it onward to Béth-Élam. He explained the fellowship that was being formed, and the calling to make a pilgrimage to the north. No fellowship had attempted it before, and no-one had succeeded as far as news travelled. He hoped that he would get his wife's blessing and if not, her consent by going along. When Jaddamiah had finished his writing, he thought to himself, 'Seven more days and I would be away from home and family for two full months . . . the longest I have ever been separated from my family'. Those were his thoughts as he sat alone at the hearth.

His attention shifted momentarily, so he opened his journal again and turned to a clean page as he started an attempt to sketch the Dragon, so he could, in his way, prove to those who doubted what a Dragon looked like, what Anusillu looked like.

———❖———

He brooded for 6 days; hardly leaving his room, hardly getting a breath of fresh air. The Dragon slaying consumed his thoughts.

He scribbled on bits of paper, wrote out strategies and plans, crossed them out and started over again. Iníon snuck away early after breakfast on the morning of the 22nd of October, for she knew he was up to something. She went as far as the furthest east side of the Dhana Hrada. She then went by way of a secret stair; to the Ælves it was called 'The Stayr a Fow a Skydnya'. How she came to know of it was not told in folktales. No human had ever been up it nor down into it. Though she was half-Danann, it did not secure her entering it but, Iníon was valiant and very audacious. (Sometimes we do things we don't know the reason why only to find its design leading to a larger way.)

No one in Weir knew of it but, on the far eastern side of the lake, some of the water fell into a deep pool. There was no way down to the pool which was some 33ft down; the sheer rock was slippery and taking a plunge down meant you would not be able to return, there was no place for gripping of fingers, no place for clove hitch or alpine knee or campusing, only danger, falling and drowning from exhaustion in the end. The stair ascended out of the lake, right out of it as if ascending from beneath the water. She walked under tree cover along the shore, then made sure no one was following. The maiden then hastily left the cover of trees, rock-hopping till she could jump no further. Iníon then took the cold plunge and swam the 100m towards where the steps crept out of the water. Wet and bedraggled she felt for the steps beneath the water and got up, looked back once more to the western part of the lake then, finally slipped away under the oak trees. They clung to the narrow-stepped path like moss to rock, tall and narrow, columnar they grew, regal Pennsevik oaks, fully clothed. It was a steep stair that wound and turned back on itself. If one tried to look out from it, for some reason the lake was completely obscured, 'surreptitious' she thought to herself. She was still dripping when eventually she reached the topmost part of the stair. There it took a steep plunge down along a rock wall toward the bottom, one could only access the pool from that position. The lake side the water seemed to seep through a thin fissure, one could only hear water cascading faintly from one side and out on the other side of the rock wall kissing the lake. She nimbly descended, quietly. When she stood before the deep pool and held her bow firmly behind her back as it was strung over her shoulder, she wasted no time for thought. She dove down the 33ft and slipped into the water like an eel. The water was brilliant, dark blue and icy cold. While she allowed the buoyancy of her lithe body to take her to the surface, she noticed that she had to keep her eyes shut for the water was filled with luminous light that was almost blinding, for that pool was named 'The Pool of Kelel'. Iníon resurfaced in the fresh air, she swam towards the curtain of water and entered it, there behind the curtain was a sizeable balcony and as soon as she climbed up the steps and stood on the balcony, water fell from her long hair and soaked garments and filled the labyrinthine markings on the floor. They immediately illumed, forming beautiful isograms and the contours of a pavonated, arched door was revealed to her. On the large stone itself, engraved was a strange glaive resting on its point, at the top of the glaive were Vasinsurapuspa or as they call it in those regions 'Bán Ghrian Ròs'(ghrian like Ryan) and wings encircling. A rush of joy, expectation and a shudder of discovery ran through her being.

She needn't say anything for she was Ælve-friend, the Duir opened, it was the way to the 'Cave of Alli'cient'.

When she stepped over the threshold the heavy duir closed with a thud. Iníon found herself in absolute darkness, darkness not even her keen eyes could penetrate but, for some reason, she was unafraid for the air seemed friendly. It was filled with an unfamiliar fragrance, for Bán Ghrian Ròs did not grow in Weir but, she knew that she deeply enjoyed inhaling the fragrance. Of a sudden, the large base of a tree begun to illume, and soft light crept up the tree, creeping to all the branches till the tree and the whole room which was large and round, was filled with warm, gloaming light. Before her stood a tall form dressed in a dark hood and cape. The hood obscured his face. He rested both hands on the hilt of a sword, the self-same sword she saw engraved on the duir of the cave. The sword was at least 6ft long; the cross-guard was long and ended in some sort of floral embellishment. From the rain-guard to the fuller it was kræfted of some black metal, between the fuller and central ridge the blade was quite narrow and between the central ridge and point the blade, was broad and sharp. She was impressed, for Iníon fell somewhat short of being a hoplophile. In the stillness of the cave and her proximity to the glaive, she felt the harmonic balance of it. The vibration was so strong that she was sure she could hear music from the weapon. No words came from the dark stranger that stood before her, and by his composure she did not want to antagonize him so, she commenced with the first word, "I am Iníon-Dé Danann, half Danann, daughter of Eirmægden from House of Hrosweard. I come in peace, seeking a boon for a friend."

Her voice quivered, whether fear had crept up in her she could not tell. The large wings of the dark stranger stirred, then he answered in a distinctively, deep voice, "Few have come, none have left. What have you to offer *half Danann*?" Iníon stepped back, removed the quiver from her back and laid it down on the floor, as she untied the leather strap on the outside of the quiver, she noticed that the surface was made of emerant. She retrieved what she was searching for and gave a sigh of relief, it was still dry. She stood up and untied a neat bundle; first she unwrapped the large oak leaf, then she unfolded the blue cloth and held it up to the stranger. Nestled in the nearly damp cloth were 3 slices of honey cake, it smelled good. The dark stranger did not stir, he only replied, "You may pass, I have no wont for the viand of the Eldiëni." She neatly folded the cloth over the honey cake and gently hid it in the pouch of her quiver. She stepped around the dark stranger and walked in the gloaming light past the illuminated tree, she did not recognize it for there wasn't a single leaf on the tree. As she walked out of the circular room, she followed the sound of the water that ran in a rill at the base of the wall of the passage, which had substantially higher vaulted ceilings. She didn't walk more than 100 meters when she came to another hall, that one larger than the first. It also had a large, illuminated tree growing at its centre. She saw 3 Ælves seated on ornate seats at a rectangular well, they were staring into the water, what they were staring at she could not see, but one, an Ælfennes, got up and carried a golden thurible. Blue smoke twirled out from it. The Ælfennes carried it towards the mysterious tree and hung it on one of the branches. She then approached Iníon and said in a gentle, melodic voice, "To what doth we owe the honour of the visit for such a one as yourself?" Again, she repeated herself, "I am Iníon-Dé Danann, half Danann, daughter of Eirmægden from House of Hrosweard. I come in peace seeking a boon for a friend." Her voice no longer quivered for she was distracted by the beautiful, glowing face of the Ælfennes and her manner of speech. She also wore an elegant silver-grey peplo, she stood with her left hand in a strange manner, a single, thin diamond band glittered around her finger. When she spoke, Iníon found herself stepping back a pace for a large, white crane with a crimson head, was in her hand. Also, a pale outline of blue glowed in the form of the Frawahr in her forehead. "And I am Fenna. I readeth thy mind, our hands art not our eyes. We art forbidden to touch the one thee cameth to seek a boon for. But per adventure thee wish for something else. Something Elvysshe!"

"What is your meaning?" inquired Iníon thoughtfully.

"Thou bringeth honey cake. Those who enter the 'Cave of Alli'cient' must travel 9 days and need drinketh the waters of Forgetfulness, then only can they drinketh the waters of Memory."

Iníon contemplated those words, she didn't move. Long had she desired to look on her father's kin, long and alone has she waited at the rim of The Pool of Kelel, only to turn back on numerous occasions. She looked into the bright, serene face of Fenna and nodded. "I accept," she said softly, so softly that she barely heard herself saying it. Fenna opened her hands and held them side by side, palms up. Iníon removed the honey cake and placed it in her hands. Iníon noticed that the water well into which two Ælves were scrying began to flow faster and louder, they got up from their seats and joined Fenna. In that manner, Iníon was led away out of the existence of the world of the Eldiĕni and dwelt for 9 days with those Master Spirits of the Cave of Alli'cient.

When Eirmægden rose from sleep, she found that her home was quiet, except for the feint tinkering of belts and buckles and sword or blade. It was only feint so, she didn't yet realise that it was her guest. In fact, she had a notion that perchance it was her daughter heading out into the wilds for the day. She arose and slipped into her gown and walked over to the closed door of Iníon's bedroom (a closed door being out of the ordinary) and gave a soft knock on the door. There was no reply so, she opened the door and found the room empty, the bed was unmade, and it seemed that her daughter had rushed out. She entered the room and stood in the stillness and listened. She decided that the sound came from a floor down. As she was about to sing in her silvery voice, for such was her custom when contemplating, she noticed a dim light forming over Iníon's bed, up against the ceiling. The light slowly descended and drew her fascination. As it descended, she saw that it was a fluffy, white feather, reddened at the tips. She grabbed it in the palm of her hand, closed her fingers about it and waited. The feather felt warm against her skin, she uncurled her fingers and looked at the Heka-en plume.

Eirmægden sat down on the edge of the bed and smiled, though her serenity had been moved. She knew what that meant, because long before, which now felt like ages, Iníon's father augured that if the eolas in their daughter's being were strong enough, it would lead her to seek out 'the secret pool'. Eirmægden found those words feathering over her lips, "Tá eolas agam ar an áit seo."

Tears rolled down her flushed cheeks; she brought her plaits forward to her bosom and lay down on the bed. She toyed with each plait in turn between her fingers and lingered in thought, moments fleeting as the years. Soon she realised that both plaits were loose and her long, silky, ebony hair was undone. She got up from the bed and went down the stairs. As she tip-toed, the tinkering had grown considerably louder. She asked Jaddamiah if all were ok, but he didn't respond so, she proceeded to the kitchen and sang a song of bitter-sweet strains.

There is Castan smoke sweet on the air;
Though day is breaking no hearth is bare
I fumble down stairs, still dreams in my hair
Plumed convoys call us to duty
Is the red dawn a mark? Is one to find their passing?
Shall the Ælves not save us by a compassing.

Are these the days portending that all has changed for-ever?
Is all well still? Wood-smoke still sweetens the air,
Though vain glories leave men russet and bare
Without returning to those Halls of Healing;
Hath some phantom come to remove their masks stealing?
I will sing my songs! Stop? No never!

Ere the horse maiden's song is over
Can the day turn for better then?
Or shall the Wyrm seduce more men,
Like the Castan smoke in the air;
It lays my senses bare.
Or does my song reveal the dreams of a foolish lover. . .

Jaddamiah was cautiously optimistic, and when he thought that he was ready, he listened till Eirmægden stopped her singing, and as she walked back upstairs, he snuck out like a burglar. As he tried to push the bedroom door closed as quietly as possible, he opened it suddenly and went back inside and sat down at the desk and wrote;

I know my street and all its gardens;
Innocentia, without any wardens.
I have heard the lilting of the housewives,
Watched the knaves take honey from the hives.
I go now to slay the dragon,
If I fail, I beg your pardon.

Will victory stay away the wolves and monsters?
Let this verse be neglected by critic and monsters.
And to my hostess;
Clink! You have given me the mostess.
If there is no one to beguile my fate with song,
Let them be there for destiny erelong.

When everything in the house was quiet, when even the midday meal was standing cold on the kitchen table, Eirmægden knew that all was not well, and it was when she stilled her thoughts and a chill draft rushed suddenly through the hallway, that she grabbed her cape and rushed out the front door. Outside she discovered that it was quite separate from her world, the one in her home; for people were rushing in one direction, and that direction wasn't necessarily safe. She tried to ask a passer-by what on earth was going on and the person looked at her as if that was the daftest question in the world, *in Weir.* Just then Nanu came down with the flooding crowd. She didn't mean to go along with the boisterous crowd, only to tell Eirmægden that she thought it was unwise to follow the crowd and that she would leave Weir to travel to her parents in Bútangyð, some 60 miles from Nilbud.

"But what of the. . ." asked Eirmægden, interrupted by Nanu placing her finger on Eirmægden's lips. "I will return erelong. I must make haste, perchance I will take the paths of the weald," she said in a hurried fashion. The women embraced and Eirmægden lost view of Nanu as she pressed into the oncoming crowd.

Eirmægden had more thoughts on Jaddamiah Jabberwocky, on his safety. . . perhaps also, just perhaps some curiosity too. So, she followed at a close distance behind the last line of the throng. The crowds couldn't see the new from the past, their self-esteem stopped them. They remembered the past attempts of the dead and the wounded soldiers, the bravedors who attempted to slay the dragon. They blindly hoped that Jaddamiah Jabberwocky of Béth-Élam would slay their foe and, since their self-esteem was principally grounded in their memory, which was a past thing and the past things fear the new, they deadened their fear by placing their faith in an attempt that had been attempted before, and Anusillu knew that. The crowds came with pitchfork and spade, with stick and brick, also the twelve Weir guard were present but, the Weir guard were mostly comprised of old, weary men. In the background the 6-man, hand-pump-brigade were waiting. It wasn't their desire to see the ancient, slumbering town burn to the ground. The dragon gave a sadistic laugh and begun to sing;

"The Moon doth shine as bright as day
Have your supper, and go to sleep
Be warned! There is a dragon in the street.

They came with sword, they came with lance,
They came prepared and took their stance.
Up from Élam a Jabberwocky came,
A gold purse promised, to find himself a name.
I'll crush his bones, and watch him cower,
And eat him as pudding within the hour."

"Boo! Boooo! Boo! Bobolyne! Booooo! Rakefire! Gobermouch!"

The crowd jeered and swore at the immovable dragon. Someone in the crowd cottoned onto the word 'Gobermouch' and someone else repeated it, until everyone shouted in unison though, unison was hardly the word to use just then. Gobermouch-gobermouch-gobermouch-gobermouch-gobermouch-gobermouch!

Dead with *the Gobermouch*! Rakefire! Gobermouch! Rakefire!"

The Dragon yawned and called out at the end of the yawn; his yawn and his mocking jeer faded into one, "Muckspouts!"

The Dragon gently laid his head down on his front talons and closed his eyes, or so it appeared. Meanwhile Jaddamiah held Mordēre in one hand and 'Heavenly Ember' in the other. He so wished that he had a lance right then, he looked over to his left and there to his surprise lay a bloodied lance in the open hand of a Yeager, not blood of the Dragon of course but, the victim lay beside it, vultures and eagles had already come to gather the carrion. Of that carrion, closer to the town, the ambulance men had tried to clear it to give those men some sort of burial and since most of the towns' people of Weir believed that the land of the dead was beneath the earth, it seemed fitting to dig graves to provide the deceased with easier access to the nether world.

'Now is the moment' thought Jaddamiah to himself. 'This is it!'

He said loudly in his head. He lunged forward, taking aim at the Dragon, but Jaddamiah had never thrown a lance before, he did not know that speed and power were required for hurling a lance.

And sometimes '[1]a great dominance of power can be foregone for mastery'. He held the lance up over his shoulder; he wasn't to release it just then. Jaddamiah was looking for that weak spot, the spot he and Iníon forced but, the Dragon didn't move. Jaddamiah strode gently, placing each foot down premeditatively. Elsalah was sailing into the sea in the west while simultaneously the full Tally-of-Years was rising. The crowd was quiet for, as Jaddamiah moved stealthily past the Dragon's tail, they drew closer, plucking up courage for they found strength in numbers and sticks and stones. Anusillu turned its head still feigning sleep. Jaddamiah moved ever forward, lance in hand. No sound was heard except his beating heart; never was he more present than that moment. For all his life he was living in a past or a future, a time that never was. It was the desire of the Eldiĕni.

---

[1] Quoted directly from Glórgalaloy of Ukhahlamba

Then clear as day, he saw the spot where the 'heavenly ember' was dislodged but, he spied a peculiar thing, a second scale was already beginning to form in its place; a thin membrane, but was rejuvenation nonetheless. Jaddamiah's heart sank; he thought that he had the upper hand. Involuntarily the lance set flight from its master's hand piercing the cool evening air, only a mere moment had passed but the lance stuck in the softer tissue of the Dragon. There was a great roar from the crowd, they rushed forward with brick and stone, pitchfork and spade, some grabbed weapons lying about and rushed towards the Dragon. Others who came with torches, flung it at their enemy but, many things were not what they seemed. The Dragon stood up on its great, five-toed feet, its talons grating the flag stones, undoing myriad of them. The lance fell out. Although Jaddamiah had keen eyes, he lacked mastery. Weakness in the core created dimness in the transferring muscles, so diminishing the force and reducing performance.

The large, flavescent collar glittered in the moonlight as the head turned downward, the collar spread out making a rattling sound behind its neck. With one foul swoop from its caudal spade, shimmering with Meline anger, twenty or thirty attackers were flung north and south; some falling ka-plash in the river. Still other bodies fell ka-plunk against the bridge, bones in places never heard of, broke. The Dragon, fully angered, drew in the aethyrs and distilled it within its molten core. . .

Jaddamiah saw another chance, and rushed forward with Mordēre tight in his grasp, he wouldn't lose his sword that easily.

He jabbed twice. Anusillu elbowed him. The pain was excruciating, Jaddamiah could hardly stand. Several of the crowd helped him up, placed his sword back in his bloodied hand. "Go smite the Dragon!" they shouted courage. Then it ushered forth, like a river of torrid odium; fire upon fire upon fire. Fire and flame. . .issued forth like blood on a red Moon passing through feverish skin.

It burned the trees, it set fire to the grass, but its holocaust was not indiscriminate passion. No!

Someone found the need to run. The Dragon set down its heavy paw. . .slowly. . .and pressed the ambush attendant to a pulp, while languorously turning its head and spreading the inferno towards more lodgings. "Bombard a drab mob!" exclaimed the Dragon in a rambunctious roar. An insulant dog stood barking before the mountain of luteous scales. "Goddamn mad dog!" shouted Jaddamiah rushing for it, and took it out of harm's way. "Tirrit! Tirrit! Tirrit!" screamed the women folk while seeking places to hide. While yeoman and lavender, farmer and apprentice hurled their tools of trade at the Dragon, while an apiarian emptied his skep in the hope of stinging the Dragon, for the swarm only to sting the towns folk in the frenzy of Dragon ambush. The battledore maker beat the Dragon's tale, only to be kicked like an item under the rug, for he was company unannounced. Jaddamiah had hurled a second lance at the Dragon, that time with a rasp to the eye, just there where the soft tissue was. Some wise ropers brought out the ropes, harnessed it to hooks and uselessly tried to hook the Dragons ankles; the hooks wouldn't sink in and as the Dragon rushed forward towards Jaddamiah, the ropers were dragged over the broken and dishevelled flagstones. It wasn't pleasant to say the least, and if truth be told, the Dragon was toying with everyone.

Jaddamiah had regained his composure, Mordēre in one hand, 'heavens ember' in the other which, in after years would come to be known as 'Anuagirru'. All was permeated with blue light from the full, blue Moon.

In a place far away, many, many miles, 1600 miles in fact, situated on a hill, in a town called Pravalha, in a domed fane something stirred. 3 Djedi were going about their daily business, which was usually reading or being out amongst the grainnewich seeking new meridians, or perhaps amongst trees. They didn't notice it at first, two of them were busy inside, one was out and about. While they were accompanied by the stillnesses in the song of the spheres, one noticed on the others golden hennin, that the stars and planets were beginning to move from their meridians. As one affects the other; one was glowing very blue, the light caused that part of the hennin to pulsate. The Djedi looked in amazement, he pointed towards it on the other's head, his excitement hindering him from words. The other turned around, then round again, and raised his left hand up to his hennin and felt it.

"Is it the Moon? Is it the Moon!" he exclaimed in a musical, low voice. "Which Moon is it — which one!" he exclaimed again.

The one who discovered the phenomenon replied, "It is Midhe." In his voice there was a kindling hope. "Yes! Yes! But which Moon is it Šyvasgaldur?" asked the other. "Well. . ." he said, then paused. "For us it is the 'Row-se Moo-oon' you know," replied Šyvasgaldur, dipping his fore-fingers into the fob pocket under his hacele. The Djedi dressed in brilliant blue hacele, Bhlegaldur, pulled his lips west towards touching his nose and thereby shutting his right eye, was working it out as quickly as he could, which usually wasn't very fast, for he did not like working much with numbers. While this was going on, Šyvasgaldur walked to the table plied with many tomes, took out a round, golden object from his fob pocket which was glowing with a pale grey light, it looked like a pocket watch. He flicked it open with his bony thumb and said, "Have you worked it out yet Bhlegaldur, for Galdramaður is coming. Make haste!" He put the hennin on his head, the motifs on it also started moving, some brighter than others. There were 1,739 Sun and half-moon symbols decorating the cornicle surface. The symbols or shapes did not appear all at once, only when needed or summoned. His grey cape was wrapped tightly around his shoulders, buttoned down to just below his navel. He took his tall staff which lay on the table and stood at attention, waiting for Bhlegaldur and the arrival of the other Djedi.

"It's a Blue Moon! We must make haste!" exclaimed Galdramaður, materializing out of thin air. The two Djedi looked at each other than at Bhlegaldur but, he was not there, he had already pertessered to the vicinity of Weir.

The 3 Djedi stood high on a Puttinghoch under the moonlight, above the town of Weir. They didn't have to go down into the raucous for though their eyes were ancient they were as keen as that of Ælves. Bhlegaldur leaned on his staff and said,

> *"When the Tally-of-Years is Blue*
> *And a Dragon feigns his slumber,*
> *When Elsalah is slow to go under*
> *Strife will gain footing in Eridu."*

"That prophecy has now come full circle," answered Galdramaður, the tallest of the 3 Djedi. The Sun had just about gone under and the 3 Djedi observed, they were not alone for long. When they pertessered from Nyamaloka, Queen Estatira had felt a disturbance in the aethyrs, and that occurrence showed her that her 3 Djedi were no longer in Ninfa. It was seen in one other place in the deep, deep south, there in the Ondervelden. In the Realm of Ukhahlamba slumbered a mirthful place, last homely realm before the 'The Purple Sea' from which no Ælve returned. There in Ukhahlamba under 'The Tree of Dragon Blood' by a spring pool, from that hall came 3 maidens, who were named 'Glórgalaloy, Golseret and Ghaliyahanga'. The Djedi were glad to see them but did not speak. The Djedi did not desire to enter into their realm often and the maidens did not speak much either because they had the ways of The Hush.

Jaddamiah was in the thick of it; many towners were dispensed of by the Dragon, the bridge was consumed, so others fled across the river, others drowned whilst trying. Mordēre 'the biter' was wielded, gleaming and striking, its bearer with sword only, for he found 'heavens ember' somewhat of an impediment, a lesson learned later. Without the mastery of warrior or Yaeger and valour his only armour, the grandfather cut the leviathan but, cutting a Dragon was mere pin pricks and he was no pincushion. The residents of Weir had fled, so that liegeman without military custom, who owed service to a nobleman, pressed on bloodied and bruised.

On it went stroke after stroke, Hallux and Phalanges, Mordēre against hallux and phalanges against Mordēre. The thought of children, wife or grandchildren behind him, no thought but the conquest as his only last, great achievement. The Dragon was toying but, toying was dangerous; once more Jaddamiah the Jabberwocky smote Anusillu at his weak spot, molten gore gushed forth. The angry Dragon struck Jaddamiah with its horn core.

Jaddamiah was flung like a ragdoll under a fallen tree trunk where he lay at the gates of poisons slumber. The wound burned and it swelled and festered, a fortune for him to lay and ponder on deeds bringing bale-woe. The atheling wyrm was no lord of ingle but a caliginous Prince of Ēl Elyōn, the Most-High God — The Meline Dragon. Thus, from high stone arch, from strengthened pillar to post, from wood beam to joist, he crushed shingle and eave, for his wounds were an agitation, and flowed in waves of vexation. Fully vexed and blood horde, Anusillu returned to his prey.

Jaddamiah Jabberwocky had laid too long. Self-pity and anger led to self-cursing, and glittering Mordēre lay beckoning, 'Come take me! There's chance yet for waxing, once in a Blue Moon a small hand can wield a great candle.' Grimm and compassionate 3 Djedi, 3 Apir-El looked down on the palaver; whether sorrow or approbation? Old El would tell but, so they summoned the Parliament of Skaði.

Thunderous bird wings and piratic plumes spiralled down with heavenly music; care was given where care was taken, but oft the blind see without seeing. Nilam-Hrada was a foreboding. The Parliament of Skaði woke them; those from the heights and the deeps, Andvariah and Loki came, winged and horned glorious.

Jaddamiah's wound grew fatal, alone he thought, 'With sorrow I'll suffer. Townsfolks failed me; injury wakes me, what a cost to be furnished with gold purse. . .' Ready they were; Andvariah and Loki each to a Realm Mistress and Master, "where would you go. . .it's of your choosing". Those were the words that pressed on the feeble pretender liegeman. The Djedi staffs turned to Djed, gleaming green of emerant emblazoned, cautioning Loka-ākāśa and Rakshasa-Loka; "Be still, hold your hastening, we place footing where Ælves have yet to tread. . .and all existence, life or dread, is Ælve footing." So spoke Andvariah and Loki, 'fire of fire', with voices falling like stars. Glórgalaloy, with words falling from her coral-like lips spoke these words, "Hush my brethren, there is time. . ."

And the sound of her voice was like the sprinkling of Fáerië dust on children when they fall asleep. Then it was that Jaddamiah heard a voice as of in the distant night, he reached inside his pocket and retrieved the blue, velvet cloth. He undid the string around the object, hastily discarded the remnant and looked feebly at the glister of the pale, apple-white, tinted absinthian fluid in the phial. "Hertia Underhill! Hertia Underhill!" He exclaimed with delight. "Bless you — bless you. . ." he said with each gulp from the phial. The fluid coursed instantly through his body, he looked at the veins glowing green through his torn jacket and shirt. He turned his hands over, looking at his glowing veins. It vanished as quickly as it appeared. The pain from his wounds felt like it was dissipating. He got up and rushed to his blade, "Mordēre!" he shouted, "Mordēre come! Vidazati! Quickly, let's advance to our war-target." The Dragon then turned, full in its anger, up-right and powerful it stood on its hind legs, tail supported, and wings uncluttered like coverlets of doom. Exposed where 'heavens ember' had been cleft asunder, the magpies encircled, their claw talons enraged while still singing, agaping their rostrums, descending upon the Dragon's head. So angry he was that his nostrils exuded like sulphured fumaroles, scorching the birds. Feathers burned in the fire lay on the ground but, they were not careful of glory, their lives a portent for future compeers of all good things spent unwisely—

²One for sorrow,
Two for joy,
3 for a girl,
Four for a boy,
Five for silver,
6 for gold,
Seven for a secret,
Never to be told.
Eight for a wish,
9 for a kiss,
Ten for a bird,
You must not miss.

But those were not 6 or seven or eight, nay, they were thousands — twenty thousand and ninety-six to be exact. "For the eyes! For the eyes!" shouted Jaddamiah. In lemniscates the parliament descended on the draggish orbits; picked at it and stabbed it, scored it and tore it.

The lids of iron snapped closed on the feathered foe but too late, the Dragons eyes oozed and bled, its sight impeded. Jaddamiah slashed at the feet, dislodging a hallux, he cut at its wings and slashed at scaled things. Anusillu exhausted, took one deep breath, but Jaddamiah hopeful and bold, 'a glimmer' he thought, for the latest of world-deeds. Skaði's vast-numbered forces encircled Jaddamiah, with sword and plumed shield, he advanced once more. Fire erupted, a fire volcano, it rained down from the cruel monster burning and searing the first plumed defence but, 'heavens ember' proved a fate, for the flames returned, rebounded back at the Dragon. . .All a-light as the livelong night was nearing its end, he clung to the worm of life. With one great leap, its wings took to flight, in anguish, in flame, setting a trail on the aethyrs burning, while Jaddamiah fell down, exhausted, in a circle of plumes. Andvariah had vanished but Loki remained a moment longer, slowly fading like embers of a fire, his words rang in the hearer's ears, "Why go wandering at night when consumed by fire?"

---

² The rhyme with the lyric was first recorded around 1780 in a note in John Brand's Observations on Popular Antiquities on Lincolnshire.

Here now ends that which has been told
Of how the Ring was found;
A Herstory. And is followed in Book Two
Which is dominated by the birth and History of Normagest.
Also, the return of Jaddamiah Jabberwocky, The journey of The Ring Bearer
through the Realm of the Eldritch and The War of The Fauns and Trees.

Book Two is called *Normagest.*

A Cautionary Note

An Index, a Glossary, a Summary exists only because the mortal does not understand the language of the Dragon, the Ælve, Nature.

The mortal finds himself faced with the problem with the limitations of language, which is descriptive and informationally based. This inherent disability makes human language inadequate to meet the desired end, since all authentic wisdom is "meaningful" and not "informational." It can only be comprehended at the level of <u>Being</u>, and not through merely intellectual faculties, for this reason we are pressed to Indexes, Glossaries and Summaries.

Of Elves and Ælves

For Dreambook the author has chosen to use and start from the premise which is Elven or Elve; that is to say, the correct way as the Ælves would have it, it would not be elf. From Elve, he progressed to Ælve/Ælven, a more archaic form in English (yet even older than English or Anglo Saxon) and Ælves denoting many, whether they be Male or Female.

When speaking of a male consciousness it would be Ælve, and for singular feminine (femi-neen) Ælfennes. The plural female consciousness is noted as Ælfenna. If he is bordering on neologism then he needs be forgiven for this is not preference but rather what must be. Now, to say that one group is female consciousness and the other male consciousness has nothing to do with biology or reproduction for both male and females Ælves can take on the appearance of another and for most part on seeing them the first time, would be confusing as they may appear androgynous, which is again nothing to do with them, but more to do with our perception of Them.

A word must be said about the spelling for Dwarves also; the word dwarf will not be found here, it simply is Dwarve or Dwarves in English for it is what they are, [1]'by names and images are all Powers awakened' this quote does not belong to the author but the words of it are most true. And for the word Ælves we apply the same rule.

---

[1] From The Golden Dawn $0^0=0^0$ Hall of Neophytes

The Ælves

Irisian eyes

This term means that the Ælves have no sclera nor pupil. To say that light enters their eyes in order to see, is perhaps incorrect. Light pours forth <u>from</u> their eyes. These Celestial Beings do not depend on Memory nor information to see. Their eyes are of Water and Fire, perfect light, in perfect equilibrium, that is to say, they see without seeing, and to coin a certain graphic phrase, 'darkness is as bright as day' to them. Whether the Iris is white or blue or purple or green depends entirely on the Jurisdiction of the Ælve or the Realm which inhabits them or from which they reside in/from. Having said all this, it is without impediment that they can appear ab-normal; as a normal body with flesh and those things seen on those who are flesh and blood. They have no blood, neither heart nor soul found in them.

Vowels for the Ælves of Kur Udor (The Watery Mountain) and Jinbōchō

<u>There are no silent syllables in the language of Jinbōchō.</u>

a as in "father"

e as in "whey"

i as in "Antique"

o as in "boat" (but rarely found)

u as in "Zulu"

<u>Consonants for the Ælves of Kur Udor (The Watery Mountain) and Jinbōchō</u>

X as in German "ach"

CH (Same as above)

K (Same as above)

SH as in "Shall"

SS as in, perhaps, "lasso"; a hissing "s" common to Arabic languages

Z as in "lots"; a hard "ts" sound, not quiet as in "zoo"

Runes

Rune ᛉ: Algiz, Pronounced 'Awl-gh-eeze': A powerful rune of protection.

Calendar of MONTHS

The Months of the Year as spoken by those in the Pradeza of Ninfa and the Principality of Palador.

English	Ancient	Ninfa/Palador
March/April	चैत्रः	Chaitraḥ
April/May	वैशाखः	Vaiśākhaḥ
May/June	ज्येष्ठः	Jyeṣṭhaḥ
June/July	आषाढः	Āṣāḍhaḥ
July/August	श्रावणः	Śrāvaṇaḥ
August/September	भाद्रपदः	Bhādrapadaḥ
September/October	आश्विनः	Āśvinaḥ
October/November	कार्तिकः	Kārtikaḥ
November/December	मार्गशीर्षः	Mārgaśīrṣaḥ
December/January	पौषः	Pauṣaḥ
January/February	माघः	Māghaḥ
February/March	फाल्गुनः	Phālgunaḥ

The Months in other Dialects

Eldiĕni	Éirvana	Alkana	Ninfa	Aontroim	Palador
January	Enáir	Farvardin	Farvardin	Genver	Farvardin
February	Feabhra	Ordibehesht	Ordibehesht	Hwevrer	Ordibehesht
March	An Márta	Khordad	Chaitraḥ	Meurth	Khordad
April	An t-Aibreán	Tir	Chaitraḥ	Ebryl	Tir
May	An Bhealtaine	Mordad	Jyeṣṭhaḥ	Me	Mordad
June	An Meitheamh	Sharivar	Jyeṣṭhaḥ	Metheven	Sharivar
July	Lúil	Mehr	Mehr	Gortheren	Mehr
August	Lúnasa	Aban	Aban	Est	Aban
September	Meán Fómhair	Azar	Azar	Gwynngala	Azar
October	Deireadh Fómhair	Dey	Dey	Hedra	Dey
November	Samhain	Bahman	Bahman	Du	Bahman
December	Nollaig	Esfand	Esfand	Kervadu	Esfand

Glossary

Adeirhve: To build with numbers(dominoes)

Anlaas: Broad two-edged dagger

Abnu Zabarkizag: The stone that reflects earth and the stars

Adi la basi alaku: To bring to naught (die)

Adown: Pronounced, "Aw-done" or "aahdawn" meaning strong, Master (as in Lord but without the servant/bread insinuation)

Aerendgast: Literally errand spirit, a word pre-dating angel. In this context the errant spirit is Angel but, the teller refuses to use the term Angel as it is a modern, religious reference.

Aírþa: The Earth (Gothic)

Aferian Nibala: Noble transport

Aggy-jaggers: Eerie sea mist that forms along the shore and steals inland

Agsweran: The name of the sword belonging to Dalethdir of Hesperus. One of the Ælves who accompanied those of Palador; from Old Noraquilon agi "awe, terror" or ag "edge of a sword and Old High Noraquilon sweran "to hurt".

Ahua Awer (S)Twer and Elládunu: The first Crystal is basically Aqua Aura Quartz. The second is Carnelian. Both these words have their origin in Latin. The author is trying to refrain from using Latin as far as possible. Chalcedony, a word of uncertain origin could also be used but, that point is perhaps debatable. So, the author chose the word Elládunu, (of a red light). Ládunu a rock rose found in Sumeria; family Cistaceae. Both crystals combined in the Cupolas created Pure Light as those crystals are Water and Fire.

Algumes Māluku: The act of walking over crystals. So that one can augur.

Alkana-Landras: A kind of Physalis alkekengi

Aylmeri: Common term for folk who like falconry. Aylmeri type jess is made of high quality calf leather and greased. Invented by the British falconer Guy Aylmer (1887-1954). It is known for its characteristic of being a jess made of different elements; the anklet is reinforced through a metal ring, leaving it fixed on the bird's tarsus. The metal ring that is used is of a type known as an eyelet which allows the jess to pass through a hole in the middle known as the aylmeri, which can vary in size and thickness depending on the size of the bird. This item is composed of anklets and the jess, but do not include the metal eyelet rings. The calf leather is of greater softness and flexibility thus benefiting the tarsus of the birds, thus facilitating a better handling of the bird and ensuring its health. It is necessary to grease this regularly to maintain its durability and quality.

Amala Vartula: (The) Amala = Crystal + Vartula f. ball at the end of a spindle to assist its rotation. In the speech of Jinbōchō it would be known as Šegnuru (cold light). Unlike the one at Zamm whose creator was the Dwarve king Nshidimzu father of Buzur Vartula was kræfted by the Ælve Alalĝar.

Amanuensis: A scribe

Āmeiza: A term for tourists meaning 'ants'

Anadi: Without beginning

Anbar: Heavenly metal

Anekamudra: Having many names

Avadhuya: Shaking (of the earth)

Anvahr: Make-up

Aproneers: Shopkeepers

Arachniform: Shaped like a spider. Messages left by the Paladins in spider webs.

Ati dura: Very far away

Avra k'davra: I will create as I speak

Avrek: The planet Sirius

Ažididan: Generally, the Greek word Derkesthai is used but, I chose not to use this word as the Greeks were late comers in writing and language. The word Ažididan: *Aži* (nominative *ažiš*) is the Dagian word for "serpent" or "dragon". It is cognate to the Deru Dagian word *ahi*, "snake," and without a sinister implication and didan, to see clearly. The Ælves have this 'dragon sight' as they are the Children of The Dragon.

Baile: (BAL-yeh) – Place, home, homestead, farmstead, village, town. Where we come home.

Bandhamudra Nigra: Binding Contract

Battledore maker: The beaters used on clothes and carpets etc to remove the dust (later made the paddles used in washing machines)

Belum of Haasil: The Siriun Grand Master always re-incarnated with 18 000 strands of DNA {sleeping strands] upon Eridu.

Blenk: Light snow, similar to the 'blinks' or ashes that fly out from a smokestack (Exmoor)

Brague: The beautiful black horses of The Hrosvyras, meaning High spirited {plural – Bragii}

Bur hurkel: To remove the heinous person (a reference to Female Wulvlingas)

Bútangyð: (ð as in 'th') Without strife, a town some 60miles from Nilbud

By jas: The will of the Immortals, (the laws given by heaven for men on earth)

Capillaire: Sells or makes capillaire: a drink made from clear syrup flavoured with orange flower water

Cara: Noraquilon for friend

Catur Padmini(The): Four Petal Lotus

Cenllif: A strong flowing stream, a torrent

Cep: 'Penny bun mushroom' because of its shape.

Certes: In truth/certainly

Chādor Tamaashaa Kardan: The Veiled Watchers. The Guardian Ælves

Chakavak: Lark

Claker: Magician

Cosset: Treat with excessive indulgence

Coydencroyscee: a crossroads for trees/or a crossroad of trees

Daeges Eage: "days eye" = daisy. The word "daisy" comes from Old English Daeges Eage, meaning "day's eye." Our word, "day," comes from the word "dawn." The term "day's eye" refers to the way the flower opens its petals in the morning and closes them at night. The daisy is believed to have been in existence for over 4000 years and worldwide there are about 200 species.

Dagga: Most commonly used word for marijuana

Dama: Home

Dap: To dip gently into water; to fish with a surface fly

Dar Chakavak: The Door of the Lark

Dearovim: A way of expressing sympathy for someone undergoing a rough time.

<u>Devadāru</u>: Deodar or Cedar Trees (The Tree of the Gods)

<u>Devaka</u>: Celestial, Divine, god

<u>Dhana Hrada</u>: 'Booty Lake'

<u>Diehm</u>: Means "famous", derived from the Noraquilon elements theud "people" and meri "famous".

<u>Dina Majjari</u>: Day flower or in common speech = Jasmine

<u>Dimtu Ilimmu Shumsuene</u>: Tower of 9 names

<u>Drover</u>: Sheep or cattle driver

<u>Drycræft (The Book of)</u>: Skilled in Magic

<u>Duirparina</u>: Oak of deception

<u>Duram</u>: Far from

<u>Dynyansek</u>: To fascinate. To fascinate is to bring under a spell, as by the power of the eye; to enchant and to charm are to bring under a spell by some more subtle and mysterious power. [Century Dictionary] Words are like a veil, few look behind them so many are deceived. The strength of etymology is like an ice-berg for in the depths lay the true peril and the true light. "*to fascinate*", according to the Dictionary of the <u>Royal Academy of the Spanish Language</u>, derives from the Latin "*fascinare*" and has 3 meanings: 1. Deceive, to hallucinate, obfuscate. / 2. Attract irresistibly / 3. Make evil eye. Fascinate/fascinares foundation lies in the word <u>fascinum which in turn is</u> an ivory <u>phallus</u> used in certain ancient erotic rites. The phallus is used to ward off 'the evil eye, the hex or curse', which brings the reader back to The Edifice of Dynyansek in Midhe over which The Dark God Kašadom rules.

<u>Earer</u>: A Ploughman or Tiller

<u>Earrach</u>: Spring

<u>Eang Bont</u>: Wide bridge

<u>Eldiĕni</u>: The name that Ælves call mortal folk. Another word is used but rarely by those Ælves in Midhe or Palador. Aleidhiath is the word which means the folk who decay.

<u>Elferingewort</u>: Faerie Lore ... called "elf rings" or "elferingewort" (translates to "a ring of daisies caused by elves dancing")

<u>Elffreondspedig</u>: 1520s, from hob 'elf', and freondspedig 'rich in friends.' Hobgoblin Friends.

<u>Elvysshe</u>: Mysterious

<u>Elru'u</u>: (Ill luck to the) friends of Ælves. In the common tongue, I suppose it would be elwyn.

Emmets: Archaic word for Ants

Erlance: The first part of the word is an acronym for emission of radiation (an emission of radiation spear). It emits a lethal blow of celestial light. Depending on the constitution of the subject or victim it could either paralyse, incinerate, evaporate of put out of existence the opponent.

Eow: Old English, dative and accusative plural of þu/thou/you which also looks like it sounds like the Gaelic tú.

Eyne: Archaic – plural for eyes.

Fægenimen: From Middle English nimen to take away also niman; carry off; take possession of, also raise aloft (a weapon) or take the high road from Middle English Dictionary

Fámsanúfhálat: Heterochromia iridium. Person with different coloured eyes.

Féirínóblath: (Jasmine) Flower of the Goddess Flora

Feorr: Far, at a distance

Fernem: Far

Ferruginous: Of the colour of rust; impregnated with iron

Féth fíada: A magick mist that the Tuatha de Danann used to make themselves invisible to humans. Because Maxim Xul had fallen (he wasn't human), they caused a triple féth fíada as a normal one was inadequate.

Fir fer: Fair play

Fish Fag: A female fish monger

Flumadiddles: Utter nonsense or ridiculous

Frawahr: Commonly called, The Winged Disc. (Pronounced as furōhar in classical Alkanina) One of the most ancient symbols.

Funambulist: A tightrope walker

Gabeler: A collector or gables or taxes

Gates of Ābee: (The water-y gates) Ābee = watery

Gätker Yic (The Principality of): Surrounded by mountains

Gaurjalakula: Gargoyle

Ghobfrændi: Friend of Goblins from *frijand- "lover, friend" (source also of the word frændi).

Goldenrod: Dark, golden yellow

Golestān: In the speech of Ninfa, Alkana it means owl

Haimamarga: Haima = golden + Marga(m) way

Halkyondhra: Fáerië Circles (Mushrooms)

Halls of Irkalla: Irkalla = Underworld - Loki's Realm

Irkalla Irkalla: Sumerian, The language of Jinbōchō AND Loki's Realm

Harrani Si-il: Road + to split; to tear apart; to go away, absent oneself (cf., sila also Street).

Haycock: Conical pile of hay in a field

Heliotaxis: Response of an organism to the sun's rays

Houguehūs: Hougue (old Norse word), mound or hill + hūs = house

Hour is Hora-Al: When Gnani the Hobgoblin speaks these words to Hyperion, he is stating that the time is altered here. In the tongue of Palador or Ninfa this experience is called Zamm; 'a space of Time'. This area when passing through it; between Albtraum and the village of Zamm, one may or may not experience Hora-Al or Zamm-Time. Hora may be a translation for season or seasons. (However, one can never trust translations, but we do our best). Al is a PIE word with root meaning 'beyond'. So, this area along the River Næddre is beyond mortal Time.

Ḥqêl Dmâ: Akeldama- meaning 'field of blood'.

Hrosmaw: A direct translation would be horse-boy. A horse or cow herder, particularly found on the plains of the Hrosvyras.

Hursagga: An archaic Sumerian word for hill

Idein: To see – from the etymology of the word Idea

Eli Baltuti Ima"Idu Mituti: Dead Will Be More Numerous Than the Living

Illaliazu: Il = ælve + lal = honey + Iazu (one who knows oil; physician) The Ælves Honeyed Oil.

Ilubit Tuklati: Crystal Alexandrite

Itimamitudagur: The Dark Place of the Dead Reptiles

Izvira-ehir: Exposed to the king's ear

Jesses: A short strap fastened around the leg of a hawk and attached to the leash. To put jesses on (a hawk).

Jalakukku: Black headed gulls

Joon: Pronounced 'jān' of endearment or respect + mitra = meaning friend

Joulupukki: Billy goat

Kakkishu: Rat. Búbgaz 'The Destroyer' used the word as a term of derision towards Hemming.

Karkadann: A type of sword-horned animal on long, thick legs.

Kelel: (The Pool of) Secret light; from the old Noraquilon word Kel for secret/ The secret (Kel) of Ælves (El)

Khemitian: An ancient people in the deep south now called Egyptians.

Khthōnic: Deities or Spirits of the underworld (We have Mr H.P. Lovecraft to thank for the popularizing of this word or any form of it.

Kinnikinnick: It is a word from the region of The Hushas.ene which literally means "what is mixed," referring to the mixing of indigenous plants and tobaccos. (Also, Sumac or Dogwood and Bearberry)

Koweth: (Male) companion, comrade, friend, mate

Kuhmaskan: Mountain house

Kurnugia Dúr.gar Zalmat-Qaqadi: The Underworld throne (from the verb to sit) of the Dark Race

Kurva-vaste: Two + (to wear clothes) two pieces of cloths

Laksmi Kuvela: (Charm of the) Blue Water Lily

Lampyglowdia: A lamp that glows as it passes - direct translation. Glow-worms.

Laulu Lumessa: (Finnish) Song in the snow

Lesewut: Nilbudian word for "reading craze" (literally) used to describe a specific period in the intellectual history of Nilbud from the late eighteenth century onward.

Leśyā: Karmic Stain

Liemduwëi: Directly translate this mean 'your tongues essence or 'the spirit of language'. It is a combination of glossolalia and telepathy yet nothing of the two. One can only draw from what one already possesses or from memories one already is conscious of. So those individuals in Eridu, having a connection above the threshold of consciousness, are drawn to the Ælves and so with that in mind Liemduwëi is experienced

Lītūtu Da 'Āmu: Star Oath

Lohavara: Gold

Loka-Ākāśa and Rakshasa Loka: Andvariah's Realm and Loki's Realm

Lokarahu: Jörmungandr = Uroboros, the serpent chasing its tail

Lytherenna: To spell

Nasta Limmers: Literal meaning is 'lost mongrels'. A kind of Reptilian Hybrid. The Minions of Merodach-Baladan. Nasta is reference to the star system Sirius, for this creature co-mingled with the Siriun by co-ersion and manipulation.

Mal de vivre: Depression of spirits from loss of hope, confidence, or courage; dejection.

Mångata: Pronounced; 'moo-aang-gaar-tah'.

A road-like shape created when light reflects on water from the Moon. Most commonly refers to the reflection of the Moon and the wavy, generally deltoid trail leading up to it when looking from the coastline off to the horizon.

Matsyahrada: King of the Lake (The sacred place belonging to Bllömpotvölle)

Matsyavana: King of the Grove - matsya (m)king of the + vana = grove (n)

Meal-drift: High wispy clouds

Mellish: Brightly coloured and flowery

Men-Nefer: The Capital of the Khemitian lands (meaning The Generation of Harmony)

Mêrênuššu: (The Garden of) "My name is Sanballat of Mêrênuššu." which if Dheya understood correctly was. . .'I am the enemy in secret and this is the garden of desolation or this garden is in a state of desolation'.

Mergwarch: Mer = to rub away, harm + gwarch = of protection (in the Ancient tongue Pradezini (Dagian) Protecting.

Mey Booie: A slang phrase (a black speech) used by The Kwizir for woman's breast. Literal: my breasts. (pronounced my 'boo-hee')

Meystornurímgeké: Astro/loger/logical

Mino: My mother

Morsdarack: (Death) dead oak

Morpheus: World of the High Ælves. Also known as Lampadais. Morpheus is the higher vibrational name for Aldebaran.

Mpese: Original spelling Mpɛsɛ. In parts of Ta-merri children are born with naturally locked hair and are given a special name: 'Dada'. There are also those offspring of the Sons of The Earth and those children of The Mountains of Vakratuvakra who are specifically named The Dada, and also the Orisha of the deep ocean, who wear locks. These folk refer to dreadlocks as Mpɛsɛ, which is the hair style of The Djedi and even common people.

Murmbheslenti: After a wave has crashed, the last remnants of water rubbing over the sand that reaches the furthest point on the beachfront before seeping away.

Mush-dagur: Gecko, Lizard. Dagur = zakur "dog" in Basque. A type of Hybrid Reptilian Being for DreamBook

Nagaghosa: Mountain Hamlet

Nakālu: To bewitch

Napa-Tu: Fire Crystal

Naraizaoha: Or naraupaoha or naravegaoha = a rickshaw

Navapur: New fortress

Ngíz-al Lycurgus ina Awilumur: 'Watch Lycurgus the man-wolf'

Nilaksa: Blue eyed gulls

Nilamsaras: Blue lake

Norlündir (The): The Ælves of the North Sea on Hesperus, in The Ring Nebula of Lyra

Nshidimzu: Dwarve who fashions from the deeps

Nyth: Nest

Omdreylya Stayr: To revolve, the stairway that goes round and round. The name those at Jinbōchō gave to 'The Stairway of Tiemugara'.

Orchaiomelelvenotolkienarate: Which means 'in the old sweet style of Elven maidens in the works by Tolkien'

Patravaha: Postman

Pandura: Pale white gulls

Pano ine ndine: I am here (from Chichewa; an Ondervelden dialect)

Parliament of Magpies: Magpies often appear in large assemblies in Spring, looking stately and cawing at each other. Chs. 21 & 32) According to Alice Karlsdottir, the Old Norse noun skadhi is a word for magpies. This was chosen for the DreamBook because it feels correct and true.

Parizád: A beautiful person or born of a Fáerië

Peely-wally: Telling tales as all children do. When they "tell on" someone else.

Pertessered: Drifted upward. Translocation of sorts.

Poke: An archaic word for bag or sack like "Pig in a Poke".

Puttinghochs: From the Collection of Words by S.B. Engelbrecht - meaning a flat, grassy clearing, situated high above on a crag or elevated location. (like golf putting green)

Prabartanā: Persuasion

Prusten: The word is Noraquilon and means to puff and to blow.

Rángárang: Of different sort/kinds

Rasala: (A city of Ninfa) simply meaning Grass.

Ratha: Two-wheeled wagon

Rahu: Dragon + ucca (m) height = Dragon Heights (Rahu-ucca)

Reimfor: A fortune telling rhyme. Reim related to Old Provençal word 'rim' (masc.) measured verse and 'fors' which is luck, chance, fate.

Revedh: Meaning strange, astounding, or a wonder.

Ṛbhú–Zaila: Ælve Hill

Rjóður: The rjóður ("to clear away") – Dukkǭ (dog) A nickname, Beautiful, red dogs owned by the Hrosvyras, The Horse Lords of Hros. Rjóður *m* (poetic) one who reddens, smears with blood (used in kennings). They never went to war or into battle without these dogs.

Sag kata (The): n. Narrow passage

Saĝsiĝĝar: To bend or lower one's head (before someone/something)

Samacapada: Fair and square – honest – genuine

Sambaddha: Belonging to + daru = wood (n) (m) = Sambaddhadaru

Samsum: Noun. Physics. An effect whereby heat is given out or absorbed when the power in a Sun passes across a junction between two worlds. This process, known as the Samsum effect. Depending on the type of planet/s associated with increased heat below or above ground it effects the vegetation, water or ground even air casting a great 'V' swirl across the planets' surface

Sanamzuka: 'Zuka' for short – cloth covering the bosom (like a bra)

Sandhana: Making peace with

Sanúf Áyán: Of different colour eyes. Some folk who are superstitious call this, 'Ramad' which is to say, 'a disorder in the eyes'.

Śapatha: m. An oath, a vow

Satyam, Satyam: This is true (an expression)

Satyam Kar: To make come true. A device for telling the dates of days, months and years. For having it manifests reality. A device for telling time, giving meaning to space. That is why in the tongue of Palador and Alkana its meaning is 'to make come true'.

Sea-Cat: In Midhe they call a certain whipping device a 'Cat o' 9 tails' - it does not resemble a cat at all (at least none that the authors seen) but it does resemble an Octopus in the many pain-inflicting extensions it has from the handle.

Segaisslat: (Pronounced – Ser-gay-lart) Wisdom's rod or the Hazel Rod. An oath for Celestial Beings which binds them to the condition of a Realm.

Scrithers: From the Collection of words by S.B. Engelbrecht - the sound insects or scorpions make when moving over hard surfaces.

Scrumping: To steal fruit

Sidhamidha: Sacred wood as in forest

Sidhamidha Torana: The secret road of the Queen of Ninfa; meaning the tunnel of the sacred wood.

Sight before hearsay: Old Danish proverb

Silvaearn: The Eagle of the Trees

Sphulligini: Sparkling (something akin to fission power)

Stayr a Fow a Skydnya: The stair of the cave of descending.

Sun-Scald: A patch of bright light found on the surface of waters.

Susvapnah: Sweet dreams/ of good dreams (a greeting in Béth-Élam and some other Pradezas. The Hrosvyra also use this term and sometimes also 'breadwiddion melys' which means the same thing.

Svadurasa: Having a sweet or agreeable taste

Sylwar-barthed: Inosculation

Tá eolas agam ar an áit seo: I am familiar with, am acquainted with, this place.

Tapiens: Like a Petunia

Tarast: A G-string (also Ġeyn- Tar literally gee-string)

Teyrngwarch: Sovereign, monarch + gwarch = of protection

Therians: (Slang) Therianthropic is the correct usage

The testimony of one eyewitness is worth more than the hearsay of a hundred: Old Sicilian Proverb

Tiemugara: (Tibalgara – Sumerian; 'bal' means to revolve (The Stairway of) Found at Vel Samoda. 'Ti' is the Sumerian Cuneiform for life (the double helix) 'emu' means to turn (as a helix twists and turns) + 'gara' which is the Yoruba word for crystal.

Titan: Live (those live in heaven) *to bring to life, for those the Ælves used Titan and they live for-ever.

Tulwar: Is a type of curved sword or <u>sabre</u>.

Trayodaza: The 13

Umsundulu and Hei: (Hallo of) meaning worm and tree

Ussušuha: 8 handed fish

Vakrapuri: Twisty town – puri m.

Varasura: Turn to the Sun (The ancient flower of the Ælves)

Vargdarreh: Valley of the waterfalls

Vasinsurapuspa: Also called 'Bán Ghrian Ròs' = white flower of the Sun. The common name is Elder/Ælve Flower. Those who are in love call it 'Luibh an Ghrá' or 'Herb of Love' because of its intoxicating, heavy fragrance. The fragrance is a mixture of honey and ancient Black Flower and is most intoxicating and lingers long in the summer sunshine. This Elder Flower must not to be confused with Sambucus. Sambucus is a genus of flowering plants in the family Adoxaceae.

Vel Domas: Veiled dome

Vel Samoda: Veil of Joy

Vesi-viitta: Water Cloak (of Finnish)

Videlicet: Pronounced 'wi-dey-li-ket'; (English 'vi-del-uh-sit') an unwanted guest at 3 in the morning.

Vimāna: Space ships

Virya: Energy (a poor word in comparison to what it really is). It is the Perfection of Energy devoid of any earthly fire because that Element amongst the Stars has not been allowed in mortal hands. It cannot be rekindled by temporalities;

Vimzinpuspa: 'Twenty flower'. Marigolds from its original name Cempaspuchitl is the name given to Mexican marigold flowers (Tagetes erecta). The word "Cempaspuchitl" comes from the Nahuatl (the language of the Aztecs) word zempoalxochitl which means twenty-flower - zempoal, meaning "twenty" and xochitl, "flower"

Voogabool: Cave-axe

Wanderpel: A Bird of prey; *pel Proto-Indo-European root meaning "pale." It may also mean to thrust, strike, drive.

Proto-Indo-European root meaning "pale."

Weepy: A land rife with springs

Winterburna: An ephemeral stream, dry in the summer and running in the winter.

Wirlonaa: The wolf forsaken or forsaken werewolves.

Wonty-tump: Molehill – (Herefordshire)

Wulfmaer: Wolf Famous

Wynebau Gnomes: Those Gnomes who spend most of their time on land rather than under it.

Wynebau: Surface

Xul-Kappu: Means 'evil wing'. A large 6foot Scorpion (found in Eridu in days of yore, possibly a species of Eurypterus)

Yanagola: To journey in a circle

Yath-Atatham: Adverb - as it really is

Yanavidhu: The March of the Lonely

Yavana Yahva: Yavana f. curtain + yahva m. flowing waters

The Curtain of Flowing Waters

Yett: A yett (from the Old English and Scots language word for "gate") is a gate or grille of latticed wrought iron bars used for defensive purposes in castles and tower houses.

Yuvasuravira: Yuvasura = ale + vira = root of ginger

Zantabhavena: Quietly

Zapta: adj = Taken as an oath

Zenzizenzizenzic: The eighth power of a number: For example - 10 to the 8th power is 100,000,000 — Which is an equation of 10 x 10 x 10 x 10 x 10 x 10 x 10 x 10 OR consigning 8 zeros after the 1.

Zésàndara: Zésàn, and ancient name for Tanzania (Tanzanite) and 'dara' (for dark or dark blue).

Zythepsarist: A Brewer

A list of Sentences

'Ana zu nacham nin' = For your comfort lady

'Annitu! Annitu! Beleti Immaru ak ina isu' = Behold, Behold – Lady
Light of the forest

'Atö thin aŋuen' = There is more

'Bhavata etad na kartavyam amba' = Do not tell Mother

'Negeltu, mi!' = Awake woman

अन एविल् देअथ् विल्ल् सेत फ़ोर्थ् व्होम् थे बलादे पिएर्चेस् = 'An evil death sets forth when the blade pierces'

"Me ngíz-al ngishnugal golyó ene' = We watch light, (the) light of trees in marbles

Female Names

Aspas: Guard of strength

Blaiddfamdis: Wolf mother of the slain

Bluen: Feather

Bleddyn: Normally (m)BLETH-in "wolf-like" Blethyn

Búbgaz: To slaughter

Dhara Móðir: Earthmother

Dyddanwy: Delight {dee THAN wee}

Ekam Audapana: Pegasus in Greek. This word is synonymous with springs and fountains.

> Therefore, in Ninfa she is called AudapAna : adj. raised from wells or drinking fountains + Ekam n = one

> Ekam Audapana which means; 'One raised from wells' or 'fountains' which is interesting because there is some kind of union between Merlin the second Element. Pegasus 'equivalent in Norse Mythos is Sleipnir which means Gliding One which would be in the tongue of Ninfa Ekamesa which is one gliding. Or gliding one.

> It could also be pataGga adj. horse + bhAj adj. belonging to. . .

Fenna: Guardian of Peace

Féhmiaælfwine: Woman friend of Elves (She was born in Nilam Hesperiis)

Glórgalaloy: Is a name comprising of 3 phonemes; composing a name which describing the individual's spiritual/character qualities as well as reference to her lineage.

Glór- Gaelic for voice

Gala = Gail/Gale: from gala "to sing, chant," or(enchant) the wind so called from its raging or on the notion of being raised by spells (but OED finds reason to doubt this). Or perhaps it is named for the sound, from Old English galan "to sing," or giellan "to yell." The Old Norse and Old English words all are from the source of yell (v.). In nautical use, between a stiff breeze and a storm; in technical meteorological use, a wind between 32 and 63 miles per hour. Old Armenian լոյս(loys), for bright/light

Golseret: Rose faced

Ghaliyahanga: Ghaliyah Female fragrant = South Dagian +

Anga light (also: space, sky, transparent)

Gluggivængr: Wind eyed Wing. Pegasus.

Göbel-Malu: Bright Hobgoblin with the long hair

Hyldeblomstdrik: (Danish) Elderflower Tree also called Hagradama = disfigure make ugly uglify + mother

Iníon-Dé Danann: (ee-ni-yan) Daughter of the People of Dana

Lusinfiodh: (Woodland Ælfenne), light. 'fiodh- Fee-ode' = forest

Lyadalagapē: The Beautiful Wolv Lover

Malina-Chada: Black Feather

Malina-Kama: Beautiful Feather

Morkaél: Maiden loved of Ælves

Merthblaidd-ddyn: Werewolf of pleasure

Ninduglilene: Nin = lady + ene = plural Ladies. + dug which means to speak. (Speak into or out of existence-Manifestation) + lil = air/ghost or spirit.

Ninéderim: The first lady of man (first created)

Ninsar: (Edin of) Goddess of Flowers (Flora) Edin = plains of flora.

Norns (The 3): "Amser' What Once Was - Amser = Time.

"Ferne' What Is Coming into Being. 'Future' pronounced Fer-ne

'Carma' What Shall Be.

Okunoku: The Element of Fire (Lorelei)

Olwen: (The Path of) shining track

Orla: (Orlagh) Meaning 'Golden Princess'

Puru-Ambas: Celestial Waters

Þrúðr: Strength/strong (pronounced 'throod')

Puratana: Means Ancient

Sprites

(Of Alkana) Rügfeydah, Hunnahveydah and Lurlluhrlian;

> Meaning of names is unknown in mortal speech. Rügfeydah; A possible reference towards The Woods (Sylvan Realm) to do with the trees.

Vardhaka: Old age (12th Queen of Alkana)

Vēḍu Vīrü: Strong white Willow

Male Names

Andhrimnir: The one exposed to soot (he cooks for the Paladins)

Anusillu: Heavens Shade. The Dragon that attacked Weir sent by Ēl Elyōn, rendered in English as "God Most High" "The Meline Dragon "who is also the usurper of Ēl Elyōn"

Arka Naravahana: Singer of a Prince. Naravahana m. of a prince; The swan at The Palace of Ninfa; Prince, with reference to the Ælve Baldur, for his name means Prince. Arka Naravahana was Baldur's swan.

Banû: Builder, creator

Bhelaribhus/Rbhus: Restless, who shines brilliantly

Bēlu ēpišu: Master Builder of Damasandra and Merodach-Baladan

Bīnudhē: Tree Doom (tree, timber, medicine, magical purification) + *dhē-, Proto-Indo-European root meaning "to set, put."

Búbkalu: He who "makes those who run stand still"

Cayden: Great fighter

Dal: Meaning door, or rather entrance; the "door" of my lips

Damasandra: A great Guardian once. Some thought it was Procrustes in much later tongues of men. Also called Kašadom which means to 'overpower with doom'. His name is synonymous in Old English with dom "law, judgment, condemnation." In some tongues the word stems from PIE root *dhe-* "to set, place, put, do". Also related to ruin and destruction.

Danmala: In the tongue of Alkana 'dan' means giver and 'mala' is a garland of flowers. Father of Hyperion who is mother of Normagest Illyrian

Dayaal: Kind hearted. Father of Elhama

El-Ashhal: The Ælve with the blueish black eyes.

Elmerkar: Ælve hunter (not hunter of Ælves)

Eynon: (Brother of Elhama) literally means "anvil" and suggests the qualities of stability and fortitude.

Invidia: The equivalent of Nemesis. To look against, to look at in a hostile manner. It is associated with jealousy or envy and also the Evil Eye. The jealousy here is not merely a negative feeling against one who has what you have, but a feeling that what another has is unjust or undeserved, offending one's sense of justice in the world.

Heilyn Surbaer: (Sadrada of Ninfa) Meaning of his name is 'steward of the southern light'.

Laegel: Green Elve from laeg meaning green and el meaning Elve or light. (He is from The Elves of Hesperus)

Liulfr: Old Norse personal name, meaning "shield wolf."

Lucht Siúil: Traveller. "Loo-ch-ed soo-eel". Jaddamiah Jabberwocky says this to be his name when asked by the Meline Dragon.

Lycurgus: He who brings into being the works of a wolf

Maredudd: Pronounced: 'mah-RE-deeth'. Meaning sea lord (Son of Nanu)

Mihi: Guardian Elve at the palace of The Queen of Ninfa his name means 'beautiful sun'. Mi = beautiful + hi = Sun or Sunlight or day. (He is from the Ælves of Hesperus)

Nāṣiru: Preserver

Nunzalag: Radiant Prince

Mussuku-Emētu: Mussuku; Of repulsive appearance + emētu, a mother-in-law

Sebelo: Meaning half. In some tongues the name means 'venerable'. While in others it means 'God of the earth'. Elo means half in Pleaidian - It is a ranking which indicates that the person has reached a high evolutionary level

Thumia: Desire or passionate desire (epithumia)

Urinšeg: Eagle of the Snow

Vala: Meaning 'Chosen'.

Vana: Meaning 'harp with 100 strings'

The Hobgoblin Horde

1. 'Gwalather' (gwal-LATH-ə) means 'leader'
2. 'Gugu' means 'treasure'
3. 'Geet' means 'song'
4. 'Gnani' means 'knowledge'; Wisdom; One Armed with Knowledge
5. 'Göbel-Malu' (f) means 'bright, long haired'
6. 'Galchobhar' means 'eager helper'
7. 'Galton' (English) means 'from the town on the High Ground' (He and his tribe live in Zamm)
8. 'Gaagii' means 'raven'
9. 'Garšausis' means 'long ears'
10. 'Galeme' means 'big/great tongue'
11. 'Baddar' means 'on time/punctual'
12. 'Gamba' means 'warrior'
13. 'Gul' (f) means 'rose flower'

Place Names and Sacred Edifice

Aik (Forest of): Entangled trees

Avinirnaya: Indecision

Ayodhya: Means 'that which cannot be subdued by war'

Dome of Kala: Kala f. elements of the gross or material world

Drastumanas: Wishing to see (a tall mountain peak from where one could see Sudinnipat-Somadhara (The Stone that fell from heaven)

Giridvara: Mountain Pass

Ilat Elnabha: Ilat = Supreme Central Sun (or Eltarā = Sun of Suns)

Irkalla (Halls of): The Underworld

Iza Ramatarā: Supreme Dark Star (The Planet of a Million Years)

Mutterseelinallein (The Abyss of): Mutterseelinallein is the quintessential word when it comes to describing loneliness. Although it is a German word, it has been derived from the French idiom – 'moi tout seul' means 'me all alone.' When you are mutterseelinallein, you are completely, utterly alone; it is the very foundation of despair. (See Languageoasis Blog Translation You can trust)

Nilbud: Without flowers, the capital city of Midhe

Nabholihvara: Towering Gates

Skallagrimmr: Grim cliff

Tara: An ancient name for the Consciousness that is called Earth

Virana: Fragrant grass

Stars and things that Glister

Alhalsu Tamtu: Alhalsu = fortification + tamtu = sea (in the future it shall be called Larimar)

Amala Somadhara: Crystal of heaven

Azvapadin: Meaning horse footed. (known in the future as Alpha Centauri)

Dhisana: The Chalice, knowledge, wise, dwelling place. . . from Old English mæl, "measure, mark, appointed time

Ezeru-Izar: The cursed star or Star of the crossing. The 12th celestial body in the Solar System with an orbit of 26 000 years. It is also known to those in Midhe as 'Halálseren' meaning Death Star.

Izi S'uba: Fire Agate

Mul Lunergal: The Constellation of Andromeda. Lunergal = great watcher of man.

Multanaddassi: To throw down the stars. A Meteor Shower of both Perseus and Leonidas.

Sudinnipat-Somadhara: The Stone that fell from heaven

Sunnestede: The standing still of the Sun. An equality of Time (night and day)

Sylperdarn: Loosely translated it would be wormhole, though a Sylperdarn only occurs amongst forests and trees. This must not be confused with a Le Badhaprapta. But a Serenperdarn would be that which transports some between the stars. Like Wormhole – Piluceda.

The Piluceda under the correct hand can connect at times with the Sylperdarn.

Talaith: 'Diadem' (a crown or headband worn as a sign of sovereignty; royal authority or status)

Tarala: Ruby

Vidazati: Bite to pieces

Wizards

Bhlegaldur: Blue Magic

Šyvasgaldur: Grey Magic

Galdramaður: A wizard, enchanter, magician

Armament

Abnu Zabarkizag: The dagger gifted to Jaddamiah by Eirmægden.

'Heavens Ember': That came to be known as 'Anuagirru' held at Jinbōchō in after years. Hence the word Anuagirru for this was the speech of the Ælves of Jinbōchō. Anuagirru as a name in a kind of direct translation means 'heavens watered fires' for the Dragons' scales represents water. Its breath is fire therefore being an embodiment of Perfect Light.

Mordēre: The sword of Jaddamiah Jabberwocky

Sagitta: The Arrow

Appendix on The Word 'Dream'

By the time the author came to the completion of the first book he was hard pressed to continue with the spellings 'Dream' and 'Dreamn' or 'swefn' wanting to replace them with 'Dreamn' and 'swefn'. I was asked to continue with the former spellings as it had set a certain tone in the book, this is what the Ælves (wanted). Wither he will continue to use those former words in the next book, we shall see. For he feels that 'Dreamn' which is appropriate as it would denote rejoicing, music and therefore; c. 1300, "to own, possess, enjoy the possession of, have the fruition of,"

To him this sounds more appropriate and swefn would then be 'sleep'. The whole thing reminds him to much of The Nightmare by Henry Fuseli. But having said all this, always respectfully he must consider the Wisdom of the Ælves for they are simple Immortals yet, not simpletons. And their voice is softest with admonition. We will press them for a change if possible. . .

Printed in the United States
By Bookmasters